continued . . .

S0-AHB-283

Praise for *Wraith*

"A highly original addition to urban fantasy . . . I look forward to reading more about Zoë Martinique and her world."
—Patricia Briggs, #1 *New York Times* bestselling author

"With a quick-witted heroine and truly frightening baddies, Weldon offers a fantastic kickoff to what promises to be a vibrant new series."
—*Booklist*

"Launching with a bang, this new detective series/urban fantasy crossover plunges its astral-traveling heroine in the middle of the action. Martinique is strong, resourceful, self-deprecating, and fascinating."
—*Library Journal*

"Weldon's lively debut . . . keeps Zoë and her readers off balance with brisk pacing and brain-wrenching plot twists, drawing the story to a satisfying close while leaving enough loose ends to set up Zoë's next adventure."
—*Publishers Weekly*

"Interesting, off-kilter characters . . . I can only hope that we will see more of Zoë Martinique and her family . . . Everything is so matter-of-fact that you come to quickly accept these fantastical trappings—not because of *Buffy* and other TV shows, but just because, well, it seems so solidly real within the context of the book."
—*SFRevu*

"This fresh urban fantasy series keeps the action intense with its first-person point of view. Heavy on pop-culture references and quirky dialogue, it features original characters the reader will want to befriend. With a penchant for finding trouble, like Kim Harrison's protagonist [Rachel Morgan], and witty banter akin to that of *Buffy the Vampire Slayer*, Weldon's astral-traveling heroine, Zoë, makes this series a hit."
—*Romantic Times*

"[A] worthwhile debut that bodes well for disembodied adventures to come."
—*Kirkus Reviews*

Ace Books by Phaedra Weldon

WRAITH
SPECTRE
PHANTASM
REVENANT

A ZOË MARTINIQUE INVESTIGATION

REVENANT

Phaedra Weldon

ACE BOOKS, NEW YORK

THE BERKLEY PUBLISHING GROUP
Published by the Penguin Group
Penguin Group (USA) Inc.
375 Hudson Street, New York, New York 10014, USA
Penguin Group (Canada), 90 Eglinton Avenue East, Suite 700, Toronto, Ontario M4P 2Y3, Canada
(a division of Pearson Penguin Canada Inc.)
Penguin Books Ltd., 80 Strand, London WC2R 0RL, England
Penguin Group Ireland, 25 St. Stephen's Green, Dublin 2, Ireland (a division of Penguin Books Ltd.)
Penguin Group (Australia), 250 Camberwell Road, Camberwell, Victoria 3124, Australia
(a division of Pearson Australia Group Pty. Ltd.)
Penguin Books India Pvt. Ltd., 11 Community Centre, Panchsheel Park, New Delhi—110 017, India
Penguin Group (NZ), 67 Apollo Drive, Rosedale, North Shore 0632, New Zealand
(a division of Pearson New Zealand Ltd.)
Penguin Books (South Africa) (Pty.) Ltd., 24 Sturdee Avenue, Rosebank, Johannesburg 2196,
South Africa

Penguin Books Ltd., Registered Offices: 80 Strand, London WC2R 0RL, England

This is an original publication of The Berkley Publishing Group.

Copyright © 2010 by Phaedra Weldon.
Cover art by Christian McGrath.
Cover design by Judith Lagerman.

PRINTING HISTORY
Ace trade paperback edition / June 2010

Library of Congress Cataloging-in-Publication Data

Weldon, Phaedra.
    Revenant : a Zoë Martinique investigation / Phaedra Weldon.
        p. cm.
    ISBN 978-0-441-01865-9
    1. Martinique, Zoë (Fictitious character)—Fiction.   2. Single women—Fiction.
3. Astral projection—Fiction.   4. Atlanta (Ga.)—Fiction.   I. Title.
    PS3623.E4647R48 2010
    813'.6—dc22
                                                        2010008672

PRINTED IN THE UNITED STATES OF AMERICA

10   9   8   7   6   5   4   3   2   1

For my father, Leonard C. Weldon, Jr., my mother, DeLois,
my sisters, Amber and Tara, my brother, Marc, my husband, Ernest,
and my beloved and most precious gift, my daughter, Indri.

Why, then 'tis none to you, for there is nothing
either good or bad but thinking makes it so. To me it is a prison.

—William Shakespeare, *Hamlet*

1

SUPERMAN makes this shit look easy.

Flying, I mean. Just points his beefy hand out with a mighty fist and away he goes. Up, up, up. I do the same and crash into—*through*—and past a building. I guess this is a good thing since I don't actually break anything in the process. No bones or concrete.

Though that last condo I blasted through had some seriously questionable stuff happening in that middle unit—was that a cat-o'-nine-tails I saw? I tumbled out and put the brakes on, backpedaling in midair as I concentrated on the darkened world, looking for the telltale signs of the Fetch I'd been chasing.

What's a Fetch? Hell if I knew. The only intel I'd been given was that if I could catch them easily, I would graduate from grasshopper to padawan. Yes. I know. Mixing media here. It's good practice, going after the small baddies. Gets me in shape for the big baddies, right?

What I did know about Fetches was what I'd read in the Dioscuri notes the Society of Ishmael had let me read. Was still reading.

Nasty little suckers. Really nothing more than a stray bit of Abysmal essence discarded by its creator. They were a lot like Daemons, brought into existence to spy or do icky things. Some were used as assassins. They weren't given forms like me or you—but left naked in a way so they could blend into their environment. This one'd been made out of office supplies—like an Office Depot transformer. And every time it'd gone through a wall, its accouterments had been ripped off, and then it'd pulled whatever else was nearby to itself, giving it form again. Last time I checked—this one was made of toilet paper—two-ply.

Oh—let me explain. My name's Zoë—and you'd think I'd get tired of reintroducing myself. But see—I never know where people join the adventure. Or tragedy. Depends on how you look at it.

Martinique. Last name.

I'm a twentysomething former retail salesgirl turned Wraith.

Wraith. That's what I am. All because—and let me make sure I got this straight in my own head—I was born an Irin, the child of an angel, and was touched by the Abysmal plane.

Got that? Good, 'cause I ain't repeating it.

"Hey—lover—" came a deep voice to my left. A voice that rightfully belonged to a detective I knew but was being used by my companion at the moment. I was hovering as I got my bearings, my arms crossed over my chest, and turned my head to take a look at my enemy, my nemesis, and the reason all this shit had happened to me.

Let me introduce you to that part of the Abysmal plane I was touched by.

The Archer. TC to me and my buddies. Trench Coat.

That would be the bald guy with sunglasses hovering to my left. Not that he knew what would happen back then—or I. But apparently we're irrevocably linked together in all sorts of oogy ways. Before he touched me, I could go out of body, or OOB as I called it. Astral projection. But then things changed—*I* changed when he marked me. I glanced at the light red hennalike tattoo of his handprint on my left wrist, could only imagine the streak of white in my otherwise-dark Latina hair.

My being was now a miasma of both planes—existing as one. Mutt.

This bastard next to me had kidnapped my mother's soul. And then I lost my ability to OOB because of a spell my mom did when I was a child. Because of this, my dual soul split down the middle. And the evil half of me possessed the man I loved.

Detective Daniel Frasier.

Love.

My . . . darker half drove him to do things against his nature. To kill. And enjoy it. The consequence of that was madness—and an undying passion to kill *me*.

He tried, but killed his captain instead. Kenneth Cooper.

That's when I started seeing the skulls. Death masks. I'd seen them before—on people—when they were about to die. Now I saw them on everyone. I didn't go out much anymore. Not in the daylight. I didn't want to see them. Not anymore.

A week later, I learned I no longer needed to go OOB to go Wraith. And Archer was there. Waiting on me.

Daniel was insane and committed to an asylum. Out of state. Away from me.

That's my life experience. Getting one's heart ripped out and stomped on a few times. Oh yeah—and condemning one's soul.

Oh—but we haven't confirmed that one yet. That whole condemnation thing. Seems to be one of those vague provisos in small print. In a language nobody speaks anymore. Except for Rhonda. And a guy named Dags.

Dags.

No, no, no . . . not going there. *That boy is gone. Out of the city. Out of my life. No thoughts to him. Nope. No, sireeee.*

I moved a good one hundred feet or so above the reconstruction of the Bank of America Building. I sort of blew it up a month or so ago when I rejoined with my darker half. The Abysmal part of me. The media said it was a tornado.

Man . . . my life's so screwed up. Most women when they have a bad day throw clothes all over the floor. Me? I screw with construction. Can't say it wasn't my fault. Because it was.

TC moved closer to me, dressed in a long black trench coat, drivers' gloves, and dark glasses, hovering eye level with me. Vin Diesel—with a smirk. "I lost it."

His smirk deepened. "Because you're not *looking*." He pointed past me to my right. "There."

I turned my entire body, my wings working independently to keep me afloat in the air. I saw it, an iridescent paper-covered blob moving below us, back into the building. I dove down after it, managed to go incorporeal long enough to move *through* the building's walls, then *through* the offices, right on its tail.

Stay with it, TC said in my head. That was getting annoying. One of these little new things that kept cropping up since rejoining with my Horror self. Oh . . . might need to explain that too, huh?

Maniacal laughter echoed through the halls.

Uh, hold that thought.

Wasn't sure if the laughter belonged to the Fetch—or something else. The little fucker blasted past me and through a door at the end of a long hall. I willed myself forward, imagining myself as a bullet, and sieved easily through the door. Wood. Easier.

Though . . . I always felt like I needed to pick splinters out of my teeth afterward.

I stopped abruptly. The thing wasn't moving—just hovering in the center of some schmuck's office. A piece of toilet paper fell from its body and drifted to the floor. In the darkness, the Fetch glowed a soft aqua green through the paper. Usually, whatever it attaches to itself forms into some sort of face—and this one was no exception. The paper looked as if it'd been moistened and molded into some old bald guy with a look of surprise. Made me think of a sand sculpture on the beach.

A beat later, I realized the face wasn't looking at *me*, but up at a point above my head. It looked as if it wanted to scream, to bolt out of there—but it was frozen in place.

Every Wraithy hair on my back and arms shot up as I was overcome with the freaky factor—

There was something *behind* me. Above me. Something this Fetch was so scared of it couldn't move.

TC—

Get out of there! came his reply in my head—his response so loud I felt it reverberate against my skull.

I turned just as something struck the side of my head, the force sending me to the right of the Fetch and into the wall—oops—I'd forgotten to go incorporeal. But then—I was a little preoccupied with whatever it was that'd just knocked the shit out of me.

I landed on top of the office-desk bureau, doing some serious damage to the wood, then bounced forward onto the wheeled chair, which popped out from under me. I settled on the floor with a cracking thud.

Ow.

Laughter filled the awkward silence after my ten-scoring nose-dive, closely followed by the scream of the Fetch. How did I know it was the Fetch screaming? I'd popped off a few of them. There is nothing more disarming than their cry of pain. Imagine taking a million nails and pulling them down a chalkboard.

Your hair standing on end now?

That's what I heard as I moaned and righted myself, feeling my wings pull in and vanish. I could tell from the dark charcoal color of my taloned hands I was still Wraith—sans flight apparatus. Twisting my neck to the left and right, I started to push myself up from behind the desk.

"Stay down!" TC yelled, and the mental force of his warning yanked me back into a crouch.

I sensed that the Archer was in the same room—and peered up over the side of the desk as I heard the sound of scuffling. For me, seeing at night was the same as seeing in the day—only with the added shadows and wispiness. I could see TC wrestling in midair with—

My eyes bugged out.

What the hell is that?

From what I could see, he was doing an alligator death roll in midair with—*red hair?*

Standing up to my full height—which is nothing to sneeze at—I moved closer, waiting for the opportunity to wail on the big red hair ball. Seriously—it looked like the comic character Dawn's red hair had walked off her head and was attacking Vin Diesel, wrapping itself around his neck, his body, his arms and hands.

But he wasn't exactly losing though. He was yelling at the top of his lungs, yanking the hair out by its roots. Of course when he let go of it as if to throw it away, it just got right back up and rewrapped around him.

"Zoë—"

I blinked. "What?"

"Kill it!"

"How?"

"Yell at it!"

Well now, how in the hell was I supposed to do that and *not* hit him?

Boy . . . that was a reversal of roles. I could remember that night months ago—with Daniel's broken body at the base of that building—taking aim at this asswipe and screaming him into oblivion.

And now I was *afraid* of just nicking him.

"Zoë!" he bellowed. "Stop fuck'n around!"

Asshole.

I held out my arms, took in a deep breath—

Abruptly TC was tumbling in midair toward me. I squeaked and went incorporeal just before he sailed through me and into the wall behind me, physically smashing into the bureau I'd already mangled. I winced as I re-formed and looked around for the thing he'd been fighting.

But—it wasn't there. Besides the creak of wood and TC's muttering, there wasn't a sound. The shadows that usually moved like liquid mercury along the periphery of my vision crept out from their hiding places. A sure sign that whatever that was—

It was gone.

I moved to the pile of gooey, gloppy toilet paper and pointed. "Ew."

TC righted himself, his shades gone from his face. He looked like he wanted to wrap a tree around someone. As he stomped closer, still muttering, I pointed to the floor. "Uh . . . Fetches don't usually do that when you kill them."

He was looking back at the pile of cheap pressboard and bent over to retrieve his glasses. Finding them, he plucked them from a pile and turned to me, wiping them on the edge of his black silk shirt. "I've told you already—you can't kill anything Abysmal or Ethereal, you just sort of pop it out of the form it—"

TC stopped when he stood next to me and looked down at the pile. His eyebrows arched, and he hooked his shades on the back collar of his coat. In silence, he knelt beside what was once the Fetch and rubbed at his chin. I knelt beside him, looking at him, then looking at the pile, then looking at him.

"Well?"

He continued rubbing his chin. "Well—" He looked at me. "This is bad."

"Bad as in 'wow, whatever that is kicked this shit's ass,' or bad as in 'uh-oh, we're all gonna die'?"

He pursed his lips and gestured with the index finger of his left hand. "The last one."

That wasn't what I'd expected. "Wha'?"

TC looked up at the air, his expression serious. Now, let me really drill home how odd that was to see a serious expression on the Symbiont's face. Normally, TC's expression rests between mildly annoyed to annoyingly smarmy. Angry—he does angry well. And pissed off. Smirking too. The king of smirking.

Though Dags had a nice smirk.

Phhhtt . . .

Watching this lack of anything definable on his face made those hairs on the back of my neck rise. "TC . . ."

"I—" He was shaking his head as he looked at me. "I don't know what that was." He shrugged, the leather shushing. "I've never felt or seen anything like it. The closest in smell is . . ." And he looked at the pile. "I don't know. It's like it had the darkness of the Phantasm's soul, but it had the strength of an Ethereal."

I searched his face. "Like a Horror?"

"No . . . not a Horror. This was something . . ." TC sighed. "I need to find out what it was. Because this . . ." He nodded to the pile in front of us next to my killer bunny slippers. "This ain't right."

"Did it kill it?"

"Yeah. It did kinda kill this Fetch. It mutated it. It's all but dead. It won't ever corporeally form again. I'm not even sure there's much of a sense of being left in it." He raised his left hand, and a red light sparkled from his palm. Within seconds, the thing pulled and twisted into that light until the only thing left was damp toilet paper. And by the time TC lowered his hand, even the paper was dry.

"Won't that give you like . . . indigestion?" I asked.

He shook his head and stood. I stood beside. And no matter how big being a Wraith made me feel, he always managed to make me feel small. "I don't think it will. I'll give it back to the Styx when I leave."

At that moment, my watch went off. I cussed and lifted my left wrist, looking at my Harry Potter watch—the only watch of its kind that could move with me through the planes and still keep on ticking. My best friend and magical MacGyver, Rhonda Orly, had fashioned it for me. In the beginning of my Wraithdom, I'd used it to warn me when I'd been out of my body long enough so I wouldn't experience the lethargy and illness that always seemed to accompany staying out after curfew.

"When're you gonna tell 'em?" TC said as he moved to the office window. The moon was waxing, close to full, its glow making an ethereal halo behind him, casting his face in slight shadow. He looked . . . impressive.

I pushed the alarm button. "Soon."

"You said that last week."

"So this is this week."

He shook his head. "You sure they have no idea you're sneaking out at night moonlighting with me?"

I shook my head. "No."

"And you're sure they don't know you can go Wraith—without slipping your mortal coil?"

"No." Which was the truth. I really didn't know. But I doubted it.

He reached behind him and retrieved his shades. Sliding them on, he turned his face to me. "I wouldn't be so sure, lover." He smiled, but I could tell he was thinking about that hairy thing he'd just fought.

"So sure about what? Mom's and Rhonda's reactions?" I made a noise. "Oh, I'm sure they'd be pissed and try to exorcise me."

"No." He shook his head. I couldn't see through those shades. "Don't get comfortable, Wraith. Palling around with me isn't safe. You're still a threat to the Phantasm, which makes you a threat to me. You shouldn't trust anyone—especially me." He gestured to the window, and the glass shattered outward—freezing in midair just outside. He didn't have to do that to leave—he just wanted to make an impression. "And you won't find the answers to your future on that old society's books."

"Will you tell me what you find out—about what that was?"

He looked back at me and faded away. The glass fell straight down to the asphalt below.

Don't trust me, Wraith. Don't trust anyone.

2

I felt like I was twelve again—sneaking back into my room while Mom slept. And I knew she was still sleeping 'cause I nearly jumped out of my body when I heard her snore.

Yes—I live with my mom. And it's not what you think. I did have a condo a few months ago—but after Archer took Mom's soul when her body was hijacked by a rogue spirit whose body was destroyed (Charolette and Bertram—otherwise known as Bonnie and Clyde), I had to tuck her body into a long-term-care facility.

Not cheap.

So I sold the condo and moved into the Botanica and Tea Shop. The shop itself was a converted house on Euclid—with two stories, a basement, and a wraparound porch. I forget the name of the style of house. Ask Tim and Steve, Mom's resident ghosts and the former owners of the house. They could tell right down to the exact type of paint you need.

Since Mom's return—and all the other disasters that've cropped up—I haven't spent a lot of time looking for a new place. I need one. This being in one's twenties and living with Mom sucks. Especially because—well—I've gone through a few more changes since the last time we spoke about my being a Wraith.

There are three bedrooms upstairs. Mom's master is to the left of the steps if you come into the house in the more traditional manner. It has its own bathroom tucked inside. The other two rooms share a bath to the right. Sometimes Rhonda stays over—but having seen her new palatial digs with her uncle's group, the Society of Ishmael, I can't understand why she'd want to. I mean, she's got a tub the size of my bed!

Sieving through my bedroom window was simple, and I landed silently beside the bed. I felt like some creepy vampire entering a maiden's room, ready to bite her neck.

Heh.

I can think of a neck I could bite.

Shaking my head to clear the sex visual out—'cause for some reason sex just sets off the Wraith-dar, then I'm like off the charts in oogy—I did the mental shrug I'd started using to shift my body back to the physical plane. I watched as my hands and arms became their plain slightly olive shade—though I had been darker in my younger days. I felt the weight of being physical pull me into the carpet as my bunny slippers took on a more normal look—not all toothy and Tim-Burton-looking.

I used to dress in black—black pants, turtleneck, and slippers. I'd recently started using a black catsuit I'd found at Throb—one of Atlanta's kinkier stores—which oddly enough I found comfortable. I still braided my hair and decided after seeing the split ends it was time to pay Jameal a visit.

Sighing, I started pulling off the suit as I made my way to the bathroom. Stripping down, I tossed the suit in a small bag I kept under the sink, then stood up—

Directly into the path of Tim and Steve.

Squeaking, I jumped back, and of course did that modified Eve pose to cover my now bare who-who and hee-hees. Not that these two would care either way.

"This has got to stop," Steve said as he crossed his arms over his chest. Of the couple, Steve was the more mature one—not so much in age before he died, but in personality and responsibility. He had that sort of take-charge persona that I think Mom liked. In fact, Mom thought he was hawt.

Tsk.

Getting a little irritated—since this was the third time these two had greeted me after a night's work—I stopped trying to cover myself and set my hands on my hips. "Oh? Why, Steve? Wait . . . I know the answer." I held up my right hand, index finger in the air. "Because I shouldn't trust the Archer."

"Not just that," Tim said from his more distant position by the shower. He was smaller than Steve. Slighter build, with dark eyes and dark hair. I'd always felt closer to Tim and his more gentle mannerisms. He moved forward, becoming almost totally corporeal in the bathroom light. I watched him as he grabbed my robe from a hook and handed it to me. No repulsion. No hesitation. Just purpose. "The fact you're not moving out of your body anymore. You need to tell Nona, Rhonda, and Joe."

"Why?" I took the robe and pulled it on before moving to the mirror and turning on the water. I needed to wash my face before I slept. I wanted to take a shower—but the sound of the water running would wake Mom, then she'd be all up in my Kool-Aid about why I was up at six in the morning taking a shower before going back to bed and sleeping all day.

I splashed water on my face and looked at them in the mirror. It always amazed me they had reflections. At least when they were corporeal. Pumping soap in my hand, I scrubbed at my face, hoping to get rid of any lingering piece of that Fetch's gooed-up remains. I *reeeeally* wanted a shower.

"Oh, let's say," Steve said, "because even though you've been a bitch now and then, they've always stuck by you. Rhonda's your best friend, Nona's your mom, and Joe's hopelessly in love with you."

Och . . . here we go again. I rinsed my face and grabbed a towel off the nearby hanger. It smelled of Downy and my mom's herbs. "Steve, this is really getting old."

"I'll say," Tim said. "Your sleeping till three in the afternoon is driving everyone nuts. And then you spend the nights over at Rhonda's reading over those old Dioscuri notes."

"No, not that," I said, and tossed the towel on the sink. "I mean about Joe. Just stop that already. Joe is a friend. He's dating Rhonda. End of argument."

"No," Steve said. "Joe is in love with you. Dags is in love with you. Rhonda is in love with Dags. You're in love with a crazy person. *You* are an *idiot*."

Giving him my righteous bird finger, I turned and exited stage left into my room.

One thing about ghosts—they tend to do whatever they want. *Damn them.*

The two were already in my room before I could cross the threshold. I made a shooing gesture at them, dropped my robe, and changed into my Danny Phantom tee shirt and a pair of old cotton loungers I'd snatched from Daniel.

Daniel.

Thinking of him always sobered me. And not in a good way. More of a self-involved guilt trip. I'd tried to see him since he'd been shipped out of state into Maryland. But he'd refused. Screamed in his now-volatile state of crazy.

A crazy I'd given him. And I couldn't take back.

"I'm sorry," Tim said, quietly. I knew he realized where my mind had wandered.

Looking at him, I smiled and moved to the bed, plopping down and turning on my headless-Mary lamp. My old dry-erase board lay at the foot of the bed, my last scribbled FUCK YOU still visible in red ink. "You know I have to know everything my great-uncle did. I wanted to know what it was he did to my dad. I wanna know what else is out there. The man was a bona fide nut job." I paused. "But he kept good notes on everything he'd seen in the Abysmal. Categorizing them. Labeling them. Listing their abilities. The hierarchy of things."

"Have you read the notes on the Ethereal?" Tim said quietly. "Those are just as important, if not more so. You're so focused on the Abysmal, you're missing the bigger picture. The Ethereals—especially the Seraphim—those are the ones you can't trust. More so than anything the Abysmal can cook up."

I rubbed at my face. I understood what Tim was getting at—my dad was an Ethereal being now—had been when he'd conceived me with Mom. What I didn't want to tell them was that I *had* read a bit on the other plane—my great-uncle took copious and detailed notes—and it scared me more than Daemons, Symbionts, Fetches, and Phantasms.

A *lot* more.

I chose not to answer his question. You know, I'd noticed a lot of that lately—me actually *not* talking. I mean . . . I had my voice back. My voice. And I was choosing not to use it.

What was up with that?

"Zoë." Tim sat on the edge of my bed, not making any sort of dent in the comforter. That told me he was simply solid but not corporeal. Ah . . . didn't know there was a difference, did ya? Neither did I. I had learned a lot during my time as a Wraith.

Too much.

I looked at Tim, raising my eyebrows and stifling a yawn. I was soooo tired. "I'm gonna fade out if you don't speed up the question, dude."

"You need to at least tell Nona about your new condition."

I shook my head.

"Have you even tried to slip out of your body?"

To demonstrate, I released my physical self. It plopped back on the pillow, eyes half-open, while me the astral self continued sitting up. My lower half was still in my body, so it kinda looked like I'd half taken off my Zoë suit.

Actually—it was kinda creepy.

"Stop that," Steve said, joining in the conversation and no longer hovering in the far corner. "Doesn't it worry you that it's that easy to just slip out?"

I leaned back into my body, felt the connections resume, and sat back up. I'll admit there was a more pronounced feeling of "ick" every time I did that. But—why should I care?

Really?

"What am I supposed to do about it? Every time I had the opportunity to be normal—something always managed to step in and screw it up."

Tim pointed at me. "There it is again."

"What?"

"That not-caring attitude. Zoë, you've always cared." He lowered his hand. "It's Archer. Hanging around with that Symbiont—his evilness is rubbing off on you."

I snorted. "Hardly. And we're not really hanging around. He's teaching me."

"He's teaching you?" Steve spoke up. "To what?"

I wasn't liking this. Getting the third degree in my own home was unacceptable. Well . . . Mom's home. I turned and pushed my feet under the covers, yanking up my pillow. Glancing at the window, I could see the outside getting lighter. *Argh. Maybe I should just, like, limit my outings at night to twice a week.* Sleep was something I was sorely missing.

"Fine. But if you don't take care of your physical body, Zoë, your astral self will suffer."

Ah, foreshadowing. Too bad I already knew that.

I knew Steve had left. There was always a lot less pressure in a room when he left. *Overbearing* came to mind. "Tim?"

"Hrm?"

I turned then and saw he was still sitting on the edge of my bed, watching me with those huge brown eyes. "Do you know all the different kinds of things there are in the Abysmal plane?"

He shook his head. "I only know what I've learned from you, Nona, and Rhonda. Steve and I didn't even realize there was an Abysmal plane until Nona moved in, and we met you." He moved his head to the side, his dark eyebrows flattening. "What is it?"

"Well." I sat up, wrapping my fingers together like I used to do when I was little and had to tell Mom about something I saw. "We were chasing a Fetch tonight—"

"A Fetch?" Tim leaned forward. "Who was it after?"

I shrugged. "We didn't know. Archer spotted if first hanging about in a shrub while we were talking. I supposed it was after one of us."

"I don't think so." Tim shook his head slowly. "From what Nona and Rhonda have said, those things are pretty much used for long-distance hit-and-run against physical-plane beings—so—it doesn't make sense that it'd be after one of you." He frowned. "Is that what's got you spooked?"

"No—" I opened my mouth, then shut it. "It's what showed

up while we were chasing it. I can't—I just can't wrap my head around it."

"What?"

I pursed my lips and frowned at him. "Hair."

His reaction was what I'd pretty much thought it'd be. "Hah?"

"Yeah . . . hair. Big red hair. Or that's all TC and I could see. Whatever it was—it demolished that Fetch into ectoplasmic goo and was able to hold TC off in a fight. It was strong."

"Did it destroy the Symbiont?"

I heard that bit of hopefulness in my little buddy's voice. TC wasn't exactly his favorite person. In fact, he wasn't anybody's. Not even mine. "No—but I could tell it unnerved him. And then it was gone. Just—*vanished*. TC said he'd never felt or seen anything like it—though he did compare its strength to that of the Phantasm."

"You think it was another Horror?"

"No." I chewed on my lower lip. "I don't know what it was. TC told me to scream at it—you know, use that voice. And when I started to—that's when it left. As if it knew what I was about to do."

"Maybe it did."

My phone rang then—scaring the bejesus out of me and Tim. I squeaked and jumped up, looking for it. I usually kept it in my jeans . . . which I'd tossed . . . Ah! In the closet!

Of course.

My iPhone. Yay. I looked at the incredibly bright screen. Joe Halloran.

I glanced at the time on the phone—6:22 A.M.

This couldn't be good. I pressed the answer button. "Hello?"

There was a familiar pause as an automated male voice started speaking. "Zoë. Meet me. Down. At the. Morgue. Lex. Has. Our. Kind of. Trouble. Call Rhonda. Need. *Book of. Everything*."

I disconnected. Remember how I said TC had a voice and it wasn't his? It was actually Joe's voice. And now Joe was the silent detective. He was lucky Mastiff was a good partner—and the new captain was hearing impaired.

Though—I wasn't sure he liked me yet.

And Lex.

Lex Takashi was the creepy criminal biologist at the Dekalb morgue. I'd met her—it—back when Daniel killed Boo Baskins. Only we didn't know he was doing it at the time. Lex was also a friend of Joe's and was the one who'd originally helped him brew up his concoctions that bring accidental astral walkers back into their bodies. That was how Joe and I met—that night in the morgue when he'd assumed I was one of those accidental tourists on the astral plane. He'd used his potion, and I'd come to life.

What I had learned about Lex just the previous week was that she carried a Symbiont inside of her. But not the kind of Symbiont I was accustomed to. Though my only experience with one was TC. And to be honest, we only called him a Symbiont because Rhonda's big *Book of Everything* did.

But Lex seemed . . . different. Her Symbiont called itself Yamato.

And I wasn't really ready to know just *how* different. I pulled up Rhonda's number on the iPhone and pressed the CONNECT button. Within seconds, she answered—and sounded wide-awake.

I yawned as she agreed to come get me. I was without wheels (I'm broke!), and Mom hid the keys to Elizabeth. Evidently, I forgot to put water in the radiator.

"Oh," I said. "And bring the BBOE."

"The wha'?"

"That big-ass book you have covered in human skin."

She laughed. "So we're going to see Lex again?"

"Uh-huh," I tossed my pants on the bed—those were dirty. *Do*

I have a clean pair somewhere? I rummaged in my closet as Tim continued to sit on my bed.

"Don't forget to bring your stakes and garlic."

I grabbed a pair of pants off the floor and sniffed them. *Ah. Downy. These are clean.* "My what and who? You expecting Dracula or Lestat to show up at the morgue?"

"No. For Lex." I could almost hear the twinkle in Rhonda's voice. "You *do* know Lex is a vampire, right?"

!!!

3

MOM was up the moment she heard the shower—told you.

I hadn't slept—so I needed the water to wake myself up. When I bounded downstairs, she was in the kitchen and insisted on making one of her calorie-loaded breakfasts. "Uh-uh," I said, my own stomach twisting up at the thought of buttered biscuits and eggs. Normally, that image would have sent my slobber glands into maximum overdrive. But—not this morning. I was too tired and too keyed up.

Between the earlier attack of the killer hair and meeting Joe down at the morgue (I'm ignoring the vampire crack from Rhonda . . . lalalalalala—dinosaur), I just wasn't in the mood. Instead, I gave her a rundown of what Joe had said on the phone— or what Joe's voice-box had piped in.

"Be careful with Lex," Mom said as she handed me one of her specially brewed teas. I swear I thought I saw a ghost of a skull and crossbones poof up from it. I took it—but I sure as shit wasn't going to drink it. "Not all the First Borns are sane—and Lex is the worst of them."

I pulled my gaze from the floaty smoky poison symbol and frowned. "First Borns?" I knew what that meant. Had read about them in the Dioscuri notes. They were the first creatures created by the original Phantasm, before there were real solid borders between the planes. According to my great-uncle, the Phantasm then sent his children out—no one's sure how many—into the physical plane to experience life for him since he was unable to exist in body outside of the Abysmal.

But then something happened to the Phantasm, and the First Borns were hunted down. They retreated into the bodies of their hosts, burying themselves so deep inside, merging with the souls trapped there, taking in blood to mask their existence within, creating something old, ancient, and full of legend.

Vampire.

I shook my head. "You believe all that stuff about vampires? I mean, granted—Lex is one spooky bitch." Correction. One spooky *tall* bitch. Taller than me. And I'd wondered—albeit briefly—when we met if it wasn't really a man in drag. It was good drag. But suspicious.

"Zoetrope," Mom said, using my name again. *Yiiiiiick.* "After everything you've seen—all that's happened—you don't believe in vampires?"

"Mom—please." I pushed the toxic tea away with my finger. I wondered if I could toss it in the money tree on the counter. No . . . that would be a crime against Chinese superstition. And just plain meanness to the plant. "Symbionts, spectres, spooks, Horrors, Fetches, Daemons—all that I can relate to. There's no universal legend attached to them. Or rather, no, like, worldview of them. Not like the Wolfman, or the Mummy, or Dracula. So—believing vampires are real? Uh-uh."

"It's not like Dracula—"

There was a honk from the back of the kitchen, outside the door. Rhonda was there. I grabbed up my backpack (small, black, and covered in Jolly Rogers—borrowed from Rhonda's old stash), kissed Mom on the cheek, grabbed Tim's rock, and held it up. "I'm taking this," and I bounded out the back door and down the steps, again feeling the gentle tug on Mom and Jemmy's wards on the house.

Rhonda had made good time getting to the shop since she now lived in her uncle's secondary estate in Alpharetta (I kinda knocked down the first one—oops)—a thermos of oolong tea out and ready for me (I would have preferred coffee, but Rhonda was all about this keeping the mind and body in sync shit lately)—and a granola bar.

Ick. Twigs in a wrapper.

I'll pass.

Tim appeared ghostylike in the backseat as I tossed my backpack into his middle. He frowned at me and vanished—but I knew he was still there. I had his rock.

Rhonda was dressed in her usual—black hoodie, jeans, anarchy shirt, black nails and lipstick, dark makeup even at the butt crack of dawn. A month ago she'd gone through this weird transformation when she'd housed my mom's soul for a bit when Nona ran away from TC—but couldn't get back in her body. Rhonda had actually started looking basically normal—new haircut, clothes, shoes—but now she was pretty much back to her old self.

And looking nothing like the leader of a secret society should.

This morning her hair was in pigtails. Her earlobes had skulls and crossbones in them. "You tell Nona?"

"Uhmhm . . ." I sipped the tea after pouring it into the thermos lid. *Mmmmm. Nontoxic.* "You know she'll be on the Internet or on the phone to Jemmy in less than an hour." I managed to get my seat belt fastened before Rhonda took off, snapping my head back on my neck.

We drove in relative silence as Atlanta woke up slowly on a Wednesday morning. Traffic grew increasingly thick as she took Ponce into Decatur—luckily it was heading in the other direction. The silence continued, though it wasn't as thick as Rhonda's nonspeak. She was thinking, wanted to ask me something.

But . . . I could wait it out.

Whistles

I finally refastened the lid on the thermos and put it between my legs before holding up my hands. "What?"

Rhonda was actually smirking behind that dark lipstick. "You have got to be the worst liar I've ever met."

"Hah?" I played it off not guilty, but my mind was barreling zero to one hundred toward the door handle—in case she decided to zap my ass.

Oh. Yeah. There have been a few changes with Rhonda's little magic as well. Zapping being in the top five.

"This sneaking out at night?"

Man, I was sure I looked guilty as hell. I stared at her, trying to figure out exactly *how* she *knew*. I threw Tim an accusing stare, but he only shrugged his half-visible shoulders.

"Don't look at him," Rhonda said. "He didn't tell me anything."

I decided that being silent and feigning innocence was the best course of action. There it was again—that really weird insane desire for me to be quiet. Hrm . . .

"Zoë—who is it? Is it Dags? I mean—I understand it. I don't like it—but I understand the attraction. I have it too—and I don't think it'll ever go away."

If you could actually see the face I was planting at that moment as I stared at her. I mean *stared* at her as if she'd grown not just a third eye on her forehead but a whole other face.

And she was still talking!

"—he was in town. It's not that I keep spies on him or anything. I mean—well, yeah, I do—'cause he's got the Bonville Grimoire and all locked inside of him. But I also worry about him. So if you're sneaking out to see him—"

"Wait!" I put up a hand as she made a really scary last-minute turn to the right. "Stop—please. Before I totally hurl on you. You—you're accusing me of sneaking out and meeting Dags somewhere? Oh man . . . this is too rich. Of all the people—" And then her words hit me. Time delay. You know—me using my single brain cell to power my mouth and not my ears. "Wait—Dags is in town. And you have people spying on him?"

Aw, man . . . talk about someone 'et up with guilt. Her face literally flushed pink . . . no . . . make that Day-Glo red. *Look out, Rudolph! You got competition!*

"Damnit, Zoë—stop playing the fool on this. If you're seeing him, then tell me."

"Hey, if you got spies on him—then how come you can't tell if we've been together?" It's not that I really cared—since I hadn't seen Dags in over a month. So if she claimed at all that's where I've been—I'd call her a liar to her face and explain afterward.

Maybe.

But she didn't accuse me of anything. "Zoë—look, we know he came in at Hartsfield-Jackson Airport at nine or so Sunday morning. So he's been here for a few days."

"Where's he staying?" Whoa . . . why did I ask that? It just blurted right out. Kinda like vomit. Blap.

"Not funny—you know where—"

"I am not seeing Dags!" I yelled.

Tim sniggered from the back. I pointed at him. *You, be quiet.*

We were both quiet for a while, getting close to the morgue.

Then, "Zoë—I can't help it. You got a piece of him that I'll never—"

"Stop." I put up a hand. "We already agreed not to do this, Rhonda. What happened between me and Dags was just sex. A onetime thing. Okay? Nothing more. I love Daniel. Yeah—he's a bit nuts at the moment, but you know we all go through phases in our lives—"

"I just . . ." She sighed and kept her eyes on the road. The sun was about up now, and I could see everything with a monochromatic overlay. Color, but muted. "You've shared something I'll never have with him. He'll always hate me—because of what I did to him."

When Rhonda referred to what she "did to him," I was sometimes in the dark about that myself, not having been with her, Dags, and Joe during that little mishap. Where was I?

Oh, at home, looking for Mom's soul, unable to OOB, and totally pining away for a man who was already possessed by my darker half and killing people.

Yeah . . . that was normal.

"He doesn't hate you." And that much was true. Dags had said it. He didn't hate Rhonda. She did what had to be done, to save him and protect the Grimoire. But—what I wasn't going to tell her was how he told me he loved me. And he would love no one else.

Moment of awkward.

Rhonda pulled into the empty parking lot of the Dekalb County morgue. Well, not really empty. Joe's truck was there, alongside a Bentley. I stared at it as I got out, taking note of the license plate. D8d Dock.

How droll. Had to be Lex.

I followed Rhonda to the building as the front door opened, and Joe stepped out. He was as smarmy as ever, his long face holding the expression of one who has grown impatient. His hair was spikier than usual, and he needed a shave. He wore his usual uniform—plaid shirt, jeans, boots, and badge on a chain.

How redneck.

Joe motioned for us to follow—not having a voice to speak with and, noticeably, no dry-erase board. We moved along the halls as we had a month before, and again I caught the smells of disinfectant. And death.

On that first visit a month ago, I wasn't Wraith. I couldn't see or sense anything. This time? Watching the shadows creep and move along the floor made my skin crawl. Their motions weren't fluid like normal, but jerky, as if frames from the picture had been removed. Great effect on-screen. In real life?

Not so much.

As before, we moved through a set of double doors where the polished tile became dingy and worn. The odors changed, and the whole presence felt—

"Zoë?" Rhonda stopped and looked back at me. I hadn't realized I'd stopped walking.

For the first time—I could sense it. There. Ahead of us. A heavy, heady essence of old things. Worn things. Used. Time marching across the planes.

Joe snapped his fingers in my face, and I blinked, looking at him. His eyebrows arched in question. Rhonda looked concerned.

"What is it?"

"She senses me," came the melodic voice of Lex behind Joe and Rhonda. They turned, parting in front of me so that I could see her with my Wraith eyes.

I don't know what I expected—having sensed her power. Or was it something else? She looked as she had that first night. Tall, flaw-less, with perfect movement as if each step were a practiced varia-tion of the next. But there was something else . . . something . . .

Old.

Lex moved toward us, her body never making the bobbing motion of walking like a normal mortal would. She glided closer, her lab coat pristine as it moved with her, as if it were a part of her.

Joe waved at me to get my attention, and I looked at him. He raised his eyebrows, and signed, *"Is that right? You can sense her?"*

I nodded, my gaze drawn back to her.

"She senses my age—" Lex said, blinking lazily at me, looking down at the child who plays where she doesn't belong. "And the kinship we share on the First Tier."

That jogged me out of my catatonia. "First Tier?"

Rhonda spoke up. "It's what the First Borns call the Abysmal plane."

Lex's eyes grew amused. "It is what it is. My home." Abruptly, her face split with a smile, and she held out her hands, her expres-sion growing serious again fast. "Come—I have something to show you. And perhaps the little Irin child can confirm what I suspect."

She turned, and I glared at Rhonda, who shrugged and fol-lowed Joe into the examination room. What I did notice this time meeting up with Lex was that her voice sometimes had this duality to it. Like there were two voice tracks, speaking in unison.

Lex had the regular room with its stainless-steel tables, drains, and pipes. Areas for washing the bodies and diagnosing cause of death. But just behind that, past the rows of toe tags, was the "other" examination room. This room was marked private, and according to Joe, no one—not even the Chief Medical Examiner—went inside.

Actually, once through those doors, I couldn't blame him for not wanting to go in there.

The room itself was small—not so much a broom closet but close. Enough space for an examination table—with straps, I might add—and a shelf full of things I doubt any medical professional in today's world thought about using. It actually looked straightened up today. The walls were painted with symbols I'd only seen in Rhonda's book. And in the book Dags carried inside of him.

Not that they meant anything to me.

On the table lay a nude girl—nude from the waist up. Seems showing breasts was now considered the norm. How European.

Her eyes were open and milky white—telltale sign of death. Her skin was chalky and her lips blue. But what got my attention wasn't the color of her skin or her hair—but the intricate markings carved over every inch of her exposed flesh from the collarbone down.

. . . help . . .

We gathered around her, with Lex at her head. I glanced across the body at Rhonda, whose eyes had grown to the size of chicken eggs. She pointed at the body, her finger getting close to the flesh.

"No!" Lex snapped, and grabbed at Rhonda's wrist with lightning speed.

Joe, Rhonda, and I all jumped. I never even saw Lex's hand move—it was just there—keeping Rhonda's hand above the body.

"Sorry," Lex said as she let go. "But the ritual is still active. If you look with your sight, you can see the essence lingering."

Rhonda swallowed and pulled her hand back. I watched her as she narrowed her eyes and looked at the body. Joe and I glanced at each other—him shrugging. Obviously, he wasn't as interested, having been there a while already. "Oh . . . you're right. There's a . . ." She straightened up and looked accusingly at Lex. "It's gold. Why is it gold?"

"First Tier and very powerful," Lex said as she crossed her arms over her chest.

"Abysmal magic?" Rhonda said.

I frowned. Abysmal what? Was that possible? I looked around for Tim, then realized I'd left the rock in the car. *Crap.*

"Wraith," she said, and my gaze snapped to her. I had no choice in the matter. "Reach inside."

Uh . . . what?

I shook my head. "That's gross."

. . . alone . . .

I wondered if I was hearing things.

"Do it."

And I did. Of course . . . I could actually have just made my body incorporeal and slipped my hand in—but I hadn't shared that little tidbit yet. So I held out my right hand, allowed my astral hand to sieve out. It looked really weird—as my physical hand relaxed away. Kinda like shirking off a flesh glove.

Scrubbing bubble——*ewwwwww.*

With a glance at Rhonda, I paused. "Now . . . how come I can stick my hand in there, and she can't touch the flesh?"

"Oh, just do it, chicken shit," Rhonda said.

Oh . . . you are so gonna get it.

Lex nodded, and I took a deep breath—

—And plunged my hand into the iciest, murkiest, nastiest gunk I could have imagined. Even before I could yell, I was yanking my hand out, the cold actually burning my astral arm.

"MOTHER GUPPY FUCK AN EGG GOD DAMN—"

Yes! I could cuss out loud again. And I did, waving my now-frozen hand around the tiny room.

"What happened?" Rhonda was saying, her eyes even bigger.

You know . . . if they got bigger than that . . . she'd look like Mr. Magoo.

Lex nodded to the body as I held my physical hand and hissed as I eased my astral one back into it. Ow. Fuck. Damn. Ow. Burns. She then motioned for us to look and tilted the girl's head to the side.

There . . . blatantly obvious against the white skin . . . were two distinct puncture wounds.

"She was drained of blood and her soul destroyed."

4

I tucked my still-stinging right hand under my left arm, and said, "You telling us that a vampire did this?" I gave her my *you're shitting me* look. "I thought *you* were a vampire."

Lex nodded. "Yes. I am. But a vampire didn't kill this woman. Yet it was made to look as if one had."

Okay. I hadn't expected an outright admission to being a blood-sucking creature. But there it was. I knew *what* they were because of the Dioscuri—but ever having met one? Other than Lex?

Nope.

Joe reached into his shirt pocket and grabbed his pad and pen. He scribbled. TELL THEM.

I looked at Lex. "Tell us what?"

Lex looked uncomfortable, which was uncomfortable for me too. My hand tingled when I took it out from beneath my arm, but it was better.

She indicated my hand. "What you physically felt inside of this body—the burning ice—was my blood. It was the spark of life that kept the flesh from corrupting."

Oh. Kay.

"This girl—this woman—was my companion. Mialani. She had been with me for a little over a hundred years—the longest living ghoul in existence."

Rhonda nodded slowly, as if she got it.

Well, I didn't. "Okay—lesson here. This woman was a ghoul? Like in a zombie ghoul? Did she have a Symbiont too?"

"No," Rhonda and Lex said in unison.

Freaky.

Rhonda glanced at Lex and spoke to me. "First Borns—when they join with the souls of their hosts—change the chemistry of the human body. It's not a fast process—and it takes time. But over the years, the human body changes to adjust to the creature dwelling within it. The blood changes, the organs, the brain, it all shifts into something a bit more than *Homo sapiens*."

I pursed my lips, then went into full-on boo-boo lip. "Mmm-hmmm . . ."

Lex took it up from there. "The word *vampire* does, and does not, fit what we are. I joined with this body over three hundred years ago. It is, for all practical purposes, no longer human. But in order to stay anchored to these bodies—to remain hidden from prying Abysmal eyes—we take a sustenance from the blood of others. Without it, we—the First Borns—would lose control and release the body. The host would die as the physical being tried to return to its natural state."

That sounded . . . awful.

They were like vampires, and as she said before, not like vampires. "I take it the First Born is the key."

"Yes," Lex said. "My First Born—Yamato—is more than a mere parasite to me. She is me, in so many ways. And when she joined with me, she brought with her all the joys, tragedies, and experiences from the previous hosts. Knowledge was mine. Our bodies are like yours, Wraith." She smiled. "Human . . . but also Abysmal. We—as I said before—are sisters."

Joe and Rhonda looked at me, and I shrugged. *Help! Stop pointing that out!*

"A ghoul," Lex continued as she put her hand lovingly on the girl's head and smoothed out her hair. "We can't make others like ourselves. We live in seclusion away from the Phantasm's eyes. But we can make a companion—a creature of legend—if we choose. Mialani was beaten in her home village—having bedded a man besides her husband-to-be. She was then stoned. But before she was burned—I came to her and offered her a life with me. I gave her a taste of my blood—and her dying corpse was reanimated and given life. And as long as she drank a single drop from me every month, she remained as beautiful and young as the day she died."

I realized my mouth was hanging open, so I shut it. "She was literally—the walking dead."

Lex nodded. "There are drawbacks, of course. If she were to have missed a drink, madness would take her, and she'd have gone on a killing spree to relieve her hunger." She waved her hand. "But that rarely happens. We're careful about our ghouls and take care of them. And you would never know you'd met one unless they told you, and you wouldn't believe them."

Wait . . . can we go back to that whole madness thing and killing spree for hunger?

Joe pointed to the girl, and Lex nodded. "Someone killed Mialani in the old way. Using a ritual devised by the present Phantasm to annihilate all First Borns within the planes. The draining of blood, the carvings, the spell—it's all here. Only Mialani wasn't a First Born and so suffers a fate worse than the death of a First Born."

"And what's that?"

Lex looked at me, and I finally saw the sadness locked away behind that Symbiont's eyes. "Her soul is now seared to the flesh. She cannot move on. She is there—calling out to me every second as her body dies. And she'll feel it worse than you, Wraith. Even after the flesh melts away, and the organs return to dust, she'll feel the bones as they decay until piece by piece she'll become sand, and disappear."

I knew I shouldn't have asked.

Rhonda sighed. "Lex—you think someone targeted Mialani purposefully? A message?"

"Yes." Lex nodded. "There are two other bodies like this one—south on Tara Boulevard. But they were humans, so the souls weren't touched. They were drained of blood."

"Is that part of the ritual?"

"Yes and no," Lex said. "You can drain blood from a body in a thousand ways. This killer is using the bite marks to send a message. Somehow, they have found the old texts about the spells and are using them. I feel they're incomplete though—or else there would be a First Born body and not that of a ghoul. Draining the body of blood weakens the First Born's hold, then the symbols are carved in, locking the soul in place. Once the ritual is complete, the First Born is obliterated."

Something TC had said earlier that morning touched off my question meter, and my left hand shot up. *Okay . . . so we're back in school?* "Wait . . . I thought Abysmal creatures couldn't be destroyed. That even if I release them in the physical plane—they simply re-form into the essence of life and reshape again. You're saying this ritual actually destroys them?"

Lex nodded, her eyes sharpening as she watched me.

I pressed my luck under her scrutiny. "So—if the ritual succeeds, does the First Born become little more than slime?"

"Zoë!" Rhonda barked.

I looked at her. "What? I'm asking a question here—getting answers."

What are you up to? Joe's voice was loud and clear in my head. He'd been so quiet, I'd forgotten he could do that.

Moi? *Nothing.*

Zoë—

Shhh.

"Insensitive . . ." Rhonda was saying.

Well, that might be . . . but there was a really weird similarity here between that thing TC fought and what I'd just learned.

TC?

I booted Joe out of my head as painfully as I could and smiled when he nearly dropped his notepad. Served the perv right.

"You can save her, Irin Daughter."

It was a good beat before I realized she was talking to me. I looked at her—blinked. "Huh?"

"You could release her from the pain."

"But you just said there was no release," Rhonda said.

"There is no release that I can give her." Lex looked directly at me. "But you can."

I took a step back, my arm tingling from the burning cold. "No . . . I can't touch that. I can't release her—she's buried too deep."

Please . . .

"But you can—if you do not surrender the flesh."

I blinked at her. "Surrender the flesh?"

"Your flesh will protect you."

Now—I kinda got what she was meaning. I just hoped the other two didn't. As in she was saying I could release her if I didn't go OOB and used my Wraithiness in the flesh. Which—of course—I had no intention of doing.

Sensing there was a tense moment, Rhonda spoke up. "Lex—the symbols. Can you read them? Do you know if the ritual is complete?"

This seemed to pull big bad vampire girl's attention away from me, and I half listened as I stared down at Mialani's face. I strained to hear her—to sense her there. But the truth was if she was buried in that muck—I might never have found her.

When were you going to tell us?

I jumped at Joe's voice and looked at him. He stood at the body's feet, his arms crossed, his eyes intense on me. I lowered my gaze. *You read my mind?*

No ... I've known Lex a long time. I know what she's implying. He paused. *So you can go Wraith now, without going OOB?*

I didn't nod. Didn't need to.

Well ... congratulations there, kiddo. Hope you find your new life fulfilling. And with that he moved out of the room.

Lex and Rhonda stopped talking as he left, and Rhonda looked at me accusingly. "What did you do?"

I was irritable because of no sleep, hungry, angry, and just plain ... oh, my sugar was just messed up. I moved around the body and out the doors to follow Joe. He wasn't inside, so I went outside and found him just by the curb, looking up at the sky. It was foggy out—and there were cars starting to fill the parking lot. Employees getting in to work. Seeing a man there with a gun in a shoulder holster meant nothing to these guys.

I stood behind him. *I'm sorry.*

He whirled on me then, his eyes flashing. *Sorry? Something this important happens to you, and you don't share it with us? Why, Zoë? Why? What happened? When did it happen?*

I held up my arms. "I don't know—well, yeah, I kinda do. It happened the first time that day at the warehouse with Holmes.

When Daniel saw me. I—I actually released Holmes with a touch—without slipping the meat suit. And then I got so scared and things got so crazy and you disappeared and Daniel disappeared, then I got sick and couldn't OOB . . ." I let my voice trail off—not really sure what else to say.

Joe came to me then, a daunting man with broad shoulders and a musky, manly smell that I always liked. He smiled down at me, and I wished I could hear his voice again. He reached out and took my chin in his hand. *I told you why I left. When I kissed you—I knew it meant more to me than it would mean to you. Your heart was Daniel's. And I needed space. And time.*

I looked up into his eyes. He really was a nice-looking man. Even with the smirk.

But how did I tell him . . . this close to me . . . that sometimes . . . in my dreams . . . I wished he would kiss me again?

Oh, that was easy. I didn't.

I couldn't.

It wasn't fair. And it wasn't real.

"Hey, what're you two doing?"

Joe and I jumped at the sound of Rhonda's voice. And I knew he was feeling as guilty as I was—though nothing had happened between us. He was dating Rhonda. And that was okay. Even though I knew where Rhonda's heart really was.

And so did Joe.

Shit . . . when did this turn into *Days of the Scooby Gang's Lives*? Or *As the Scooby Gang Turns*? Or even *One Wraith to Live*.

Bah.

I turned to her. Lex wasn't with her. "Us? Nothing. Did you find out anything else helpful from dark and spooky in there?"

She's really a nice lady, Zoë.

I glanced at him. "Uh-huh. She tasted your vintage, Joe? She's a First Born, and no matter how fancy you dress that up, it's still a Symbiont, isn't it? Well, we've had our run-ins with those, haven't we? Not to be trusted."

Oho! And where was this self-righteous lying indignation coming from? My conscience did a double snap and put its hands on its hips. *Girl? Who you been hopping around with lately? The tooth fairy?*

Rhonda approached us, passing me to stand close to Joe. They kissed. I seethed.

Welcome to real life.

"Zoë, I don't think I'd use the term *Symbiont* with the First Borns. They're different, stronger, older. Now, on what's happening, from what Lex knows, the symbols aren't complete. They should be carved over all of the flesh—face included. It's her guess and mine that whoever is doing this doesn't have all the pieces—might not have all the ritual."

"Well, for what they do have"—I glanced back at the morgue door—"it's enough."

Rhonda was at my side. "Can you help her? Mialani? Lex was so convinced you could."

I didn't meet her eyes. Rhonda had an uncanny way of telling when I was lying. Me to her? Not so much. I'm more the gullible type. "I think she'd like to believe I could—but what I touched—" I held out my hand. The ends of my fingers still tingled at the memory—the feel of that body's insides. Usually, there wasn't any feel. But it was more like she'd been stuffed with radioactive Jell-O.

Ew.

Joe waved at us, then signed, *"So what's the game plan?"*

I looked at Rhonda. I wasn't the boss. Didn't think I ever was.

She sighed. "I told Lex I'd do what I could to look up any

mention of this First Born ritual in the Society's texts. Zoë—you read anything in the Dioscuri notes?"

"Nope," I said. "But then—I'm only like—" I held up my left hand and indicated a small amount. "This much through it. But I can skip around, see if there is."

Joe held up a hand before reaching into his shirt pocket for his small notepad and a pen. He scribbled something down and handed it to Rhonda.

Why was I suddenly put out that he handed it to her and not me?

Rhonda looked sharply at Joe. "You sure?"

Joe shrugged and signed, *"Why not?"*

"Why not what?" I said.

"Joe suggests we get hold of Dags." She paused, and I made the hugest effort to keep my jaw closed. "He has a wealth of knowledge in that Grimoire—and he might have something there that could help us figure out this ritual—or the symbols."

Uh-huh. I crossed my arms over my chest and glared at Joe. Bring Dags in. Right. Because you know your girlfriend has the hots for him. Smart man.

Not so much.

I shrugged. "Might. You think he'll help us?"

"Why wouldn't he?"

I blinked. "You talked to him?" My thoughts ran straight to the letter Dags had left me before his disappearing act out of Atlanta again. His confession of love. To me.

"I talk to him all the time."

Uh . . . s'cuse me? My gaze snapped back to her. "You do? You spy on him, and you talk to him? What'd he say? What's he been doing? Why hasn't he—"

I almost said it. Almost confessed I'd called him on my own.

Called him several times over the past month. Left messages with questions. But he'd never called me back.

Joe touched my shoulder and frowned at me. *Zoë—Rhonda has Dags watched because he's carrying something very dangerous inside of him. And she talks to him all the time because—*he shrugged—*he works for her.*

I gaped at him.

He frowned. *Didn't Rhonda tell you? Dags McConnell is an employee of the Society of Ishmael. She's his boss.*

5

I absolutely freak'n hate surprises. Which is kinda funny given I tend to live my life through trapdoors.

But there it was—again—another surprise. Another tidbit of news that I was ignorant of. Dags was working for the Society—and he'd been in contact with Rhonda.

Not me. Not the one he'd slept with.

Oh no.

Rhonda.

Not that that instance meant anything. No. I was over that. A moment of weakness. I mean, come on—with the way things had gone with Daniel, my libido had been starving for attention. And I was sure it would've been better sex with Daniel.

Sex is sex.

Right?

Uh-huh. If that were true, why did I feel so damned bad all of a sudden?

Driving back to Nona's, I was quiet. Which—given the return of my voice a month ago—was an odd thing. And I felt Rhonda sometimes glance over at me. I knew Tim was there, still in the car. We'd given him the 411 on what'd happened inside after he berated me for not taking his rock in. Well, sorry. Sue me. I had a whole bunch of other things on the brain, you know? Like . . .

Why the hell did it bother me that Dags had talked to Rhonda and not me?

And why the hell—

"—didn't you tell me you'd been talking to him this whole month while he never answered or returned my phone calls."

Silence.

That's when I realized I'd finished my thought aloud.

Fuck.

Awkward.

I glanced at Rhonda. She was stiff and white-knuckled, her gaze fixed on Ponce.

What do I say?

"Zoë—" Rhonda began, as we neared the left turn onto Moreland Avenue that would take us into Little Five Points. "When Dags agreed to work for the Society—it wasn't really a request. It was—" She pursed her lips. "It was a demand. A condition."

I was narrowing my eyes at her suspiciously. If there was one thing about Rhonda—she was full of all sorts of land mines. And I'd blasted my ass on a few of them these past few months. "Care to elaborate on that?"

"You understand what I mean when I say that Dags is carrying something very important. Right?"

Ya.

"And you understand that this something important is, in essence, keeping him alive."

Ya.

"And you know that there are members of the Society who

have concerns about a guy so young—infused with all the spells and powers—whose very soul is split between the Abysmal and the Ethereal. I.e. Alice and Maureen."

Uh . . . ya . . .

"But did you know that over half of the council within the Society voted to destroy Dags—to retrieve the Grimoire in order to keep it safe?"

Uh . . . ya . . . no. "I didn't even know you had a council in the Society."

She glanced at me with that *are you nuts* look she'd been giving me a lot lately. "Yeah . . . you don't think that I like *own* the Society of Ishmael, do you? That I'm the numero uno grand muckety-muck?"

Funny . . . I think I actually mentally called her that once.

Ah! Mental note: *Rhonda is not the grand high muckety-muck.*

Uh . . . Addendum to mental note: *find out who is.*

I waited for the rest of the story. "So . . . and?"

She stopped at the light to the left of the Vortex and I got the craving for good hamburgers. But it was still too early. Only 8:30 A.M. Though the streets down here were already getting crowded with people. Working or not working, Little Five was always alive. "So and—I'm really only a figurehead. Having been the niece of one of the founding members of the Society. And because I have a personal relationship with the Wraith."

Awwww . . .

"And I own the controlling financial interest in the Society."

"It has money?"

"Loads of it. And my uncle made sure the older—" She clammed up quickly and looked around as if those very older people could pop out of the air. But then again, in my story, they could. "The more power-hungry members of the group couldn't gain access to it. Oh, they're not as bad as that, Zoë. Close your mouth."

"You make it sound like Congress versus the White House."

"Well, in a way it is. My uncle had to deal with this on a daily basis, but he also had to deal with people like Bonville and Rodriguez—and thankfully those assholes are dead."

Hear! Hear! I'd been present when Rodriguez exploded. Oh happy day! "But the monster grew another head?"

She laughed at that. "Yeah, it did. The council is made up of seven individuals—each of them having had something to do with your great-uncle's first experiments. Like working in the lab, or being there hands on. All of them live in different states. There are seven members to prevent deadlocking. No tie votes."

"Is that a good idea?" Tim said from the back.

"Dunno." Rhonda shrugged as the light turned green, and she waited for the slowpoke in front of us to move so she could turn right onto Euclid. I looked past the cars to the left, where Moreland continued on, and saw the Zesto's sign. *Mmm . . . a milk shake sounds good. And they have the best.* "It's kept them moving all these years. And my uncle was good at keeping them corralled. Though it has been the cause of Machiavellian machinations of biblical proportions at times." She laughed.

Tim laughed.

I didn't get it. What's a Machiavellian? Was it like the Merovingian in the second *Matrix* movie?

"So what exactly was the problem?" Tim asked.

"Well, fear mostly." Rhonda turned the Beetle into the back driveway of Mom's shop/house. That's when we noticed Mastiff's car. Joe was already here as well. The boy must've done warp two to get here before us. Rhonda ain't no slow driver. She parked it and released her belt. "It's like this." She half turned in her seat as I unfastened my own belt. "Dags ended up with the power they'd all wanted—especially once it was known that the Bonville Grimoire was indeed the original Cruorem's bible. All those old spells, incantations, stories, histories—very important stuff. Hell, it was in that book I learned how to create a Veil." And to demonstrate, she held up her right hand—and it disappeared in the air between us.

Seconds later, she pulled it out but was clutching an umbrella. Demonstration over, she tucked it back into the invisible Veil.

"Oh, so it's like having a Clarke Belt surrounding you all the time?" Tim said.

Oh, I know that! Clarke Belt was the name given to the area that surrounded the planet that allowed geostationary orbit.

Named after some writer or scientist named Clarke.

And something to do with Sri Lanka.

Wow . . . I really needed to organize the junk folder in my head.

Rhonda was smiling. "You could say that. But—when it came down to it—it wasn't that they really saw Dags as a threat. I mean, they kept him locked up at the mansion for a week examining him after it happened—and they determined he wasn't possessed. It's just that he had the power, and they didn't."

As we got out of the car, the Georgia June thick air hit me in the face. Instantly, I was coated in a thin layer of sweat. God, if there was one thing I hated, it was the Southern heat. Like moving through soup. Even at eight in the morning. And it was just gonna get hotter by the time August got here.

Meh.

Tim vanished—and who could blame him. It was cooler on

the other side. Not this thick. I grabbed up the rock and shut the door before scooting up to Rhonda as we neared the back porch. "Wait . . ."

She stopped at the lower step and looked up at me. "Huh?"

"You said—" I licked my lips. The hair under my ponytail was already sticking to my neck. At this rate I was gonna need another shower. I was already walking in that dream state of no sleep. "You said they kept Dags at the mansion? Like . . . as a prisoner?"

She looked sad. "Almost. Honestly, Zoë, I didn't know what the asswipes were doing in the beginning. They snatched him out of the hospital after we got him away from Rodriguez—and he wasn't used to the changes his body went through."

I narrowed my eyes at her. Cicadas buzzed from the brush nearby between Mom's home and Jemmy's. "What do you mean?"

"Well"—she shook her head—"when they took him from the hospital—he defended himself."

"Uh-huh."

"He made one of the members disappear."

!!!

Oh. My. God. There was so much I didn't know then about what that boy had gone through. From being branded by the Cruorem as a Guardian, to having the Familiars sealed in his palms, to Rhonda fusing the Grimoire to his very soul. And yet—when I'd seen him again that night, I'd nearly barbecued the house doing magic—

The softness he'd shown me. The care and the kind words. It was like none of what he'd gone through mattered. If any of his experiences left scars, he kept them on the inside, never bringing attention to them. "What—what did he do with that member? What happened?"

"They're vague about it—" Rhonda looked irritated. "I had to scry to see for myself. And what I saw was unforgivable."

I waited. Then leaned forward. "Care to share it with me?"

She balled her hands into fists, her backpack on her left shoulder. Her skin looked even paler in the June morning light, and I couldn't see her eyes through the shades. "They came into his hospital room—six of them. One of them had a syringe ready. But Dags woke up—" She gritted her teeth. "He opened his mouth to say something, and one of them slapped a pillow over his face as the others held him down. They were going to shoot him full of something—but then the syringe and the one holding it vanished."

I blinked. "Just . . . poof?"

"Yeah. Poof. It freaked them out. They ran out of there, and Dags managed to catch his breath and call Joe. We came and got him, then the council called and demanded he be brought in for examination. Bastards. Joe stayed with him, you know. Didn't leave them alone with him."

"Joe did?"

She nodded and looked at me. "There was one thing—"

And I never discovered what that one thing was as the back door opened, and Joe and Mastiff walked out.

Mastiff was a tall man—Joe's height. With a medium build and close-cropped hair, his dark skin was smooth in the sunlight. I always thought of him as a young Denzel Washington. Same bright beautiful smile. Only this Denzel knew about the bad things.

Hell—he'd been shot by one. Daniel Frasier.

We looked up at them as Nona came out to stand to their left. "You two need to get in here for this. We have a problem."

Rhonda and I looked at each other. "We do?" I asked.

Mastiff nodded and looked at me. His suit was impeccable—

down to the starched white collar. An opposite to Joe's more mountain-man casual. "Especially you, Zoë." He sighed. "Daniel Frasier disappeared from the Mt. Sounder mental facility in Maryland three days ago. He was spotted in town last night, asking about you."

I blinked. Daniel . . . escaped from a mental hospital?

Joe smiled. *Meet your new bodyguards.* He pointed to himself and Mastiff. *The new Crocket and Tubbs.*

6

I never watched *Miami Vice*. But I knew the characters. And these two were more like Starsky and Hutch. The remake version.

After Mastiff's initial blow, Mom hustled us inside. Jemmy was there, puttering in the kitchen. The shop wasn't officially open till after ten since it was a Wednesday. I could smell the aroma of buttered eggs, biscuits, bacon, sausage, orange juice, and spicy gravy before I even came through the door.

Okay. Before, when we left, I wasn't hungry. But by then I was *starving*.

And with the news of Daniel's disappearance and reappearance—food was the best form of comfort. Right?

About that—

"The word is no one saw him leave," Mastiff was saying as he buttered a biscuit. If there was one thing Joe's new partner enjoyed, it was Nona's breakfasts. Good old Southern boy at heart. "Since his internment, Frasier's been the model patient. They took him off the tranqs about a week after he arrived, and he's been very docile. Almost agreeable."

I frowned, remembering that day in front of the Foxx—leaving the Bridgetown Grill and Daniel wielding that gun—rounding it on me . . .

Cooper jumping in front of it. Daniel firing—and then screaming at me.

Blaming me because he'd shot his boss.

And then the death masks came . . .

". . . till midnight. All the beds are checked every two hours. So"—Mastiff shrugged—"they're not sure how he escaped. No sign of forced exit. All doors locked. And no one saw anything."

I blinked. Looked at him. "Nothing? Not even a scratch or a sign that he'd cracked that lock?"

Mastiff shook his head as he bit into the fluffy biscuit, butter squishing out on the sides.

Joe was across from us, his plate barely touched, his arms crossed over his chest. He was staring at his food but not seeing it.

I decided to intrude on his thoughts. And why not? He did it to me all the time.

What are you thinking?

Eh? He kept his head tilted down but looked at me across the table. *Trying to figure out if maybe Daniel was possessed by a Horror again. I mean—is it possible?*

I pursed my lips. *I—I don't know. If he was—it wasn't from me.* Not this time. No. I was whole. Literally so. *Maybe it's something else?*

Or maybe he really did figure out a way to get out undetected. He could have sweet-talked a staff member.

True. I didn't like the way that sounded—making Daniel out to be a whore-dog of some kind. But . . . *You think maybe he did, and they let him out, then relocked the door?*

Joe nodded.

I voiced this to Mastiff, who nodded.

"Yeah, they thought about that. And the room's been finger-printed. But—that's not really going to prove anything. They have an accounting of staff who regularly go in and out of that room—not to mention patients who wander in during the day. And as for the security cameras—they conveniently went on the fritz for that period of time." He used his right hand to gesture while holding the biscuit in his left. "One minute he was in the bed. The next—he was gone."

Nona set her fork down and picked up her coffee. Tim sat beside me, listening and watching. Mastiff couldn't see him unless Tim wanted to be seen. Steve was apparently absent. Lately, he hadn't joined in any of the reindeer games. I wondered why. "Now—how was he spotted here in Atlanta? And how did he get here?"

Mastiff shook his head. "He was spotted on a closed-circuit video screen. Here." He wiped his hand on his napkin and reached inside his suit jacket. He pulled out a five-by-seven picture and handed it to Mom. "That was taken at a convenience store on LaVista yesterday. So he's in the area."

After looking at it with her eyebrows arched high, Mom handed it to me. Rhonda started for it, but I snatched it back. Mine! When I looked at it—my heart leapt into my throat.

The image was grainy—like any photo taken as a capture from video. But it was him, standing on the other side of the register purchasing something. He looked good, his hair longer than it had been, cupping around his face. He wore a gray hoodie of some sort, with a blazer.

He looked good. Not crazy. "So when you catch him," I said, handing it to Rhonda, "what are you going to do?"

"Bring him in for questioning."

Joe sat forward quickly and waved at Mastiff. He made the sign, "What for?"

"Oh, come on, Joe. You know we can't talk about that in front of the ladies. Or at breakfast."

"You mean question him about the bodies with the drained blood and the wacky carvings?" Rhonda spoke up, her attention still on the photo.

The expression on Mastiff's face was priceless. He blinked a few times and downed some OJ. "Uh . . . how did . . ."

"Society," I piped up.

He nodded. That seemed to explain a lot in this group. Not that the rest of the Atlanta PD knew about them or their purpose in the South. Most of the members—including Rhonda—came from money, and with money, well, you gets respect.

And with the way my account is looking lately—I'll be missing that respect bus for quite some time.

Joe was waving again and this time grabbed up the pen and notepad by his plate. He scribbled. I used to scribble too. WHY 4 THOSE? NO EVDENCE HE WS INVOLVE.

I winced at his misspellings. I used to do that too.

Mastiff shrugged. "Not my call. Talk to the captain."

I could tell by the look on Joe's face that was exactly what he was going to do.

"Anyway," Mastiff said, "one of us will be with you at all times, Zoë. Or at least our presence will be known."

Ominous.

Not.

"Are you first on duty?" Jemmy asked from where she'd been eyeing the poor detective from her perch beside Nona. *Yeah . . . he's cute, Jemmy, but a half and more younger than you. Down girl. Woof.*

Mastiff nodded. "Yes. Halloran here was up early with the latest body." He winced—but I wasn't sure if it was from the taste of

Mom's coffee or the fact that we already knew about those. "I've put in to have the other two bodies moved to Dekalb. Made it a central hub of activity for the time being."

So all the bodies were going to be in one place.

Rhonda asked, "You mean like that'll be done today?"

Mastiff nodded. Rhonda looked at me, and I thought, *Uh-oh. What is she plotting?* I was making nefarious plans to grab Archer tonight and show him the bodies to get his opinion. And to find out if he'd maybe gotten an idea on that hair-monster thing. Pick his Symbiont brain about the First Borns.

But why is Rhonda curious?

With a full stomach—I was ready for sleep. Whether I wanted it or not. I gathered up my dishes, dropped them in the sink, and turned to find Rhonda directly behind me. I backed up, blinking. "Hello?"

"Going to bed?"

I looked past her to the tea shop, where everyone was gathered at the main table still eating and talking. Except for Joe, who was watching us. Refocusing on Rhonda, I nodded. "Yeah—like you said. Sneaking out. Tired." And I even yawned on cue. Not made up.

But she wasn't moving out of my way.

Instead, Rhonda narrowed her kohl-rimmed eyes at me. "You weren't sneaking out to meet Dags—not like I thought. You didn't even know he was in town."

I didn't have time for this. If I didn't get at least a few hours of sleep, I was never going to last tonight while zooming to the morgue. I sighed. Okay . . . a half-truth was better than a no truth. Right? "Okay. Fine. No, I wasn't sneaking out to see Dags. But first you have to tell me how you know. You keeping spies on me too?"

Rhonda's reaction was perfect. She actually looked stunned.

"Well, no . . . it's just that you're always sleeping. So I figured you were doing something at night and not sleeping."

"I'm practicing—okay? I went nearly a month with no OOB, then poof"—I held up my hands for emphasis—"I'm not only a Wraith but part of a Horror. And then I'm slammed back together. So, yeah, I've been out practicing. Learning what it is I can do."

She almost looked . . . happy. At least she didn't look mad anymore. Instead, she reached out and hugged me. And I mean gave me the huge squish. I returned the hug, feeling a bit awkward. Then she pulled back and smiled. "I'm sorry. I just—I lost you for a while, and it was awful. And I thought because you felt you couldn't trust me—you'd leave me out of what's happening in your life. And I'm still interested. I still want to help."

I grinned. "That's good. But the best way to help right now"—I reached out my arm and pushed her to the side—"is to let me get a few hours of deep sleep." Moving past her, I waved at the table. "Mastiff, you'll have a great shift. I plan on sleeping all afternoon."

"What about helping me?" Mom said, looking mockingly upset with a hand to her chest, her eyebrows raised.

I went to the steps beside the kitchen and waved them off. "Get Steve to do it. He's great with the customers."

Which was far from the truth. Already, the man had managed to frighten off two pregnant women and a gaggle of Girl Scouts. All because he appeared in front of them and said boo.

But even as I fell into my bed, my mind gathered up all the events and mushed them together in a single troubled list.

Daniel was missing—either having escaped by mundane or extraordinary means.

Something unknown attacked Archer and killed a Fetch—something that had visibly upset the Symbiont.

Someone was using an old ritual created to destroy First Borns—and had killed a ghoul. They'd also made it look like vampires had done it. Why?

And to top it all off—why hadn't Dags returned my phone calls?

Suddenly unable to sleep, I pulled my iPhone from my back pocket—hey, I could talk again, so I had gone after the coolest phone I could find—and pulled up his number. I didn't have a picture—not a single one. I only had my memory of him. And even that was getting fuzzy, even after one month.

What I could remember was his touch—gentle and soft—and his warm body against mine.

I hit the CONNECT button and waited. It rang once, twice, then the same message in his voice mail, "Greetings and salutations— you've reached the voice mail of Darren McConnell. I'm not available to take your call—"

I disconnected. What was the point in leaving another message? I'd already left five.

7

MOM tried to wake me up at some point—yammering about a guest downstairs. One of Rhonda's friends—but I was having none of it. I wanted sleep, and nothing was going to get in my way.

Eventually, I did crawl up from the depths of unconsciousness. It was dark outside, and I stumbled to the bathroom to shower and change into my usual black clothes. After tying up my hair, I meandered downstairs to a completely empty shop. There was a note taped to the microwave from Mom.

> *Why are you always so tired? Are you not testing your sugar?*
> *Gone to dinner with Jemmy and Missus Parks. We'll be back late. There's a plate of food in the microwave.*
>
> *Mom*

I opened the microwave and pulled out a massive helping of fried chicken, mashed potatoes, green beans, and biscuits. Uhm . . . this might have looked appetizing an hour or two ago. But now it was more like coagulated grease and starch. Stepping on the garbage-can release, I raked all of it in, gave it last rites, and closed it up. Tossing the dish in the sink, I looked in the refrigerator. Hum . . . sandwich meats, cheese, fruit—chocolate cake!

Win!

I pulled out the plate with half of a hunk on it—looked like my Mom's devilishly rich chocolate mousse cake. Mm . . . a piece of this, then a dollop of whipped cream—and coffee. Needed to make coffee.

I stood, shut the door, and turned—

And let out a thunderclap of a scream.

TC reached out and capped my mouth with his hand. "I hate it when you do that."

I stood in my mom's kitchen, holding a plate of chocolate cake with Vin Diesel's hand over my mouth. Life was not exactly boring, was it? I reached up and pulled his hand back. "Then stop popping in and out like that without warning. I was getting something to eat."

"No time," he said, and stepped into the front area of the tea shop, looking around. "We need to get to the morgue."

Okay, that got my attention. I set the cake on the counter and followed him. "The Dekalb morgue? You mean where the bodies drained of blood are?"

He spun so fast I didn't see him move. Instead, he was in front of me before I could take a step back. Sometimes being with Archer was a lot like playing with a half-feral tiger. Not something you wanted to take lightly. "You know about the bodies?"

I blinked and finally stepped away, my back against the dessert display cabinet. "Well, yeah—I saw one of them earlier today. Drained of blood, bite marks, and symbols carved in their skin."

His eyes narrowed. Dead eyes. "So you know about the Revenants?"

I shook my head slowly. "No . . . I don't think anyone brought them in." Uhm. "Who are they?"

He turned away from me with a disgusted noise and sneered. "Deserters is what they are. Weaklings. So afraid of taking what they deserve, they hide deep inside the souls of the physical plane. We call them Revenants because that's what they are—revenants of an age long gone from the planes."

I had to wonder if he was talking about the First Borns— and I also decided to play it dumb. Not a hard stretch most days. "Uhm . . . you care to help me out on this? Joe brought me and Rhonda to the morgue to see the bodies—see if maybe Rhonda knew what the symbols meant."

He turned to me, and it was the most serious I'd ever seen him. "They mean destruction. Annihilation."

"I thought it wasn't possible to actually destroy or annihilate anything—"

"You *can't*!" he boomed. And I pressed myself against the display. *Yow.* He advanced on me and pointed to the floor. "Not normally. Not without Ethereal help. But with those symbols, you can. That spell—that ritual—is forbidden. Forbidden for anyone to perform it except the Phantasm itself."

"Why?"

"Because it *can* destroy. It exists for the sole purpose of destroying—annihilating—*Revenants*."

Not to repeat myself but, "Why?"

He fixated on me. "Haven't you been reading those damned Dioscuri notes? Don't they have any mention of the Revenants?"

I shook my head. "No." I omitted the info about First Borns.

"That's why I'm asking you why. You need to help me a little here."

He pointed at me, and for the first time I noticed he was wearing a really large silver skull ring on his middle finger. "You listen fast, girlie—we ain't got a lot of time here." TC lowered his hand. "They call themselves the First Borns—the first creatures ever formed by the first Phantasm—"

"The first—"

"Shut up!" he interrupted.

I did.

"They're powerful—more so than any other creatures conceived. They were given the ability of free will—not something any other Abysmal creature has ever had." He grinned and pointed to his chest. "Until me."

"I think a thank-you for that is in order." He wouldn't be the way he is now if it weren't for me and my Irin DNA. Or—that's how I'd figured it out.

He literally waved that comment away with a hand gesture. "When the first war between the planes erupted—these First Borns were soft, having lived with the monkeys for centuries in the physical plane. They didn't know how to fight and weren't able to defend the First Tier, so the Seraphim won."

"Seraphim . . . as in angels?"

"Yeah, don't ever want to meet one of those." He frowned. "Never mind. You already did. But what I'm saying is that the Phantasm was destroyed, and a new one came to power. It was smart enough to know that if these First Borns continued living—and banded together—they could, in fact, destroy it. So the Phantasm sent armies of its own creation out to destroy what few First Borns were left after the war."

I looked up at him. "That can't be the only reason. I mean . . . it's the Phantasm."

TC nodded. "You're right. Rumor amid the planes was that the first Phantasm knew its life was coming to an end—one of its First Borns possessed the gift of prophecy—and so it supposedly gave the Last First Born the key to their creation. The secret of how to create creatures with free will."

"I thought there wasn't any such thing as free will—that it was destiny and fate. Or that's what my Mom's always saying."

"That's what the Ethereals would want the worlds to believe. If you set up a play and tell the players they have to act out that same performance every night or die—then there's no variation. Nothing to worry about. And they can sing and laugh and be merry in their little kingdom. But if you introduce creatures with free will—"

"It upsets the status quo," I said. I thought I'd almost gotten what he was saying. "This new Phantasm wanted this secret, didn't it?"

"Yes. And so it ravaged the mind of every First Born it killed to find it, to find the Last First Born."

"Go on."

TC shook his head. "The cowards learned how to hide. They buried themselves so deep inside of human bodies, merging together with their souls. They created a new race of beings. Revenants. Once inside, they were hard to find. It was rumored the surviving thirty or so had done this to themselves. So the Phantasm disobeyed the covenants between the planes and created a spell that would eradicate the First Borns—the Revenants—burn their existence into ash within those human bodies. It was this disobedience, the creation of this spell, that started the whole border patrol." He smirked at me.

"The Irins were born to prevent the Phantasm's armies from over-running the other planes while hunting down these Revenants."

Uh-huh.

"The new Phantasm managed to destroy a handful before the spell was stolen and hidden away."

Wait. What? I shook my head. "Someone *stole* the spell? How can you steal a spell. Didn't he like commit it to memory?"

"You can't memorize these things," TC said. "Safety catch or something. Ever wondered why witches and sorcerers write it all down in books? Or even why that Grimoire exists? Because you can't memorize it. The Phantasm wrote it down and gave it to his own army of Symbionts—and it was returned every day in order to guard its safety. But—somehow it was stolen."

Weird.

"The Revenants, unfortunately, weren't able to keep their existence secret for long. Their very essence prevented them from remaining invisible to the eyes of the Ethereals, who also believed them to be abominations. So they discovered they could mask themselves by drinking blood in order to keep themselves human." He made a face.

"You actually look disgusted."

"I am. I like overshadowing physical beings—but not fusing with them. It's disgusting. But it diluted their power. Diminished them. The Phantasm forgot about them as they disappeared, no longer a threat. But now . . ." He growled, and I pursed my lips. "But now it looks as if something's found that spell—and they're using it."

"On these Revenants?"

He didn't answer. I moved forward, my hands crossed over my chest. "What about this has got you spooked?"

Archer snorted. "You don't get it, do you? How spells work."

No.

"The creator of a spell is as vulnerable to it as the one it's intended for." A creepy, slow grin cracked his face. "It means there's a weapon out there—to kill the Phantasm with. And I intend on finding it."

8

WELL, this was just all kinds of phucking phantastic.

I eyed TC, still unsure if I should trust a damn thing he said. Honestly—he was making the hairs on my arms rise. It all sounded like a lie—but not the kind he'd make up on the spot. More like a lie he'd been told and committed to memory.

And it raised my hackles.

Mental note: *what exactly* are *hackles?*

"So"—I held up my right hand, index finger in front of him— "let me get this straight. If I create a spell—first off, I can't memorize it, so I have to write it down."

He sighed, crossing his arms over his chest. If he had a watch, I was sure he'd check it. "Yes."

"And—if someone did steal this spell—they could use it against me."

Again, a sigh. "Yes. Can we go now?"

I winced. "Why in the hell do you want me to go with you so bad?"

Now that produced an even bigger sigh. More like a groan.

"You cannot be that thick. How much of those notes have you read?"

"Obviously not enough," I said, putting both my hands on my hips.

"As a Wraith, you possess certain abilities no one else has. Even the Phantasm."

That much I'd gathered over the past seven months. When he didn't continue, I leaned toward him. "And?"

"And nothing—I don't know what all you can do." He smiled. "But I do enjoy finding out. Let's go."

"Wait, wait, wait." I pulled my arm away from him. He was getting mighty grabby lately. "You haven't told me why you want to get to the morgue. If these are bodies—why are you so eager to see them?"

"Not the bodies," TC said. "The Revenants. I'm more than sure there is at least one there—" He paused. "I can't sense them. Not like I can sense other Symbionts. But why else have them brought to that morgue?"

"Oh, I don't know—to keep them all in one place maybe?" I wasn't real thrilled about going back to the morgue, and I was sure Lex was still there. And if she was, she'd want me to stick my hand in that sticky, oogy, cold, nasty . . . thing again. If there was a soul in there somewhere, I hadn't sensed it. And I really didn't want to get that close to it again.

"Are you scared?" He raised an eyebrow at me, and though I hated to think it, he looked damn good in the light of Mom's tea shop.

"I've already seen the bodies. What's there to be scared of?"

"Exactly." He turned and vanished, though his thought lingered in my head. *Let's go.*

I really hated being pressured into doing something I didn't want to do. But then again—what he'd just told me kinda sounded like what I'd read. But from a different perspective. The Dioscuri described the First Borns as the survivors of the first Phantasm war. But how did my great-uncle arrive at that conclusion in his notes? Had a First Born told him?

Lex's conversation with me earlier kept surfacing as well. It also hadn't escaped me that Lex was one of these Revenants. The whole vampire thing sort of gave it away—that and knowing about this spell. And if I understood the logic, the First Born inside her was called Yamato. But Lex had called it a Symbiont—was that the same thing as a First Born?

And TC's opinion of them seemed a bit prejudiced. Man . . . who knew there were so many layers to the Abysmal plane? I didn't even want to get into the Ethereal.

Really.

I didn't.

Becoming the Wraith while in body—how can I describe this? Or even relate the first time it happened after all that Horror craziness last month? I'm not sure there is a way. The first time came when I wanted to go back to the explosion, to see for myself what had happened. It was after Cooper died, and I wasn't feeling right. I'd kept seeing the death mask—skulls—everywhere I looked.

I'd been standing in my room at Mom's, then I was moving up through the roof, through the attic (needed a cleaning!), and into the sky. Hovering.

It'd been almost instantaneous. I'd wanted to be OOB, and I'd planned on lying down on the bed to leave my body in a comfortable position. But—as I'd hovered there above the building—I realized I still had it.

I STILL HAD MY BODY!

And as I looked at it—held out my hands and arms—I saw that

my skin was no longer its natural olive, but black and mottled. My clothing had changed as well. It was still my usual—dark pants and shirt—but my bunny slippers had red eyes and fangs.

And my nails—I'd seen those talons before. When I'd killed Rhonda in her uncle's home. I'd seen this body before. And I knew that spread out behind me were wings so much like the ones I'd first had that same night, and again while battling the Horror.

I didn't know what they looked like. Not sure I wanted to.

So once again I stood in my mother's house, shifting my body from physical plane to Wraith. From human—to not so human. From innocent.

To damned.

Going OOB had nothing on this sensation. Before it was like stepping out of a second skin without feeling. Removing shades from my eyes so that I could see the shadow world around me.

But like this? This was different. Like this I could feel. And I could smell and taste, and I could see. See things I really didn't want to. Sense things just along a certain perimeter around myself. And as I stood there and changed and the world around me grew and shifted, I sensed something—

What's that?

I opened my eyes and looked around the shop. Shadows moved and warped, some sprawled across the floor like dark dry ice, while other things—and there was no other phrase but *other things*—called out like haunted cicadas and a preternatural catbird.

Yeah. Who knew the Abysmal plane had a sound track?

I pushed up, rising through the ceiling, through my bedroom, and finally into the air above the shop. I hovered there, only slightly aware of my wings beating softly behind me. I could sense and see others below me, driving, getting out of their cars, grilling on back porches.

It was June now . . . and summer was here.

I should be grilling at my condo—long sold. Rhonda inside making her killer frappuccinos, Mom making roasted potatoes, with Dags outside with the—

Wait.

WTF?

I said Dags, didn't I?

Shiiiitt. I mean Daniel. DANIEL. He would be outside grilling, and I would be happy and not bothered by any of this shit.

. . .

It really bothered me that I said Dags.

Skip it.

It was June and damn hot. Let's stick with that.

And those below me? If they had noticed me at all, it would have been the distant beating of wings. No, I didn't make that up. TC told me.

Now the dogs? I could just breeze by overhead and set one of those things off in a New York minute.

Something . . . I rose higher and hovered again. What was it I was hearing? Or smelling? Or both? It felt . . . familiar. But somehow . . . not.

Will you stop fucking around?

Cursing, I moved farther up and followed TC. I couldn't really see him, but I could sense him. And though directionally if I wasn't on a Georgia road, I would get lost. I don't do aerial travel. So I just followed him and eventually touched down in front of the morgue.

Parking lot was empty, kinda like it had been this morning. Even the Bentley was gone.

"I don't sense anything," TC said. He stood in front of the double doors, but he wasn't making any moves to go in.

He might not have—but I was registering something. And it had the oogy meter of doom pushing into the red. It was that old smell again—something ancient.

In fact—it felt a lot like—"Lex?"

TC turned to me. "Who?"

"She's the—" But then I thought better of saying anything. Lex had gone through centuries hiding her identity. And since TC had a less-than-stellar opinion of First Borns—Revenants—in general, I decided it wasn't my place to out her either. It was also apparent I could sense her and TC couldn't, giving more credit to his story of how the First Borns burying themselves in humans made them difficult to find. "No, it's nothing."

"You got something?" He looked back at the door. Why wasn't he going in? I'd never known TC to hesitate.

"No," I lied. I wondered if Lex was inside. I assumed that if she was, then, being a Revenant, she could take care of herself around TC, right? I don't know why I was suddenly nervous about the two of them meeting—maybe it was TC's original reaction to the thought of Revenants around.

I moved past him to the door. But as I put my hand out in front of me, intending to move through the interior door—a small cry reverberated within my mind. I hurried into the lobby and listened again. The sense that something was here increased as did the sound of someone's cry.

TC moved beside me, watching. "What do you hear?"

"There's someone crying for help . . ." I moved slowly through the corridors, listening for the voice, aware that the presence I'd been feeling was getting stronger and stronger. In my head I saw it as a pulsing, moving black mist. It was stationary—staying put. And I was pretty sure it sensed me.

But it wasn't afraid. Not like me.

Again a voice cried out in my head. A woman's voice.

I moved into the morgue, past the tables of bodies. The lights were off, but I didn't notice. Lex's private room was before me, and I paused only for a second, TC at my side, before I charged in—moving through the door—and stood at the foot of the table where Mialani lay. I was pretty sure I looked scary with my whole Wraithy goodness up and open, but I felt like a male peacock trying to frighten away any adversary in my yard.

The voice crying for help was stronger than before—loud. And full of terror.

I realized within seconds that the voice was Mialani's.

A man stood beside her—nonthreatening—simply bending over her with his hand on her forehead. And he'd been talking to her, softly, reassuringly. So this is where that old smell was coming from. That sense of old. It was the same sense I got from Lex—the essence of old ghosts and age.

He was medium height—and well built from what I could see. He dressed nice, in an expensive suit. I could smell a soft cologne as he moved though he didn't look at me. Didn't even turn. His hair was dark—cut short in back and on the sides. I could see a well-trimmed sideburn against a strong profile.

A familiar profile.

Wait—I'd met this guy before.

Abruptly, he turned his face and looked at me, grinning. "Good evening, Zoë. I told Mialani if she called out to you, you would come. We need your help."

TC appeared between us, actually hissing like some B-movie vampire. "You! How dare you show your face!"

Oh, get over yourself. I stepped up and moved him out of the way as my wings vanished, and I slowly became myself. Just me. Zoë. I continued moving closer until we were face-to-face.

Yeah. I knew him.

He was an old acquaintance of Rhonda's—someone I'd met back in August of last year. He'd come to Atlanta asking for Rhonda's help in finding someone.

I grinned at him. "Jason?"

He smiled back, white glorious straight teeth and a dimple on each cheek. "Hey, Zoë. It's nice to see you again."

Everything I'd felt since arriving at the morgue coalesced around him—and I realized Lex wasn't here. I wasn't sensing *her*.

I was sensing . . . "Jason . . . you're a . . ."

He moved away from Mialani and tilted his head to the side. "A First Born. Revenant." And then he smiled. "A vampire."

9

TC rushed at Jason then, his fists out. I really don't know what the asshole intended on doing to Jason at that moment—basically because TC never carried through with the action. Abruptly, Jason wasn't there anymore, and TC moved past me and through the wall.

Jason reappeared to my right, standing close. "I hadn't known you'd be bringing the Archer with you. I see a lot has changed since the last time we met." He eyed me. "Including you."

He was referring to our first meeting. Back in August, Rhonda had introduced me to Jason Lawrence and Nick Shay—old friends she called them. Jason's looks were classic—with an almost European accent to them. Tall, broad-shouldered, chiseled features with short, curly hair. His eyes were brown, much like my own color, and he'd been dressed just as immaculately.

Whereas Jason appeared to be in his early thirties, his friend Nick had the appearance of a twenty-year-old but the air and mannerisms of someone much older. Nick had had more of a swimmer's build, with long blond hair kept back in a ponytail. Electric green eyes and almost iridescent skin.

The two of them had disappeared with Rhonda, just when I got my job from Maharba to check out a house on old Web Ginn House Road.

I hadn't seen him since, and because I'd not been Wraith at the time, I hadn't known about . . . this little twist.

We stared at each other. Me more drawn to the darkness that seemed to surround him, just as it had Lex. But where Lex's presence felt ominous and foreboding, Jason had a different air. Not quite as . . . old.

"You've gone through some changes," Jason said. He glanced at where TC had vanished. "But I didn't expect to see you with him. Does Rhonda know?"

I cleared my throat, very much aware he and I were the same height. "*Know* as in would she report it to the Society?"

His eyes flickered—the only evidence I had that I'd hit a nerve. *Booyah.* "You know about that?"

"I found out the hard way, Jason." With a glance back at Mialani, I nodded. "You do that?"

"Me?" He looked back as well. "Drain Mialani? No. But you know I didn't. The spell is used to destroy us."

"Revenants."

"First Born." He sighed. "*Revenant* is such a nasty word. But it's what the Phantasm calls us when we go underground, so to speak. As do his servants." Jason crossed his arms over his chest, and I noticed his suit—*Was that Hugo Boss?* No tie, though. He was playing it casual. "And vampire? Well"—he shrugged—"it's stereotypical. I know in our own history we sort of perpetuated that myth on our own."

And then I got it in one of my rare moments of brilliance. "Hide in plain sight."

He grinned. I'd always liked his grin.

"And Nick? Is he a vampire too?"

"Nick is a ghoul."

I blinked. I knew that.

I looked at Mialani. "Like she was?"

"Yes."

And then another thought popped up in this really freaky brain of mine. "So . . . do your kind always choose same-sex companions? I mean . . . are you and Lex gay?"

Jason's laughter carried around the room. Well, I'm glad he had a sense of humor about it. "Oh, Zoë—I have certainly missed your naive honesty."

My what?

"I could go into detail about the complexities of knowing me for a long period of time, or about the histories of Mialani or Nick. But for the moment—Mialani's soul is in danger."

Huh?

Soul?

What?

"Uhm . . . ghouls have souls?"

"Lex told you how we create ghouls, didn't she? About how the First Borns—or Symbionts, as I've learned the term—inside of us change our bodies, and our blood becomes in a sense a sort of fountain of youth?"

I pursed my lips, remembering the squishy inconsistent stuff I'd touched when I'd put my hand inside of Mialani's corpse. "I'm not sure I'd call it a fountain of youth—'cause you're not really keeping them young. My understanding of it is that drinking your blood kills them."

He nodded. "Yes. It does. It's toxic to the human body, but the essence of the Abysmal plane that lives inside of our blood—inside of our bodies—clings to the human soul, anchoring itself as well as the soul in place. And because it lives to preserve, it preserves their bodies as well."

"So . . ." Wow. My head was spinning. I really needed Rhonda to be there and explain this to me in English. "What you're saying is like with Mialani." I moved past Jason to stand by the corpse. "When Lex gave her blood, it finished off what those others had started. It killed her. But the blood itself grabbed hold of her soul and kept it there—and continued to regenerate her body."

He nodded, his arms still on his chest. "In a sense. But the blood can only accomplish so much before it needs to be replenished."

"Hanh?" I turned a face to him. "Replenished? You mean that drinking-your-blood thing."

"Zoë." Jason lowered his arms and took a few steps toward me. "A ghoul if properly created can live as long as the vampire who created it. A ghoul has to feed regularly from the vampire that created it in order to maintain its aesthetic." He shrugged. "And its sanity."

I held up my hand. "That's where that whole killing spree thing can come in, right?" I said, remembering Lex's remarks from earlier.

"Yes." Jason nodded. "It's a very complicated process—but we can go into it later. Right now, you need to release Mialani's soul."

"Her soul?" I looked back at her face. "Is—is she what I'm hearing?"

Before he could answer me, another voice interrupted him, shattering the relative calm in the morgue as TC came barreling out of the wall he'd disappeared through. I'd kinda wondered where he'd gone.

The Symbiont became solid enough to tackle Jason, the two of them flying past me to crash into the back wall and the cabinets and instruments set up there. I shifted into Wraith as I moved to them, but stopped as a deep, cultured voice spoke to me—inside my head.

Please, Zoë. Release Mialani. If you don't, her soul will remain trapped in that body even as it's embalmed, then entombed. This can't be her fate.

I looked around the room, almost in a crouch as I looked from the two on the floor trying to kill each other to the body. "Who—"

My name is Mephistopheles. I am Jason's—Symbiont. Yes, yes, let's use that term since it's familiar to you. And I know you have the power to release her. I beg of you . . . I can hear her suffering.

Jason's Symbiont sounded like Ian McKellen? What was up with that? And since when did Symbionts care about anything or anybody but themselves?

"Zoë!" Jason called out from where he and TC were on their feet staring at each other. TC's back was to me, his hands out. He was actually raising his hand where I knew the red light would come. "Listen to Mephistopheles! Release her!"

"Don't do it!" TC said without looking back at me. "You release that soul, and you'll be releasing the tainted blood that kept it alive!"

Why did that sound like bullshit?

Because it is, came Mephistopheles' voice. *Release her, Wraith. It is what you do.*

Again I heard the cry—the echo of a woman's frightened voice. I turned to the corpse then and, without thinking, shoved my hand into her.

The burning returned—though not like before. Nothing like before. No.

THIS WAS FREAK'N WORSE!

And it wasn't just contained at my arm. This pain started spreading upward—into my shoulder, then my chest.

You feel pain because it is the Irin in you—that which is Ethereal cannot bear the contact of the Abysmal.

Okay—I liked the sound of Mephistopheles' voice—*butnotrightnow!* "What—what do I do!"

"Stop!" TC screamed, both out loud and inside my head.

Destroy the link between the two—sever the bond.

Okay, I thought, *sever the bond.* I assumed that was the bond between the Revenant blood and the soul, meaning what was binding her to the body. *And if I do that—what happens?*

Did it really matter? No—I just wanted to get my fucking hand out of that burning, nasty goo!

I hissed as I reached around inside the body—half-corporeal, half-noncorporeal. A soul—most of the time they resided in the middle, at the solar plexus. But—I wasn't finding it. And the longer I stayed with my hand in that goo, the faster the pain spread up my arm. I needed to find the soul right away.

Think—think—I told myself.

Blood was the glue.

So—blood was associated with the heart.

Ew.

Can it be hiding there?

With a yell, I moved my hand from the corpse's middle over to the chest and felt something solid—like finding a chunk of rock in toxic pudding. With tears streaming down my eyes, I grabbed hold of the rock—

My fingers buckled into it as I yanked it up through the butchered skin until I was holding it in my hand—Mialani's heart.

It was little more than a wad of congealed goo with a solid

center. And as I held it I could see her there . . . faintly. An amorphous creature surrounding the burned and bloody thing in my hand. Without any idea what I was doing, I crushed it.

There was a scream—my scream—as my own heart contracted in my chest. It felt as if my rib cage had been turned into a bear trap and was crushing my heart and lungs inside of it. The heart evaporated in my hand until there was nothing left, and I was bent over on the floor—no longer Wraith—but just plain old Zoë.

"Stupid . . . so stupid," TC was saying. "You don't fucking get it, do you?"

I wasn't getting anything at the moment—I was trying too hard to pull air into my crushed lungs. I was gasping for breath as I tried to stand and failed. My knees and legs were rubber, and I was aware of a foul smell.

"Just do it, TC." Jason's voice was angry, and very powerful. "You don't have a choice."

And then he was beside me, inside me. TC. The Symbiont was a part of me. I could feel his frustration as well as his fear as the pressure on my chest eased. I wasn't breathing on my own—but with him. And he was filling me with warmth.

I—I couldn't ever remember TC overshadowing—me.

"I'm not," he said in my ear, and I realized he was no longer in me but kneeling beside me, and anger radiated off him in waves. "Don't be so fucking stupid again."

And he was gone.

I lay back on the cold, dirty tiled floor, staring up at the bright lights above me. That smell—what was that smell? Jason was suddenly hovering over me, his left eye bruised below his cheek. He grabbed my arm and helped me sit up and away quickly as something spattered beside where I'd been.

He pulled me in his arms—hands like ice against my again-human skin. His chest was hard like a wooden board and cold beneath his thin shirt. I wasn't uncomfortable against him—but was more enjoying a feeling of safety as I stared at the muddy black goo dripping from the table.

We both stood, with Jason still holding on to me as I turned and gasped. Mialani's body was no longer on that table. Instead, there was a melting pile of viscous, black—well—it looked like something you'd scoop up from the bottom of the Chattahoochie River.

Nasty!

Ew!

"What—"

"Without the soul," Jason was saying as he led me away from it, "there's nothing to prevent time from reclaiming what it rightfully possesses."

And then it hit me—*that* was Mialani. Or what happens to a body after being denied the process of decay for a hundred or so years. I put my hands over my face and coughed. Jason moved behind me and steered me out of the room, past the tables of bodies, and out through the lobby door into the night.

The cold air was like a pleasant slap in the face—and I'd much rather smell the pine-scented air of Georgia than the odor of putrid flesh. I coughed a few times as we moved to the curb, and a huge black Cadillac pulled up next to us. Jason moved to my right and opened the door, gesturing for me to get in.

"Where—"

"Back to Nona's," he said with a smile, and he put a hand on my arm.

We need to talk, came Mephistopheles' voice again in my mind. *And I can't think of a better way to get there but in style.*

I grinned despite my stomach doing flip-flops. I did not feel good. And I'd never been inside a limousine in my life. Crawling in, I fell into the soft leather seats as Jason piled in behind me. As I looked for the seat belt, I noticed a red mark on my host's shirt. My eyes grew wide as the black glass between the front and back opened, and another familiar face peeked through.

"Nick!" I heard myself say.

He grinned at me and winked before taking a look at Jason. Two seconds, and the smile faded. "Jason?"

"I'm good." Jason waved at him. "Just get us over to Nona's. And call ahead—" He winced as he moved enough for me to get my seat belt fastened. "I'm gonna need a little of Kitten's magic."

Nick nodded and turned around, pulling the limo forward and out of the morgue parking lot.

Once we were clear, I turned a sideways look at Jason. He looked a little paler than usual—and Jason normally had a complexion similar to my own. He leaned his head back, pressing his hand to his chest.

"What did TC do?" I heard myself ask. I couldn't remember what had actually happened once that bastard had charged back in. My attention had been snagged by Mephistopheles' voice and Mialani's screams.

"He stabbed me through the heart," Jason said in a soft voice.

!!!

No worries. I am healing him this very moment. Though . . . having Kitten's help will be a bonus.

There were a billion questions running through my head at that moment; why did TC attack like that? Why was he so against me setting Mialani free? Why did the Phantasm want the Revenants dead? What was this first war? There was a Phantasm before this one? How long had Jason been a vampire? Was he one back in August when he visited Rhonda?

Did Jason understand the spell and magic used on Mialani? How had he known to come?

But the first question that came out of my mouth wasn't any of these. No . . . I was so typical.

"Jason—who's Kitten?"

He opened his eyes and grinned at me. "You don't know?"

"Don't know what?"

"About Kitten?"

I blanched. "Oh—Rhonda? You call Rhonda Kitten?" I couldn't imagine anyone calling Rhonda Kitten—and living.

"No." He shook his head and lifted it, looking at me very serious. "Zoë—Kitten was my pet name for Nona."

Pause.

"When we were lovers."

10

I'VE always felt there would be a limit to the ew factor in my life.

And to be honest, I thought I'd already reached it. And I think I rationalized that the instant had been so traumatic I'd core-dumped it from my memory.

So I wasn't prepared for that.

Wasn't eeeeeeeeven going to acknowledge it. No. I sat in that limo in complete silence, all the way back to Mom's. Yeah . . . I had my mouth open. But still.

I could feel Jason grow silent beside me. Even the Symbiont inside him was quiet. I think Nick was a little nervous and turned on the radio. I concentrated on Anastasia's "Everything Burns" and tried to puzzle this one out.

My mom.

And Jason.

Exactly how old is he?

And when was this supposed affair?

Nick expertly pulled the limo into the back of Mom's shop. All the lights were on inside, and the moment we parked, the back door opened. Mom, Rhonda, Joe, Lex, and Jemmy came piling out of the door. Rhonda was the first one to Jason's side of the limo, bending down and inside—with Mom right behind her.

And I watched my mom—really watched her face as she looked at Jason. And I saw—

Zoë?

I jumped at the familiar voice in my head. I turned to see that Joe had opened my door and was leaning in, looking very worried. I grinned at him and took his outstretched hand. "I'm fine," I said, as he helped me out of the limo.

And nearly fell flat on my face as my knees buckled beneath me. I suddenly did not feel so good. Aches, nausea, and a driving headache. Joe scooped me up in his arms—probably the only man I knew who could besides Jason—and carried me inside the house as I struggled to maintain my dignity and not throw up all over him.

We moved through the kitchen and into the botanica, and Joe sat me in my papasan chair. He removed my shoes and quickly covered me with a blanket before shoving a thermometer between my teeth before I could say a word.

Jason, Nick, Mom, Rhonda, and Lex bustled in next, with Jason helped along by Nick. My eyes widened as I saw the growing red spot on the front of his shirt. It was also evident that Jason, his eyes closed and his head lolling to one side, wasn't moving anymore.

Nick put him on the couch to my right and immediately unfastened his shirt, exposing a well-developed six-packed chest covered in dark blood. Rhonda moved in quickly, kneeling in front of him with a jar of something—foul-smelling. Eh . . . whatever that was, it reminded me of sewage. And it was turning my already-nauseated stomach over further as the thermometer beeped and Joe snatched it out. I hadn't realized he was still kneeling beside me.

You have a fever.

I looked over at him. I sort of knew my temperature was elevated. I had a headache. I was sore, achy. Flu symptoms. But—I also somehow knew it was in some way related to my freeing Mialani. Had to be. Which also made me stop and pause. Didn't—hadn't I in the past felt, like . . . euphoric after releasing a soul? Wasn't there always a surge in power and the onset of Mr. Tingles?

Yes . . .

Or at least those were my memories. So I wondered why I felt as weak and frail as a newborn kitten? Why Mialani's soul was somehow different?

Rhonda stood suddenly, her left hand a bloody, gooey mess as Mom moved in and knelt—not an easy feat for a woman with her breast size—and held her hands out over Jason's body.

What was she—

Jason is in shock, Mephistopheles' voice said softly to me.

"I thought you said you were healing him," I said aloud. Nick looked over at me, and I could feel Joe's eyes on me as well.

Rhonda turned and frowned. "I haven't said anything like that."

I waved at her. "Not you." I pointed at Jason. "Him . . . or I mean Mephistopheles."

Lex's eyes widened, as did Nick's.

"You can hear him?" Lex snapped.

I gave her a half-snark look. "Yeah. And he said he was helping Jason earlier, but now he's in shock."

I am. My blood, my bond with him, is what is keeping him from leaving this body. But it is at its base a human body. And not quite old enough to regenerate easily. He paused. *He needs . . . I need . . .*

I sort of knew in my head what Mephistopheles didn't want

to say as I watched my mom's hands glow a soft blue. Her eyes were closed as she moved those hands over his chest, never touching him.

"He needs blood," I said.

Lex hissed.

But Mom held up one of those hands, commanding silence. "Yes. Mephistopheles, can you take control?"

Take control?

What the fuck is that?

And then, abruptly, there was a shift in Jason's body—not something physical because I realized I was seeing this on a different plane—as the skin took on a soft glow. And then, to my horror, Jason sat up, his eyes closed, and my mother continued to hold out her right arm.

Jason's eyes opened. I gasped. They were milky white, much like Archer's. Shadows gouged out the hollows of his face, making him look darker.

Malevolent.

He reached out with his hands and took Mom's arm.

Okay—so I'm not always up with what's going on in front me. I'm more like the movie watcher with her popcorn and soda being dragged along with the audience for what comes next.

Same then. Too late, I realized what was about to happen.

"No!" I shouted, and tried to hop off the papasan so I could pull my mom away from him.

But Joe was holding me, his arms wrapped around my shoulders.

Jason leaned in to my mother's wrist, staring at it. I expected fangs to either materialize or slide down from beneath his lips. In amazed horror, I saw her skin split so much like a seam giving way under tremendous pressure—and blood come rushing out. He brought her arm up to his mouth and began to suckle that wound as Mom gasped and leaned her head forward.

Every bad vampire movie I'd ever seen in my short life sprang to the forefront of my thoughts. I yelled out at him to stop and pushed at Joe. Rhonda was beside me, as was Jemmy, as Joe pushed me back into the papasan and tried to shush me in my mind. I gave him a mental smack as I clawed at him to get to my mom.

Too late I felt the shift, triggered by my need to get to my mom. I'd fought to bring her back, had teetered on the edge of despair when TC took her, and I was not about to let her die in front of me just to feed some damn vampire.

I could see my hands moving from human to Wraith. From flesh to dark shadow. I heard Rhonda gasp as Jemmy cursed softly under her breath. I felt their hands fall away as I stood—

—and faced down Lex. I saw *her* then—Lex's Symbiont, Yamato—an image of power superimposed over Lex's visage. She was as tall as me—and powerful. I could see and feel the vibration of her surrounding me and the room.

STOP! came Mephistopheles' voice in my mind.

I winced.

She winced as well.

I moved to the side to see that Jason was no longer feeding from my mother's wrist. Instead, he was sitting up on his own, Mom's head in his lap, and he was stroking her hair. Nick hovered over the two of them, one hand on Mom's neck, the other tilting a watch where he could see it. He looked at me, his eyes widening for an instant, and nodded.

Your mother is fine. She knows me, almost as well as Nick does. Trust that I would never harm her, Zoë. Never.

I stared at Jason as he stared at me. Abruptly, the whiteness left his eyes, as did the shadows in his face. His eyelids fluttered as he fell back, Nick catching him and easing him down. Jemmy moved in to rouse Mom, the two of them moving away.

It was then I realized I stood in front of the papasan transformed into a Wraith.

The new Wraith.

Rhonda was staring at me with a mixture of horror and fascination. She pointed. "You—"

Lex sighed. All trace of her Symbiont gone, tucked safely inside. "The Wraith has finally emerged, I see. Mephistopheles told me what you did." She bowed deep and with a great deal of composure. "I am in your debt," she said upon rising. "Mialani meant the world to me, and I'm happier knowing she is now free and not forced to endure eternity inside of a rotting corpse." She pursed her lips. "If you will excuse me—I need time."

And she was gone.

No smoke. No moving out the door with a dramatic slam.

Just . . . gone.

Much like TC loved to do.

Rhonda, Jemmy, and Joe were still staring at me, giving me a wide berth.

Finally, Jemmy cleared her throat. "You—you think you can tone that down a bit, girl? You're sick. Longer you stay like that, the longer it'll take your body to recover."

I looked at her, seeing her for the first time with these new eyes. Jemmy's aura was so much like my mom's. A mixture of orange, yellow, purple, and indigo. So much transition. But—at her core—something else burned bright. A vague light I'd never seen before flickered, then disappeared, like a candle being snuffed out.

Tim and Steve appeared behind them. Steve looked indifferent—but Tim's face reflected to me what I must look like to them. I sighed, took a deep breath, and shifted again.

Instantly, I was falling back, my knees completely useless, and Joe was there, taking me into his arms. It was hard to focus as the shadows I'd seen only seconds before filled the edges of my vision.

"She's going out," Jemmy said, as I felt Joe move with me. "Get her upstairs. Gonna need to let her sweat out the fever."

Fever.

I wanted to tell them I was fine, but then my stomach rolled to the left, and I nearly threw up on Joe. I held on to him as we moved up the stairs, each step accompanied by nausea.

It's okay, came his tentative voice in my head. *I've got you.*

I moaned. God . . . I hadn't felt this bad since those one or two times I'd stayed out of my body too long and had to deal with the physical consequences. I felt soft sheets on my skin, but it was getting harder to keep my eyes open.

And I was . . . cold.

Very cold.

Pressure on my chest opened my eyes. I saw Joe, and Rhonda. Jemmy was on my right and made a noise. I'd wanted to ask what was happening . . . but that didn't come out. I was horribly sick to my stomach and couldn't move.

I am sorry, Mephistopheles said again in my mind. And I could feel his emotion in his voice. *I was dishonest with you.*

I blinked a few times before closing my eyes. What was happening to me? There was no way I was going to stay awake no matter how hard I fought.

Dishonest?

Yes. The Archer's protest was valid to some degree. He knew what would happen if you released Mialani. He knew how it would affect you as well as himself.

I wanted to know, but I also wanted the dark oblivion I could see coming for me.

Mephistopheles paused. *When you release a ghoul, Zoë, you don't receive the benefits of its soul's release.*

I waited long enough on the precipice of that darkness for his explanation.

You take on its damnation.

11

USUALLY, it's during this time I have some weird, wacky dream. Something that shows just how crazy the internal workings of my head can be. Yeah . . . well . . . I wasn't disappointed.

I wasn't on the back porch of Mom's house this time—nor was I beside a babbling brook or even running through some deranged cave or other freakish nightmare place. This time I found myself in one of the squares in Old Savannah.

And you know how I knew it was a dream?

It *wasn't* stiflingly hot like Savannah usually is in June.

I was dressed in my usual: dark pants, shirt, and bunny slippers (happy slippers with pink noses), and the sun was somewhere above the canopy of magnolias and Spanish moss. There weren't any people out. No bums in the square, no shoppers, no elderly couples taking a siesta.

I couldn't tell which of the squares I was in. No landmarks. Not even a sign.

Instead of just standing there, I started to walk around, looking for someone.

Anyone.

"Zoë?"

Ah—I knew it!

I turned—expecting to see Rhonda or Mom, or even Joe or Jemmy, Steve or even my dad. I wasn't expecting the mature, white-haired woman standing by the nearest tree. Her hair had a soft luminescence to it as it flowed down over her shoulders and seemed to disappear into the white—uhm—clothing she was wearing.

I tilted my head to the left, still trying to discern exactly what it was this person was wearing.

"You don't recognize me, do you?"

My gaze traveled from her clothing to her face, and I concentrated on it. She had brilliant blue eyes, and wasn't as old as I originally thought she was. But as to who she was? I was drawing a wholesome blank. I shook my head. "Hint?"

She smiled. "I'm a Guardian Familiar."

Oh. Shit! "Alice?"

She nodded. I smiled. *Hooo-kay.* So . . . I was dreaming about one of Dags's Familiars. *How wrong is that?*

"We need to talk—but I'm afraid I don't have much time in this realm."

"Realm?"

"Dream time."

Oh. I nodded. *Okay, I'll play along.* "You can do this? Come into someone's dream?"

"Not everyone's dream. But Darren shares a deep affinity for you—and you for him—so that makes the communication ea—"

"Wait." I put up my hand. "Hold it. I do *not* have an affinity for him."

"Yes, you do."

"No, I don't."

"Yes, you do."

"No. I. Do. Not."

She glared at me. I sighed. "Go on." Wasn't this *my* dream?

"As I was saying . . . it makes it easier for me to find you when you are dreaming."

I won't say I wasn't a little happy that I'd somehow established some kind of link with Dags—even if it was through some weird Familiar dream-link-thingie. And nothing was going to stop me from saying, "How is he?"

Saying hell. I *blurted* that out.

Blah.

What I didn't expect was the confused look on Alice's face. She opened her mouth, then closed it, and half turned away. "He's not dreaming."

"Not dreaming?" I frowned "You can tell?"

"Being"—she looked back at me—"what I am. I'm a part of Darren. Both Maureen and I are. It's a symbiosis in its own way. Though—since he was fused with the Grimoire—our impact on his life lessened. He can survive without us—though maimed. But without the Grimoire, he will die."

Yeah . . . I'd been told that. But I was still fuzzy on the details. Dags had his own stories to tell. "And you can see his dreams?"

"I could if I wanted to, but I don't. I'm not that nosy." She shrugged. "But the point is, he's not dreaming. Hasn't been for several weeks. It was spotty at first, and I'd noticed he was having trouble concentrating. But now—"

"Is it affecting his abilities?"

"Yes. Mostly with Maureen. He rarely uses his left hand when fighting, and I'm getting overtaxed. When he does call on Maureen"—she frowned—"there's something wrong."

"Can't you just talk to Maureen? I mean, are you two like sisters in this? Share the same condo? Chez Dags?"

She smiled at my quip but shook her head. "Maureen doesn't know either. She's just as surprised. And I know if she lies." Alice shook her head. "We're not sure what to do—so I wanted to see if you could help us?"

Us?

"Why hasn't Dags answered my calls?"

Whoa. Wow. Where the fuck did that come from? I had to look inward at myself. *Jealous much?*

Alice's confused expression spoke volumes. "You called him? He said he hasn't heard from you since last month."

"I called him!" I held out my arms. "More times than I'll admit to. He's been in contact with Rhonda though."

"Well, he's working for her group."

I hated that. "So has she noticed anything different?" *And now that I know about this not-dreaming thing, I intend on asking Rhonda about it too.*

"I don't know. We've been in California most of the month. The SOI had him procuring another Grimoire—though not as powerful as the one he carries."

"Did he get it?"

"Oh yes." She looked distracted. "I have to go—"

"Wait." I tried to take a step forward but found I didn't have any feet. Figures. Damn dream. I was apparently growing out of the square itself. And my happy, pink-nosed bunny slippers had hopped off somewhere. "Alice—was that what you needed to tell me?"

She wasn't looking at me anymore—she was walking away in a lazy stroll, through a hedge made of azaleas that turned from pink and red to black and white. The trees turned gray as well as the world became monochromatic—looking a lot like an old horror movie.

And as if on cue, a hand popped out of the ground to grab at my feet. I squealed a little. Okay. I flat-out shrieked because I really wasn't expecting skeletal hands. And then—

I sat up in bed, and something cold and wet fell into my lap. Blinking, I looked down to see a folded washcloth in front of me. My head felt as if someone had stuffed it full of styrofoam pellets, and they moved from side to side when I moved my head.

"You're awake," came a melodic voice to my left. I realized then I was in my bed at Mom's. And I was dressed in a set of very soft cotton pajamas. Uh . . . where did these come from? I narrowed my eyes to the voice and saw Jason move to sit on the bed beside me.

He looked incredible—much better than the last time I'd seen him. Eric Bana in the Hugo Boss summer collection.

Niiiice.

Sans the jacket, of course.

He reached out and took the cloth from my hands, but then immediately put his own hand to my forehead. I realized then I was wet. I mean—my entire body was covered in a heavy layer of sweat, and the pajamas were sticking to me in all the right strategic places. "Fever's broken. That's good."

Fever?

When he pulled his hand away, he got up and moved into the bathroom, which joined my bedroom to the adjacent one where Rhonda sometimes crashed. I heard water running as I threw off the heavy cover. Yeah, I was covered in perspiration. I needed a shower.

But when I stood to move into the bathroom, some asshole

moved the floor on me, and I went down, my knees giving first. I never actually hit the floor though—as Jason was instantly there, holding on to me, his arms around me. With a sigh, he nearly picked me up and sat me back on the bed.

Next, he leaned down to my eye level and pointed a finger in my face. "You—sit. It'll take you maybe a day to get up to speed—if I'm right about your Wraith ability." With that, he turned and went back into the bathroom.

I stayed put. Not because he told me, but because I was still focusing on not falling in a seated position.

When he came back, he had the washcloth again and a bowl of water. Setting it on the nightstand, he started moving the cool cloth up and down my arm, then moved it to my face, where he pulled my hair away and started wiping it all down.

I wanted him to stop because I felt twelve and helpless. But I was getting very light-headed and nearly fell back again. Jason was there and moved me into the bed.

"Please . . ." I managed to say. "I'm hot. Don't put that quilt back on top of me."

"I won't," he said, and continued to dip the cloth into the cold water and rub it over any exposed skin. "Breaking a fever like yours was hard. Just sit back and relax. Joe went to get you a glass of water with cucumbers."

Cucumbers?

Jason laughed. "Don't make that face. It's good for you. And you need the liquid. You're dehydrated."

I watched him, again amazed at how incredibly beautiful he was. Oh, don't get me wrong—when it came to beautiful men, I was surrounded by them to hear me talk. From Daniel's boy-next-door look to Joe's rugged manliness, all the way to Dags's pretty-boy face.

But this—

This was a vampire. A First Born. A Revenant.

I cleared my throat as I watched him with droopy eyelids. "What happened?"

"To you? Or to me?"

"Both."

"Well, for me"—he wiped my forehead one more time before setting the cloth in the bowl—"when Archer came at me, he initially stabbed me through the heart with a rod of rowan tree."

A what? He had a stake? Was Jason kidding? And where did a Symbiont stash a stake in his coat?

"Apparently, when you pushed him through the back wall, he traveled to England and snatched a stake from a magic house over there. It hurt, and it did some serious damage to me, as in Jason. But as for ending my life?" He smiled. "Not yet."

"But why did he try to kill you?"

"Oh, I wouldn't say that he was trying to kill me. It was more like"—he smiled—"sibling rivalry."

I reached up with my left hand but couldn't get to his chest. Reading my actions, he pulled up his shirt to expose a well-toned chest and a healing hole to the center right from my point of view. "I guess healing fast isn't true about vampires?"

"Revenants." He smiled. "It's not my favorite word—but *First Born* has a pretentious ring to it, don't you think?"

I couldn't help but smile. He had a way about him. Something kinda sparkly in his eyes, and I was disappointed when he pulled his shirt back down. Lemme tell ya . . . the Revenant's got a serious six-pack, ladies.

"I've glanced over the Dioscuri notes on us"—he gestured to himself—"and they're vague at best. Your great-uncle wasn't as curious about us as he was all the other little critters on the Abysmal plane." Jason gave a short sigh. "I've already explained a lot of this to Nona, Rhonda, and Jemmy. Lex, of course"—he looked directly at me beneath his dark brows—"is forever in your debt. She felt Mialani's release, as did I. Now, knowing that her companion is in a better place, she feels she can fight whatever this is that's coming after us."

As I rested there and watched him, the sweat on my body cooled, and I started shaking. *Meh. This totally sucks.* Jason stood and pulled the cover back up and handed it to me. "Sorry," I said. "Body can't seem to like hot or cold."

"No, no." He sat back down. "It's perfectly normal. For you. Zoë, there are degrees to what I am. Abilities, strengths and weaknesses that all have to do with age. Age of the Symbiont and age of the host."

I wasn't really sure this was a good time for an episode of *Life as a Revenant*, but I was willing to do anything to keep him sitting there. And no, it wasn't because he was nice to look at, or that I really needed to know what the fuck it was he and Lex were, but because I had every intention of getting out of him *when* it was he'd boinked my mom!

He looked in my direction for a bit, but not at me. I knew his mind was somewhere else, remembering something else. "When a Symbiont, or First Born, fuses, or merges, or joins—pick a word—with a human, body and soul—and I do mean soul—the human doesn't gain all the benefits of becoming a Revenant all at once. It happens in stages and over time, as the Symbiont's Abysmal essence changes the human body's DNA. You grow stronger, more impervious to age and disease. You find you can do things—like jump higher than an average human. And the older you grow, the more you change, and the stronger the Symbiont becomes."

Like this irritating stake wound, Mephistopheles said in my head. An echo of Jason's voice. *The Archer's aim was accurate, and it might have killed a much younger host. But Jason has reached his century mark, and so I am able to control a bit of his physical health. My being has changed his blood, and is healing the wound. It's not instantaneous yet—but given time, it will be.*

I understood that. Or I'd read enough vampire or fantasy books to get it. "So—you can withstand a fire?"

Jason shook his head. "Probably not. If my body becomes too badly injured for Mephistopheles to heal, then I will die."

"And what happens to him?"

"He finds a new body."

I had to ask. "What if he can't find one?"

There was a slight laugh in my mind. *I always find a body. But I do not take it. My hosts give me life voluntarily.*

"He finds us at our weakest," Jason said. "But not in a bad way. I wasn't the healthiest candidate. But his former host had been stabbed repeatedly on the docks in Manhattan. I was there . . . homeless. A vagrant. And I was dying and didn't realize it. He offered me a future when I didn't have one." He looked down. "I couldn't see one."

I had this feeling there was more to Jason's story than he was giving me. But I didn't want to pry. "Why do you drink blood? I have the reason that TC told me. But you tell me. Is it really to maintain humanity?"

He looked at me. "Yes."

Wow.

"When I said that age is a plus, I also mean it's a detriment. As our bodies change, we grow less human. The Revenants discovered a long time ago that by drinking human blood, they could maintain the status quo, so to speak. If we don't drink blood, then our bodies will undergo a dramatic change."

"You mean a physical change?"

He nodded. "Yes. Not so different than your own change now, as a corporeal Wraith. But not something we can hide as you do. So we drink it to maintain the balance. Like the other night— when your mother offered me blood—she knew that if I didn't get it, Mephistopheles' blood would start to change me physically because it's a fight of the fittest. Whose blood is stronger. So she gave me hers willingly, and I was able to stay human."

Well, there was my in . . . but my curiosity level of what he was talking about overpowered my when-did-you-boink-my-mom level. "If you'd have changed into this other . . . this thing like me . . . would you not change back? I mean, I can change back. Pretty easy."

Jason looked more serious than I'd ever seen him. It looked interesting on him. "Not easily. Mephistopheles is strong, and he's never tried to override *me*"—he put his hand to his chest—"Jason Lawrence. If I were to lose that much control, survival would kick in. It's a natural response. I could eventually change back, reverse the body shifts. But as I am—unlike you—I am more human than Abysmal creature."

I sighed and closed my eyes. Geez, I was tired. And I was pretty happy Jason was okay.

"There's one other thing, Zoë."

Uh-oh. I looked at him. "Is it about my mom? This whole dating-her thing?"

"No—but that is something she and I need to talk to you about. My concern is what's happening to you on the Wraith side. The physical transformation rather than the astral one." He cleared his throat. "Your relationship with the Archer, to be exact."

I thought about TC. About his seemingly uncontrollable dislike for Jason. For all Revenants. His attack. And then how he—

"Jason—TC was the one that helped me. After I released Mialani."

"Yes."

"He's never done that before."

"No."

"But you seemed to know he could." I pushed myself up on my elbows and narrowed my eyes at him. "What is it you're not telling me?"

He took in a deep breath and clasped his hands together in front of me. "I'm not sure how to tell you this—but as a preface: did you ever wonder how it was that he could do what he did with you? That of all the Symbionts out there—you had a run-in with one that, when he touched you, you changed?"

Honestly—that thought had never crossed my mind. I shook my head. "I didn't know that no other Symbiont could have done what he did." I leaned back, held out my left arm, and looked at the handprint there. It was faint now, and looked almost gold. "I was out of body, and he tried to take my soul. But when he touched my astral body—"

"The shock from touching the living plane changed both of you." Jason nodded. "The Archer is a liar above all things, Zoë. Dedicated to self-preservation. He is also one of us." He lifted his shoulders and stared directly at me. "He is the *Last* First Born."

12

IF there was one thing I'd been expecting in terms of waiting for the other shoe to drop—that wasn't it. In fact, that was nowhere near what I'd expected to hear from Jason. And I'm sure my face showed it as he moved in a little closer and reached out for my hand. Again, I was surprised at how warm it was and how pliable his skin was in comparison to Lex's.

"Zoë, I know that probably sounds made up—"

"Uh . . . yeeee-ah," I said. "You're trying to tell me that TC—the freak that derailed my being some Irin or such—is actually one of you?"

I could hear Mephistopheles grumbling somewhere, under his breath. Something about asses and donkeys.

I like him. He's my kinda disembodied voice.

Jason's eyes narrowed, and I kinda figured he and the Symbiont hijacker were in conversation, privately. I also figured that I could hear Mephistopheles only when *he* wanted me to. Finally, he gritted his teeth and looked at me. "Apparently Mephistopheles isn't that fond of calling the Archer what he is."

"Neither am I," I said. "But this—How can he—But I didn't—"
Och. This was getting me nowhere.

"Zoë." Jason lowered his shoulders. "When the first Phantasm created them—the First Borns—he created a limited number, and even now that total is unknown. But Archer was created last before the original Phantasm was destroyed. He was never allowed to mature or grow up outside of the next Phantasm's influence."

"So that's why he was doing the Phantasm's work?"

"He was for so long controlled by the Phantasm—until he met you. And then everything changed."

I heard Joe's footsteps before he came in, a tall glass in his hands. He stopped in the doorway and grinned. His hair seemed droopier than usual, and I wondered if he'd run out of gel. He held up the glass as he stepped forward. *Jason said this will help you feel better.* And he handed it to me.

I took it. The glass was clouded with condensation, and I could see the cucumber floating inside with ice. "Cucumbers."

It's actually pretty good. Nona put a bit of sweetener in mine. Though I don't think that's a good idea for you.

I cocked an eyebrow at him just as his phone went off. He held up a hand and pulled it from his back pocket. Joe couldn't talk on the phone—having no voice. So he and Mastiff used texting in order to communicate. I watched as he looked at the screen, then moved out of the room.

Jason gestured to the glass. "It's really refreshing. Vitamins."

I stared at it and, with a shrug, tasted it.

Smack, smack. Hrm . . . not so bad. Cucumber wasn't a flavor I usually chose over strawberry or vanilla, but this would do. Abruptly, I was parched, and I drank the whole thing down before realizing I could get—

"Uh, Zoë, you might want to slow down before you get—"

Och. I winced and pressed my fingers to the bridge of my nose as an old familiar pain centered there.

Brain freeze.

Jason took the glass and waited patiently for me to refocus on him. "Be careful."

"Just go on."

"Those of us born before him were released as free spirits into the planes. Back then, there weren't barriers, or Guardians, or any real rules regarding realms."

I rubbed at my forehead. *Oh man* . . . What a headache I was getting. *Maybe I should check my sugar?* "In the good old days?"

"Maybe." Jason shook his head. "My memories of those centuries aren't as clear—too many years have passed from host to host. But there were no borders. And the Phantasm worked in tandem with the Seraphim."

"The angels?"

The look he gave me was soooo condescending. Oh. I hate that look. It was bad enough when TC did it. It was just intolerable for someone with Jason's face to do it. "No, and yes. Much about the Seraphim is a misconception. Misinterpreted. Creatures like the Seraphim aren't a grouping of angels—as literature would have you believe—but the culmination of eternity wrapped up into a single entity. Many as one."

What was that emoticon that meant complete incomprehension? Oh yeah.

O.o

'Cause that was the look I gave him.

And to his credit, he didn't look impatient. He looked more determined. "Okay, take the Phantasm. The term itself has a plural connotation to it. Phantasms in lore have sometimes been labeled into a swarm or a group. Same as the Seraphim. But in truth, it's really just a title."

A title. "You mean like president or Speaker of the House. The position remains the same but different personalities inhabit it."

He grinned. "Yes. There have only been to my knowledge—or to Mephistopheles' memory—two Phantasms. The one that created the First Borns. A war happened—not unlike the most recent Bulwark—and the present Phantasm took control."

"What happened to the first Phantasm?" I was still waiting on the explanation of TC being a First Born, but I still wanted a bit more history. More than the Dioscuri notes could give me.

"That creature—" He hesitated, and his eyes took on that whole MEGO look. I knew it wasn't because I was boring him but because he was obviously talking to Mephistopheles. *Wow . . .* I wondered what it was like to constantly have some sort of presence in one's head. I didn't wonder for long, as I was immediately reminded of my overshadowing people, with my voice in their heads. Ick. "That creature isn't with us any longer."

"The new Phantasm kill him?"

"No—" He shook his head and refocused on me. "I can't really say. Even Mephistopheles isn't sure what happened. They only knew the moment their creator was no longer in power, and they had become a hunted group." He gave a short sigh. "But do you understand the concept of the Seraphim?"

"Yes," I lied. I wanted to get on with the story.

"Sure. As I said—both planes worked together. Not always in harmony. The Phantasm created his first brood to go into the planes and experience life. Primarily physical existence."

"Now," I interrupted, "my understanding is that the Phantasm can't actually touch or influence this plane."

"Right." Jason nodded. "Neither can the Seraphim. Their very being isn't able to connect to this plane. If they ever tried—the worlds as we know them would cease. And so would they."

"Wait." I held up a hand. "Can we back up with the cease? You mean like—end. Poof?"

"Yes. Poof. Which is why they both made their soldiers, their scouts, extensions of themselves through which to experience things."

"The Seraphim too? It makes Symbionts?"

Jason nodded slowly. "Yes."

Jason checked his watch. A Rolex, I noticed. He patted my thigh. "I'll be right back. Rhonda was making you a snack." He stood and left the room.

I was feeling . . . punched in the stomach. My head was a jumble of things, from the scene in the morgue with Jason and Mialani and TC, the dream with Alice about Dags, and now trying to understand that somehow TC was a—First Born?

I heard the tray before Rhonda came into the room with Mom in tow. Rhonda wore a pinched expression, which only complemented her black tee shirt and cargo shorts. She wasn't wearing her usual black lipstick or black nails, and her skin looked even paler than when she wore makeup on it.

Mom—well, Mom was Mom. She wore a pair of jeans and a tee shirt, though the shirt was pretty much stretched to its limit over her breasts. I watched her come in, then, "Hey—that's my tee shirt!"

She only waved at me as she came around the right side of the bed, a thermometer in her hand. I pointed at it. "I don't need that."

"Yes, you do." She pressed the button and heard the beep. She leaned over me. "You can open wide, or I can use this one the way I did when you were a baby."

Oh, I opened wide. And while I lay there with a stick under my tongue, Rhonda set a tray of Mom's goodies at the foot of the bed. I recognized her lemon cake, salmon and salad, soft yeast rolls, a fruit salad of strawberries, pineapple, and blueberries, and a carafe of what I figured was tea.

I was wondering who the feast was for until my stomach betrayed me with a vengeance. Rhonda grinned at me. "I see your stomach is better."

Nodding, I sat up. The room didn't tilt on me the way it had, and the stick beeped. Mom pulled it out in time for me to grab up the roll and bite into it.

"You're still at a hundred," she said.

I pointed to the carafe and looked at Rhonda, the question in my eyes, did my mom make that?

'Cause she was notorious for her really nasty tea concoctions. Rhonda glanced over at Nona, who was pressing buttons on the thermometer, and gave me the head shake. No, Mom didn't make the tea. *Yay!* So I poured myself a small mugful and sprinkled in some Stevia.

Jason came back in, a mug in his hand. I frowned. Revenants eat?

Ah, no, we do not eat, came Mephistopheles' voice in my head. *But our hosts must for at least the first two centuries. Jason is still young and has an enjoyment with beef.* There was a pause and a chuckle. *As do I.*

Somehow that was just wrong. But I wasn't going to figure it out just yet.

He looked at Nona. "Good?"

"Well, good for what we started with Wednesday."

Wednesday. I looked at Jason and Rhonda. "What day is it?" Oh God, please no. Tell me I didn't lose days again?

"Saturday," Rhonda said. "It's about seven thirty in the evening."

Shit!

I set the mug down, my appetite vanishing. "What the hell happened?"

Mom and Rhonda crossed their hands on their chests in unison. Now I know the two of them shared Rhonda's body for a while, after Mom's soul escaped from TC, but this whole thing with them doing similar movements and saying similar things—CREEPY. "Apparently you did release Mialani's soul," Rhonda said. "But it had a real blowback effect on you. Usually you get more powerful—that whole euphoric thing you loved to tell me about."

Well, that worked with what Jason had said. "So I got sick."

"You got deathly ill," Mom said, and sat on the bed beside me. "I think I'd gotten used to you being so strong as a Wraith, that nothing could hurt you."

"I'm not sure I want to do that again anytime soon," I said, and realized then that I hadn't gotten the end of the story from Jason. Crap. I looked at him. "You gonna finish?"

Jason had been sipping his—coffee? "Oh. Yes. Sorry. Ah." He set the mug down on my nightstand and put his hands together. "To bring you up to speed—after the usurping Phantasm took control, he sent his armies of creatures out to hunt and destroy the First Borns. All but a handful survived those first centuries, until they learned how to merge with human souls."

I'd heard most of this before from TC, but it felt like Jason was being a little more Revenant-friendly with his retelling. "The Phantasm somehow gained the knowledge of spell casting, Seraphim-style—and created a spell that destroys or obliterates Revenants. It managed to dwindle down the ranks to a rumored twenty or so Revenants before the spell was stolen."

I nodded. "TC told me about the spell being stolen. And so the Phantasm stopped hunting?"

"Well." Jason shrugged. "There didn't seem to be a purpose any longer. When First Borns go Revenant, their power is diminished as they grow closer to the physical plane. The Phantasm turned its attention to that last offspring. The Last First Born, who fell under the Phantasm's spell, became his right hand. His Metatron, as you might believe."

I looked at each of them. No news there for them. "So TC is that Symbiont."

"It explains his being stronger," Rhonda said. "Different than the rest. I mean . . . in all this time of your traveling around OOB . . . it can't be that you've never encountered one before and nothing happened. With it either in body or out of a body."

I had to agree. "So this Phantasm now has had TC with him all this time, knowing he could be a threat."

"TC—" Jason smiled. "What you call him?"

"Yeah." I nodded. "When I first saw him, he was like Vin Diesel in a trench coat. So I just referred to him as Trench Coat. TC."

"But you know he's called the Archer—and what that means."

"Well, yeah." Though I couldn't remember where that name came from or who told me. *Yikes . . . there goes my perfect recall.* "He's a rogue, a betrayer."

"And who do you think gave him that name?"

I blinked at Jason. "Oh man . . ."

"Yes." He nodded. "Because he fell into the control of the Phantasm, we knew it was a voluntary control. He chose to do the Phantasm's bidding for his own gain. He was the last, and he was the most ruthless of us all."

Mom looked at Jason. "Mephistopheles—if the Archer is like you, why didn't he ever become a Revenant?"

I wondered why Mom addressed the Symbiont and figured she could hear him too. Until I watched Jason's face change, and I was reminded of those lucid moments downstairs, when my mother gave her wrist to him. A darkness came over his face, something alien. Something . . . wrong. And for an instant I was a little afraid of this Symbiont, of this creature that stole Jason's natural life and drank the blood of living beings. *Because to join as you see here, lessens us. We diminish little by little as the lives of our hosts bury our own memories. He is far more powerful as he is, remaining Abysmal.*

It was a voice I heard with my ears, and in my mind. I don't know why I assumed the host controlled the symbiosis, but it became painfully clear as I watched and listened that Mephistopheles could take control of Jason anytime he wanted. Yet, he chose not to.

"You mean by not fusing, or joining with a human soul," Rhonda said, "he kept his power intact. But used it with the Phantasm. Willingly."

I shook my head at that—I'd had conversations with TC several times—and he'd alluded to waking from a deep sleep when he touched me. I suspected that for a long time he'd been in the Phantasm's service because he was forced.

But then, I was wrong a lot. And voicing this opinion just then, probably not a good idea.

And then my mind started working on its own—this was where Rhonda usually chimed in—but over the past months I'd experienced so much and my own curiosity about my mother and my father . . . of what I was . . . I wanted to know.

"Mephistopheles," I said. "How does the fusion happen?"

Jason/Mephistopheles laughed softly. *Ah, you are seeing the greater picture. You understand now why he was able to heal you in the morgue, why he did not want you to release Mialani.*

Oh hell yeah, I got it. I got it big-time.

Mom held out her hand. "What is it?"

"TC kept himself free of joining with a human host for centuries," I said as I watched Jason's face. "But"—I looked at Mom, then Rhonda—"when he touched me—"

Rhonda hissed.

Mom put a hand to her mouth.

"Why didn't we see this before?" Rhonda said.

"Because we didn't understand the Dioscuri notes," Mom chimed in. "Is this true? Mephistopheles—is Zoë his host?"

"No."

I looked at Jason. That was his voice and not the Symbiont's. "No?"

He shook his head. "The Archer has joined with you, but it's not a complete fusion. It's more of a connection. But one he desires, and one he fears. His link to you is a true symbiosis, not a parasitism. You both draw from each other, but you also give each other strength. Whereas our merging engages the human and diminishes the First Born."

"But that doesn't make any sense. Why haven't all of you become like Zoë?" Rhonda said. "When he touched Zoë, she became a Wraith. A new creature. When the Symbionts joined with the others—"

"Humans," Jason said. "Just plain humans. Creates us."

"And when he touched my child," Mom said. "Who isn't human—"

"But an Irin," Rhonda said, and lowered her shoulders. "Something different happened."

Jason nodded. "If he'd joined with a normal human, he would have been like us. And the Phantasm would not fear his power. But because his touch created a Wraith"—he smiled—"he fears you most of all."

I felt as if I'd been kicked in the stomach—again—though I did like knowing more about TC. And don't think I wasn't gonna ask him about this when I saw him again.

Which brought up: "Mom"—I looked at her, then glanced at Jason—"you and I need to talk."

I thought—for a second—Nona Martinique was going to do some sort of dodge like she always did when she didn't want to talk about something. But Joe took that moment to come into the bedroom holding up his phone, his expression hard. Rhonda took the phone at the same time I heard his voice.

There's another body.

"There's another body," Rhonda echoed.

Jason was on his feet within seconds, his eyes wide, his hands out to his side. It looked as if he'd been slapped, hard. Mom was beside him, taking an arm. "Jason?"

He ran his fingers through his hair and looked at Mom, then at me. "Oh God," he said. "It's a Revenant."

13

I wasn't all that and a bag of chips when we left Mom's house at about eight thirty or so—me, Joe, Jason, Rhonda, and Tim piled into Jason's Lincoln, with him at the wheel. Mom insisted on staying home in case we needed her. But I sort of got the feeling Jason had confused her on some deep emotional level, and Nick volunteered to stay with her. And to be honest, I was still confused as well. And I really wanted to get one of them alone long enough to get the details.

Which seems kinda Jerry Springer when I think about it now.

My mom and a Revenant.

Ew.

We traveled in Jason's Cadillac, with him at the wheel. Joe sat in the front, and Rhonda and I were in the back.

I looked at Rhonda, and said in a low voice, "Dags is working for you, right?"

She glanced at me. "Yeah."

"He talk to you? About things? Like him and the girls? Maureen and Alice?"

"Yeah . . . sometimes. Though I usually just talk to them my-self." She frowned. "What is it? You're not all freaked-out because of it, are you?"

I shook my head. "No. But do me a favor—find out if he's dreaming."

Her expression was priceless, a mixture of WTF and HUH? "Dreaming? I just ask him that?"

"Yeah. Ask him if he's dreaming. Or if he's sleeping. When you talk to him again."

Rhonda nodded. "Okay. But why?"

"I dreamed about Alice," I said as I looked at Rhonda's eyes. "She said Dags wasn't dreaming."

"Oh, Zoë." She grinned, and her tone sounded like Mom's did sometimes, when she was about to shake her head at me and go "tsk-tsk" because I had said something stupid. "*You* dreamed about Alice? You know how whacked out your dreams are. It was probably nothing. Of course he's dreaming. We all dream."

"I didn't have a whacked-out dream." I gritted my teeth at her, and I guess something went wrong with my eyes because hers widened. I could feel that bit of the wild inside of me, and I backed off. "Look—I think it was the real thing. You want proof." I twisted in the seat because honestly, if I paid attention anymore to Jason's crazy driving, I was gonna puke. Man, no wonder Nick did most of the driving.

I vote Nick back on the island.

Rhonda was waiting.

I pointed at her. "You sent him off to California to find another Grimoire, but not as powerful as the one inside him."

Her expression? Golden. After her eyes bugged back in her head, she leaned in to me. "How did you find out? Did you go OOB and spy on me?"

Go OOB and spy ... why hell! Why didn't I think of that? Shit.

Evidently my expression was enough to convince her that wasn't what I'd done. "You trying to tell me it was the dream? Alice told you this?"

I nodded. "Yeah."

She looked away, then back. "Did he get it?"

I narrowed my eyes. "Is that a test?

"What do you mean? If Alice told you where he was, did she say whether or not he got it?"

I stopped then—a little confused. "Didn't he?"

She put her hands up. "That's the problem. We don't know. Last I heard from him concerning this new Grimoire was Wednesday. Then he vanished for a few days before he called and said he was in town. But when I asked him about the Grimoire, he avoided the question."

But ... didn't Alice say he found the book? So ... why hadn't he told Rhonda this? Unless ... he was in trouble. Something was wrong. But that didn't fit either. If he was in trouble, then wouldn't Alice have been more specific?

Oh ... this is already turning out to be one hell of a week. Starting out like it always did, with a bunch of crap that makes no sense. But eventually, it'd all come together.

Or not.

It was just before nine when we arrived. The morgue parking lot was empty except for the Bentley outside and Mastiff's car. Jason didn't bother parking and simply stopped the car at the curb so we could all pile out. Once again, we were through the doors and into the back area of the morgue. This time I remembered to take Tim's rock, so he was a half-visible presence moving around the place like a six-year-old in a fun house. Yep, doesn't get out much, does he?

Lex was in a rage—and I knew this because her skin was flushed. No, this Revenant of an indeterminable age wasn't pale at all. Her eyes glowed red from deep inside, and I knew then that the Symbiont—First Born—dwelling in there was pissed. Off.

A male body lay on the table this time. He looked to be Jason's age. Blond, well maintained—even though the age of the body was up for question. His face was ruggedly handsome. He would fit well on a beach anywhere in the world—except for the fact that every inch of his flesh was carved up with symbols, and he was obviously drained of blood.

Help . . . me . . .

The call was deafening and rattled in my brain. I put my hands to my head and crumpled down on my knees. Sonofabitch that *hurt.* It was so different than Mialani's cry for help. Like comparing the pad of a cat's foot on the roof with an elephant's stomp. Jason was beside me, as was Joe, both of them pulling me back on my feet.

What gives? Can't a girl crouch if she wants to?

Help . . . me . . . please . . . pain . . .

"AAHHHHHH!" someone yelled out.

Oh wait. That was me!

"Zoë." Jason's voice was in my left ear, and I could hear Mephistopheles' echo inside of it. *You can hear him . . . you know what you have to do.*

Do?

Is he kidding?

I pulled away from him and shook my head. "Not just no but *hell* no!" I shouted, lowering my arms. "I released a ghoul's soul and lost almost three days. You tell me I took in Mialani's damnation, but you don't explain it to me. And now you want me to release *him*?" I pointed at the body where Lex was lurking.

"If you don't," Jason was saying, "they'll both be trapped in the rotting corpse."

"And?" I pointed to my chest. "What about me? You didn't hear me—I lost three days. What will I lose if I do this? A month? This isn't a ghoul. This is a Revenant. No fucking way. You say they'll remain in the rotting corpse. What then? Bodies turn to dust. Can't they just get out once that happens? I mean, no vessel, no trap, right?" Made sense to me.

"Points in the planes where such a diminishing occurs become traps themselves. The two of them will remain locked where the body is interred, or burned. Forever stuck in limbo in that spot," Lex said from where she stood. "It will truly be death for a First Born. You can't let this happen."

I sort of compared it to Tim and Steve, being forever trapped inside of their house. I mean, what happened if someone tore down the house? Would they just stay there?

"Never thought about that," Tim said from the corner. "Not sure I want to."

Zoë, Joe said in my head. *Before, Lex said that the ritual obliterates First Borns. Does she mean this ritual is right? That someone got the rest of it?*

I relayed his question, and Lex shook her head. "No. If it had worked, then the soul and First Born would not have remained. There would be nothing left. Much like the Horror and the way it eats souls."

Wow. It seemed to me this way, being stuck in a rotting corpse or the same area of space and time for eternity, was a worse punishment than obliteration. "So basically they still don't have it right. They don't have the full spell."

"No," Lex said. "But they're getting close." She glided along the floor to me. "You can hear him. You can speak to him."

Him? "You mean him the soul or him the Revenant?"

"Aether." She looked at me with wide, red-fire eyes. "The First Born. He is the *first* of us to merge with a human soul to create a Revenant. He is the primordial essence of how we became what we are. If you can speak with him—"

Joe snapped his fingers. *Zoë, if you can talk to him, maybe you can find out who did this to him. He had to have seen who or what.*

"You want me to do what?" I looked past Lex to Joe. "Look, right now, whoever's voice I'm hearing isn't doing anything except screaming out. I'm not sure I can actually carry on a conversation." I was also remembering the pain I'd felt when I'd touched the ghoul's body with my OOB self. *Uh, no thank you.*

"It's not the same." Lex had reached out and grabbed my shoulders. "This is a First Born, the most regal of all the Original's creations—you must free him!" And she shook me. Hard.

Look, I'm usually a very patient person. Well, maybe not *very* patient. But I can put up with a lot. And sometimes I'm a little clueless. Okay. A *lot* clueless. But I'd had a lot happen to me over the past months. Not only physical changes but mental as well. And my heart—

My heart wasn't something I understood anymore.

And, well . . . I'd been pushed around enough. By TC, by Rodriguez, by the Horror (which was really me, and if I thought about it, could totally screw up my thinking), and now by some Revenant I had no loyalty to.

I put my hands on her forearms as she shook me.

"Lex, stop!" Jason was beside us, pulling at Lex.

Joe was also there, trying to pull her off me.

But Lex was lost in her own misery, her own despair at the loss of her lover, and at a possible threat to her very existence, and on one level I understood this. That didn't mean I liked being shaken. I pushed at her arms as I yelled at her. "Stop it!"

"You will free him! You must free him! You're nothing but a mutated bastard that should never have been born!"

Okay. I was pissed.

And, unfortunately, like most of us with Latina blood, I had a short fuse at times. So screw what I just said on being patient. I was fucking PISSED OFF. Calling me a bastard was a direct insult to my mom, and my dad, who just happened to be Ethereal.

I pushed away from her, but she pushed back, and before I knew it she was lifting me and slamming me against the back wall.

Jason shouted.

Tim gasped.

Joe tried to stop her but was flung backward by some invisible hand and crashed into the wall beside the room's door.

I felt a growl start deep in my throat as I shifted—not just physically but mentally as well. My strength increased, and I wound my arms around, twisting out of hers, and pushed her so hard she flew back into the table where the body rested. Her expression and face became feral, and I recognized the emergence of her First Born, the seed of her power, showing itself for the first time.

And to be honest, I thought Lex was a whole lot scarier.

She hissed at me, and I could actually see blurs in the air as she threw something resembling shirukens at me. I put up my arms and felt stinging along my forearms. Checking, I saw that my skin had split just as my mother's had when Jason fed from her. *Is this a Revenant's power? If so, I really need to figure out how to create a mind shield or something.*

"You will free him!" she shouted at me, her voice and that of the First Born's echoing in my head.

I held out my arms as blood dripped on the floor and saw my talons grow. Oh, I was ready to slice and dice this bitch's flesh to ribbons. But before I could get a running start to launch at her, something coalesced in front of me, blocking my view.

Trench Coat!

He was there in all his sexy glory, his coat flared out behind him, his shades in place and his hands to his sides, palms facing Lex. "That's *enough*, Yamato!"

Everything just stopped at that moment. Tim appeared to be as startled as me as he yelped and vanished.

I peered out from behind TC and watched as Lex's expression switched from lividly angry to seriously confused. She was standing up by then, wiping the blood from her nose. Her nose? Did I hit her? I didn't think so. Joe and Rhonda stood just beyond her, their eyes as wide as goose eggs. Tim wasn't even corporeal anymore. And Jason—

He was beside Lex, pointing at TC. "Just stop, Archer—this has to stop. Bickering among ourselves isn't the way to solve this."

But Lex's arm was raised again, and she was pointing at us. "You will make her do it! She has to release him! Aether cannot end like this!"

. . . Please . . . help us . . . So much . . . pain . . .

I put my Wraithy hands up to my temples and twisted them to see the slashes on my forearms. The blood was starting to flow, and I couldn't figure out how to make it stop. When I was OOB, the injuries echoed back to my body, but they were basically echoes.

Yeah, they were physical, but I always managed to heal. But being in physical form—

Abruptly, TC turned and grabbed my arms, and was facing me. His hands squeezed the cuts, and I yelled out because that hurt. I could see his expression go from anger to irritation behind the glasses. "Luv—don't ever go head to head with a Revenant. They ain't got nothing special 'cept this skin-lashing thing. If you want to crush 'em"—he grinned then and pulled his hands away from my no-longer-wounded forearms—"you gotta do—"

He spun around and pushed out his left arm. "This!" The red light shot out of his hand as it had that first night we'd met, when he'd tried to take me. It blanketed Lex with an eerie glow, and she snarled and growled but didn't attack back.

"Archer!" Jason said, sounding like a dad scolding a son. "Stop it."

TC looked over at Jason. "Nice to see you, Meph. Nice bod—though not as nice as that last one. Sorry we didn't hook up in Manhattan. She get popped?"

"Might not have happened if you'd've kept the date. But we're not here to talk about Lacey," Jason said. "Let Lex go. You have to realize what's happening here."

Rhonda stepped up and pointed at TC and then at Jason. "Am I right in thinking—you two were—"

"That was a long time ago," Jason said.

TC snarled. "It was just one night, and my ride was horny as hell."

I blanched as I realized where Rhonda's mind had gone—OMG. Because, evidently, TC and Mephistopheles-in-Lacey had once—"You two—had sex?"

TC looked at me and held out his non-red-glowing hand. "She meant nothing to me."

"Yeah." Jason crossed his arms over his chest. "I tried to warn Lacey you were nothing but a player."

Oh . . . gross. I glared at Jason. He'd had my mom . . . and he'd had . . . the Archer? "Whore dog."

But Jason only smiled at me, looking for all the world like the Cheshire cat. "Ever heard of the pot and the kettle, Miss Martinique?" He raised his eyebrows.

Not understanding, I looked at TC. He shrugged and pointed to himself and then me with his free hand. "Remember that we— you and me—"

Oh.

Jason laughed. "I can see you left a memorable impression on the Wraith with your sexual prowess, Archer."

Sexual—

OH!

That first long night out of my body, when I woke up dead in the morgue.

God . . . when did my sex life become so damned complicated?

14

NOW, bad relationships could affect a situation. Bruised feelings, toppled egos. All that shit. So if these two had a history, then I figured this situation could go good, or it could go bad.

I was thinking that, with my luck, the bad would win.

Luckily TC lowered his hand, releasing Lex. Lex started to go after him, but Jason quickly reached out and grabbed her arm. "No!"

. . . No time . . . left . . .

Gah . . . there were two voices in my head. The darker, more powerful one had to be Aether's voice, and the smaller, more frightened one was that of the man on the table. Deep down I knew I had no choice but to help them. But I didn't want to. I was too scared to. *Och . . . damn me and my mortal conscience.*

"She's not going to do this," TC said in his deep voice. "It's not her fault or mine that Aether got himself into this situation. He was also stupid and cocky."

"Cocky?" Lex said. "You're the cocky one. The betrayer. We all know it was you that showed that bastard where we were, showed him how to find us so we had to hide in these forms." She tapped on her chest. "We had to become something base, something else. You betrayed us all!"

"I did not betray anyone!" TC boomed, and stepped forward. I swear it looked as if his coattails were alive and fanned out to either side. "I wasn't myself. You think I enjoyed those centuries under his power? Under his control?"

Lex spit in front of him. "Bullshit, Archer. You weren't under anyone's control. No one believes you!"

"That's the truth!" TC moved in closer.

Okay, I'd already been through fourth grade, and I got past this whole "yes you did" and "no I did not," and didn't particularly want to repeat it. I moved from behind TC and neared the body, ignoring the WTF looks I was getting from Rhonda. Like I knew what the children were fussing about? Instead, I moved in close to the body and stared at the symbols.

In this form I could see things I normally couldn't see when just plain old human. When I looked at Mialani on Wednesday, the cuts all over her body looked like regular cuts (I wasn't going to say normal cuts because there was nothing normal about having things carved all over one's body), like someone had used a razor blade or a very sharp knife and carved them in.

But when I looked at Aether's body—the human host's body—each of the cuts sparkled as if sprinkled with white glitter. The closer I got, the more every line twinkled at me. And as I looked at the body, a soft, purplish glow seemed to infuse it. I only half paid attention to the Revenant and the First Born arguing at the foot of the gurney. It was a small room.

Joe came to stand on the opposite side of the gurney. I looked at him. He was glaring at me. Though not with the same angry intensity that Rhonda was as she took up a position behind him.

Can you ask him?

I realized at that moment that I'd already made up my mind to do just that. If there was any way to find out who was doing this, then I really didn't have a choice, did I?

Crap.

I raised my right hand and pressed on the man's chest, and gasped when it went through the flesh. I immediately cringed, expecting to feel the cold fire I'd touched before when I'd touched Mialani's body. I was pleasantly surprised when that didn't happen. Instead, I felt—

Nothing.

Well . . . it was kinda like putting my hand in a vat of cotton candy. If there was something there, it was just that hard to catch.

"Zoë?"

And abruptly I wasn't in the morgue anymore but in darkness. And I mean dark. I couldn't see anything, not even a hand in front of my face, which, of course, I was waving. I could still hear Joe, and Rhonda, and was that TC yelling? But it was like a bad long-distance connection. Suddenly, I realized I wasn't alone.

How?

Because something was humping my leg.

I looked down, and of course I couldn't see anything, but I could reach down and feel it. It was furry—

Ouch!

And it had teeth!

I growled at it and used my left hand to grab it. Within seconds there was a gold flare, and the thing was gone. But the golden light had illuminated someone standing in front of me.

With a shrug, I held up my left hand again. The mark of TC's handprint glowed and illuminated a circle around me. They were still there. A tall man I recognized as the man on the table, then an even taller, more physically buff guy beside him. I supposed this was the actual First Born. What disturbed me most what that they looked like corpses.

All pale and stiff.

I waved. "Allo?"

The smaller dude stepped forward. "Are you real?"

Trick question? The apparition asking if I was real? "Yes. You—" Wait. I had no idea what the name of the host was. "I'm Zoë."

"You're the Wraith," the taller one said, and his voice held a bit of an echo in the darkness. "I am Aether."

"Hi, Aether. Yes, I'm a Wraith. And I'm here to help if I can— but before I do, I need to find out who did this to you?"

The smaller man nearly disappeared, and the expression on his face frightened even me. And I didn't scare easy by then. Well . . . that might not be all true. "No . . ." he said.

Aether reached out and took the younger man in his arms, like a father would comfort a son. "Easy. It's okay." He looked at me, and his face was still half-hidden in shadows. "We don't know."

I pursed my lips and felt my wings unfurl. Ooh . . . sometimes they had a mind of their own. "Wait . . . you're a Revenant. Sharper hearing, seeing, senses period, right? Like a vampire. And someone snuck up on you, killed you, drained your blood, and carved symbols into your flesh, and you never knew who?"

Aether shook his head. "Whoever it was drugged my host and I was blinded. Before we could regain any sensation, the blood was drained, and my host's body died, though my presence kept his soul here with me. But without his eyes, as you can see"—he looked around—"we are in darkness. I can only tell you that it wasn't anything I'd ever encountered before."

"Meaning it wasn't from the Abysmal plane?"

"Nothing that I had ever known, but then I have encountered several of his beastly creations before." Aether turned his head in the shadow as if to look away. "He himself is an abomination."

Well, this was a dead end. Literally. Whoever or whatever was attacking was making sure it wasn't identifiable. But still . . . to sneak up on a Revenant? I somehow got the idea that wasn't as easy as it sounds. At least not with someone as old as Aether. And I could sense that age while I stood in front of him. "Are we inside the body?"

Aether nodded. "You can release us. I can sense that." He paused. "But there is a price."

Hooo boy. "I released Mialani's soul Wednesday—and just woke up today. I'm not sure how well I'll be able to release the two of you."

"It's not that kind of price." Aether moved closer, and I took an involuntary step back. He scared the crap out of me there in the weird funky golden darkness that I was illuminating.

"I have an idea of what kind of price," I said, and held up my other hand. I felt and heard my wings rustle. "Damnation and all that."

"No," Aether said, and stopped coming closer. "That's not what I mean. The price is not for you to pay, but for me." There was a pause, and I felt somehow that he was coming to a decision. "What

I can tell you about who did this is what I sensed, but not what I know. The presence was not familiar, but it did have the taste of something Abysmal, as well as Ethereal."

Well, I hadn't expected to hear that. "Both? Something in between?"

He nodded. "And it was terrifying. It wasn't anything in physical form, but something that entered my host's dreams. It paralyzed us, wrapped itself around us until this darkness came, and we were trapped. I knew then there was no escaping this body, and so we have been here ever since."

Was part of both planes, was Abysmal and was Ethereal. That much confused me. But what bothered me was the description of how it wrapped itself around them. Reminded me of the image of that thing me and TC had encountered that Wednesday morning. "Uhm . . . did it look like hair?"

Aether tilted his head to the side. "I'm sorry?"

Wow, Revenants were polite. Wonder where TC went wrong.

"Did it look like a huge wig of long hair when it wrapped itself around you?"

"I don't know," Aether said. "I couldn't see it. Neither could my host. But I could sense magic. Strong magic. Even now, it's eating its way through the flesh to us."

Hrm . . .

I thought of something he said. "What do you mean the price is for you to pay?"

He came toward me again and stopped. I held my ground this time. "It means I must lose this world." And his voice was sad inside my head. So very heavy with regret. "I won't be able to return to it. My essence will become part of the darkness of the Abysmal, and I will no longer taste the fruits of this world, know the desires of the human heart, or be able to feel a lover's caress on my lips. But—I will remember it."

I felt my breath catch in my throat as I understood what he meant. For him, this was the end of the ride. "And your host?"

"He will ascend as he was meant to do." Aether turned and held the smaller man close to him. "As they were all meant to do." He pulled back from him and touched the smaller one's chin. I could feel the fear vanish. "But I will remember him. I will remember all of them."

Oh, this was intolerably sappy. I held up my hands and waved. "Wait, wait, wait. Are you telling me that you'll return to Abysmal goo, and he'll move on?"

"Yes."

"You can't just pop out and continue as you were before?"

"No. Not as the spell is written now." He looked at me, and I could almost make out sad golden eyes. "I don't count this as a curse, Wraith. I count this as a blessing. If this spell were correct, I would no longer exist, and neither would my host. Please"—he sighed—"release us both."

Oh boy.

And here's where it got sticky for me. I wanted to, and I was scared to. And could anyone blame me?

But no matter how scared I was, I knew there was no way I was going to run away from it. I couldn't. And so I'd lose a few more days. Bah. I needed the sleep.

With my left hand still out, the pattern of TC's hand grew brighter, intensified the golden light. Aether pulled his host closer and pointed to my hand. "Touch her—and the pain will vanish."

Hesitantly, he came to the light, and he was an exact replica of the man carved on the table. He looked at me with sadness and took my hand. There was a sharp intense pain in my gut that grew, a stabbing agony—

Which dissipated the second Aether touched my hand as well. In fact, the pain disappeared altogether just as the soul vanished, and there was nothing there but Aether and me, holding hands.

"You would have been a great Irin, Zoë Martinique," he said in a soft voice. "I would have loved to—" And then his eyes widened as if a great secret was revealed to him. "Oh no . . . that can't be. You can't let him do that! You must get away from—"

A huge bright golden light blinded and deafened me as he disappeared, and abruptly I was tossed backward and landed on a cold, hard floor. I looked up, blinking at the fluorescent lights, and recognized the smells. Morgue again.

TC was hovering over me, as were Joe and Rhonda.

"She's human again," Rhonda said.

Joe nodded. *You okay?*

"No," I said aloud, as it felt like every nerve ending in my body had gone to sleep. That whole pins-and-needles thing. "But it's not like it was with Mialani."

"Of course not," TC said as he offered his hand and pulled me up. His touch made the tingling sensation go away as I stood. Jason and Lex were near the body and I didn't need to take a peek inside to know the Symbiont and the host's soul were gone. Lex was sobbing. Jason looked . . . worried.

Why does he look like that?

"Why is that?" Rhonda was looking at TC, her stance a bit tense as she faced him. "Why was it so bad for her to release the ghoul and not the First Born?"

"Two different somethings," TC said as he stepped back. He was looking at me, and I realized I wasn't in Wraith form anymore but just plain Zoë. "Ghouls are abominations. Souls trapped within dying bodies, and the blood of a Revenant is what keeps it together. Otherwise, it would break down like it was meant to do." He looked at Rhonda with his shaded eyes. "But a Revenant possesses the body, envelops it and fuses with the host soul. It's not what you would call natural for this world, but more natural than the ghouls. Releasing the ghoul causes loss of essence from the Wraith. But release of the First Born . . ." He looked at me and gave me a half smile. "The Revenant gives up a part of itself to her for that release. As well as its place in this physical world." He glanced back at Lex. "Oh, knock it off, Yamato. Aether can't hear you anymore."

"Fuck you. *You're* the abomination. The betrayer."

I sighed. *This is gonna be a long night.*

Joe moved into my line of sight. Ah, a cooling sight for a starving girl. *You learn anything?*

And always the detective.

I shook my head. "No. Aether said they didn't see the attacker. It came while they slept and wrapped itself around them. They were locked in unconsciousness while it was happening." Or that was how I interpreted it.

Lex wiped at her face. "So they couldn't tell you *what* it was?"

"He said it was both," I looked at Lex. "Abysmal and Ethereal."

That got everyone's attention. In fact, they were all staring at me. "What?"

"Zoë," Rhonda stepped forward. "There aren't many creatures from both planes. That contain both essences." She glanced at Joe. "There are two. There's you."

Uh-oh.

"And there's one other," TC said with gritted teeth. "That damned book boy."

Oh hell.

Dags.

15

WE didn't talk much more in the morgue after that. Especially since the body started releasing a whole bunch of toxic gases on its way to goo-land. Once the Revenant and the host's soul were gone, there was nothing keeping it together, so back to its primordial elements it went.

Gross.

We drove back home in silence. The moon was up high in the clear sky over Atlanta. I craned my neck in the backseat to get a better look at it. The clock in Jason's dash read 9:42. My thoughts strayed to Daniel.

Where is he?

What is he doing?

Is he running for his life, hurting other people? Or himself?

Have they caught him yet?

Does he still hate me so much to want me dead?

I think most people would see me as stupid to be worrying about a crazy guy. Especially one who had tried to kill me and succeeded in killing his friend and boss. But Daniel's insanity was partially my fault. I'd brought him into my life, and he'd paid that price. And when I thought about Dags and what he'd gone through, I had to wonder if his knowing me had anything to do with the situation in which he found himself.

Being a book and all.

But then again, he was shooting light out of his palms before we ever met at Fadó's.

Whatever was happening, I refused to believe it had anything to do with him. It wasn't possible. The girls—his Familiars, Alice and Maureen—would never allow it.

But if that was true . . . then why had Alice come to me in that dream?

The argument with Lex in the morgue before we left returned as well. And I really wanted to hammer Joe in the head for being so damned loyal to Lex.

"Oh . . ." And her eyes had lit up. "I remember him. He shone brightly the last time we met. But—I never understood why. Why is he like that?" she'd asked after I had blurted out his name.

Rhonda had remained quiet, as had I. But Joe?

What an idiot.

He'd relayed the state of Dags's existence to Lex the same way he had to me. It was obvious Yamato could hear him. And I could hear him as well, like overhearing a conversation in the next room.

Dags was accidentally made into a secondary watcher during a botched ritual by a magician named Bonville. He possesses two Familiars who balance out the Abysmal and the Ethereal. Bonville owned a Grimoire passed down in his wife's family. But there was a nasty group of people called L-6, who wanted that Grimoire, led by a man named Rodriguez. He learned that Rhonda had the book in safekeeping and kidnapped Dags as leverage. Dags was tortured violently, and, in order to save his life . . . Joe had sighed, and I could sense he was still a bit put out by what Rhonda had done. *To save his life, Rhonda used one of the spells in the Grimoire to fuse Dags with the book.*

Lex's eyes had widened as she looked at Rhonda with an almost renewed awe. "You are truly a witch. A bender of things. Wicce."

Rhonda had looked uncomfortable.

"This is interesting," Jason had said, rubbing one finger against his jawline. "This individual has a Grimoire fused into his soul's grounding to his physical body."

Rhonda had nodded. "I thought it was the best place to hide it from Rodriguez at the time."

At the time, yeah, but a month or so later, that man, Rodriguez, had exploded in my mom's bedroom, with TC's help, from the inside out.

I had *not* liked cleaning that mess up.

Ew.

Jason had moved closer to Rhonda. "Does he have access to the spells?"

"I think he does." She had looked at him. "Oh, Jason, you don't think this spell is in that Grimoire, do you?"

He'd shrugged. "We'd need to find out. Clear his name."

"I want him," Lex had said as she'd come to stand by Jason. "I will take the book."

"No, you won't," I'd heard myself say. *Ooh. Whups. That was my outside voice.* "You won't touch a hair on his head. Got it?" *And where exactly is this bravado coming from?*

She'd glared at me. "If I find he is responsible for this, I will do as I please."

"No." I'd moved closer to her and shifted, the Wraith coming to the front. I'd been a little worried at how easy this was getting to be. "You touch him, you deal with me."

Jason had easily slid between us. And I had to admit we'd probably looked like odd opponents. Lex with her beautiful Asian Amazonian looks and me with my weird, gray, winged self. "Both of you, stop it. We have no proof this man is involved at all. We will simply set up an appointment to see him and find out." He'd turned to Rhonda. "He works for you, right?"

She'd nodded. But I had seen in her face she wasn't happy.

That was when we'd left. Noxious gas. Left Lex to clean it up. *Good riddance.*

Even as we entered the house, I was still feeling a bit conflicted about Dags. Unsure what was happening. The description Aether had given me sounded a lot like that thing TC and I had encountered. But TC had been able to diffuse it. Send it on its way. And he was a much younger Symbiont than Aether. But then, TC had never joined with a human soul.

Though . . . he had *touched* one.

Mine.

Oh hell, I wish someone would fucking make up a guidebook or a sourcebook on this freak'n game and let me read it!

Jason and Nick went into the botanica as I went to the refrigerator and grabbed a pint of Starbucks Java Chip. I'd wanted to go take a long bath and sort through this, but apparently Mom, Rhonda, and Joe had different plans.

I put Tim's rock back where it belonged, and he appeared near the fireplace. He looked thoughtful, and I didn't disturb him. He'd talk to me when he was ready. He'd witnessed it all.

Mom had tea ready, and we all sat in the botanica. I was in my papasan and refused to touch that tea. I wanted my stomach intact, and the Java Chip was improving my mood epically.

Rhonda was in the kitchen on her cell phone. Jason and Nick hugged each other near the door. Nick waved at me, went to Nona and gave her a kiss on the cheek as well as a hug, and then left the house. A few minutes later, I heard a car start up outside.

I looked over at Jason. "You two have a spat?"

He shook his head. But it was Mom who answered. "He wants Nick as far away from here as possible. After what happened to Mialani"—she looked at the Revenant with a sad expression—"I don't blame him. Nick's too precious to lose."

"It would . . ." Jason fixed his gaze on me. "It would destroy me."

Mom settled in her high-backed chair as Joe plopped down on the couch. Jason moved to stand by the fireplace, an imposing if not handsome picture.

"Okay, I've left a message," Rhonda said as she came into the room. "But he hasn't been answering my calls right away."

At least he answers them. Putz.

Rhonda pointed at Jason. "You get Nick out of here?"

Jason nodded.

"Good. That's one less person we have to worry about."

"So," Mom began. "My daughter."

Uh-oh.

"When were you going to tell us about this new ability you seem to have? You can go Wraith without going OOB?"

I smiled at her. "Actually, I wanted to surprise you."

"Consider us surprised," Rhonda said as she moved to sit on the couch beside Joe. "Care to regale us with the tales of you sans OOB, now that we have a moment to listen?"

I looked at her. "Sorry."

"So when did this happen?"

I looked at Mom. "Shortly after Cooper was killed. I wanted to go to the morgue and make sure he was really gone—and not trapped—"

"Why—had you seen him?"

"No. I just wanted to make sure, okay? And when I tried to go OOB"—I shrugged—"poof. I did it in body."

"Interesting," Jason said. "And the Archer? I'm sure everyone would like to hear about your apparent relationship with the betrayer."

"TC?" Mom looked at me with wide eyes. "Zoë—"

"Look"—I held out my hands—"TC has been helping me learn how to use my power as a Wraith, okay? He's done nothing wrong here."

"You *trust* him?" Rhonda said.

"Hell no," I lied. Because in a really fucked-up way, I did trust him. And I had no idea why. Though now that I understood his existence a bit more, things were starting to fall into place. "But he's taught me a lot about flying, about fighting, and about sensing Abysmal creatures. And he's basically healed me twice."

"Well, that's because you're almost like a host to him," Rhonda said, "if I'm understanding all of this right. But he's only doing it because you give him power."

Well, we kinda knew that anyway so—

Wait a minute.

I felt my eyes widen as that point drove itself home. I looked at Joe and Rhonda, who were both looking at me the same way. We all realized that Lex and even Aether had said that by fusing with a human soul, they'd diminished themselves. But by touching me, TC had grown stronger.

When I put this to Jason, he frowned at me as if I were six. "You already know the answer to that. Because you were an Irin. Not just a normal human."

Oh. Yeah. That's right.

Nuts.

"But Jason," Rhonda prodded. "If TC became that much more

powerful simply by touching Zoë—and he is a First Born—then why hasn't he ever tried to fuse with her? What kind of creature would that create?"

Uhm . . . yikes?

I looked at Joe. He was staring at me. And I wasn't sure I liked the look in his eyes. *What?*

Nothing, he said back to me. *I'm just thinking.*

"I'm not sure what would happen," Jason said. "But I'm not positive I want to find out. Zoë." He looked at me.

I pulled my gaze from Joe and peered suspiciously at Jason. "Uh-huh."

"Has Archer at any time actually tried to join with you?"

I pursed my lips. "Define join."

"I'm not talking about sex, Zoë."

Well, that silenced the room. *Tadah. Thank ye, I'll be here all week.*

Mom sighed. "Honestly, she gets that from her father."

Oh, now *you* talk about him, Miss Former Burlesque Dancer. "Honestly, Jason, he's never broached the subject. It seems whatever it was he wanted, he took from me that second encounter, when it looked like I'd died." I'd had no memory of what'd happened for those hours prior to waking up in that drawer/box in the morgue. Not immediately.

But over time, and with a bit of prodding from Mr. Trench Coat himself—things had become crystal clear. We'd had sex. And a lot of it. And I had enjoyed the hell out of it. Which really pissed me off.

But in hindsight, if he'd ever taken anything from me except my voice, I never knew it.

"Can you call him here?" Jason asked.

"In my house?" Mom thundered. I was sure Mom was less than

eager to see him, seeing as he'd yanked her out of that man-made, man-parts puppet that Bertram and Charolette had stuffed her into. TC had never apologized for that. In fact, he felt no remorse. Especially after possessing her body to communicate with me.

That was gross.

I'd never told Mom about that. Didn't plan on it either. I was sure the woman would insist on some Indian voodoo ritual inner-body cleansing, and I just wasn't in the mood to eat dates and flax-seed. *God, I need to get my own place again.*

I looked at Jason. "I don't think that's such a good idea. But I can ask him."

"You really think he'll be truthful?" Rhonda asked.

"No," Jason and I said in unison.

"Jinx!" I shouted at him.

He grinned but kept quiet.

I liked him.

"I will ask him, though." My stomach growled at that moment, and I put my hand on my middle and set the empty ice-cream container on the hearth beside me. Mom had cakes and cookies, but I wanted real food. I hadn't really eaten much of anything since I woke up. "I want a pizza."

"A pizza?" Rhonda said. "Sounds really good."

"We could head down to Savage," Jason said. "They're open till ten thirty."

I grinned. A vampire who loves pizza. "With garlic."

He matched my smile. "Always."

Well, that blew that myth right out of the water.

Walking around the corner onto Moreland to get to Savage was kinda fun. Just the four of us. Mom insisted she had work to do and was on the phone with the Geriatric Scooby Gang when we left. Tim bowed out when I grabbed his rock, and it made me wonder if he had to come when I took the rock or was it just simply like an express train to wherever I was.

We got a bench table in the front. I ordered pepperoni, Rhonda and Joe got a sausage, and Jason ordered a white-cheese pizza. A couple of Cokes and we were seated and talking. Sometimes it was just good to get out of the shop and away from Mom's potions and herbs.

Not to mention those wacky wards she had up that tended to twist my stomach sometimes.

Joe sat back in his chair, turned sideways with his Coke. He'd gotten really quiet inside my head, and that was spooky. I wanted to know what he was thinking, but that would be me overshadowing him, which means he'd fight me, which means I'd have to go OOB—

Wait.

Or would I?

How does that work with this new power?

Is it necessary to be noncorporeal? Or can it be done while Wraith?

Oh . . . so many questions. And for the first time since this whole ride began, I was interested. Really interested.

Jason spoke up as he sipped his Coke. It was interesting watching him do this. It was like each sip was ecstasy. "We have four bodies. Two were human, one a ghoul, one was a Revenant. All of them had a form of this ritual applied to them. But we know it wasn't the right ritual or the full ritual because the First Born wasn't obliterated."

"The big question is who is doing this?"

"Well, I'd say first off it's the Phantasm," Jason said. "I've been on the phone with three of the others discussing the possibility. And since all the deaths are centered here in Atlanta, we've come to the conclusion that it centers around the Wraith."

Hrm. Hadn't considered that myself. But it was odd that all these killings were here in the South, when I was sure the Revenants were all over the world. But, to think it was because of me?

Naw.

Really?

"Why do you think that?" Rhonda said. "I'm more inclined to believe it has to do with Archer."

Jason nodded. "The two Revenants I spoke with had letters delivered to them, telling them the spell had been discovered here, in Atlanta, and they had a chance to destroy it once and for all."

Me, Joe, and Rhonda, we all looked at him as if he'd grown a third eyeball. "You are kidding me," Rhonda said. "Have you called all of them? All the remaining Revenants?"

He nodded. "I have, and three have responded. The others are talking to each other." Jason had a frown on his face as he focused on the pizza joint's front door. I was aware a couple had come in and were arm in arm. I leaned forward. "And?"

Jason looked at me. "And I don't think it's got anything to do with Archer, or you, but something else entirely."

"Care to share?" Rhonda said. "Because I'm at a loss on this one. I've never heard of this spell, Zoë here can OOB without actually OOBing, we've got a dead ghoul and a dead Revenant—the oldest of the First Borns at that. And now you tell us that all of you received letters to come here? To find this spell? Where were you supposed to look?"

Jason narrowed his eyes. "Well, to begin with, Aether wasn't the oldest of the First Borns. He was the oldest Revenant. And where do you find a spell but in a book?"

"A book?" I frowned. Well, that made sense since Archer had said that spells had a catch and had to be written down. So they were looking for a book. "Where is this book?"

Jason pursed his lips as he looked at each of us. "In the weird-est place I never would have thought of." He turned in his chair and pointed to the couple. "In him."

We all looked past Jason to the couple settling into chairs at a table near the counter. She had fire red hair and a bright smile as her date kissed her ear. And he—

HE—

OMG

"Is that—" Rhonda said in a low voice.

I nodded. Yes, it was.

It was Dags.

But who the hell is the redhead?

16

I held up my hand for the table to be quiet though I didn't take my gaze from the two of them.

The redhead was beautiful, with a very petite figure, a good inch or two shorter than Dags, and wore a soft light green summer top that revealed well-toned arms and an ample breast size.

Since when did he go for the boob-enhanced type? I glanced down at my own. They weren't overtly large, or enhanced, but they were nice. He seemed to like them before.

And Dags—he looked *happy*. He wore some sort of shirt that I couldn't focus on and a pair of jeans. His hair looked the same—shorter than when we'd first met and just a bit grown out. He looked like Dags. They sat with their backs to us, and I was more concerned over where the redhead was putting her hands.

Why are you staring?

It took me a moment to realize that was Joe's voice and not my own conscience. I turned back around and glared at him. "I am not staring."

"Yes, you are," Jason said. He had a very lazy, quizzical look on his face. "You know that boy? He's carrying a very subtle but dangerous power around him."

"You can sense it?" Rhonda said.

"Any Abysmal creature for miles can sense it. He should learn to cap it." The Revenant sat forward. "I take it this is the Guardian?"

I sensed she nodded. I wasn't looking. My attention was too focused on Dags paying attention to the redhead. Didn't he notice us sitting over here? Couldn't he like, sense me?

Even a little?

And why was it bothering me?

I wonder if he's actually sitting *with his last job,* came Joe's thought. *Maybe she's the reason he's been kinda incommunicado?*

You shut the fuck up! Oh. Wow. I did not mean to respond that emphatically.

Yay! I finally got to use that word!

I glanced at Joe. He didn't have happy face on. He had grumpy face waiting in the wings. And he was still looking at me funny.

"Well"—Rhonda stood up—"I'm his boss, and I'm having a word with him."

Joe yanked her back down by her jeans. She turned and glared at him, and by golly, he glared right back. *Booyah.*

"I need to go to the bathroom," I said, as our pizzas arrived. I stood and moved around the pizza dude and went quickly by their table, keeping my back to them as I went to the bathroom. Of course I really didn't need to go—but it gave me a great vantage point to watch them. From there I could see Dags's face. Watch his expressions. Feel my heart thunder in my chest when he reached out and touched her arm.

"You know you could always blast him," came a voice beside me.

I knew it was TC, but he still startled me. I smacked the side of my head against the wall I was near, then glanced over at him, cowering in the doorway with me. Though, honestly, he was way too big to cower. "I'm not gonna blast him."

"That's book boy."

"Yeah."

"Who's the squeeze?" He smirked. "I noticed it's not you."

I shoved at him and was a little surprised when my shoulder made contact. "Why are you here?"

"Got a bit on that thing we saw the other night."

"That hair monster?"

He grinned at me beneath the shades. "Yeah . . . the hair monster. Anyway, apparently it's been hiring, then killing Fetches and Daemons all over the city."

I made a face. "Hiring? You mean like paying them?"

"Well, pay for one of those things is more like offering up a blood sacrifice. Or a fresh heart."

Ew. I shook my head. "I'm not that concerned about the currency, but the fact is it's hiring. Not creating. I thought those things were created."

His grin turned sly. "You see my point. Whatever it is, it's either *choosing* not to make a Fetch or a Daemon, or it *can't*. And if it can't, then it's not wholly Abysmal."

"And second, what's it hiring them to do?" I looked at him. "Did you find that out?"

His grin vanished. "Still working on that." He looked over at the other table as they happily dug into pizza. "Let me give you a word of advice," he said, but kept his shaded gaze focused on the table. "Revenants are only out for one thing. Survival. You think you did a good thing today?" He looked at me. "Releasing Aether?"

I shrugged. "I guess so. I mean, if I hadn't done it, then they'd both be trapped inside that body forever."

"Naw." He shook his head. "That's not true. Revenants can hop bodies, abandon them if they want. Of course, after using a body far past its expiration date, things can be quite ugly when they leave it."

Oh God. I made a horrific face. "They do that?"

"Some do. Luv, not all Revenants are like Mr. Knight-in-Shining-Armor over there. Some are downright insane. Just like the human race, you got your bad apples."

"Like you?"

"Me?" He grinned. "I'm a one of a kind, thanks to you, luv. But"—he held up a finger—"remember what I said. Trust no one. Something is spiraling in on Atlanta—otherwise why start taking out all the Revenants. There aren't that many left."

I glanced over at Dags and the chick. They were ordering now. And he hadn't even noticed I was there. And I remembered the conversation from earlier with the others. "You think maybe whatever is coming is coming for me? Or you?"

He shook his head. "I'm not sure what's up. I just know if whatever it is finds that spell, I'm ganking it on the spot, then I'm gonna do me a bit of magic myself."

And he was gone.

"Zoë?"

I nearly came out of my body, literally, at the sound of my name. I turned and stood from my cower and found myself face-to-face with a pair of incredulous gray eyes. Immediately, I had images of two bodies, arm in arm, in front of a fire . . . touching, needing, wanting . . .

"You okay?"

I blinked. "Y-yeah. Sure. I'm great." I then noticed that the red-head was behind him. "Who's the chi—your friend?"

"Oh." He moved out of the way so I could get a better look at the competit—uh, I mean girl. Woman. Person.

GAH.

"This is Stella Rosenburg. She's my landlady."

Landlady?

Stella offered me her hand and had a grip to rival Superman's. "I'm so happy to meet you. Darren talks about you all the time. In fact, so much that me and the girls feel like we know you."

The girls?

I guess my expression repeated my thoughts because Stella stepped in close, and whispered, "The Familiars," in a conspiratorial fashion.

I nodded slowly and smiled as she pulled back. Dags was watching me, his eyes bright. In fact, he didn't look like anyone who hadn't been getting a good night's sleep. Maybe not dreaming was a good thing?

I know I'd be a lot happier some nights if I didn't dream.

Dags put a hand on Stella's back. "Zoë, you look good. Better than the last time I saw you."

I stood up straight and looked at him. "So do you—seeing as how the last time I actually saw you it was in ICU."

Dags had been with me and Joe and TC on that roof. He'd been thrown around like a rag doll by TC, and later wound up on life support at Piedmont. And then, one day, he'd gotten up and walked out. Mom had said he was fine and out of Georgia.

"Yeah . . . well . . ." He shrugged. "Rest time was over. So." He looked around and noticed the table in the corner. "I see the gang's here. And you've got a Revenant with you."

"You *know* about them?"

He nodded. "The Grimoire's got all sorts of information in it. And oddly enough, bits leak out now and then, and I know things."

Okay—I have never been told I was terribly bright. Nor have I ever tried to be. But sometimes there is a glow, a spark of OMG that comes to me when I get an idea that makes me feel all good inside. "Dags," I reached out to put my hand on his shoulder. When he pulled away—I forgot what I was going to say.

We stood there looking at one another. Just inches apart, but somehow it felt like a lifetime.

Okay. That was hokey. Even for me.

But . . . it was true.

He swallowed and looked away first. "I—I've been busy. You?"

I nodded. I watched his eyes—so gray they resembled polished metal at times. There was no denying Dags was one of the prettiest men I'd known. The fact he was compact made him all the more adorable. Yet, every time I tried to remember that evening by the fire, and enjoy it, I'd see Daniel's hard expression when he'd walked in on us.

And then I'd see his body riddled with holes. I'd thought he'd died.

I nearly did.

But he didn't.

And now he was insane.

"What were you going to say?" Dags spoke up.

I blinked, refocusing on his face. "I—the Grimoire. Does it have really old spells?"

He arched his dark eyebrows. "Yeah."

"I mean like really, really old spells."

He nodded again. "Yeah."

"I'm talking beginning-of-time old spells."

This time he gave me a warning look. "What are you getting at?"

I reached and grabbed him whether he flinched or not, looked at the tall redhead, said "'Scuse us," and pulled him to the table. Once there, all eyes turned to us—especially Rhonda's and Jason's—but for different reasons.

Dags pulled his arm away and nodded. Gave a little wave. "Hi, all." He turned to Jason and offered his hand. "Dags McConnell. I've never met a Revenant before."

Jason returned the handshake and offered Dags a seat beside him, where I had been sitting. "And I've never met a living book before. Please, sit. And bring your lovely companion."

Before I or Rhonda could protest, Dags turned and motioned Stella over. She nodded, grabbed their drinks, and sat down on the other side of Dags. Leaving me with no room on the bench.

Whoopee.

I shoved Rhonda over into Joe and put on a smile I was not feeling. Again introductions were made to bring Stella, Jason, and Joe up to speed.

"So," Rhonda said, with her elbows on the table. The pizza was suddenly forgotten. Oh, except by Joe, whose conversational skills of late were definitely negated. "Why haven't you returned my phone calls?"

Dags's eyes widened. "You called me?"

"Yes." She glared.

I glared too. I'd called him, and he hadn't answered me either.

"But I haven't gotten—"

And then Stella the bella raised her hand. "I'm afraid that's my fault."

We all glared at her. Except Joe. And Jason. I noticed he was kinda leering. Was he hungry for something besides pizza?

"How is it your fault?" Dags asked.

"I blocked the calls," she said. "You were so tired and needed the downtime once we got here. And those two numbers just kept showing up. So while you were resting, I took your personal cell and blocked the numbers on it. So you weren't showing the calls."

My mouth opened into an O.

"Those *two* numbers?" Dags frowned. "I'm sure Rhonda called—since I was working for her. But who else called?"

I didn't raise my hand.

Stella shrugged. "Dunno. That number wasn't as persistent. But"—she smiled—"Alice and Maureen both thought it was a good idea."

I remembered why I brought him over. Man, the memory's got like a ten-minute time delay lately. Need to check on that. "Oh, wait. Rhonda—the Grimoire in Dags. Do you think it could possibly have the spell in it?"

Everybody sat forward, and I was amazed that no one else had thought of it. Well, except for Lex.

"It'd have to be a really old book," Jason said as he narrowed his eyes at Dags, focusing on his middle. "I can sense it, but I can't see it. How do you see it?" He directed that question to Dags.

"Well, I more or less just know it's there. There's a constant warmth from it, not unlike the warmth I get from Alice and Maureen."

I thought we were gonna have to explain the girls, but Jason only nodded. "Yeah . . . I've heard about them. The Familiars. You do realize that it's been nearly a hundred years since a Guardian had Familiars? Hell, it's been that long since there's been a Guardian."

Dags nodded. "I'm learning it. Slowly. The book itself helps and lets me take a peek at something inside now and then."

Does it have like a table of contents? Joe bit into some pizza.

I relayed the question.

Dags grinned. "I heard him, Zoë. And I think I have an answer for him." He leaned forward across the table, his right hand out, palm up. We all leaned in to see a set of concentric circles forming in a white-blue light. I'd seen them before. A circle in a circle in a circle. But they were different now—the edges of the circles bordered with symbols that looked a lot like—

"Hey, aren't those like the ones on the bodies?" Joe said.

"The symbols themselves are universal in arcane magic," Jason said. "Just about every magician—ceremonial or otherwise—uses them to—"

It was about that time we all stared at Joe.

And he was staring back, a slice of pizza in his hand, held up to his mouth. He blinked and lowered the pizza to the table. "You all heard that."

We nodded slowly. *Mother Guppy!*

Rhonda looked at Dags, her eyes wide, but then narrowed in an accusatory fashion. "How? I've been trying to restore his voice for over a month. And you do it in a second? With a glowing, spinny light show."

Wow, that sounded like I said it. Though I would have said glowing, spinny light show *thingie*. All thingies are fiendish.

And I was watching his open palm. The circles were still spinning, only in the center were triangles, moving through and around each other. Wow, if it got any brighter, he'd have to douse that.

"I found the spell while doing something else," Dags said as he watched his palm. "About a week or so ago. Couldn't wait to get back here and show you."

But Joe wasn't paying attention. He was clearing his throat through a whole bunch of "mememememes" and "aahhhhhhs." I laughed at him as he stood up and started reciting Hamlet's soliloquy, then launched into Princess Leia's message to Obi-wan.

Man . . . what a geek.

Rhonda jumped up and hugged him. He hugged her back and sat down with the coolest grin on his face. I hadn't noticed that he'd not been smiling lately, and who could blame him? After losing his voice, he'd lost his partner to madness, and had his friend and boss killed. Wow.

He pointed at Dags. "You—I'm not gonna hug. Too manly for that."

"I'm not really done yet," Dags said, as the circles spun faster.

Stella looked behind her to make sure no one was looking, but as a civilian in all this, she didn't seem to mind. It was like she'd seen it before. Jason sat forward, his face darkening, and I realized Mephistopheles was present and watching. Carefully.

Abruptly, the circles vanished with a sparkle of light, and our ears popped.

Sticking his pinky in his ear and wiggling it, Joe said. "WTF?"

"Oh, I made sure it couldn't be taken again," Dags said as he started wringing his hand as if to get something yucky off of it. "Voices carry power in the planes. Not all creatures have them. Hence the Archer stole Zoë's, then Joe's."

"Well, in truth, Archer has a voice." Jason as Mephistopheles spoke up, enhancing the echo I heard in Jason's voice. "The Phantasm simply took it."

I blinked. "So he's not gonna have a voice anymore?" Oh, I will so get into trouble for that. And the bastard will come after Dags.

"Unfortunately, he will. What I just did—because they were linked like that—gave TC back his voice as well."

Shit.

"You saw that spell and recited it?" Jason/Mephistopheles asked. Echo.

"No," Dags said, and looked at the man to his right. "Spells like those can't be memorized. Safety precaution built in. They're written."

So TC had been truthful in that.

"Then . . . how?"

Dags sighed. "Well, I see them in my mind. See the written spell. And then I just know it. It doesn't last long. Like, that spell I just used? I'd have to call it back up again. I can't remember a word of it. The Grimoire is full of them."

Joe took a sip of Coke. "Okay, then, what I said earlier. Is there a table of contents? And hopefully everything's laid out as per simple, basic, really hard, and arcane?" He grinned and looked at us. "I love to hear my voice."

We know. Oy.

Dags shook his head. "No, I'm afraid not. It's more of an intuitive thing. They come when I don't call them." He held up a finger. "If I don't know them. Now, the voice one came up the other day when I was looking for something else. Cross wires. So I remembered it and could recall it." He closed his eyes and rested his elbows on the table. Dags rubbed his forehead.

"You need to lie down," Stella said. "It takes a lot out of you. Especially with—"

Dags looked at her and shook his head.

I waved at him. "What?"

"It's—I ran into a little problem on the last thing Rhonda sent me after."

Rhonda started to get up. "Then we have to talk—in private."

Dags held up his hand. "No secrets, Rhonda. I need help. And it might mean we put our brains together. You're not calling the shots on this."

Whoa. I don't ever remember him talking to Rhonda like that. Hell, I couldn't remember him talking to anyone like that. I looked at her, and it was evident she was just as shocked. I also knew his tone wasn't going to sit well with her. "Excuse me? I'm your employer. I call the shots on everything."

"Not this time."

"Mr. McConnell, did you procure the item?"

He sighed. "Yeah, I procured it. The problem is I'm not sure how to unprocure it."

"I don't think that's a word," I said.

Rhonda glared.

Sheesh. And they call me scary.

Jason held up a hand at Rhonda, silencing her next outburst before it started. "Dags—what happened?"

He stood then and looked at Stella. She looked worried and nodded. With a glance around, he started to unbutton his shirt.

Joe choked and held up his hands. "Hey, dude. Not while we're eating. We can't—"

He never finished it.

But it didn't matter. What stopped him stopped all of us. With wide-open eyes and mouths, we stood en masse and stared at Dags.

I think I've mentioned before that Mr. McConnell has a most

beautiful chest. Short, compact, well proportioned, and an incredible girdle that just begs touching.

All of that was still there. But what marred that beautiful scene was—well—what looked like the corner of an old, brown leather book, sticking out of the center of his chest.

Joe sighed. "Well, that's not something you see every day."

17

"IS your . . ." Rhonda started and stopped. She was staring at it with ill-contained horror. "Is it the Grimoire?"

Grimoire, hell. I pointed at it. "You're walking around with a book sticking out of your chest, and you're here getting pizza?"

Oh, come on. You were thinking it too.

"He's starving," Stella said in a soft voice, and pulled at Dags's arm so he'd lower his shirt. He then sat down as we all did. "He hasn't been able to eat in two days."

Once again, I say, he looked good to me. Might be starving. But looked good.

"Stella"—he gave her a sideways smirk before looking at us— "it's not all that bad. I've been able to eat soft foods. But nothing that needs a lot of digestion."

"You didn't answer me. Is the Grimoire coming out?"

He tilted his head to the right side. "You held on to that book for weeks, and you can't see this is not it?"

Touché. I snapped my fingers. "The thing you needed to unprocure."

"What exactly happened?" Jason asked. He reached over and grabbed a slice of his pizza from the wire frame. "I for one am starving as well and wish to hear this tale. It's one thing to be told someone lives with a book fused to his soul—but to actually see it sticking out? Quite . . . entertaining."

"I know." Dags winced. And for the first time I did notice the dark circles under his eyes. The gaunt look of his cheeks. On second thought, he didn't look *that* great. Was he casting a glamour spell? "As to how or why it happened, I don't know. I will say the book was right where Rhonda said it would be. But when I touched it—" He looked down.

"Just touching it did *that*?" Rhonda leaned over the table and pizzas to pull at his shirt again. He hadn't buttoned it up yet. I was getting an appetite, but not for garlic and cheese.

Dags nodded. "Once I got into the old theater, I could actually sense it. And it wasn't like most things that have magical ability—it was a little stronger. It didn't call or make itself known. More like"—he shook his head—"it had power and *knew* it did. It was content to just *be*."

Now, I'm not sure about anyone else, but that made no sense to me. I nodded as if I was, like, smart but grabbed a slice of pizza to alleviate boredom. I think only Rhonda understood most of it since he was out doing her bidding. And besides, of all the oogy things I'd seen in the past seven months—the book sticking out of his chest had to top them all. And it wasn't like an axe protruding, or even a knife. The skin around the book wasn't bloody or anything. It was . . . kinda like it'd *grown* there.

Dags shrugged. "Alice and Maureen checked it out first, and neither of them sensed anything. I said the incantation like you specified, reached out, and touched the book. There was a very bright flash of light. Alice and Maureen shouted. I woke up on the floor, no sign of the two of them, and realized I had this poking out of my chest."

"Does it hurt?" Joe asked. Simple. Like a six-year-old.

"I know it's there." He sighed. "And like I said, it's sort of interfering with digestion. I haven't been able to call on the girls since. I'm not sure if the book is hindering them or me."

"How did you get past airport security with that sticking out?" I blurted.

"A book doesn't register on a metal detector. And this thing is so old, there aren't any metallic pieces. From what I can tell, it's all handwoven, handcrafted. I don't know if what happened is a protection mechanism." He looked down at his chest and moved the shirt again. "And honestly, I don't think regular people can see it—people who haven't been touched by the Abysmal or don't have some other wacky ability going for them."

Stella raised her hand. "That would be me."

Rhonda frowned at her. "You can't see it?"

Stella shook her head.

Weird.

Rhonda said, "But Nona needs to take a look at it. Maybe she's seen something like this before."

I doubted it.

"I'm more inclined to believe, or suspect," Jason began, and I could still hear Mephistopheles echoing in his voice, "that whatever spell Rhonda used to seal the Bonville Grimoire in place has also attracted this book. That when Dags touched it, the books tried to merge."

Rhonda nodded slowly. "But why stick out like that?"

"He's not exactly a big guy," Joe said as he grabbed for a second slice of pizza. "I've never seen this Bonville Grimoire, so maybe there's not enough room? Like sticking a book on the same shelf and space as another, larger one?"

Jason and Rhonda looked at him wide-eyed.

He held the slice just in front of his mouth. "What?"

"You might have nailed it," Jason said. "It makes sense. I can sense the larger volume, the one fused to his soul. This one . . ." His voice trailed off as he stared at Dags's chest. "There's something familiar—" He shook his head as if to clear it and looked at Rhonda. "I do think a full examination of both books and their contents is in order. As for the question if either of them contains the spell we're looking for—we won't know till we can take a look at what's inside."

I'd never considered Jason ominous. Though I hadn't really known him that long. Yeah, we'd met briefly like ten months ago and back then I'd had no clue about him or Nick. Wasn't Wraith. But I do think if I'd heard him say that back then, I'd still have gotten this creepy feeling at the base of my neck. "When you say examine them—exactly how do you mean?"

"I'd like to know that myself," Rhonda piped up.

"It's easy. We remove both of them in order to take a look at the contents."

Silence. Then, "You can't do that, Jason. I thought you understood that when I joined the two of them, it was to save Dags's life. The Bonville is grafted to him, in the same way Mephistopheles is grafted to you. Without him, you would die. And without that book—"

Jason held up a hand. "Wait. I didn't mean yank the books from him. What I mean is see if there is a way to remove one, examine it, then replace and look at the other? Or perhaps Dags can view the contents of the books mentally? I mean, they are a part of him."

I raised my hand. "Um . . . first off . . . I'm not really good at magic stuff—"

Dags snorted. I shot him the bird. I knew he was remembering a month back when he'd saved me from the Coyote flame after my attempt at magic. *Jerk.*

"But what exactly *is* the book sticking out? We know the big book inside is full of lots of stuff, and it's powerful enough to keep Dags's ticker going. This small book—and I say small because I saw the other one, and it was a monster—does it have the same kind of magic?"

Rhonda sighed. "I get what you mean, Zoë."

I blinked. *You do?*

"Is it like substituting a healthy heart for perhaps a diseased one. Or even a subpar one."

Dags raised his hand. "Do I have a say in this?"

Jason nodded. "Of course. But you also have to understand our situation, Mr. McConnell." And Jason gave him a very concise and well-worded explanation of the past four days' events, starting with the human victims brought to the morgue. Once he'd finished, Dags looked a bit bewildered.

"A spell to kill First Borns? You do realize that these things can be reverse-engineered, right? That if the Phantasm created this thing for that purpose, it can be used against him."

I knew that. TC had told me.

"This is getting weirder by the minute," Joe said. "And now that I can talk, I'm going to. Phanty creates this spell to get rid of his competition, and you have to write spells down because they can't be memorized." He held out his hands. "So, if this spell is that important, how did he lose track of it? Because it's obvious someone has it, or part of it, but it's not working since we've got souls in limbo and not on the redacted list."

You know, one of the things I loved most about Joe was his ability to put things into perspective. And into plain English.

"The first objective, which I plan on passing on to the Revenants I can get hold of," Jason said, "is to figure out who or what has this partial spell. Big question is whether the Phantasm is pulling the strings, or are they being pulled for him."

"If it means the destruction of Revenants," Rhonda said, "and someone else is doing it, I doubt he's going to raise much of a fuss. I mean, he'd get his way."

"You've met the present Phantasm," Jason said. I had to nod. I'd met him on several occasions. He was kinda nuts. Like Joker nuts. Not Nicholson, but more like Ledger. "He loves control. Power. And if he doesn't have this spell, it's because it was stolen, not because he lost it. Once he realized someone else had it, he did everything he could to get it back. One, because in just general terms of the power, and two, because yes, it can be used against him."

"Yeah, but whatever or whoever has it isn't exactly targeting the Phantasm," I said. "We got four bodies. One a ghoul, the other a Revenant." Well, in truth the only bodies we had so far were the two humans. The others turned to goo. "So I'm getting it's not a friendly ghost."

Jason laughed softly. "You may be right, Zoë. But in any case, it looks as if it's experimenting with what it's got." He wiped his hands on a napkin. "I think it might be best if we grab leftovers and head back. Let Nona take a look at Dags."

I noticed the way he said Nona. All sweet and affectionate. I made secret plans to corral my mother and get the skinny on this whole seeing-Jason-the-Revenant thing, which I knew nothing about.

Dags offered to drive Stella home first, then come back to the shop. Rhonda volunteered to go with them. I think the purpose was twofold. One, because she's got the world's biggest crush on him, and two, to make sure he *did* come back and not disappear.

But when we got back to the shop, Mom wasn't there, but Mastiff pulled up as we piled out. Joe swore under his breath. "I'm not sure how I'm gonna explain this one."

"Aw," I said, and patted him on the arm. "I think he's a grown man and can take it. Just hope he's not gifted enough to see that book sticking out of Dags's chest."

"Halloran," Mastiff said as he got out of the car, "we have a problem."

Don't we always.

Joe held up his hand. "Before we go into anything—"

Mastiff froze in midstride. His eyes were wide as a grin spread across his face. "You—you can *talk*."

Joe nodded. "Long story. No time to get into it. And I don't want to make a fuss."

Oh yes, you do.

"No, no. Not a problem. Though explaining it all to the captain might take some fancy footwork." He looked past us to Jason as he moved around to the car. "I'm sorry—I don't think we've had the pleasure."

"Oh, Detective Mastiff, meet Jason Lawrence. An old friend of Nona's and Rhonda's."

The two shook hands and sniffed butts. Geez. The solidarity of the guy teams. Was amazing sometimes.

Mastiff turned back to Joe. "We've spotted Frasier."

Heart . . . sinking. Pounding. I stepped forward, a hand going to my heart. "You have?"

"He was actually spotted in a morgue in Cumming earlier this evening." Mastiff looked apologetically at me.

"Someone see him?" I asked.

"No, but cameras in the parking lot picked him up entering, then an hour later exiting. The police didn't find anything suspicious inside. And the ME insists nothing was taken."

In a morgue. Oh man, that doesn't sound good. What was he up to? What could he want in a morgue? Rhonda and Dags pulled up then, Dags behind the wheel of a Ford rental. It was gray—close to the color of his eyes. They caught sight of Mastiff and asked questions to get caught up.

"How long ago was it that he was spotted?" Joe said.

"A good three hours. We didn't get the call for identification till half an hour ago. I was going to drive up there and check it out. Need a partner."

"I'm there." He turned to me and pointed at the house. "You good? It'll mean no bodyguard for a while."

"I think I can manage, Detective," Jason said with a grin. "And we'll keep you informed if we learn anything." I knew Jason was talking about the book in Dags's chest.

With a nod, Joe moved to Mastiff's car, and the two drove off.

I looked at the house. "I wonder where Mom is." We all moved to the back door. I hesitated. Something felt off.

"What is it?" Rhonda said.

"Do you sense anything weird?"

"Weird? Oh, come on, Zoë. This is your mom's house. Weird doesn't describe it."

True dat. But. "Why are all the lights off? Mom never turns the kitchen light off—it's why she bought that energy-efficient one." And then the hackles along my back rose. Someone was in the house.

Jason seemed to sense it as well. A different presence, and I could see the subtle transformations about him that warned anything or anyone around he wasn't human.

Beware.

Rhonda and Dags both seemed to arm up with magic as her right fist glowed green, and the inside of his palms hummed a brilliant blue-white. But still no sign of Alice or Maureen. I moved my body into Wraith form and went as incorporeal as possible but still visible to them. Wow. I was getting pretty good at this.

"Revenant."

It was a single word spoken from Jason, his First Born's voice echoing from within the timbre.

There was a Revenant inside. I looked at him as the four of us stood outside the back door, at the foot of the porch steps. "It's not Lex?"

"No."

"Anyone you know?"

He nodded slowly. "Inanna. And she's very . . ." He hissed. "Frustrated."

Uh-oh. I wondered what frustrated meant to a Revenant. From his reaction, it couldn't be good. I know for me it meant sex. WANT. I hoped Mom was still out with Jemmy somewhere up to no good and not inside, like, dead on the floor or something.

"She's looking for something," he added as a side note.

I pursed my lips. "The book?"

"Yeah." He shrugged. "Or it could be me. I'm afraid she and I didn't part on good terms the last time we were together."

"When you say together"—I tilted my head and my wings rustled—"you mean like together, together. How long ago?"

"Last host."

"You mean like with Archer."

"Kinda . . ."

"But you were a girl."

He looked sideways at me. "Your point?"

"Hey," Rhonda hissed. "This isn't the time!"

Oh man, I was intrigued by then. Jason squared his shoulders and took the first two steps. "Inanna, I know you can sense me. Please, there is no one here to harm you."

There was a deep laugh from inside, kind of like the dude from the 7-Up commercials. Reeeal spooky. Man, if that's Inanna, then she's got one hell of a sore throat. I glanced at Jason. He seemed not to notice. Rhonda? She was pale, but I knew that face. It was the one she used when she attacked soap scum.

Abruptly, the back door burst out and something man-sized and dark flew at us. I yelled and launched myself up, grabbing Rhonda and taking her with me because she was closest. Rhonda's reaction to being hoisted into the air was a deafening shriek.

I looked down to see what looked like a man in a black, hooded robe, tackle Jason to the ground and hold something up over his head. Dags was moving closer to them, his hands transformed into balls of light.

"What's going on? Put me down!"

I hovered a few feet up and watched as Dags hit the robed guy with a few blasts of light. It appeared to have some effect on the dude in black because he fell off Jason. I took that moment to land us far enough away that the intruder couldn't immediately attack.

Boy was I wrong. I'd barely got us to the ground when parts of my body began to burn. I looked down to see slashes again, just as Lex had made before. Blood flowed out as I put myself in front of Rhonda, our initial position protecting her from the largest of the attacks, but I could see deep gashes tearing at her jeans.

"Zoë!"

I turned to see Jason back on his feet. He was motioning me to move. "Get Rhonda and Dags out of here!"

Rhonda was easy, she was behind me. But Dags had engaged

the guy. I could see the air almost waver every time he sent a slash at Dags, but the Guardian was blocking them with the light of his palms.

I turned to Rhonda. "You run! Call Mom! I'll get Dags!"

She nodded and didn't argue. *Yay.* Then I moved a few inches from the ground and barreled into the dude in black, tackling him and sending both of us into the side of the house, putting a dent in the wall where the botanica's books were. The impact wasn't as painful as I thought it'd be.

What I hadn't expected, though, was the speed with which the guy recovered. He was up and back on his feet, a gun in his hand.

And he fired it at Jason.

The Revenant went down.

Then Robe Guy turned it on Dags.

"NO!" I bellowed, and moved in front of Dags. Robe Guy fired several times at me, and I felt the strikes like pins and needles in my flesh. But I'd had it. I opened my mouth and SCREAMED—

18

THE power of my scream wasn't lost on the Revenant. He vanished in a whirlwind of dirt, debris, and old copies of newspapers Mom had stacked on the back porch. When I ran out of breath, I turned to Jason and knelt beside him. Three large, bloodied holes decorated his shirt, and he lay on his back panting. The body that was Jason Lawrence was shaking.

Rhonda moved to the other side, and Dags joined her a few seconds later, moving a little slower than usual.

"We need to call—"

I looked at her. "Call who? Nine-one-one? I don't think so, unless they know how to treat vampires." No, calling anyone was a bad idea. Unless it was Mom.

Mom!

I held out my palm. "Give me your phone."

She did as she started pulling Jason's shirt away from him, exposing the bullet holes. I pressed Mom's speed dial, but Jason's hand grabbed at my wrist.

I looked down at him. "No need . . ." And he smiled. He was shaking. But he was also *smiling*.

I closed Rhonda's phone. "You mean to tell me you can withstand bullets but not a stake?"

Rhonda sighed with relief as the bullets started pushing out with sickening squishy noises. I was reminded of the bullets falling from Daniel's body when the Horror possessed him. The pinging noises as they hit the floor. "I guess bullets aren't as effective?"

Jason finally sat up with a little help and nodded. "They hurt like a stone bitch—but Inanna didn't want to kill me. She just wanted to stop me to go after her real target." He shook his head. "Or I should say he. Looks like she managed a male this time."

"Real target?" Dags asked.

Jason finally stood with a groan. I did as well and felt my body shift back to human. Dags remained on the ground, looking up. "The real target is you. I told you I could sense the book, and I'm sure most everyone else can too. He probably thought you had it in your possession—not that you were possessed *by* it."

I held up my hands, looking at the slashes along my arms, legs, and forearms. They weren't as deep as Lex's. Just surface cuts that would cause agony if covered in salt. I noticed Rhonda's were the same. Sliced clothing, but the wounds beneath weren't dangerous. I thought about the guy in the robes. I'd seen that type of robe before. "Uh, Rhonda, did that robe look—"

"Familiar?" She was dusting herself off and examining a long slice on her upper left thigh. "Yeah. Those were ceremonial robes. A lot like the ones Bonville's followers used." Rhonda looked at Dags. "It looks like there are still neophytes out there, Dags. And they're still wanting that damn book."

The look on Dags's face caught my attention. He was pale—

too pale. I knelt beside him and put my hand on his arm. He started to pull away, and I pulled him closer. "Talk to me. What's wrong?"

His gray eyes focused on mine. "I think—" He blinked a few times. "I think I got hit."

"What?"

I helped him lie back on the ground and moved his shirt away. And there, beside the book, was a hole. Blood had pooled from it, but not a great amount. *Phock!*

"Oh shit." Rhonda moved in, her hands glowing green again. She closed her eyes as she held her hands over the wound and the protruding book. Dags made an odd sound and closed his eyes. I pushed at his shoulder, but he didn't stir. I looked at Rhonda. "What did you do?"

She opened her eyes, and her hands stopped glowing. "We need to get him inside. I tried to remove the bullet—but I think I failed."

"Son of a—"

"Just shut up and get him inside!"

Wow, it'd been a while since I'd seen Rhonda this take-charge. Still in Wraith form, I put my right arm under Dags's shoulders and my left under his knees, my wings flapping slightly to balance the weight.

"Zoë, let me get him," Jason said as he came closer.

I nearly growled at him. "I've got him," and with ease I lifted him, moving quickly to the door. My heart thundered hard in my chest, and I remembered the helplessness I'd felt a month ago when he'd been in ICU. And I'd been unable to do anything for him.

I turned sideways to get him through the splinters and spires of broken wood. Mom's stained-glass window lay in a tangled mess on the first porch step.

Wow, she was gonna be *pissed* when she saw that door.

* * *

"**WHAT** THE HELL HAPPENED TO MY DOOR?"

I winced. She was going to blame me. That much I could see coming. I could be in a different state, and the woman would blame me for everything.

We were upstairs in my room when she and Jemmy came in. Rhonda had called her and told her what'd happened, and she and Jemmy had made record time coming back from the herb man's house. Though why buy herbs this time of night? I decided it really wasn't a good idea to ask.

The minute they saw Dags—and Mom got a load of the book sticking out of his chest—the two of them grabbed Rhonda and went into a powwow in the other room. I pulled a chair up next to my bed and watched Dags breathe. He was stable but unconscious. Rhonda had been a basket case with a purpose since getting him inside.

I'd thought nothing of undressing him, wanting to see more of him. Rhonda seemed a little nervous and bolted from the room when I removed his pants. *What? He's wearing boxers!*

Uh . . . no. He wasn't. *Wow* . . . I didn't know Dags went commando.

I got him under the cover and downshifted into just me. In this form—me—my eyesight wasn't as defined or shaped to the things that lurked in the shadows, but was still aware of them. And they of me. As Wraith, I could see the book burning bright in his chest. But I noticed as me—

I saw something—it just wasn't a defined book. It looked more like—

Well—like when a TV network pixels out a brand logo sometimes.

I blinked and put my hand on the area. My hand looked fine, but the skin beneath it was just blurry—except for the bullet wound, which was trickling blood—no book. *Nada.* Shifting back to Wraith, there it was. Downshift, blurry.

What the hell?

"You're going to get dizzy doing that," Jason said as he came in with a pan of hot water and clean towels. He had a pack of sterile gauze tucked under his arm and tape carried on a finger. "You can't see the book as a human—I mean you should see something."

"Why is this?" I took the pan from him and set it on the night-stand. Headless Mary was watchin' me. "I mean, before when I would OOB, I could still see things when I was back in my body."

"I don't know the rules when it comes to how your perception works," he said. "I just know that when I am not a part of another's soul, my own perceptions shift and change. Like this." He set the rest of the stuff on the bed. "I'm locked into what Jason perceives. Looking through the eyes of a human in the physical plane. Maybe your own perception has moved with your change."

The way he was taking about Jason, I thought I was speaking to Mephistopheles. I watched his movements—patient and deliber-ate. There was no hesitation as he opened the gauze, neatly fold-ing each piece before he set it upon one of the clean towels. This wasn't the first time I'd noticed his elegance, and I wondered at that moment if the dance of this seemingly mundane action reflected Mephistopheles' centuries as a human? Living day to day in a human body.

I shifted again, so I could see the book. And I found if I looked harder, I could kinda see where it entered his skin and ended, and then, "Jason, I think I can see the other book."

"You can?" He moved from the opposite side of the bed and came to stand to my right. "You can see the Grimoire?"

I narrowed my eyes as I focused on it. It was like refocusing Dags's body in Photoshop, making it transparent. And there at the center of everything was a large, tattered-looking book. He literally had a book in his—"Wait. This is the astral body I'm looking at. This book is connected to his"—I looked up at Jason—"his soul."

The Revenant nodded. "Of course. Where did you think it was?"

"I guess I hadn't thought about it," I said. "I mean—I've seen the Veil that Rhonda uses where she puts things around her to hide them. I guess I sort of thought this was the same thing."

"No." Jason shook his head, and this time I could hear the First Born clearly in my head. "My understanding—from what Rhonda told me—was that Darren was dying. Rodriguez had stripped him of his will to live—damaged his heart so badly he wasn't going to survive. His Familiars were too weak to heal him. So she used a very old spell, one she'd found in the Grimoire itself, and fused his heart, and soul, to the power of the book."

"But"—I looked down at him again—"it looks as if this new book has, in a way, fused itself to the old one."

"Oh?" He narrowed his eyes. "Interesting."

"Interesting?" I blinked at him. "Jason . . . Mephisto . . . whoever you are . . . what exactly is happening? I mean what happens if they do fuse?"

"Why don't you look inside and find out?"

Jason and I straightened and turned together. TC stood in front of one of the windows, his front shadowed from the light filtering in from the streetlamp. Jason immediately moved around me and approached TC. "Archer."

"Hello, Mephisto. I see you survived the rowan?"

Well, I guess Dags was right—he'd given TC back his own voice. It was deep and nicely melodic.

"How dare you attack *me*."

I noticed Jason's voice was no longer his own. In fact, I wasn't sure if Jason Lawrence was at home at all.

TC took a step forward, not even the least bit afraid. "How dare *you* put the Wraith in danger like that. You knew what could happen if she released a ghoul, and yet you and that damned bitch pushed her to do it. You need to learn truth, you old ass. Something you Revenants discard like old shoes."

I frowned. I was missing something here. Something important. And though I wanted to know more—*hell, add this to the list of things I want answers to*—it really wasn't the time. "Jason . . . Mephistopheles . . . not now, okay? TC, what did you mean look inside?"

TC glared at Jason as he pushed the Revenant aside and stood by me. "You still retain the ability to overshadow, as you did with Mialani and Aether's host. Take a look inside and remove the bullet. You can do it better than that witch."

I looked at Dags. He was breathing shallow. And—it made sense. I waited for a protest from Mephistopheles, but none came. He'd turned and was watching me. Taking in a deep breath, I moved my hand toward Dags's chest, just to the right of the protruding book, and pushed in. To my amazement, my hand *did* go through Dags's flesh, and into his chest. I closed my eyes and looked inside as well, using my hand as my eyes.

Amazing . . . it was like having a tiny camera attached to my fingers. Okay . . . that image was gross. It wasn't that I saw organs and blood and bone, but more of the ebb and flow of his aura as it moved throughout his body. Most of the colors for him were dark blue and purple. But in the center, below his rib cage, there was a concentration of red and yellow. Angry colors.

I could see the book—the original Grimoire—and the smaller book was somehow pushed into its side. As I moved closer I realized—the bullet was *in* the Grimoire. Somehow, an astral item had stopped a physical intrusion.

Is this possible?

In order to get the bullet, I was going to have to open the book. To open the book, I was going to have to remove the smaller one. Before I could do anything, I felt a coldness along my spine and realized I was no longer alone.

TC was inside.

What are you doing? I asked him.

Watching you. Why are you hesitating?

Because I don't want to hurt him.

Awww. TC's voice was more than a little sour. *Is the big bad Wraithy afraid she'll hurt her wuver?*

Fuck off, and I shouldered him away as best as I could in the astral state.

No chance, baby. I don't give a shit about this asshole. He bit the tip of my finger off.

That he did—when TC had tried to kill him by suffocation. I'd wondered why TC had started wearing gloves. Evidently what happens in the astral doesn't stay in the astral. *He also gave you back your voice.*

Oh . . . is that what happened? Okay. I owe him one.

Geez.

Hrm . . . looks like you'll have to remove the small book to get to the larger one.

Well, duh. I moved my hand slowly, watching Dags's reaction both in his physical being and his astral. He flinched once or twice, and when he moaned, I stopped again. Waiting, I slowly gripped the spine of the smaller book and got one freak'n hell of an electric shock. When I jerked my hand back, the book came with it, out of the astral and back into the plane of the physical.

I sat on the bed, staring at the book as my body shifted from Wraith to human. It looked less like a Grimoire of some kind and more like someone's journal. Like Jules Verne or someone like him. It was maybe five inches by eight and a half, hand-tooled leather, and hand-stitched in the binding. A leather thong held the book together.

"Let me see that," Jason said as he moved forward.

But before either of us could react, TC grabbed the book from my hands—

And was gone.

That simple.

"Shit!" I said, getting to my feet.

"Shit what?" Mom asked as she, Jemmy, and Rhonda came through the door. They were each carrying handfuls of stuff, all wrapped in blankets. They looked like the Three Wise Men bearing gifts.

Nothing could have prepared me for the look of pure incredulousness on their faces when they looked at Dags—with no book sticking out of his chest. Mom dropped her bundle. Jemmy crossed herself.

"Shit!" Rhonda said.

I pointed to Rhonda. "See?"

19

JUST as Mom was about to lay into me, two flashes of light appeared to my left. Alice and Maureen materialized, both dressed in their full Familiar regalia (which was basically Valkyrie anime strategic armor). Alice's light was white, Maureen's a deep red. Alice crouched and looked at me. I smiled and waved.

She then turned to see Dags on the bed and hissed. Immediately, the two of them shifted costumes, swords gone, and moved in to put their hands on their Guardian.

I somehow got the impression I'd popped a cork.

"Where is the book?" Mom said as she came forward and yanked me out of the way. Rhonda did a similar movement with Jason, who looked as if his entire attention was taken up by what the two women were doing.

I swallowed. "I took it out."

"How did you do that?" Rhonda hissed.

"I just reached in and grabbed it." I sighed. "The bullet is in the Grimoire, and I needed to remove the book to open the Grimoire to—"

"NO!"

GAH . . . ! If there was one thing Rhonda Orly had, it was lungs of steel. I put my hands to my head and whirled on her. Her eyes were bright and her complexion pale. "WHAT. THE. HELL?"

"Please tell me you didn't open the book?"

I frowned, keeping my hands protectively over my ears. "What book?"

"The Grimoire?"

"No, I never got that far."

Mom whirled me around to her. "Did you open the small book?"

"No. I didn't open any book. I just pulled it out, and TC took it. He snatched it—"

"WHAT!"

GAH . . . ! Stop that! Both of them yelled that time, and I moved away to stand beside Jemmy and Jason, where it was less noisy. "What is with you two?"

"How did TC get in here and get the book?" Rhonda said.

"I have this place warded," Mom said.

"Yeah, well, they don't work. He found a way in," I muttered. "And he took it."

Both women were quiet for a while as Jemmy handed me her bundle and moved to where Dags lay, his body enveloped in a soft golden light. The girls were leaning over him, their eyes closed in concentration. I just hoped Jemmy didn't bother them.

"You just stuck your hand inside him?" Rhonda was apparently stuck on that part.

"Yes, just like I stuck my hand in Mialani and in Aether's host. Now what is the big deal?"

"Zoetrope—"

God, I hated it when she said that.

"You are not to stick your hands into anyone else, do I make myself clear?"

"Wraith!" Alice called out.

I closed the distance between us. "What is it?"

"I've laid the book open just enough to remove the bullet—but I need you to reach inside and take it. Only you can do this."

Huh. You're kidding me, right?

I turned and looked at Mom. "Can I?"

She glared at me as I shifted back to Wraith and repeated what I'd done before, easing through the golden light, which kinda tickled, then through the physical flesh to the astral, where I could see the book once again. The book was half-open just as she said it was, and I could see the bullet clearly, embedded in the paper.

With my tongue stuck out, I moved closer, getting a grip on the bullet.

"Just don't touch the book," Maureen said in a sour voice.

"What?"

"Don't touch the book."

"Why not?" My hesitation caused me to move, and my knuckle touched the book.

Nuts.

Dags gave out a low moan, and I looked at his face. He winced in pain, and I felt my heart flutter. At the same time, I also started seeing flashes of symbols across my eyes, until a scroll of them appeared like a superimposed image over the scene. The scroll rolled itself up and moved to my left hand, where it tucked itself nice and neat into TC's mark.

What the—

"Zoë!"

Oh. Right. I looked down again, and this time carefully grabbed the bullet with the thumb and index finger of my hand. Willing it to stick to my astral fingers, I carefully pulled it free of the book, out of it, then through the flesh. Once it was done, I went solid again and held it out.

Dags abruptly hissed and started to move. Maureen and Alice became solid as well and pressed him down.

"What's wrong?" I asked as I moved back.

Alice looked at Nona. "We could use your help now."

And then I was suddenly shunted aside and replaced by the three wise ladies. Jason touched my shoulder and pulled me closer, his voice low. "What did you see?"

I frowned at him. "See?"

"When you touched the book. I know you touched it because of the boy's reaction. What did you see?"

I wanted to tell him. I really did. But there was something ringing in my ears, something warning me that saying anything about it was a bad idea. That what I'd seen wasn't something that needed to be known. "I didn't see anything. But it shocked the hell out of me. Just like that other book did." I tried to see around them. "But I was more concerned with Dags."

Jason narrowed his eyes, and I realized with a double take I was actually talking to Jason, not Mephistopheles. "So—I'm trying to understand the relationships. Rhonda and Joe are dating—but Joe is always watching you. You and Dags have had intercourse—"

"Who told you that?"

"No one. The astral ties are strong, especially for you." He smiled. "But you two have had sex."

And maybe a couple of months ago I'd have said yeah, we had sex. But—saying that made it sound cheap. And what I'd had with Dags—let's face it—was not cheap and dirty. "We made love, yes."

"But you pretend you don't love each other."

"It's complicated."

"I'll say. Because what's really confusing is this relationship between you and the crazy cop."

Okay. End of conversation. I was done. I held up my left hand—the one not holding the bullet. "Can we skip this subject and discuss you and my mom?"

He stared at me, blinking. "That was a long time ago, Zoë. Before your father ever entered into Nona's life."

I finally dropped the façade of sarcasm and really looked at him. "You looked the same then, didn't you?"

"Yes. And after a while, when I learned who her great-uncle was—and understanding his work—I confessed to her one night what I was."

"And she didn't freak?"

"No, but she did start wearing a lot of turtlenecks."

He grinned. I smacked him.

"Seriously," he said. "I was honest with your mother, and my honesty paid off one night when a group of Fetches came after me. I'd allowed Mephistopheles to be seen." He used finger quotes around the word *seen*. "Which wasn't smart. I put up a fight, but I was badly wounded. Your mother—having listened to me—knew exactly what to do."

"Just like she did the other night?"

"Yep." He smiled. "It wasn't long after that she went to work for Domas. And she met Adiran Martinique."

I sighed as I looked at his face. "She does love the dark ones, doesn't she?"

He echoed my amusement. "We remained friends. I've kept in touch with her, and we've perpetuated myths about us in the Dioscuri notes."

"So." I got it . . . "You put lies in there, to keep anyone from really discovering what you were."

"Exactly. And your mother has been an asset to me many times. I did what I could for the two of you after Adiran vanished. But Nona is a proud woman and wouldn't let me take you in."

I got the feeling just from looking at the man's suits and shoes that he had money. And the thought that during my youth we could have been living the life of luxury instead of scrimping by really annoyed me. But I understood her pride. And her fear. "She wanted to be free of the Society."

"And L-6 in turn." He nodded. "We Revenants have our own group and our own cliques. The older ones tend to hang together. The ones who've lived more lifetimes. All but one has answered me: Inanna. Aether's response was almost immediate, confirming for me that we had all received that note. Aether was the first to become a Revenant. Unfortunately, he is now the first to die by the spell possibly buried in that ancient book."

"Well, that book didn't look too ancient to me." I thought about it.

"You know better than anyone that items on the physical plane can look different in the astral. Ancient could mean different things."

"Maybe." But I wasn't really sold. "So, basically, someone is luring you all to one place. Here in Atlanta."

He nodded. "We noticed this as well. With Aether gone, I suspect there are only twelve or so of us."

"What about Inanna? She or he going to help or just attack every time they're around."

"I think Inanna's target was Dags because she sensed the presence of the book, as said in the note. But what I'm not sure of is why she didn't communicate with me—she was the one I couldn't get hold of. She was right there—I sensed her—but she refused to speak to me."

I winced. "I'm sorry I blew her away with my scream."

"Oh. No. You didn't. She simply left before you began."

Uhm . . . "Jason—are you saying you can literally make the physical body vanish?"

"Not vanish." He tilted his head to the side. "But we can make it look like it." He fanned the fingers of his right hand at me as if to effect a magician's magic trick. "It's all illusion, Zoë. Inanna can move with great speed. Each of us has our gifts."

"Oh," I said. "What's yours?"

He smiled. "Death."

"Oh, thank the goddess," came Rhonda's strained voice.

My attention went immediately to the bed, and I was behind their little semicircle in seconds. "What? Is he okay?"

Mom turned and put a hand on my shoulder. "Yes, he's fine. Dags has always been strong. We were worried the bullet damaged the book—since the book acts as his anchor to this life."

Jemmy ambled out of the way as well, patting my side as she passed. I felt my heart fluttering as she smiled. "He'll be fine as long as he knows you care, sugar." And with that she left the room.

Alice and Maureen were gone—maybe taking a siesta after healing their Guardian. Only Rhonda remained, sitting in the chair I'd pulled up earlier. Dags was still, his eyes closed, dark circles beneath them. His chest had been wrapped in the gauze Jason brought up earlier, and my comforter was pulled to his waist. His left arm was on top, and Rhonda had his hand in hers.

I moved to the other side and climbed onto the bed, sitting up on my knees. The braid of my hair swung around and half rested on my arm. My head was a jumble of questions—but all the wrong ones. I wasn't thinking of what happened. Why did this Revenant attack? Why was that book stuck in his chest? Why did TC take it and what will he do with it? What was *in* that book? Was it possible the spell was in it? And what the hell was with that scroll?

Those were the questions I should have been considering.

But no . . . I was thinking things like . . . did he still feel the same? Was what he said the truth? That he loved me. And that he would always love me. I remembered him flinching back. And then in the background I thought of Joe and Mastiff, looking for Daniel, who was no longer in a facility but out there. Maybe stalking me.

No one really knew.

"What—what kind of damage did I do?" I asked in the smallest voice I think I'd ever used.

I felt Rhonda's eyes on me, and when I looked at her, I didn't know how to read her expression. "You didn't do anything wrong. I did. The bullet was originally on the cover of the Grimoire—but when I tried to move it"—she gave a short sigh and looked back at him—"I pushed it into the book. The book's pages—not the actual fiber but the ink and spells on them—they're the magic that keep him alive. That keep him with us. And any damage to those spells could unravel what it was I did."

"You mean like a bullet marring the ink?"

"Yeah . . . exactly. It's all so complicated, and sometimes I'm not sure I really know what I'm doing." Rhonda reached out and brushed a stray lock of dark hair from his cheek. "I'm amazed he made it all the way back here like that—with that book interrupting his astral flow. Maureen and Alice were cut off from him, so when you removed the book, they could appear and heal him."

I thought back to my hand inside him, and of the pages the book had been half-open to with the writing on them. "So—the bullet didn't damage any of the spells?"

"No." She reached up and tucked her own bob behind her ears. "By a miracle, the bullet only touched a page with no spell. It was a blank."

I thought about the image in my head of the symbols spiraling off and onto a scroll—then moving into my mark. I held up my hand to look at it and the handprint. Before, when it was new, it resembled a really bizarre henna tat. But now it looked like faded gold paint. Was it possible that that was the spell on that page? That it'd somehow saved itself? And was tucked—inside of me?

I opened my mouth to tell her this—but the words caught in my throat. I cleared my throat and tried again. But every time I started to say something—nothing would come out.

"You okay?" Rhonda was looking at me, but she still had her hand in his. "You need some water?"

"No, no, I'm fine." So—evidently I wasn't supposed to tell anyone it was there.

Interesting.

But what does it mean?

Jason moved from the window and stood behind Rhonda. "So—there were blanks in the book? Blank pages?"

Rhonda nodded. "Weird, isn't it? Usually these things are packed full. And Nona and I and Dags had already looked at several of the spells. Dags is the only one who can read a lot of them."

"Oh?" Jason said.

I nodded. "They're written in ancient Sumerian."

His eyes widened. "Sumerian? Are you sure?"

Something in his voice caught Rhonda's attention as well, and we both looked at him. "What's wrong?" she asked.

He put his hand to his jaw and rubbed. "Most of the stories of us make it seem as if we were all made at the same time. Presto, and the Phantasm had children. But in truth it took centuries between each of us. Inanna was born during the time of the Sumerians and still knows the language."

"Nobody else did?" I asked. "Like in all those years nobody else would learn it?"

"Why learn a dead language?" Jason shrugged. "Who does that?"

"Dags." Rhonda sighed and looked back at Jason. "What has that got to do with the spells?"

"Maybe nothing, maybe everything." He crossed his arms over his chest. "Inanna was the first of us to carry an interest in magic—and it was she that discovered that magic, when brought into the planes other than the astral, could not be retained. That writing it down was mandatory. So when the spell was first used on us, she studied the body for a long time, examining the symbols and reverse-engineering the magic."

He paused.

"And?" I asked.

"And"—he shrugged—"I know she used to use Sumerian to write the spells in so nobody else could use them, and we could possibly study them. She kept a book with everything she'd learned inside it."

Mother . . . Guppy. "Are you saying that—"

He pointed at Dags. "The reason she tried to get that book is because she wrote it. That's her Grimoire."

Oh . . . shit.

20

THAT night, I slept next to Dags.

Hell, it was *my* bed. Several times I woke with my arm draped over his chest. His own hand clutched my arm, and yet I never saw his eyes open. Real solid sleep was out of the question—no dreams. Which reminded me that I needed to talk to Alice when she came out again and ask her if she'd really spoken to me in my dreams.

I think I finally dozed off heavily closer to dawn, my thoughts set on finding TC and the book.

When I did wake up, I was alone in the bed, and the sun was shining way too bright through the windows. I hissed and pulled my cover over my head. And as I lay there in the semidarkness, I noticed something missing.

No smells.

Usually my mom was pretty regular about fixing a big Sunday breakfast, and by this time—basing my time line on how high the sun was and getting in my face—I should be smelling fresh coffee, bacon, eggs, biscuits, and—

Why aren't I smelling any of this?

I sat up and looked around. Dags's clothes from the night before were gone as well from where I'd sort of piled them in the corner. With a yawn, I bounced up, used the bathroom, pushed my hair back into submission, and went downstairs. The kitchen was completely empty, and clean. No one had been in it since yesterday. The back door was also miraculously fixed. Not the same door, but the frame had been hammered back, and a new, unpainted door had been installed.

What freak'n time was it?

I checked the clock in the kitchen.

One o'clock?

It was one o'clock on Sunday afternoon?

I had slept through the whole morning? Cruising through the whole house only to find no one, I used that back door to step outside. The broken glass was gone, and so was Mom's Volvo.

WTF?

They'd all hauled ass and left me by myself?

How was this cool?

Getting more pissed off by the minute, I marched back inside and caught sight of a piece of paper taped to the microwave oven. I yanked it away.

Zoë,

We decided to let you sleep—Dags said you'd tossed and turned all night. Joe came by and helped fix the door with Jason. Dags is fine, and it was suggested we keep him at Rhonda's estate. The wards there are much thicker, and he'll be harder for any of the Revenants to trace. Just call if you need us.

Mom

I stood there in my loungers and tee shirt for a little bit. So, Dags had noticed me tossing and turning. Had he been awake the whole time? And when my arm had been around him—had he noticed that too?

I didn't want him getting any ideas. I didn't love him—not like that. But I cared about him. Like a little brother.

Riiiiiight. *And seeing him with Stella hadn't bothered you at all,* said a little voice in my head.

Oh . . . shut up. Yeah, it bothered me. More than I cared to admit. And there was a large part of me that wanted him beside me like he'd been a month ago. Telling me everything would be okay.

Holding me when I needed it. Human contact.

Or was it really Wraith and Guardian contact?

Either way, I missed him, and I wasn't going to admit that to anyone. Least of all him. I needed to keep my hopes positive for Daniel. He needed me to think about him. Daniel.

He's in the city somewhere. And the last time I saw him, he'd wanted to kill me. And so—why have my entire family and circle of friends left me alone?

The back door banged open, and I jumped—a hazard since it was getting easier to jump out of my skin. So I yelled out.

It was Joe, each hand holding two green bags of groceries. He saw me and grinned. "Oh, hi. You're up."

I nodded and immediately went to grab as many of the bags as possible to put them in the kitchen. After depositing them with me, he went back out and grabbed two more before closing the back door and locking it.

The bags were filled with herbs, along with regular staples. Eggs, milk, bread, cheese, meats. "I didn't realize Mom was this low on fixings."

"Well, some of it has to go out to Rhonda's place. Nona called me, complaining her kitchen didn't have the right bacon, nor the right eggs. So I ran over to Whole Foods and grabbed them."

"You mean Whole Paycheck?" I shook my head. "Expensive place."

"Your mom's credit card. Not mine. I eat fast food." He started helping me put away most of the items but kept a bag separate for Mom. Eventually, he stopped and watched me. I stopped and looked up at him.

"It's nice to have your voice back."

"Yeah, I kinda understand how you felt now." He leaned on the counter. "You okay?"

"Okay with what?" I grabbed up the water pot and streamed water into it. Setting it back on the burner, I turned it on high heat. I wanted tea. English Breakfast. "Waking up with a madman out there wanting to kill me? Doesn't make me happy or feel safe."

Glancing at Joe, I saw him smirk and look down. "Sorry. That was my fault. But you were sleeping so sound, I didn't want to disturb you. And I figured a few hours at the grocery would be okay. And I need to fill you in so you don't worry so much." He moved to the refrigerator and took out half a gallon of milk, then retrieved a glass from the cabinet. "Last night, when Mastiff and I got to the morgue, we found bupkis. Nothing. Eyewitnesses say Daniel was there and identified him from a photo. But they also say he walked in calmly, asked specific questions about the bodies brought in before—the ones transferred to Dekalb—and then left."

I paused. "Wait—you mean the morgue you guys went to was the one where the first bodies were brought?"

He nodded. "I didn't realize it either till halfway there." He searched through the pantry and pulled out a container of cocoa powder and proceeded to load up the glass with it. "The general idea is—Daniel's responsible for the murders."

I nearly dropped the mug I'd pulled out. "Say what?"

"The first body was found the day after he disappeared from the facility. Now he's been seen asking specific questions about the bodies—he seemed to know about the symbols and described a few. The employees he spoke to all said he was courteous and polite, and a few said the word, and I quote, 'hawt.'"

Yeah. That was Daniel. I'd always said he was hawt. And kind. But . . . "Daniel's the suspect?"

Sighing, Joe reached into his back pocket and pulled out a folded wad of papers. He unfolded them and set them on the counter. "These are photocopies of things he'd drawn on the wall of his room at the facility a week before he vanished."

I took them up and immediately recognized them. "These were on the bodies."

He nodded. "Finding that didn't help." He resumed his chocolate-milk making, pouring the milk over the heap of cocoa before fighting a spoon down into it. "And I wanted to talk with you away from all the others. Is it possible he's possessed by a Horror again? Not necessarily yours?"

I shrugged, still looking at the copies. "I suppose anything is possible, Joe. Though unlikely. Apparently, it's not that easy to make a Horror and unlikely Phanty will have the opportunity soon."

"But it is possible that once used by Phanty, Daniel could be again?"

I put the papers down and narrowed my eyes at him. "What are you getting at?"

"Nothing really—just theories. The nurses at the facility all said Daniel had all the symptoms of someone suffering from posthypnotic stress syndrome. And that five days before he disappeared, when he started drawing these, Daniel seemed lucid and cooperative. The model patient. And then he vanished."

I pursed my lips. "Sure sounds like possession, don't it?"

"Yeah, and the murders started a day later." He took up the milk and drank half of it. His milk mustache was priceless. "He's the prime suspect right now. No other leads. What I don't have in this is motivation. Though Jason had a theory." He leaned against the counter. "As a Horror, Phanty had access to Daniel's mind. What if that's what's happening now? He's using Daniel to wipe out the competition? Only he's looking for the spell of obliteration or whatever it is and is working on it through Daniel from memory."

"Makes sense that it's not working. He's only got most of it." I shook my head. "I don't know. I would say ask TC, but—"

"Yeah, about that." He set the glass down. "Why did he make off with that small book?"

"To see what was inside? Did Jason tell you that all the Revenants received notice prior to the killings that someone was resurrecting that spell?"

"No . . . but that explains their wanting grimoires. And our little buddy is a walking book."

I asked him if he'd been told about the break-in yesterday. He nodded. "And how the book inside Dags might belong to a Revenant. This just keeps getting better and better. I can always count on you to raise the spooky, Zoë."

I grinned at him. The kettle whistled, and I dropped a tea bag into the mug. After a few seconds, I poured hot water in on top of it.

Joe's phone rang, and he pulled it from his pocket. With a frown, he answered. "Halloran. What's up?"

Within seconds I knew it wasn't good news. He didn't say much, but his expression gave away everything. When he hung up, he looked at me. "Go get showered and dressed."

"What is it?"

"Another body. They found this one near here. Over at the Jimmy Carter Center."

Damn. "Lex have it?"

"Not yet. But she will. And Zoë—"

I reached out and touched his arm. "I know. It could be another Revenant."

IT was.

I could hear them calling the moment I stepped out of Joe's truck and into the morgue. Coming here in the daylight was a little different, especially in the heat. Once we were through the make-shift Dekalb security area up front, Joe led the way to Lex's area. There were bodies stacked everywhere—well, not literal bodies, but gurneys with bodies littering the area. I'd say Lex had a backup.

Moving through into the private examination room, we found Lex standing next to another carved and drained body. This one was another male. Asian. Lex looked at me with an accusatory look. "This has to stop."

"Like I'm doing it?" I said in a less-than-happy voice.

"They think it's the crazy cop. That he's been possessed."

I glared at Joe for sharing his views with Lex, though I could understand. Lex was a good friend of his. I could only shrug. "I don't know, but I don't believe it."

"He tried to kill you."

"He was recovering from being possessed. It takes time to work through the bugs. And I seriously doubt Mr. There-Is-No-Such-Thing-as-Magic has access to or possesses some arcane spell capable of destroying Symbionts—or First Borns—or whatever."

Lex only glared at me. "And maybe the spell is in the book inside your lover."

Okay, wasn't expecting that statement. I glanced at Joe, but he looked as bewildered as me.

"Lex, who told you that?" Joe said.

"No one." And I knew she was lying. "But I knew it when I met him, sensed he wasn't right. There is a Grimoire inside him, and if there is any possibility it contains the spell, then we must have it. If we can get that spell and use it on the Phantasm—"

I knew where she was coming from, and I could respect it, but, "Lex, we're not sure how to get the spells out of the book. And he doesn't have access to them on a voluntary basis."

"Then we take the book out of the boy."

Joe put up a hand. "No can do. You do that, he dies."

"So?"

Oh, piss off, bitch. I turned at that moment and left the room. Lex yelled after me, and Joe was right on my heels. He wasn't trying to make me go back. No. He was walking *with* me, through the corridor and out the door.

When we got to the car, Joe's phone started ringing. He paused at the truck door and pulled his phone out. Grinning, he said, "Lex," and put it back inside his pocket.

"You're not gonna answer it?"

"No. I'm gonna make her come out here."

Come to think of it. "Do Revenants go out into the sun?"

"Zoë, they're a product of the Abysmal plane. Nothing there likes the sun. They can tolerate it, but it gives them headaches."

HAHAHAHAHA.

Once we got in the car, Joe put the key in the ignition. "Three . . . two . . . one . . ."

And on cue, Lex came out of the front of the building, a black umbrella shielding her from the afternoon sun. She walked with purpose and anger right up to my window. I banged the lock down and was glad the window was rolled up because she nearly pressed her unearthly face into the glass.

"You must release him!" she shouted through the window.

"Release him?" I yelled back. "You talk about killing an innocent man—someone I care about—to get your book, and you want me to release someone close to you? No!"

She put her hand against the glass, and I could see her First Born shining through. Oh lawdy . . . what do normal people look like? I forgot. My life consisted of nonnormal people.

I needed a vacation.

Joe opened his door. "I'll handle this." He got out and motioned Lex to follow him to the front of the car. I watched them fight for a while. I don't know if Joe thought I couldn't hear them—because I could—or if he thought he could better handle Lex in this matter. After a few minutes of conversation in a lower voice, Lex turned and stalked back into the building.

Joe opened the door. "Okay. She's promised not to touch a hair on Dags's head."

"Or on his body."

"Or anything. She's to remain hands off if you'll come and release her friend."

I got out and followed him in. Lex was back at her position, staring down. I shifted into Wraith as soon as I entered the room and stood across from her. I took in a deep breath and allowed all the power I could muster from the physical plane to become evident to her. She took a step back as I spoke, my voice deep. "I'll release them—but if Dags is hurt in any way, I will come after you. Are we clear?"

She swallowed and nodded quickly.

Everything happened the same. His name was Hephaestus (what was with these huge-ass power names?), and his host was

Yoshi. Again, he could give me no real description of who did this to them—having been previously trapped inside of Yoshi's body. I released both of them, and again felt the surge of power as Hephaestus gave me strength. Afterward, I remained in Wraith form as the body disintegrated into goo. I turned to Joe. "I think whoever is doing this knows enough about Revenants that it's trapping them in the bodies first." I looked at Lex. "How is that done?"

She was watching the body dissolve and looked at me with distant eyes. "I—it's easy. We're still locked to the weaknesses of the human host. If the human body slips into a coma—there is little else we can do. It's like being locked inside of a dark box, with no windows or exits."

That sounded a lot like where I'd been during both experiences. A dark box. "So the human hosts were somehow put into comas or somehow made unconscious. Someone in the medical profession?"

Joe shook his head. "It's a new lead. I'll check it out. Oh"—he grinned—"Lex found a hair on this body didn't belong to the vic. It's being rushed through trace."

"Rushed?" I winced. "Joe, I know how this really works. It'll take them weeks to get through it."

"No, it won't," Lex said. "Because I'm doing the work myself alongside them."

Well, that was a comfort.

Once Mastiff arrived at Mom's, Joe left, muttering something about mending fences. Mom and Jemmy were there, and I told them what'd happened, after Jemmy made sure Mastiff had plenty of snacks and drink while he circled the perimeter of the house. The two of them filled me in on getting Dags to the estate and settled in. Jason had volunteered to work with him on accessing the book and seeing what sorts of spells were contained within, and perhaps helping him access them on call.

Mom didn't seem to like that idea, and she was doubly worried about there being blanks in the book. "I don't remember there being any blanks, Zoë. Rhonda and I went through that book thoroughly."

I suddenly had a huge brain fart. "Mom . . . when you guys were looking at the book, back when we were dealing with the Shadow People . . . you didn't happen to make photocopies, did you? 'Cause I seem to remember you doing that."

She blinked at me. Jemmy cackled out loud and slapped her knee. "Lawd, chile—I think you're right. I remember trying to get that book situated in the machine at FedEx Office. Nona here was all worried about bending the spine."

"Oh great Lord and Lady." She grinned and looked at me. "Sometimes you have moments of brilliance."

Uh. Thanks. I think?

I shucked that away. "So what we need to do is find those copies."

"Oh, I have them." Mom moved to the basement door from the kitchen, opened it, and hit the light switch. Tim appeared beside the door.

"You going down?" Tim asked.

"Yeah. Where you been?"

"Dealing with Steve."

"What's up with him?"

"Apparently you're playing favorites, always including me and not him. So he's pouting."

Oh God, I do not need a drama queen.

"Zoë!" Mom called from downstairs.

I put my hand on Tim's shoulder. Solid shoulder. I patted it again. Wow. I was touching him. "Huh . . . that's new."

He was wide-eyed too.

"You're kinda bony. Ask Steve if he was paying attention when that Revenant was in the house, okay? Maybe that'll help. Just— see if he saw anything, so we can get a better idea of what was in here and what it was looking for."

"They're gone!" Mom called. "The box is open, and they're gone!"

Tim and I looked at each other. But it was him that said, "I guess that's what it was looking for."

21

MOM was mad.

Okay, lemme rephrase that. Mom was pissed OFF. Believe it or not, Nona Martinique does enjoy her privacy. As do I—though I've had little of that lately. The thought that some Revenant had come into the house and stolen anything rankled her nerves to no end. She huffed and stomped back up those stairs, past me, and straight into the kitchen. Tim and I stayed out of her way, as did Jemmy.

In fact—where did Jemmy go?

Mom grabbed her phone off the counter—a Sidekick, I noticed—and pressed SPEED DIAL. I moved out of her way and into the tea shop. "Jemmy?"

"Rhonda—that motherfucker stole the copies!"

I was thinking Rhonda was going to need some serious Excedrin, judging by the volume of that call. *Yow.* Abruptly, I felt a cold breeze in the tea shop and moved into the botanica. There was no sign of Jemmy—had she left?

But, standing in front of the fireplace, was TC, holding up the book. I stopped in the doorway and watched him. "Well, you've got a lot of nerve coming back here after stealing."

"I didn't steal," he said, and tossed the book on the coffee table. "I borrowed. Had to have a look inside."

"Didn't find the spell?" I picked the book up and held it close to me without opening it. "I mean, you could have just sat here and looked at it."

He looked at me over his shades. Milky eyes. "Riiiiight. Like that was gonna happen with the hen party about to start. I knew the moment you pulled that plug"—he nodded to the book in my hands—"those Familiars were gonna show up. Sorry if I wasn't in the mood to deal with any supernatural PMS."

I glanced down at the book in my arms. "So—it's not in here."

"It's illegible. I couldn't find anyone who could read it. It's in code or something. And there's nothing magical woven into it at all."

"Really?" I held it out and looked at it, turning it in my hands. I half shifted (I can do this!) and stared at the book. But there was nothing of the glow I'd seen the night before. Maybe that had been simply an effect from being closer to the Grimoire? And on a whim, I held it in my right hand and opened it.

The interior was illustrated by hand, with very well-drawn diagrams. But the language—well—it looked more like a kid had drawn a bunch of pictures. I thumbed through it and shrugged before closing it. "Wow. Maybe this isn't what they thought it was."

"I would believe that," TC said. "If it hadn't lodged itself astrally in book boy's chest directly into the Grimoire, nobody would care. We need to get into that book. The Bonville one."

"Uh-uh." I shook my head. "You harm a hair on his head, and I promise I'll take you out."

He didn't flinch. He wasn't even looking at me but in the

direction of the kitchen. Ah. Mom. He was listening in on that conversation with Rhonda. Which was a good thing since I was holding the book in my left hand now and opened it back up—

—I could read it.

I blinked down at the actual English words, then closed it. Making sure TC was still looking away, I opened it again and just landed on a page and started reading silently—

> *—within the darkest heart. For if there be life without love, then there be damnation without salvation. Samael was full of loneliness and in that despair of darkness brought forth his brightest light, a child of sun and frivolity, and he named him Aether to light the way—*

I slammed the book shut.

WTF?

TC had moved away from me and was standing just at the door between the two shops, listening. I knew I should shoo him away, but—I looked down at the book again, holding it in my right hand. When I opened it—the language was indecipherable.

Huh? What? I held the book in both hands, and the text melted, to be replaced by English again. I flipped to the back, where it looked like there was a strange genealogy with names. I scanned down the list quickly, only recognizing three of them—Hephaestus, Mephistopheles, and Yamato. The list was in triple columns along several pages, with birth dates spaced a shitload of years apart.

Were these the names of the First Borns? Whose journal was this? And how was it I was reading it when I—

And then I remembered the scroll of symbols moving from the Grimoire within Dags to the mark on my arm. *Was that—could it be—*

Something like a Rosetta Stone?

To test, I held the book in my right arm—the language became illegible. When I held it in my left hand—

It was like a translation! I had to tell Mom!

And with that thought came an overwhelming need to throw up. I doubled over, dropping the book on the floor, and gagged out loud. I felt as if my stomach were going to come up through my mouth.

"What's wrong with you?" TC said as he knelt beside me. It wasn't exactly a tender moment. But it was a little odd having TC actually ask that question.

I shook my head, the nausea starting to slide away, but my stomach—

"WHAT ARE YOU DOING TO MY DAUGHTER?!"

You know . . . lately . . . Mom really had the Charlton Heston voice going on. Moses on the mountain thing. I jumped, and it looked like TC did as well as we both looked up to see her standing in the doorway, a gun in her hand. Oh, I remember that gun— she'd shoved it in my face a while back. And now it was pointing at TC.

He cursed under his breath and stood to face her, thrusting his arms out in an attempt at an embrace. "Nona . . ."

"Don't you fucking 'Nona' me. What the hell are you doing in my house, and what have you done to Zoë?"

He looked innocent enough—about as innocent as a viper could look—and gestured to me, who was still bent double, trying not to throw up. "I haven't touched Zoë, right, luv?"

I shook my head, happy the book was actually hidden beneath me. I didn't want any attention to be brought to it. And if I even thought about bringing Mom in to look at it, the nausea started again. "He . . . didn't . . ."

"I don't believe it." She moved forward until she was right in his face, the gun shoved under his nose. "I want that book back."

"Don't have it, Mom." He reached up and moved the barrel away from his face with the index finger of his right hand. "And please, don't point that thing in my face again. I was here to help, but I guess now—"

Don't tell her!

I knew he heard me—and I could feel his internal reaction of surprise before he said, *Why not?*

Trust me. Don't.

Trust you? I could hear him laughing.

Who's more trustworthy, ass-hat? Me or you?

He paused in silence. *Good point.* TC tilted his head at my mom, waved, and disappeared.

Mom cursed when he disappeared, then leaned over to touch my back. "Zoë? Did he hurt you?"

"No," I said, and tried reeeeeally hard not to hurl. *Oh God . . . I promise not to think about showing Nona or anyone the book again!*

Suddenly, the nausea was gone. Just like that.

No . . . it can't be that easy. I remained on the floor, thinking of a way to ditch the book. Because if she saw it, she'd grab it. And even the thought of that happening made the nausea rear its ugly head. "Uhm . . . Mom . . . can you bring me a flat Coke? I—I think that'll help my stomach."

I could see her beam even with my head down. She's always believed that old wives' tale to be true, which explained my aversion to flat drinks. She hurried off, and I managed to grab the book and stand. I repeated the no-tell mantra over and over again until my stomach quieted down, and started looking for a place to hide the book.

Hrm . . . Mom always said the best way to keep something from someone was to roll it up in a lie. And the best way to hide something was to do it in plain sight. I eyed the NOT FOR SALE section by the back wall—about where I'd tackled the intruder—and moved carefully there. I didn't have a key to open the glass case, but in truth one didn't exist. All I had to do was jiggle the lock once right, once left, then left again, and it would open. Listening to the sounds of Mom in the kitchen, I grabbed up a book that looked similar in size and removed the dust jacket. With a lot of work. I managed to put that jacket over the book, then wedged the two in together and shut the door.

I went down on the floor quickly just as Mom came in with the glass. I drank it and pretended to feel better. After sitting in my papasan and getting through the whole Mommy thing, she finally did settle in and tell me about the copies.

She and Rhonda had indeed made copies while they'd had the book and we were getting to know Dags back in December of last year. What they had noticed in the middle of copying was that some symbols didn't photocopy at all. Almost like they had a no-transfer-or-modify locked into their existence.

Well, those missing pieces proved to be a problem with a lot of the spells, so she and Rhonda locked them away in the basement.

"And now some Revenant has those copies."

I thought about what she'd said, about the missing pieces, about what sat in the botanica (which I planned on reading as soon as I could get back to it), and something seemed wonky. "Mom—does it really seem likely that a Revenant is going to break in and grab these copies of a book so important that he or she shoots the very person the original is connected to?"

Hroo? Did that make sense?

Mom stopped and looked at me. "Come again?"

I sat forward. "First off—if you and Rhonda were the only ones besides Dags who knew the Grimoire had been copied, then how did this Revenant find out about it? How did he or she know where to go in the house to find them?"

"I don't know—but I suppose, in hindsight, hiding them in the basement was a rather sad idea."

"But besides that, Mom, how did they *know*? Did you tell anyone?"

"No."

"I know I didn't 'cause I didn't know you'd done it. And if this book is so important—why shoot the guy keeping it safe?"

That got her. "Oh . . . this doesn't make sense."

"No, it doesn't. Unless that particular Revenant wasn't aiming at Dags at all and was just shooting to get out of there." And if I thought about the sequence of events, that felt the most likely. He attacked with those slashes, I attacked him, then he pulled a gun and started shooting. All the while he's looking to get out of there with the papers.

"I just had a horrible thought," I said.

Mom looked at me. "I've had one a day since you were born."

I stuck my tongue out at her. "What if it's not Daniel doing this, or even another creature possessed by the Phantasm? But what if it's actually a Revenant? One out to gain power, because if it can get rid of the competition—the Revenant family—then that one could do whatever the hell it is he wants."

"And have the potential to kill the Phantasm . . ." Mom was looking at me with an odd light in her eyes. "Zoë, sometimes you do have moments of clarity."

Okay, you have got to stop almost *complimenting me. It's confusing as hell.*

"There was one Revenant Jason said he couldn't contact. Maybe that guy was it?" Nona said.

"Well, that was Inanna." I shook my head.

Mastiff came in through the front door at that moment—and I had to laugh. My protection totally missed TC and had no clue anything had happened inside the house.

Awwww.

"Zoë." He had his phone to his ear.

"What's up?"

"I've been trying to get ahold of Halloran. Results came back on that hair they found on the latest."

Oh no. I just know what he is going to say. "It's Daniel, isn't it?"

"No, which is surprising." He paused. "The hair belongs to a Darren McConnell."

22

ABOUT ten calls later and Mom and I were on our way out to Rhonda's inheritance.

Did I tell you she got rich? Or that she was always well-off, only none of us knew it? Well, I think Mom did. But then I was shocked when I discovered that Mom already knew Rhonda was a spy for the Society of Ishmael. Hell, her uncle ran it, after his predecessor became stuffing for Bertram and Charolette. But here was Rhonda, still hanging with us poor people.

I let Mom drive on the way out there. It was therapeutic for her. I knew she used that time to think and had in the past come up with some stellar results. Though I had no idea what it was she was thinking about at the moment. Maybe how any of Dags's hair could be found on the body of a Revenant he'd never met?

It was planted, of course. Had to be. *But by whom?*

Too late I realized I'd left the book in the botanica. I suppose it was best—but I also felt that a lot of the answers I needed about that book, as well as the Grimoire inside of Dags, could be found inside it. I doubted I could figure out the true mysteries of life . . . all I wanted was the mysteries of that moment in time.

We arrived at the estate around four thirty—after stopping off for more groceries than what Joe had bought. I tried his phone for the fifth time, huffing when he didn't pick up, and it went to voice mail. At least it didn't go straight there—if it had, it would mean his phone was off or out of power.

I wondered if he had GPS on it—could Rhonda track him the way she tracked Dags?

The estate sat on 180 acres of land—good God.

Yikes.

About twenty people lived at the estate besides Rhonda, and she kept a condo in Atlantic Station for convenience sake. The drive to Alpharetta could get long with traffic.

High gates and two armed security guards with swirly things coming out of their ears greeted us at the entrance. They made a point of making sure we could see their guns. *Penis heads. Yeah, yeah, so you're armed. Big deal. I'm a Wraith, and I can snatch your soul right out of your body.*

Bwahaha.

Eep. That was spooky.

Mom let her eye be scanned, and the doors opened. The drive up to the palatial estate was paved, and lined with Southern oaks and magnolias, the oaks covered in Spanish moss. I think she had it like imported in from Savannah. Azalea bushes, not in bloom, also lined the path. I know for a fact Joe had gotten on to her about those bushes because they were easy for robbers or thieves to hide in, especially at night. But I guess Joe didn't get the fact that the yard itself, all 180 acres of it, was patrolled by a different kind of oogy.

No. I doubt he realized it. I did. I could sense it out there in the afternoon sun, lazily waiting on night.

The house itself was the typical style . . . estate. Huge columns. Large chandelier outside. Drive-through front. Nona pulled the Volvo up, and we got out. One of the butlers took the car and parked it as we went inside.

And how do I describe the inside?

Let's say . . . WANT.

Marble floors, highly polished, paired with marble walls. Flower arrangements that would impress even the downtown Hilton. And a state-of-the-art in-house environmental system. There were close to twenty rooms in the main house. I know this 'cause I got lost finding the bathroom. There is a solarium—my fav place. And then there's the four whole underground floors, where I assumed Dags and Jason were.

I followed Mom into the foyer, past the steps, and into the library. Again, I thought of that book and did a mental string of cursing. Once in the library with the door closed, she did that weird thing Rhonda does—waving her right hand in the air, then left (wax on, wax off); the farthest bookshelf, next to an impressive antique desk, vanished.

Not recessed and slid into the wall.

VANISHED.

I hadn't asked where it goes yet. I'm a little afraid.

If anyone knows me—they know I don't do magic well. It's just something I should NOT attempt again. For me to open the door—huh—maybe I should ask her about that since I haven't actually come in here by myself before.

Behind the vanishing bookshelf was an elevator. We got in, rode down to the fourth floor below, and stepped out into what I termed

Magical Operations or *Mops*. From what I'd seen, it was a podlike layout. The central hub was a setup of computer terminals manned by trusted members of the Society, many of whom, Rhonda said, lived here at the estate.

These people monitored Society members out on field assignments, like Dags had been on. Some are sent out to observe, like Rhonda was originally sent to observe me. And then some are there to retrieve, and some are sent to destroy. From here, Rhonda can get an update on all of them, and when she wasn't here, the whole operation was manned by a guy she called Gunter.

Though he didn't look or act German. He looked to be about in his midthirties, with piercing dark eyes and a thick goatee. He kept his head shaved and always wore nice suits. He paced around a lot with a headset on. On the few occasions I'd been down here with Rhonda, I noticed that anytime she asked him something, he had the answer for her.

He was there as we passed around the outside of this central hub, his hands behind his back, his attention totally devoted to keeping things running. Gunter barely even acknowledged our presence with a nod as we passed, but I was sure he could quote back to Rhonda when Mom and I arrived, what time we came through, and what we were wearing.

Now if he told her what we were thinking—I was gonna have to take him out.

From this central hub area were other corridors and rooms. Most of it was archive space. Environmentally controlled. In those archives were ancient texts as well as other objects—most of the contents, she claimed, were from the Library of Alexandria. Lots of things I had no real knowledge of and didn't care about.

We took a door to the right, then a left, and I found myself in what could be described as a luxury condo, complete with cushy beige carpet topped with the best of Ethan Allan.

Jason and Dags were in a room off to the side. Mom called it the rumpus room.

And I thought that sounded a bit like porn.

We stopped at the door, just inside, where Rhonda was. It was an empty room, with no furniture. Just four walls, ceiling, and floor. I noticed the whole thing was covered in soft material. Not really a padded room, but freak'n close.

Jason and Dags were in the center, facing one another. Dags was glowing—and I mean his entire body was literally glowing a bright white-blue. The girls were there as well, to either side, both in normal clothing. Both watching Dags. And they looked as if they were going to pounce if anything went wrong.

The room smelled like something was burning.

Rhonda turned and smiled at us. "Jason's getting Dags to concentrate on the Grimoire and visualize it page by page," she whispered.

Mom stood to one side, I on the other. I leaned in. "You hear from Mastiff about Dags's hair?"

"Gunter did. The whole thing's silly 'cause Stella Rosenberg puts Dags with her all the way from California. He was never out of her sight before we left with him at Savage Pizza. So we suspect someone planted it there."

Mom said, "But who?"

"Dunno." Rhonda shook her head. "I'm at a loss, which I don't like. Suspect-wise, there's Daniel."

I bristled. I did not want to believe Daniel was doing this. He was the bad guy in the last book.

"Look"—Rhonda turned to me—"Daniel's been possessed

once already. And unfortunately, he remembered everything the Horror did while in his body. That broke his mind and has also made him vulnerable to more possession. It is possible that the Phantasm is using him in order to destroy the First Borns."

"But why?" I held out my hands and kept my voice a whisper as best as I could. "None of this really makes sense. I defeated him with the Horror. Okay, sure, fine. So it's natural he'd go around finding a different avenue for chaos. But why mess with the Revenants if for centuries they've remained hidden and noncombative? It seems to me they've led very sedate, non-Phantasm-threatening lives. Why go off and suddenly decide to possess an insane person and use some arcane ritualistic spell that will obliterate them from the book of life?"

Wow . . . sometimes I impress even myself. And no, I'd never been one for putting things as precisely as I could. I've always been more of the one that prefers to put a bit of humor into the darker situations. Nervous habit. Kinda like biting nails.

I'd evidently impressed Jason as well since he turned from Dags and came toward us. He looked impeccable in his soft blue Hugo Boss shirt and casual jeans.

But my gaze traveled past him to Dags, who remained standing with his eyes closed, glowing that blue-white light, with the girls to either side.

"Zoë," Jason said. "You're absolutely right that none of this makes sense. My Revenant brethren and I—those of us left—have also discussed this at length. No one knows the Phantasm's ultimate game or end. Only that he has been—for the past twenty-odd years—a very paranoid being. Terrified that he would lose his power in the plane. And he's done several things lately—all directed at you—that lead us to believe he fears you, as in the Wraith."

I nodded. "Yeah, yeah, I got that part." I kept my voice low. "I, an Irin turned Wraith, am something he fears. And at one point he feared the First Borns. But like you said, there are so few left, and all but one of you made yourself Revenants. You made a non-threatening decision, right?"

"Yes. To him."

"Okay, and if TC is like the redheaded stepchild of the bunch and is the only one who hasn't made himself into a Revenant—it would seem he would be more of the target. I mean—he's a First Born."

Jason nodded again. "Logically, yes. And the Phantasm has gone after him, by going after you. I don't know if you've figured it out yet, Zoë, but even though he hasn't joined his life to your soul, there is a connection between the two of you. He became a Revenant on a very base level, and he realizes this now, but he touched an Irin, not a human."

Got that. Move on.

Rhonda joined in. "That base touch changed him and, I suspect, opened his eyes. Before that, even you said he claimed to have been basically a soldier for the Phantasm. A prisoner enforcer. The Phantasm even took away his voice—a powerful symbol of control."

I blinked. "And I gave it back to him."

"Well, technically Dags did." Jason nodded.

"Eventually," Rhonda said. "But even we're not sure what would happen if he and you joined completely, like the other Revenants. Whereas it weakens and minimizes them, it could perhaps turn you and him into something else entirely."

That thought made me shiver. By just touching, he and I had changed. Especially me. Wraiths were a thing of legend in the Abysmal plane, but none had existed there until I came along. *What exactly* would *we become?*

Jason said, "I'm not an expert on this—it's more Mephistoph-eles' area—but I get the impression that the two of you merging isn't something anyone wants to happen. So far, no one's captured the real attention of the Seraphim, and we've all been left alone. We should keep it that way."

The Seraphim. The leader of the Ethereal plane and the oppo-site of the Phantasm. "Yeah. But that still doesn't tell me why he'd go after the Revenants."

"Because they're the last standing threat before you," Dags said.

We all turned and looked at him. He wasn't glowing blue any-more, and he'd moved close to us. The girls were there, standing to either side.

I smiled at him.

He smiled at me. And in that smile I saw joy, happiness, fear, confusion, and sorrow.

So much sorrow. I squelched the urge to run to him and hug him. He looked incredible, dressed in jeans and a soft, light green cotton shirt that laced in front. It looked like the top of a dashiki only without the patterns.

I squelched it not because I was embarrassed, or was wor-ried about how Rhonda would feel, but because of the girls. They felt—*wrong*.

I couldn't put my finger on it then, but if I had to describe it, I'd say they seemed fake. Like two cardboard cutouts with no sub-stance. I wanted to ask him if he felt that way as well but decided to wait till we were alone.

Of course with them around, being alone was questionable.

"So the Phantasm is getting rid of anything that stands in his way?" Mom asked.

Jason nodded. "Sounds reasonable I suppose. Then all it has to

face is just Zoë and the Archer. But I'm afraid we're not going to go
down that easy." He turned to Dags. "Mr. McConnell here has been
able to readily access the book—not all at once. Apparently he's
had practice at using the spells inside during times of duress."

Dags grinned. "Meaning when I get my ass into a shitload of
trouble, the book always seems to come through."

"Except when you touched that other grimoire," Rhonda said.
She looked at me. "I want that book back from Archer. If not, I'm
afraid he'll be on my hit list as well."

I nodded. *Yeah, yeah. Catch him if you can.*

It's not like he listens to me.

I wanted to think about the book back at the shop, and I
wanted to tell everyone what I'd found, but I was also not keen
on getting sick again. There had to be a way to let someone know
what I'd found without heaving out my guts.

"Zoë? Something wrong?" Mom asked.

I looked at her and realized I'd been staring at my left wrist. At
the golden mark. "No. I'm fine. I'm worried now about who's trying to frame Dags for these murders."

"I'd say the crazy cop," Jason piped up. "And it is possible he's
being used again, by the way. Rhonda and I have discussed this at
length. If he is, we need to find him, capture him, and try and trap
whatever it is the Phantasm is using this time."

"So you think he's got most of this spell," I said. "Daniel does.
After being inside a mental ward for a month." I was hoping she'd
see how ridiculous that sounded.

"The Phantasm could have given it to him."

I wasn't liking this. And I wasn't going to believe Daniel was
possessed again. "Maybe. But why Daniel?"

Rhonda answered. "What's the fastest, easiest way to hurt
you?"

I was going to say "Go after Daniel" initially. But even as I thought it, the impact of the act faded in my head. Yes. I cared about him. But a chasm so wide had formed between us—I wasn't sure that even if he regained his sanity, we could ever close it up.

And that just pissed me the hell off.

God, I sometimes wished my life would just go back to the way it was!

You don't mean that, Mephistopheles said softly in my head. *You've done more good than you realize, in the larger picture of the world.*

I looked at Jason. He was looking at me. I looked away. "Will you tell your keeper to stay *out* of my head?"

"Zoë?" Dags said, as Jason nodded and stepped away. "What's wrong?"

"What isn't wrong?" I finally did my dramatic walkout. The problem was I didn't know where I was walking to. I turned down the hall to the left and stepped inside a palatial apartment. This had to be where they were keeping Dags.

It was more than nice, with a plasma screen, wraparound couch, fully stocked refrigerator, and king-sized bed. I was in the bathroom, looking at the size of the tub, when he came in behind me.

"Nona's going to cook," he said in a soft voice.

"Mom always cooks when she's upset."

"Mmmhmmm . . . Zoë . . ."

I turned and found myself face-to-face with him. Well, not exactly face-to-face. He was a little shorter than me. But somehow that never seemed to matter. "I was—" I started to say at the same time he said, "I can't—"

We stopped and smiled. He reached up and pulled a strand of my increasingly unruly hair from the side of my face and tucked it behind my ear. Where his skin touched mine, I felt an electric charge. His fingertips were warm. He smelled of Polo, my favorite cologne. But somehow I figured he knew that.

"You look better," I said, stopping myself from touching his face. His eyes were such a brilliant gray.

"So do you." He grinned. Oh God, that grin. "And this new ability—I'd say it's up there in the realm of the weird. You might even have me beat, babe."

"Oh, well, having one book lodged inside your soul is one thing, but to have two? That's an achievement, Mr. McConnell." I felt twelve. Awkward. A chance meeting with a crush beside my locker, and it felt like the entire world was watching. "I'm sorry it looks like Daniel is trying to frame you."

"Well, he did walk in on us after—" He paused and looked down but didn't turn his head.

OMG. He blushed!

Guys don't blush!

My heart melted. I think it was at that moment he had me.

"Zoë, I—" He looked away, and I scrunched my hands into fists. "I wanted to say I was sorry all this has happened to you."

"Sorry? Why are you sorry? It's not your fault, Dags. You've been just as much a victim of events as I have."

He turned and held out his palms. I looked down at them, then gasped. The circles that were usually displayed as tattoos were . . . gone. "Where—"

"They vanished about a week ago. Right after I found the book. What I haven't told Rhonda or Nona is—"

I reached up and put my hand over his mouth, pressing firmly. I shook my head and mouthed the words *listening devices*.

His eyes widened, and he nodded.

"Wanna walk?" I said as I took my hand away.

"First—"

That was when he reached out with those long-fingered hands and put one to the back of my neck, the other on my shoulder, and pulled me close. I knew it was coming and turned my head to match his.

The kiss—

Fireworks shot out in all directions as I reveled in the softness of his lips, the smooth slip of his tongue against mine. I felt it within me, pulling and tingling inside the darkest, neediest parts of my body. I was instantly aroused, wanting him, desiring him, and I dreamed of devouring him.

I brought my own arms up, wrapped them around him, and cradled his head in one hand, running my fingers through his silky hair with the other.

He pulled away from me for only a second to shut the bathroom door. But when he turned back, I was already unfastening my shirt, pulling it away and coming toward him, yanking his green shirt over his head. I was careful of the lacing and the bandage covering the wound in his chest, but I wasn't showing any other part of him mercy.

My need was ruthless this time—a month of lust and pent-up desire flooded forward as I unfastened his jeans. He moved out of them with a grace I'd never seen before. And even as my own passion flared out of control, so did his. We held on to each other, arms wrapped around one another's backs, our mouths pressed firmly together, tongues searching. A soft moan escaped him, the sound sending chills along my spine.

"I missed you . . ." I heard myself say. And I meant it. Oh God, how I meant it.

"Oh, Zoë . . ." His voice vibrated against my chest as he tucked his head under my chin. "I thought before . . . was a dream."

I pulled him from me and put a finger to my lips as I moved to the shower and opened it. Inside this monstrosity were five shower-heads. With a grin, I turned all of them on, setting the temperature to something both of us could stand, and pulled him inside. Again we pressed together, marveling at each other's bodies. Reaching down, I wrapped my hands around him, pulling and fondling, keeping him far enough away so that I could see his face. Again and again I pumped, caressed, and rubbed him against my thigh until it was obvious he could no longer take it.

Dags straightened and seemed to grow even with me as he turned me around in the multiple sprays of water. He pushed me forward, gently, until my hands were pressed against the tile and he was behind me. Then he reached around to caress each of my breasts, firm but with soft abandon. His left hand moved down over my stomach, and he eased his fingers so gently, so lovingly, where I needed him most. I moved my hips against him, feeling him against my backside, wanting him inside me.

As if he knew my mind, Dags gently pushed my upper back forward, forcing me to give him entry—and I moaned as he slid inside, wanting to hold him. With each thrust, he fondled my breasts, teased my clit, and pressed his lips against my back. As he moved faster, so did my own need, and I gasped as my orgasm caught me off guard—my muscles moving around him, pressing against him, and screaming as he pulled away.

Also so safe!

I turned then, nearly passing out at the rush of blood away from my head, and I held him as his body shuddered. His arms came around me, and I half held him up beneath the water as it bounced off our skins. I pulled him beneath my chin once more and kissed his face. His eyes were closed and his breathing heavy. Slowly, he opened those incredible gray eyes, flinching just a bit as the water sprayed against them.

"Zoë—"

I put a hand to his face. "I love you . . ."

I said it first. And for the first time in a long while, I meant it. From my heart and my soul. There was no doubt in my mind at that moment.

He smiled at me, that adorable smile. "I love you . . ." he said, and we held each other for a long time under the spray.

23

THAT BITCH IS GOING TO DIE!

Okay, *that* brought me out of a dead sleep.

I recognized it as the voice of Mephistopheles.

Dags and I were asleep in his bed. He stirred and wiped at his face. "What the hell was that?"

So he'd heard the First Born as well.

"It's Mephistopheles." I kissed his lips before he was fully awake, then moved out of the bed. My clothes were still on the bathroom floor, as were his. I grabbed both, and the two of us got ready to look presentable.

We walked out, hand in hand, through the door, back out to the rumpus room.

Jason was there, as were Rhonda, Gunter, and Mom. They turned and looked at us, and I realized we might look a little . . . rumpus'd.

"What?" I said with my arms out. "Why did you scream like that?" I directed that to Jason.

"Because she's insane," Jason said, his phone still clutched in his hand.

"Who?" I said, looking from Jason to Rhonda and then to Gunter.

Rhonda nodded in Gunter's direction, but she was looking at us.

Gunter gave me and Dags appraising looks but remained quiet.

Rhonda turned and nodded at Gunter. "Go ahead."

He looked around at everyone.

"They can be trusted."

He nodded. "A woman calling herself Lex wanted me to relay a message to the head of the Society of Ishmael that she and the others have Detective Joe Halloran. And if anyone wanted to see him alive again, then they are to turn over the Guardian within the hour."

Oh well, shit fuck. Now, that's just peachy.

Rhonda tensed, and Jason continued to pace, and rant. Not verbally, but damn loudly in the astral. But now I understood his outburst. Lex had gone off the deep end.

"What will Lex do if we do not comply?" Dags asked.

Gunter fixed Dags with a harsh stare, and I could only assume he was accustomed to Detective Halloran being around, since Joe and Gunter's boss were dating. "She and the others will drain him dry."

You have got to be shitting me.

No, he isn't, came Mephistopheles' voice again, still angry but not so loud. *She's let anger and fear cloud her reasoning—and turned on the only human that would have defended her.*

Jason spoke up. "She's convinced the others that the spell in its entirety is inside of the Grimoire in Dags. And she's convinced them that all they have to do is reach in and take it."

"Surely, being First Borns, they have to realize it's not that easy," Rhonda said. "It exists on the astral plane—and it's a part of Dags's astral being."

"I know that!" Jason held up his hands. "Sorry—I'm just pissed off. I can't believe she'd do this. It's irrational."

"She's hurting," Mom said quietly. "Mialani's gone, and the spell is the reason. Or a botched version of it. She's alone, and she wants revenge. I don't care how old you grow, or how wise, the heart is a delicate thing, and sometimes we don't know how to . . . ignore it."

I watched Mom and realized right then that she understood Lex's grief more than anyone. What must it have been like suddenly to be alone with a four-year-old? No one in the world to turn to who didn't want to take your daughter and experiment on her? And no one to lean on, no one to share the good and the bad.

Just . . . alone.

I felt awful for Lex. But there was no way in hell she was going to drain Joe or rip Dags's heart out. Not without coming through me.

"That isn't an excuse for stupidity," Jason said. "We don't know that the spell is in that book. From what Dags has seen, I'd say no. What worries me most are the blank pages."

"What worries me are the copied pages that one Revenant stole." Rhonda's eyes widened. "Jason, you don't think the Revenant that stole those pages gave them to Lex, do you?"

"And you think maybe she saw something that reinforces her belief that she can take this spell and use it on the Phantasm?"

Mom frowned. "Is that what she said, Jason?"

"Yes. And she's a fool. They're all fools."

Dags ran a hand through his hair. "Are they all with her? All the remaining Revenants?"

"Most of them. There were several who, when I contacted them, told me in no uncertain terms to fuck off. I don't know who's in town and who isn't. But if Inanna did take the copies and give them to Lex—Lex is no magician. Magic is something she's never fully comprehended. That would be Morgan, and if Morgan is here, that means Hermes is here as well."

I raised my hand. "What is with these names? I'm assuming you mean Morgan as in Le Fay? And Hermes as in Trismegistus?"

Rhonda's gasp was a bit irritating. "I'm amazed you knew those names."

Here. Have a bird. Middle finger, hut!

There was a twinkle in Jason's eyes. "The myths had to come from somewhere." With that he turned to Rhonda. "I'm going to need help if I'm going to do this."

"Do what?" Dags and I said at the same time.

Rhonda looked at us. And I mean she *looked* at us. And I wasn't very happy with the look on her face. "Jason has challenged Lex for leadership."

"Leadership." I shook my head. "I didn't know Lex was the leader."

"She's taken on that role with Aether gone. Usually it would fall to the next-oldest Revenant, but apparently Lex had usurped that role. So I challenge her to a battle, and the winner is king. Then I can save Joe and get them to listen to me."

I shook my head. "What about the loser?"

Jason's jaw set. "The loser dies."

APPARENTLY even though they've lived for all these centuries, the Revenant troop as a whole hasn't made it past the Dark Ages in group dynamics. They still elect a king, so to speak. A leader. And they usually do this by way of power, which is assessed through age. Which I find to be just bogus. Since, as Jason told me, the power of the First Born itself increases with age, but every time they take a new body—that body has to catch up to where they are.

And Aether was reported to be the first to become Revenant.

Which made me think back to that book and the passage I'd read . . . "And he named him Aether to light the way . . ." *Is it some kind of diary? Or journal? Ah, hell, I wish I'd brought it.*

But now, with Aether gone (released by yours truly and with no thanks for that), apparently they'd decided to go with who had the strongest host. And hands down, that was Lex. Though—whoever that was who attacked us at the shop certainly had a body capable of physical exertion. He'd been hard to hit, and strong.

Jason could only guess at how many had answered the call. Who really knew how many Revenants were now in the city? But we could only assume that those who were here were with Lex in her bid to retrieve the book from Dags with the hope the complete spell was in there. What rattled me was how—if these creatures really did believe in protecting the physical plane as well as their existence—they would do this, put an innocent man's life at risk, for an uncertain goal?

And then another of those alien, brainy moments struck me.

We were sitting out on the back deck . . . or one of them. There was a full buffet of roast beef, salmon, asparagus, Caesar salad, and garlic new potatoes. I wasn't eating because I was worried about Joe. So were Rhonda and Dags. Only Jason seemed not to be concerned and ate salmon and bread with abandon.

After he was finished, Jason moved a crystal chess set into the center of the table where we sat. They sat. I'd started pacing. I watched him move pieces here and there while on the phone.

Which was often. That BlackBerry of his was getting a work-out. He hung up. "I've gotten hold of Re and Sigyn. They know about what Lex is doing, and they said they'd be there and stay neutral."

The deck looked onto a maze, and I noticed several dead ends from my vantage point. "What does that mean?"

"Means"—Jason started pressing buttons on his phone with his thumbs—"that they'll be waiting in the wings at the event, just on the outside. Not a part of the audience."

"Where is that?"

He looked up at me. "Zoë, if I tell you now, you'll run off and try to save Joe."

"Why is that a bad thing?"

"You'll nullify this entire game."

"Game?" Nona said with a lift of her chest. "Jason, this is no game. And no matter how much you trust Lex, I don't."

Nodding, Jason said, "Which is why I arranged the rules to include Detective Halloran's return regardless."

"I'm sorry, Jason," I said, folding my arms in front of me. "But I don't trust them or her as much as you do. I'd prefer to have him back *now*. With none of this fighting-to-the-death bullshit."

Mom stood. "I agree. This is ridiculous. Mephistopheles told me himself he never wanted any kind of leadership role. For you to play with Joe's life as well as Dags's—"

"I'm not playing here," Jason said, and motioned for her to sit. "And Mr. McConnell is under no compulsion to go along with this. He can bow out anytime he wishes." He held up a finger. "But—we have *been* played. Therefore, it is time to play the player."

Me, Mom, Dags, and Rhonda glanced at each other and sat back down.

Jason pointed to the chessboard. "This contest, this challenge, is a way for me to root out the one playing the strings. To expose them." When we all gave him MEGO looks, he sighed. "Since the beginning of this, someone or *thing* has been manipulating our movements. It somehow got hold of an ancient spell known only to First Borns and the Phantasm. Anything else that might have had knowledge of this has long since vanished from the physical or Abysmal plane."

I nodded. So did Mom. Dags's hand found my knee. I didn't put my hand with his, but I didn't move his either.

"It then uses this spell—or most of it—to kill two humans in a very specific and ritualistic way that only First Borns would recognize." He moved two pawns onto the board, one square. "Then it kills a ghoul. Not just any ghoul but the longest-lived ghoul. Lex's companion. One that would garner instant attention." He moved a rook from its place and put it in direct line of the king. "Now, we have two Revenants gone, one of them was the first of us, first Revenant." He moved a knight from either side and set them all in a row across the board. "One of our own turns on us—capturing a helpless human, demanding the Grimoire in exchange for his release." Jason moved another pawn out in front between the front line and the enemy.

Dags jumped in. "You think all this has been engineered so that we'd eventually put me"—he put his hand on his chest—"the Grimoire—in the open."

"I do." Jason chewed on his lower lip. "Once that happens, and if that spell is indeed inside, it would make it easier to take. So, if we add a bit of a kink into their plans—say put in a Right of Challenge—it will delay their ultimate goal."

Yeah. But . . . "Jason—this is something all the Revenants who are around will attend, right? So—that's putting all of them in the same place."

He gave me a very oily, uncomfortable smile. "Yes. It is."

I shivered. Obviously he knew something I didn't. "But wouldn't that be bad? I mean—it makes them vulnerable."

"Actually," Rhonda spoke up, "it gives them an advantage."

"Say that again?"

"Revenants have a link to one another—kinda like a Borg-mind thing," Rhonda said as she looked at me. "Pretty much like when Mephistopheles wants to talk to one of us."

Oh, I thought he could turn it off and on, and I was right!

Dags sat forward. "Oh . . . I see. If something happens to one while you're in the same vicinity, all of you will know it."

Jason nodded. "Yes."

"So the whole battle for dominance thing is really a ruse," I said.

"No."

Eh?

"The battle is real. Lex—in my opinion—has disobeyed one of the first tenets we put forth when we all agreed to bond with humans. And that is never to barter with a human's life. Now, I've lost touch with the others over the centuries—Mephistopheles has, that is. And there may have been changes. I mean—vampire killings still happen in the world, and I sometimes have to wonder if there aren't those out there succumbing to the drive to feed and doing just that. It's just that even though the world is more connected than ever—people aren't. No one's going to run outside to see who's screaming. They're either going to think it's on the television, or they'll close their blinds and lock their doors."

I hated to admit he was right, but he was. Other than Jemmy, neither Mom nor I really knew any of our neighbors.

"It's true that Mephistopheles has never wanted any sort of leadership role. He's always been more of a lover of the arts, enjoyer of life. And even after centuries of enjoying these things, he never tires of them. Leadership means politics and intrigue. And we got a shitload of intrigue here."

I smiled. I was sure the First Born had a lot to do with what Jason had just said, but that the *shitload* comment was all him.

"So what exactly do you do for one of these battles?" Rhonda said. "Is it like a duel at sunup? Or do the First Borns fight?"

"Choice of weapon," Jason said as he sat back. "Lex will choose since I have challenged her. My guess is she'll want hand-to-hand combat."

"You mean like a bar fight?" I said. Dags's hand hadn't moved, and I finally put mine on top of his. He didn't shift his gaze from Jason, but I could see the smile in his eyes as I glanced at him.

"Pretty much. What I'm hoping she doesn't choose is swords. I'm a bit rusty on those."

Rhonda grinned. "Swords?"

"Lex was always a good swordsperson." He grinned. "She killed me once—over a misunderstanding."

"She killed you?"

"Ummhmmm. I was a knight, and she was the king. And we were both in love with the same woman." He smiled. "I was enjoying being French at the time. My host's name was Lancelot du Lac."

24

THE fun thing about Jason was that I never knew whether to believe him or not. I mean . . . I knew the First Born had lived for a long time. Maybe even thousands of years. But to think he was actually Lancelot at one time?

Phhhfffttt. Not.

Though . . . hrm.

It was decided after that to keep Dags at the estate underground. With the security in place, it was impossible for a Revenant to get in—not counting Jason, but we did test out the security using him as a guinea pig. His body recovered faster than I thought it would.

Dags and I spent a little time getting to know each other again. I was still reeling from my own verbal admittance to him about how I felt. I'd actually told him I loved him. Hell . . . *I was full-on crazy for a detective not a month ago. And now that detective is crazy.*

"You think if Daniel is being used now, that he'll remember this too?" I said, as we lounged back in a hammock in a protected grove of oaks. The sun was starting its evening descent, and the fireflies were already out, visible against the azalea bushes. A breeze helped with the June heat now and then. "I mean—he's never going to get better if this keeps happening."

Dags was quiet for a bit. "I don't know, Zoë. I can't even imagine what's in his head. To be possessed like that—and have to watch as your body does and says things that you can't even comprehend. I'm not sure how sane I'd be afterward if something like that happened to me."

I sort of found this an odd statement—basically because of the girls. He carried inside of him two spirits, bound to him in service as Familiars to his being a Guardian. And I wondered if there had ever been a time since this had happened to him when either of them had ever taken control of him.

Or if they could.

"What do you think about Jason's plan?" he asked me.

I shrugged. "I don't know. I don't understand the whole Revenant thing. I barely understand my own connection to it."

"Your connection is the Archer." He paused. "I wonder if he has a name. A First Born name like the others."

"Archer isn't it?"

It was Dags's turn to shrug. "I thought the Archer was a title given to him. Meaning rogue. He's a turncoat in a way. Having been the Phantasm's right hand."

"I think . . ." I began, trying to remember things TC had told me. "If I'm not mistaken, TC was actually coerced. Like, put under a spell. His voice was taken from him for centuries, I know that. And he was to do the Phantasm's bidding. And then he touched me—"

"And everything changed," Dags finished. "Have you ever asked him?"

Wow.

I had never thought about that. Just asking him. "Huh. No. But I might. If I see him again."

"Oh, you'll see him. He has no choice."

I moved in the hammock to get a better look. "Why do you say that like you know something?"

"Because that's how Symbiont and host work. The Archer may or may not want to admit that he's linked to you in that way, but he is. Notice how he's always around? And he's come to your aid more times than you realize. Always at the endgame."

I frowned at him. "Someone's been paying attention."

"Uh-huh. Rhonda too. All of us. And now that we're learning more about the First Borns, it's all starting to make sense. Though"—he ran a hand through his hair—"my situation isn't making sense."

Okay, moving on a hammock is just too hard. I'm gonna have to talk to him and not tip us over. "Dags—have you been sleeping well?"

I felt his body stiffen. "Why do you ask?"

"Oh, I was just curious. 'Cause I had Alice come to me in a dream and tell me you *weren't* dreaming. Is this true?"

There was a long pause. "You dreamed about Alice?"

"Uh-huh." Okay, he sounded funny, and I like face contact. I shifted in the hammock until I was sort of propped up looking down at him. *Whoa . . . we are so gonna fall.* "She came to me in a dream to tell me you weren't dreaming. That usually she can see your dreams."

He was looking at me with those metal gray eyes. "I—I can't remember my dreams, if that's what you're asking. But, Zoë, I've barely seen Alice or Maureen lately. I know they were there last night—and their power had been blocked by that book. But even now"—he held up a hand and looked at his palm—"I *know* they're there. I can feel them. But"—he looked at me—"I can't *feel* them."

"What does that mean?"

"I have a sense of knowing what I am. I know what I can do if I tried. And I know the Grimoire is there, like an echo of whispers inside of me. And if I concentrate, I can feel it. And up until a few days ago, I could feel the girls. I could concentrate and feel their personalities. Alice with her strong Julia Sugarbaker will, and Maureen with her darker, emo self. They come when I'm in danger—like earlier today."

"You were in danger earlier?"

"The Grimoire has a protection around it. Rhonda insists she didn't set it, but it's there. And when I try to access the book, it opens for me. But I can't always use the spell, and I know it's because I'm not there yet. I don't have enough . . . oh, I don't know . . . experience points yet. But when someone from the outside tries to tamper with it"—he sighed—"well, it starts to react. When Jason's First Born tried to see it—it went all haywire, and I started blacking out. The girls showed up, and at first I thought they were going to attack Jason. But they fed me energy, and though I tried to look into the book—we found blank pages."

"Rhonda mentioned that. Blank pages." I thought about the small book again.

"Have you spoken to the Archer about giving back the small book?"

Oh wow. Was he psychic too? "Dags . . ." *Can I tell him?*

Or get sick again?

Well, I needed to tell someone.

I purposefully thought about telling him about the book and what had happened to my arm.

Nothing happened. No nausea. No rolling stomach. Huh. So I licked my lips and kept going. "Dags—about that book—"

I charged on and told everything that'd happened. From the odd scroll that oozed into my mark, to TC returning the book and Mom seeing him. And then the passage I'd committed to that nasty memory of mine, and how I could read it.

Dags's eyes widened, and he tried to sit up.

Naturally, we fell out of the hammock, with me on top of him, both of us facedown. I moved away as he sat up, and we started laughing.

Then, "Why haven't you told anyone?"

"That whole sick thing," I answered. "Seriously, when I started to tell Mom, I wanted to throw up. But when I tell you—"

"Maybe it's because the translation came out of the Grimoire."

Translation . . . of course! "Dags, that makes sense. Might even explain why the book tried to fuse with you. To get to that spell in the Grimoire."

"Might." He rubbed his chin. "You need to get back to Nona's and read that book. If you found a passage that actually mentions Aether—that book might be the First Born grimoire that Jason's been talking about."

"You mean Inanna's book?" I shrugged. "He thinks the Bon-ville Grimoire is it."

"What if the Grimoire in me had pages in it from that book?" Dags grinned. "See, when me and Nona and Rhonda looked at it before, we found a hopeless mishmash of things. From Sumerian to Italian, even a bit of Sanskrit. As if it was an amalgam of things—not written by one person but by many. What if that book—the one I found—is the key to this? And what if it holds the spell?"

I sighed. "If only those copies hadn't've been stolen."

I had to wonder how long those copies had been in the

basement—and with all the activity in that shop in the past seven months. "What if—what if those pages were stolen a while back? When was the last time anyone looked at them?"

"Oh." He looked genuinely worried. "Never thought about that. It is possible."

"What if someone already took them . . . and that's where they're getting this half spell? You already said the pages of the Grimoire were an amalgam—"

"Which would make sense as to why they're only getting pieces. All those different languages?"

"Uh-huh." I stood up, then helped him to rise. "I'm gonna go back and get that book. You stay put, got it? No heroics?"

Dags put a hand to his chest. "Me? Heroic? Not a chance." He reached out to me, taking my arm and pulling me close. In an odd way, we fit together. As long as I was barefoot.

The kiss . . .

I couldn't describe it. Not if I wanted to. It melted any fears I had, or reservations about relationships. It was genuine, and soft. I wrapped my arms over his shoulders, and his arms were around my waist. There was nothing else in the world but the two of us. Not even the girls were there.

Someone cleared their throat.

We parted lips and looked to my right.

Rhonda was there. With Jason.

And for some reason, I felt bad. Maybe it was the look on her face. Maybe it was because I knew how she felt about him. But damnit. She'd been dating Joe. And she knew how Dags felt. He'd made it clear.

Hadn't he?

"Sorry to interrupt," Rhonda said, and her voice was a bit stiff. "But Jason's leaving to meet the others."

Dags and I parted but held hands. "Now? The battle is now?"

"An hour after sundown." Jason smiled. "I told you it would be better to keep the details as much a secret as possible. I have the time and place. And I wanted to know if Rhonda would be my right."

Rhonda's complexion lightened. "Don't you have one already chosen by now?"

I frowned. "What's a right?"

"No. I hadn't worried about it till now. And you seem the perfect candidate. You've known me a long time. I was going to ask you before this, but I've never been an Old Scorch rule follower."

I looked from Jason to Rhonda. "Hello. Still here."

Rhonda sighed. "He wants me to go with him to be his surrogate. In case something goes wrong." She looked at me. "You're coming too. Nona's staying here with Dags."

Hey, no fair. Crap. No time to go snag that book either. But still. I looked at Dags and pointed at him. "No heroics."

His dazzling smile was priceless. "That goes for you too."

We kissed.

And again, my toes curled.

WE rode with Jason in one of the Society's unmarked vans. When I stepped in, I was shocked to see a combo ambulance and Scooby Gang setup. Whistling, I moved to a side seat next to a gurney in the back. "Wow . . . they think of everything."

"The Society's pretty thorough, and Gunter's good with the details."

I pursed my lips. "Yeah, about him—"

Rhonda slipped into the passenger's seat and looked up at me through her eyebrows right in the middle of buckling her seat belt. "Don't ask."

Ooh.

After getting under way, I felt a slight tingling at the back of my neck.

"Hello, Archer," Jason said.

"Get out of my van!" Rhonda said as she turned and saw him.

The Symbiont was there, kneeling between me and them. His shades in place. Looking for all the world like a *Matrix* extra. "So, Mephisto—you really going through with it?"

I looked at Jason and could see his First Born come to the forefront. "Of course, Azr—"

"Ah!" TC put up a gloved finger.

I realized at that moment the Archer had a name—"Wait—what were you going to call him?"

"His real name," Rhonda said.

TC shook his head. "Nothing important. Just an old name I no longer go by."

And you don't need to know.

Yes, I do.

I could hear him laugh in my head.

Don't tell Jason or Mephistopheles or Rhonda about the book.

He frowned behind his glasses and continued carrying on a conversation with Mephistopheles. "Old Scorch?"

Why not? TC said in my head.

Jason nodded. "Same rules apply. Though I put in the stipulation that the scapegoat not be sacrificed and returned to me or my right regardless."

Because I don't want them worrying about that book right now. If it means nothing, then it's better off—Wait—what does he mean scapegoat? *What the hell is* Old Scorch?

TC glanced at Rhonda by turning his head. He chuckled and looked back at Jason. "Good right. You picked a powerful one. She know the rules?"

Your cop buddy. He's the scapegoat. The prize. Old Scorch rules.

"You'll be there for the show?" Jason said calmly, as if asking if TC was going to a movie.

"If she chooses swords, I'll be front and center to watch you get your ass handed to you." He reached out and touched the back of Rhonda's chair. "And I'll be there to watch your life get fucked up forever."

I pursed my lips. I was missing something. "Can someone please explain to me what a right is exactly?"

It was Rhonda who turned and looked directly at me. "A right is the one chosen by the First Born to succeed the present host."

Uhm. Uh.

Wow. You ain't too bright.

Fuck. You.

Anytime, lover. You and I are due. And trust me—I got a better package than book boy.

I shivered and looked at Rhonda. "Succeed them? Like if he falls, you go to battle?"

"No." She smiled. "If he falls, he dies. And as his right, I become Mephistopheles' next host."

CRAP!

25

THE very real and very disturbing thought that I could lose Rhonda to a First Born if Jason died was both upsetting and kinda exciting. I was pretty sure that if Mephistopheles did join with her soul, that would make her a vampire. *Oh God . . . how big of a dream come true would that be for übergoth girl Rhonda Orly?*

Why are you assuming Jason is going to lose? Mephistopheles sounded amused. *Please, have a little confidence.*

I felt sheepish.

I was still chewing on that when we reached the place of battle.

I'd expected something a bit more—well—more. I think I kinda figured they'd break into the Dome downtown and have the fight there, or even get into Turner Field.

I did *not* expect pulling up to Opera.

Opera was a downtown hot spot, combo nightclub and events venue. Located down on Crescent, it was a block from the Four Seasons. The club kept the hours of Thursday to Saturday, nine in the evening until three in the morning—closed on Sundays.

But tonight it looked pretty much open.

"Lex booked the place for tonight," Jason said as we got out of the car. TC vanished and didn't reappear. But I figured he was close by. "We're to go in the front entrance. Zoë. Once inside, I need you to be the Wraith."

"Why? Brute Squad or something?"

He nodded. "Yes. I have the Wraith on my side. Better they understand that. As well as the leader of the Society of Ishmael."

I guess that made us celebrities in a way?

A wrought-iron stairway led up to an entrance, where two very large men stood. They were dressed as polar opposites. One was in a tee shirt, with RULES SUCK on it. He wore red-and-black plaid pants, boots, and lots of gaskets on his wrists. His face was unshaven, and he had heavy thick eyeliner and mascara on. His hair was dyed matte black, and the cut—well—it looked like he'd used a hacksaw.

The other guy?

Armani. African-American.

Yowzah.

They nodded as we moved in, both of them stepping back as I shifted into Wraith, my wings furling behind me, my skin darkening. Even my clothing shifted to create the illusion of something Abysmal.

I am Wraith.

FEAR ME!

Right.

Once inside, we moved past a reception desk and into a side room. The floors were hardwood and already well-worn. I thought the club was called Petra's once, but don't quote me on that. I just knew I had to be here once for an Advertiser's Award Banquet and got sloppy-ass drunk. Wheee.

The walls were painted cream and red, and modern light fixtures like twinkling stars hung from the ceiling. Three more interestingly dressed people filed in, all different races. I was impressed at the rich flavor each of them brought to the table. And how flamboyant they were. It was like being in a roomful of peacocks.

And I was the old gray goose.

Jason in his Boss suit looked slightly downplayed and normal.

More filed in, and I tried to talk to Mephistopheles. *How many of you are there?*

Here? I count close to fourteen Revenants, and about fifteen ghouls.

He sounded kinda surprised, and so was I. I really hadn't considered they'd bring their ghouls with them, not after what happened to Mialani.

The group parted as Lex made her way in. She looked different out of her lab coat. Feminine in an Amazonian way. She wore a red dress—was she going to fight in that?—that clung to her curves. Her hair was pulled back and her lips painted ruby red. Wow. Mata Hari come to life.

And then I thought . . . *This might really be her, come to think of it.*

She sneered when she saw me, then looked at Rhonda. "You chose the Society's head as your right?"

Jason nodded. "And she has agreed."

"You realize that if you fail, that puts you at the head of a very powerful organization."

He smiled. "I'm not playing around here, Lex. What you've done is inexcusable. Using a human life as the scapegoat is forbidden."

"We're talking about our survival. We need that book."

With a sigh, he shook his head. "There is no evidence the spell is in that book. We've examined it; even the caretaker has looked at it. But you would take an innocent life just to see?"

"If it means preserving our own, then yes."

I looked at the others. To be honest, they didn't look too sure. They looked . . . frightened.

"Where is Joe Halloran?" Rhonda said in a surprisingly strong voice.

"He is safe."

"No fight until we see him," Jason said.

"That is against the rules."

"You disregarded rules, Yamato. You no longer have rights behind them." Jason straightened, and I could see the shadow of Mephistopheles there. Jason might seem small in stature compared to Lex—hell, everyone did—but his First Born seemed to radiate power. And authority.

"Follow me."

We followed her through the small crowd in the room and into an open area. A stage decorated the back wall, complete with ruffled curtains and a chandelier in the center. On the sides were booths, and above us a loft rimming the entire room, with smoked-glass fronts. Behind those were more tables.

"Shadow boxes," Lex said, as if to give me an answer. "That is where you will watch me win."

We moved through another door to the left of the stage.

In the center of that stage sat Joe, bound to a chair. He was slumped over, unmoving. And as I ran toward him, I could see the open skin on his neck and his forearms. "You bitch! You drank from him!"

Rhonda and Jason turned on Lex, and she took a step back before regaining her composure and standing her ground. "He was uncontrollable. I controlled him."

"Lex . . ." Rhonda's voice cracked. "Joe was your friend. He trusted you. He always came to you. How could you do this to him?"

"We are talking about survival!" Lex hissed. "Joe would not come . . . quietly."

I knelt beside him, touching him with my Wraith skin. Too late, I realized what would happen and pulled back even as I felt his soul cling to mine.

"Zoë, get back!" Rhonda yelled at me.

I did . . . feeling doubly bad. A Wraith, harbinger of death, wasn't what Joe needed right now. I moved back and shifted to myself. At least like this I could control it better. "Is—is he alive?"

Jason moved in and put his fingers to Joe's neck. "Yes . . . but he's unconscious. He needs medical attention." He turned to Lex. "I demand he be given to me now so that we can save his life."

I could see her hesitate. It would be easy to say no. But then she'd already agreed to it.

"Lex, *please*, because he was your friend," Jason began, and he looked past her and nodded to someone in the shadows.

Nick appeared then, and it was my turn to gasp. Jason had sent him away—but here he was—and from the look on Jason's face, I knew he'd called him back for a purpose. Tall and graceful, blond and well built. I'd only seen Nick once since they'd arrived. He wore jeans and a shirt, with sneakers. He looked incredible for someone who was technically dead.

And had been dead. For a very long time.

Lex turned to Nick, and I noticed her expression change. I guessed they could sense ghouls, and maybe seeing Nick reminded her of Mialani. She looked at Jason. "Yes . . . but you and your right will come with me. The Wraith stays where we can see her. Nick . . . Nick can take Joe."

Jason nodded to his assistant, and the man immediately reached into his back pocket and pulled out a pocketknife. He had Joe free in seconds and just as easily had him in a fireman's carry. With a glance and a wink at me, he moved back into the shadows.

"He'll take him to the van," Jason said. "Nick was a doctor once. He'll know what to do."

I trust him. Trust Nick. And then I shifted again, and this time felt the little surge of the small touch of Joe's soul. So delightfully rich and creamy!

We followed Lex back out, and once I was free of the back-stage, I drifted up and into one of the shadow boxes and then, just for effect's sake, perched on the railing's edge, squatting, my wings out. I figured I either looked like an imposing, menacing Wraith—or a big, dark, goofy dodo bird. I was alone there and watched as Revenants filed out of the room up front, and Lex and Jason moved to the center of the floor below. Rhonda moved to the side.

If Jason's body is killed, Mephistopheles began in my mind, *then I will move to Rhonda, and she will be my new host. I need you to make sure no one interferes with that. But I do hope Jason can win.*

"Me too," I said aloud. "I want all of us to win."

I also wanted to go back and get that damn book.

Abruptly, everyone below me fanned out, and I put my hands to my sides as I looked down. I couldn't see. I felt too far away, and levitated upward and hovered above the show below. I didn't want any glass between me and Jason if I felt I needed to get down there fast.

Lex and Jason stood in the center, and someone said something in a language I couldn't understand. And then—uh-oh—someone brought out a set of swords. This didn't bode well.

"Yamato," Emo Revenant boomed from the side. He'd been the one to bring out the swords. "Do you agree to the terms set before Old Scorch?"

Why did Old Scorch sound familiar? *Because it is one of the names given to Lucifer, the light bearer.*

Lucifer? You mean the devil?

Lucifer is part of the Seraphim, Zoë. He is the only ally the Abysmal plane has in the Ethereal realm.

"Yes, I do," Lex said.

"Mephistopheles, do you agree to the terms set before Old Scorch?"

"I do."

Emo Revenant raised his hands, the silver on his rings twinkling in the lights. "By the name of our father—Samael—commence!" He lowered his hands and stepped back.

Lex attacked first, brandishing the sword as if she were, like, born to it. She came at Jason, hacking away at him. Jason parried and defended as best he could. I moved to get a better view as I felt TC's presence. He was there, somewhere in the darkness nearby.

Looks like Mephisto's just not up to sword fights anymore.

I ignored him and watched.

Jason moved backward into a table as Revenants moved out of the way. Lex stabbed at him with the sword, but he deflected it, pushing back and rolling off the table just as she recovered and came down hard again, her sword striking the wood where Jason had been seconds before. He moved out of the way and came in behind her, his sword raised, and yelled as he brought it down. The blade would have sliced her back wide open if she hadn't turned and moved her sword sideways, blocking Jason's sword with a crash.

She then brought her heels up and shoved Jason backward, planting her shoes against his middle. He sailed back through the air, sprawling into one of the bars. I put my hand to my mouth as Lex came barreling at him, her sword out, pointy side aimed directly at him.

Jason!

His eyes came open, and he moved to the side just before the point lodged in the bar wall. Rolling away, Jason came back up on his feet, his shirt untucked and torn open. I noticed Lex's dress was also hopelessly damaged, the skirt split up to her waist. But I got the impression nobody in this room was looking. They were too focused on the battle.

Too focused. They were all paying attention to the battle.

And nothing else. And that feeling of vulnerability came back to me.

I didn't like it.

I moved up, then became incorporeal as I moved through the ceiling. Once above Opera, I continued to move straight up and felt out around me, sensing for anything out of the ordinary. I know Jason felt this wasn't a dangerous event, that all of them together was good. But I just didn't think so—

Something moved to my left below, just behind a Dumpster. There was a parking lot behind Opera, and a walkway down. Someone was there . . . lurking in the shadows. I couldn't actually sense if it was a human, or something else.

"It's just a Daemon," TC said, and he was beside me, hovering above the club. "Looks like it's found it's way into a bum. Not exactly the smartest move."

I cursed. "Stop doing that."

"Your boy's losing. Might want to get back in there." He looked at me, and it was so surreal hovering up here above Sunday night traffic in downtown Atlanta. My hair—even wilder when I was Wraith—flew out around my head in the wind. "You know . . . this just screams of a setup."

I nodded. "How many of you are there?"

He raised his eyebrows. "Of me? Just one, baby. Just one."

I stared at him.

TC shook his head. "I really mean there's just one like me. I touched you, and my world changed. Just like it did for you. I'm not like them." He pointed down.

"But we are linked, like a host and Symbiont."

He held out his hand and wiggled it in the air, gesturing that maybe kinda. "Eh . . . there isn't a book about Wraiths and Symbionts. I can say this—a prize of great power would await the Symbiont that claimed you as their host."

Watching him, I noticed he seemed . . . relaxed. "Why haven't they? No one's approached me. Even Jason didn't choose me as his right."

"Because he can't." TC looked at me and tilted his head. "While you and I are linked, no other First Born can have you. If something happens to one of us, the other suffers for it. You've already noticed that."

Nod. I had. "Why haven't you demanded to be fused with a Wraith? You already said the power would be a great prize."

I never thought I'd put the word *thoughtful* with TC. But that's what he looked like as he chewed on his words. "Because I like it the way it is. Your touch restored me to what I was before—and then some. And I"—he bowed to me—"helped to create a creature of legend in the Abysmal plane. A Wraith. The Phantasm fears you. Fears us. He fears them." He looked down. "Though I have no idea why. It's like the bully being afraid of the nerds on the playground."

I stifled a laugh. "So we—"

But his hand was out, grabbing mine and we plummeted down, back into Opera and back to the two combatants.

I have to admit—I never considered how this might end. Never thought beyond getting it over with so that Joe was back safe. So I wasn't prepared to see Jason on the floor, a sword sticking out of his middle, pinning him down.

"No!" Rhonda screamed as she ran to him, and was immediately held back by two Revenants.

TC and I materialized beside Jason. I bent down over him while TC drew himself up to his largest, beefiest form. "Let her go! You know the rules of Scorch."

"Well, well, well." Lex stood nearby, her arms crossed. "Look what the bat dragged in. Azrael—what a pleasure."

I was looking at Jason's face, hoping the death mask wouldn't appear, and looked up. Azrael? That was his name?

"You know the rules, Yamato. Release the right."

"Not until I have the boy."

TC lowered his shades on his nose. "Miss Orly—you can defend yourself anytime."

Rhonda stopped struggling and straightened up. "By the rules of Scorch?"

TC nodded slowly. "Most definitely."

Her expression changed and green fire ignited in her hands.

I was amazed at what happened next.

26

ZOË . . .

I looked down at Jason. He was looking up at me. Or rather, Mephistopheles was. I bent down over him, pushing his hair back from his forehead. He was sweating and pale. And losing a lot of blood. Shock. He was going into shock. "What can I do?"

The wound need not be fatal. But Jason will bleed to death if you remove the sword. I need Rhonda to heal the internal organs.

I blinked. *She can do that?*

Don't underestimate her, Zoë. I need her . . .

I stood just as Rhonda turned and blasted the two Revenants holding her backward. TC moved in to help her and knocked the shit out of a big, dumb, blond one who thought he could get to TC, then pulled her to him before shoving her toward us.

"You heal Mephisto—" TC said as he removed his long leather coat and flexed his bare, tattooed chest.

When did he get all those tattoos?

"I'm gonna bus' some heads."

There were a few Revenants who stayed back. Lex for one,

along with Emo. I watched the two of them move to the side and talk—but I couldn't guess about what.

Rhonda knelt, her hands glowing, and put one on Jason's head and the other on his chest right above where the sword had gone in. "Zoë, I need you to pull the sword out when I tell you to."

I pulled my gaze away from where dude was busting heads and put my hands around the hilt. "Uh . . . I'm not Arthur here. I've never done this."

"You're a Wraith, you'll be strong enough. Just wait for me."

I tensed, both hands around the hilt even as my gaze traveled back to TC as he head-cracked one of the larger ones. Oh, that was the guy in the Armani suit!

"Zoë!'

Oh! I looked down. Most of Jason's chest was enveloped in the undulating green light. His skin was pale like bleached bone and covered in a thin layer of sweat.

There was an ooomph nearby, and I looked. One of the other meatheads had TC in a headlock. They moved about until finally TC reached around and grabbed the man's—balls?

A howl sounded from him, and I winced at the thought that even Revenants could feel that.

"Now, Zoë!"

Oh shit! I yanked as hard as I could and was amazed at the resistance. With a yell, I pulled it out and staggered back. Wow . . . these things were heavy. And they'd been swinging them around like they were yardsticks. After a glance at the two of them, I bolted into the fray with TC, who was on his back beneath them.

I hacked at their backs and screamed.

And then I SCREAMED.

* * *

OPERA was a very quiet place when nobody was inside. Just us. Sitting on the floor in the center of the dance floor. Rhonda had Jason's head in her lap and was taking in deep breaths. I sat down nearby, back to human form, the sword in my hand.

TC came over, limping a little, his coat back on. He leaned over and touched my shoulder. I felt an electric current—not the same as with Dags or Daniel . . . or Joe. Something more familiar.

And then he was gone.

Rhonda's phone went off, and she pulled it from her back pocket. Looking at the display, she answered it. "Hey, Nick."

Nick. Oh yeah. He's with Joe.

"Yeah, they're all gone. Zoë did a bit of her mojo, and they scattered. I don't think she actually killed any of them, but they're gone. Jason will be fine. Soon as he gets a good drink—parking lot? Be there." She disconnected.

"Good drink?"

"He's gonna need it in order to walk out of here. I've helped with internal, but Mephistopheles is gonna have to help. He needs to have blood to ground him." She reached into her back pocket and pulled out a pocketknife.

Getting squeamish, I waved at her. "No . . . no. Don't do that. Just wake him and let him do that slash thing."

"He's unconscious," she said, then hesitated. "I don't have a way to ster—Oh yeah." She ignited her left hand and held the blade inside it. After a few seconds, she pressed the knife into her wrist. Blood pooled fast, dark and red, and she let it drip over his lips. Within seconds, the magic in the blood brought Jason/ Mephistopheles to life, and he was moving, reaching up, and grabbing her arm, pulling it to him. I could hear him swallowing and felt the warmth return to his body.

I jumped up and dove behind the bar, searching the cabinets for linens. Finding a stack, I ran back around and helped her disengage her arm from him just as he blinked and sat up. Blood colored his lips, and he looked . . . a bit frightening.

Slashed, torn, bloodied shirt. Wild black eyes, the pupils dilated and covering his irises. His teeth—wow, his teeth looked long and sharp. His hair stood up on end.

I wrapped Rhonda's wrist in one of the napkins while he wiped at his face. "Thank you. Both of you." He looked around. "I lost?"

"Yes," I said. "And TC helped me get rid of them for now." I paused. "His name is Azrael, isn't it?"

Jason nodded to me. "Yes. His given name. The one the Phantasm gave him." He stood and helped Rhonda to her feet. When she nearly fell backward, he picked her up in his arms and carried her.

"Should you be doing that?" I asked. "I mean, you just got stabbed."

"I'll be fine," he said. "I'm nearly whole again."

Rhonda's phone rang. I moved closer to her and got it out of her pocket as we walked to the entrance and stepped out into the cold night. The van was right outside, and Nick was halfway up the stairs as I answered it. "Hello?"

"Zoë?"

I blinked. "Mom?"

"Where is Rhonda?"

"She's in the van. What's wrong?"

There was a pause.

"Mom, if you're calling about Joe, we got him. And Jason's not dead and Rhonda's not a Revenant. We're on our way back—"

"It's Dags."

Oh. Hell. "What?"

Another pause. "He's gone."

I relayed the news to Jason as he and Nick bundled Rhonda into the backseat of the van. I caught sight of Joe. He was still pale, with dark circles beneath his eyes. He looked sunken. Ill.

"He'll be okay," Nick said as he put a hand on my arm. His touch felt similar to Jason's. But then it made sense, since Jason's blood is what kept Nick alive. "His vitals are stable. He only looks bad."

An IV connected Joe to a clear bag, and a small screen showed a steady heartbeat. "You gave him blood?"

"Not enough was taken to warrant that," Nick said. "But he'll be weak though back to his old self in no time."

"Zoë."

I turned to Rhonda. She was buckled in the seat I'd used on the way down. "Find Dags."

"I will."

The story from Mom was that Dags had left. None of the employees or guards had been told that he couldn't go. He wasn't a prisoner. So a redheaded woman had showed up, and Dags had gone with her.

Rhonda had been livid. "Do I have to tell them everything? Where would he go? I mean, doesn't he know that they are out there looking for him?"

I had an idea I knew where he'd go and promised them I'd go and look. Nick promised to get them to the estate in one piece. I shifted into Wraith and jumped up into the air.

I suspected he'd gone to the shop to get that book.

When I arrived at the house, Tim greeted me. Steve was still noncorporeal. "Dags been here?"

"No." Tim shook his head. "But there were some other people here about fifteen minutes ago."

I pointed to the floor. "They got in here?"

"No, but they were snooping around outside. Even up on the porch. There were some loud noises, then they were gone."

"Did you see them?"

"No."

I moved from the kitchen to the botanica and looked for the book. It was still there, and I took it before running upstairs to grab an old messenger bag of mine. After I had that, I grabbed more clothes and stuck a sign on the door outside announcing that the shop would be closed on Monday.

Then I waited.

I was sure he was coming here. I called his cell.

No answer.

So I sat in the tea shop and opened the book. It was unreadable as usual, so I held it with my left hand and turned to page one.

I do not know if infinite wisdom would have these notes delivered to eyes worthy of understanding their purpose. I am only the scribe self-proclaimed to reveal a world the other planes have no knowledge of. And to recount the tragedies that befell me and my family.

I looked up and pursed my lips. Tim was there beside me, reading over my shoulder. "Who is this?" he asked.

"I'm not sure, but I think this is technically a journal. Written by a First Born."

Our lives began not upon the same day, but as the eons of time moved the Heavens to present our names at the time of our coming. Our father, Samael, had argued long for the want of children. Of a legacy to go forth into the future and carry the past to the present. The Seraphim wrought long a great storm of opposition but recanted when it was exposed that such a creature also bore fruit.

And was not our father equal to that of the Ethereal of Heaven?

Father often told us the story of our first sister. Such a happy event was foreshadowed with tragedy, as his beloved lover within the plane of touch was murdered. Lilith was destroyed utterly by the sons and daughters of man, stoned, then dismembered. And our father mourned long and wailed to the Heavens, demanding her return to him.

But Lilith's soul rose to Heaven, and our father was alone. And so his first born was given life into the Abysmic pool of knowledge, a dark figure full of the anguish my father felt. She was not to be his pride or his joy, but to be his damnation, for he could not give her comfort or love.

He called her Sophia.

I sat up. Uhm. "If this is what I think it is—"

"You mean an accounting of the First Borns' origins?"

"Yeah," I looked at Tim. "Then Aether wasn't the first born of the First Borns. Someone named Sophia was." I frowned and looked back to the book.

Once this art was perfected, our father then created a multitude of children to go forth into the planes and seek out happiness. He brought me through the veils. I wrote each of their names just

to keep a record of their coming. Hephaestus, Hermes, Mephis-
topheles, Re, Loki, Frejya, Sigyn, Brahma, Yamato, Erishkegal,
Morgan, Dagda—so many of us through the centuries.

But none of those born would stay to comfort my father
when the others departed. So enamored of the physical
flesh were they that they soon strayed from our home, and I
watched my father's loneliness devour him. I talked to him,
fed him, and pleased him in whatever manner was needed—
and still he fell into darkness.

Until I was able to convince him to create not a child of
shadow but one of light, and put forth enough love so that
perhaps his light could reach Heaven and bring our mother
back to us. He agreed—within the darkest heart. For if there
be life without love, then there be damnation without sal-
vation. Samael was full of loneliness, and in that despair of
darkness brought forth his brightest light, a child of sun and
frivolity, and he named him Aether to light the way—

I sighed and sat back. Even as I read, it was like being pulled
into the story, of seeing them, the children as they were born. And
again I heard the name Samael. They spoke that name tonight
before fighting. Their father.

I made note of the names. Aether and Hephaestus and Yamato
I knew. If Inanna had written this text, then she was there as well,
witnessing the whole thing. But where was Azrael?

TC?

And what happened to the real oldest First Born, Sophia? I also
wondered if I asked Mephistopheles about this, he'd tell me more.

Through all of the events of eons, my brother Aether could see
the clearest, was the champion of our life in Abysmic glory.

My father had reached contentment, and I alone noticed how he no longer watched his other children, who had now vanished into the folds of physical pleasure. Even I was barely a ghost within this existence. I could have gone to the physical plane and found that pleasure, indulged in that life. But I was too loyal to my own father, and would not leave his side.

What we did know was that our eldest sibling had touched upon the magic of one of Seraphim's bastards, and upon that touch the two became as one. Sophia grew in power both in the physical and the astral once she learned of her abilities, and she tricked three of her siblings into burying themselves in the bodies of humans. Aether was the first. There they were locked in, unable to fly or to move from plane to plane. They did not possess or rule the same magic as Sophia did.

She used the weakest to threaten the strongest, forcing them into their physical bodies, until all of them were helpless and locked away in the physical plane. With that magic of the bastard, Sophia came into our home and murdered the servants in her search for our father. I was able to flee with him, taking the post of my father's position so that Sophia could not use that as a trophy.

I knew what she was after. Power. The Abysmic throne.

It was then my father created the last of us, the vessel that would house his soul and one day depose the tyrant. I aided him in this—but father was so weak from the centuries, and his allies had turned their backs. My new brother barely survived. Because of this, I was unable to complete my task, and so I changed the words my father had commanded. But still the child was weak, so I suckled it, and took it into my arms as Sophia found us. She destroyed the shell of my father first, believing him dead.

For me it was the task of wet nurse as I took care of my brother under watchful eyes. And when he grew to maturity, I was kicked out of my home to roam the planes in search of a place to belong.

Soon I found the first of my kin and saw what years of human bodies had wrought. And so I too found a home within my first host. I chose a male as companion, so long resentful of being powerless as a female. And together we lived a happy and long life.

Of my brother Azrael, I have no knowledge. But to find him and release him from what has been—

The journal ended and I flipped pages. There was more—but that was all that translated. *Hey, what gives?*

"So," Tim said. "Who wrote this?"

"I think Inanna—"

"The one that was here?" He looked at me with wide eyes.

I nodded. "Tim—it says that Sophia touched with a Seraphim's bastard. Wouldn't that mean—"

"That you're a Seraphim's bastard? No." He shook his head. "I don't think that's what that means. But who is this Azrael?"

I blinked. "Trench Coat."

"No . . . fucking . . . way . . ."

"Uh-huh . . . and I just got the feeling that we've read something very important." I grabbed the book and stuffed it in my bag. I knew then that Dags wasn't coming. Something had happened.

27

THE entire estate was on lockdown when I got there . . . Lockdown for them, not me. I glided down (having hidden the book somewhere else) and sieved through and into the foyer and—

Had about a dozen men pointing guns at me.

"Wait!" came Gunter's voice. He ran from the side and motioned for everyone to put their guns down. "This phreak is friendly."

I glared at him and let him see the full Wraith.

He backed up, as did all the rest. I shifted back from Wraith (I was liking this!) and moved to the library. I didn't need to head down as Rhonda, Mom, and Jason were seated inside. Jason was at Rhonda's massively large oak desk, and Mom and Rhonda were on the couch. Mom looked at me. "Nothing?"

"Nothing." I looked around. "Where is Joe?"

"He's upstairs asleep," Rhonda said. "He'll be fine, but he's going to be a little groggy and grumpy. I've got him under guard. He's not walking out of here."

"Yeah, about that." I moved to the coffee table and sat down, facing her. "You care to tell me how that happened?"

She glared at me, and I was all too aware that if something happened to him, she was going to blame me. Well, take a ticket. Get in line. "I didn't think he'd leave. Why did he leave?"

"And your people said he left with Stella? Anybody tried calling her?"

"Yes." Rhonda nodded. "She's at her house, and I had some people stop by. She said she dropped him off at the shop."

Which was where I was. I wondered if maybe . . . "Tim said he heard people outside just before I showed up. I'm wondering if maybe someone was watching the house and grabbed him right before I got there."

"I think that's likely enough," Mom said. "I'm not as worried about him as I was with Joe. I know that Alice and Maureen will do their best to protect him."

Only . . . Dags had said the girls weren't really there. He'd been unable to sense them. Would they be with him if someone tried to remove the Grimoire?

Okay, now I was panicky.

I stood up and started pacing. "So—what do we do? Do you have a tracking device in him? Had you LoJacked him?"

"No, but don't think I won't do it in the future." She sighed and stood up as well. "I'm gonna go check on Joe."

I followed her, keeping a discreet distance. She never looked back once as we moved through the bookshelf, down the elevator, past Gunter's station, and into a wing of palatial rooms. I could hear the oh-so-familiar beep of a heart monitor before we came to the door. Rhonda paused only once before opening it and did not bother keeping it open for me.

I stood just outside, my head down. She and I had gone through so much together in such a small amount of time. But there were times in her life I knew nothing about. A whole life of luxury seeded with the grains of power and responsibility. I knew she'd been sent to spy on me and Mom, and I'd been angry at her. And yet through my own hatred she'd kept my Mom's soul safe, while my split center had nearly killed the man I loved.

And my friends as well.

And now that she's risked so much, here I am, taking the man she loves.

With a heavy sigh, I pushed the door open.

Joe lay in a soft bed, his chest bare and decorated with sensors, their wires hooked up to various machines that I didn't recognize. She was taking care of him. Keeping him safe. And I was—

I was useless.

I stood by him, watching him breathe. He looked better, his color good. His neck had been stitched and bandaged where the Revenants had taken their fill and torn his flesh. I reached out and brushed a small strand of hair from his temple. Joe with the spiky, unruly mop. I remembered his kiss—I always remembered it when I looked at him.

"He loves you, you know," Rhonda said from the window.

I looked up from Joe and looked at her silhouette. It was past three, and dawn would greet Atlanta early, at five thirty or so. I was exhausted—more than I would ever tell anyone. My muscles felt as if they had lead blood flowing through them.

The curtains were parted—and as I came near, I realized the window looked out onto an underground pool. It was empty, and the only light came from beneath the still water. Ripples moved along the walls and on Rhonda's face as I stood beside her.

"They all love you," she said.

I caught the taint of something bitter in her tone. "I don't ask them to."

"No, you don't." Her voice was deep, and again I wondered how old she really was. Deep inside. "I watch you—have watched you—all these years. Irreverent, bitchy, bitter at times for no reason. And completely unappreciative of what you have. I don't understand most of the time, but I stayed and watched. And when I learned what you could do—I was fascinated. To have that kind of power—moving out of your body."

"But you have power."

"I have taken power, Zoë." She continued to look out the window, her arms folded over her chest, her right elbow propped on her left as her right hand fingered a chain about her neck. "Learned, siphoned, stolen. Books, mostly. And things my uncle taught me. It wasn't until I saw and touched the Bonville Grimoire that I understood it. My first spell, the Veil." And to demonstrate, she reached her right hand in the air and pulled a box of tissues out. She took a few, then placed the box back into the invisible sphere around her. "It's getting pretty junky up there . . . my own Clarke Belt." She wiped at her eyes and blew her nose.

I hadn't realized she'd been crying. "I'm sorry, Rhonda."

"Why are you sorry? I honestly can't say it's your fault. You didn't know what you were. Nona refused to tell you—she wanted a normal life for you. And I didn't blame her. I liked our life before. I liked being a sidekick. I liked being just the one that made the gadgets, knew the spells, could spout what you needed. And then the Archer came and changed everything. Daniel, then Dags." She smiled and sniffed again and folded her arms back. "When I first saw him, I knew in that instant I loved him. Beautiful, smart, and gifted with magic. I thought I could cure him, you know? Take away the pain those damned tattoos had brought him. And then—" She gritted her teeth. "And then you had to fucking take him to Bonville, who used that screwed-up spell."

"Hey, I did not take him there. He was being summoned, and that bastard dragged Dags through the Abysmal plane to do it. If I hadn't been there, holding on to him, he might not have survived at all."

"Oh yes. I know." She swallowed and continued to stare at the reflecting pool below. "I know. He's told me so many times how it was that you saved him. Back then. And then it all ended for us— you and me—after all I'd done, you shut me out of your life, and Nona told me to leave you be. Do you know how hard it was to learn that Dags had been kidnapped? That he was being physically and mentally tortured because Rodriguez had to have that damned book? It was all about that book."

I swallowed and stayed where I was. "Rhonda . . . what happened? Exactly?"

She took in a deep breath. "Joe and I found him—and you know Joe and I started seeing each other as mutual Zoë addicts recovering from your presence. He wouldn't tell me why on his part—only that he needed to distance himself." She frowned. "His exile was self-induced. Mine was forced on me. So when we found Dags . . . he was nearly torn apart. The Familiars called out to me. And we came. Rodriguez was there, torturing what was left of him. Joe shot the motherfucker—but he didn't die. He just faded away."

And resurfaced again in Atlanta. I was happy then that he'd met a messy end. Knowing that he'd tortured Dags—I called it a blessing.

"Dags was dying—the bastard had flayed his skin from his ribs, cut him up so badly." She sobbed. "I used everything I knew . . . every spell I had in me to try to save him. Alice and Maureen—nothing was working." She wiped at her eyes. "And then it called to me. Something in the book. I found myself reaching for it, pulling it out of the Veil." She mimicked her motion for me, remembering that instant. "Rodriguez came back with a gun, and he and Joe fought. The bastard called up Fetch after Fetch, but the Familiars and the cop fought that bastard off. And then, when I wasn't sure if I could save him, the book opened for me, and the spell was there."

I stared at her.

"I—I could see it so clearly in my mind. The book wanted it, called for it to be done. And I knew what it meant. I knew it meant linking his life again to forces beyond his control. It would change him, outside and in. Physically and mentally he would no longer be the same man. It never occurred to me that he would hate me for it."

I stepped forward. "He doesn't hate you."

"Yes." She nodded and looked at me, and I could see how hard it was on her. The expression on her face. "I summoned the magic to fuse his soul with that book, to keep him and it safe. I never wanted it to fall into the hands of those who would use it for bad. Ass-hats." She smiled.

I did too, though I had tears filling my eyes.

"Dags opened his eyes then, and saw what I was doing. He didn't protest, but I could see it there—the pain and agony of what I was doing."

I bit my lip. I had had no idea. None. And Dags had never really spoken of it.

"Rodriguez left again, and we managed to get Dags to a hospital. The book wasn't physical. It was on the astral. The doctors treated his wounds, sewed him up. He lay in a coma for two weeks before one day he opened his eyes and asked for chocolate-mint ice cream."

I laughed. She laughed. That was so Dags.

Abruptly, she sobered. "And when we went to see him, he looked only at Joe. He never looked at me. Never talked to me. He was fine. Never felt better, he said. And he intended on leaving for a vacation as soon as he was released. Probably to Savannah." She looked down. "And when I said good-bye, Joe had given us a few minutes. He still didn't look at me as he talked. And he told me he would never forgive me for what I'd done. That I had no idea what it was like waking to find a beast inside you, something lurking in the dark, to hear pages rustling. He made me promise him that I would never do that again. That if his life were ever to be in danger again—I was to let him die."

She put her hands to her face, and I found I was rooted to the spot. I—I didn't know what to say. Dags had always seemed so nice. To think he would speak to her—to anyone like that!

Finally, I moved closer and put my hand to her shoulder. The floodgates opened, and she was holding on to me. I wrapped my arms around her and held her as her shoulders shook. I knew the worst was yet to come.

"And now I see him . . . and he's everything I'd ever wanted in someone . . ." She spoke into my shoulder. "And he loves you, Zoë. He's devoted to you. He said there would never be another." She pulled back and wiped at her face. Retrieving the tissue box from the Veil again, she took a couple and wiped her face. "There's a song called 'Vanity' by Yuki Kajiura . . . and I play it on my iTouch constantly. It's how I feel. He loves you. And I guess I have to live with that." She blew her nose.

"Rhonda . . . I'm sorry. I never asked for this to happen. Any of it."

"And that's why I can't hate you. I've tried, you know. Even when I'm with Joe . . . I know he's thinking of you. And the sad part is that you don't even love Dags. You're still in love with Daniel."

Uhm . . . hold on. I shook my head slowly. "Rhonda . . . I'm not sure you understand."

"You had sex with Dags. I understand that. And for him it was the wish of a lifetime. But for you it wasn't that. And I feel for him. Even when he agreed to work for the Society . . . he asked if you would be around. And instead of granting what I knew would keep him happy—I sent him off on some of the most dangerous missions we had." She pointed to her chest. "Me. I sent him to California to find that damned book. I'm the one that put his life at risk again. When I saw what had happened, I was so . . ."

I held up my hand and waited for her to stop. "Just a damn minute. First, making love with Dags did mean something. I'm sorry if that hurts, but it's true. And at the time . . . I guess I hadn't realized it. But you didn't send him into harm's way, Rhonda. Dags is a big boy, and he can say no at any time, right?" I looked at her through my much-in-need-of-a-trim bangs.

"I hope so. I'm scared on this one, Zoë."

I nodded. "Me too."

Me too.

WE all turned in then—though Jason volunteered to stay up. Nick arrived as I turned in, and the two of them were going to head out and look. I wished them luck before falling into bed, and into a deep sleep.

I don't remember any dreams—at least nothing when someone shook me at the butt crack of dawn. I waved at them to stop and used a few colorful metaphors.

"You know that's no way to talk to your mother."

I opened one eye and peered into Mom's less-than-beaming face. "What is it?"

"Detective Mastiff called. He's got something he wants to show us—and see Joe, of course."

I sat up. "Is Joe okay?"

"Yes, he's downstairs having brunch."

Brunch. "What time is it?"

"A little past two."

TWO?!!?

I hopped out of bed and grabbed up my bag. "I'll be right down." Then I paused at the bathroom door. "What's he have to show us?"

Mom's face told me things I didn't want to know. "There's another body."

OMG.

"It's not Dags."

Thank you, you fucking powers that be.

"It's Lex."

!!!

28

MASTIFF was in the entertainment room when I got out of the shower.

This room was an electronic wet dream. It boasted a surround sound system that would blow the nuts off of a baboon. From space. It also had the hugest flat-panel screen I'd ever seen, as well as a remote control that did everything except wash the dishes. The room was dark due to the lack of windows, black-painted concrete walls, and soft gray carpet. Couches were placed in a near-theater seating arrangement.

Joe sat on one of them, and I immediately went to see him, giving him the biggest hug I could, then perched beside him. "You okay?"

He nodded. "Just a little pissed I got caught with my pants down, that's all."

"How did they catch you?"

"Easy." He smirked. "I went to see Lex. She gave me a beer. It was laced with something and night-night."

I looked at his face. He looked so much better, and I sighed. "You okay about Lex? Even though she betrayed you like that?"

"Okay?" he craned his neck to look down at me. "No. That bitch took a bite out of me, and I told her if she ever did that, I'd come after her."

"And because of that," Mastiff said as he stood up from in front of a VCR, "Joe's lucky he was incapacitated or he'd be prime suspect number one. But luckily, we got this." He took the remote from Nick's hand and hit the PLAY button. "This is a tape from the security cameras outside the Dekalb morgue."

I watched with everyone else, and Mom moved to sit by us. The image was grainy, like most security cameras—why is that? But it showed the outside of the morgue entrance and the back of Lex's Bentley. He fast-forwarded it to the time stamp of 5:00 A.M., and a figure in a dark coat came out, his face visible. Mastiff paused it. "Rhonda, if you'd do your magic."

I glanced back where Rhonda sat at a computer behind us. Abruptly, the image sharpened a bit and zoomed in.

I gasped.

Daniel!

"Mr. Frasier was seen leaving this building at 5:00 A.M. this morning. The former ME's time of death was placed sometime before that."

I sat forward and stared. It was Daniel all right. Shaven. His hair was groomed. And he looked . . . peaceful. Not tormented. Oh, he had to have been possessed. "But you don't have anything on him entering the building?"

"No," Mastiff said. "There was a power surge or something that knocked out the cameras for a while."

"Convenient." Jason came to stand behind Nick. "I'm not

convinced Daniel Frasier killed Lex. He's only a human, and she was—"

"A monster," Rhonda finished. "Let's go. I want to see her fucking dead body for myself."

We piled into cars and drove down to the Dekalb County morgue. The place was still roped off with yellow tape, but Joe and Mastiff got us in. Even Mom.

Lex's body was where it was found—in the back in her special room. She was naked, and splayed out on the table as if she'd been dumped there. Every inch of her flesh had been carved into, and instead of puncture wounds on her neck, there was a gash where she bled out. The drain on the floor looked used, but I had a feeling this wasn't where she'd bled out.

When I walked closer—something terrible came to me.

There were no cries for help.

I moved right next to her and looked into her dead white eyes. Nothing. I shifted into Wraith, not even caring if Mastiff saw me (*Time to be a big boy and learn the boogeywoman exists, dude*), and stuck my hand in. I felt . . .

Nothing.

Something niggled at me in the back of my head as I looked at her body. They'd strategically placed a sheet over her privates, but I moved them away and looked at the marks.

That's it!

The marks were *different.*

I'd memorized the others, knew them intimately, having stuck my hand in the bodies. But these.

"Zoë." Jason was beside me. "What's wrong?"

I looked at him, and his eyes were wide. I didn't have to say a word. Jason knew. He backed up, his hands going to the sides of his head. "No . . . no, no, no, no . . ."

I think that even up until that moment, Jason and Mephistopheles believed Lex could be healed. That she could be released to join with Mialani in the other planes. And that this would appease her. But it's hard to release something that's no longer there.

"Jason?" Nick came forward and grabbed at his friend. "What is it?"

"She's gone," Joe said. He moved slowly to her, putting his hands in his pockets. He stood beside me as I shifted back again. "It worked."

"There's . . ." I shook my head. "There's nothing there. It's only an empty shell. I'd say whoever is doing this—has the spell intact now."

"Dags . . ." Rhonda said.

I felt it too, but didn't say it. *Is he still alive? Would I know? Had they ripped the book from him and left him to die?*
It was complete. All of it.
Obliteration.

JASON took custody of the body after the autopsy. Rhonda paid to have that done by people on her payroll so that no questions would be asked when they found that the entirety of her body was decaying with a fast necrosis. It was transported to the estate, as Jason got on the horn to every Revenant in the city. This time Mephistopheles was sure they all showed up at Rhonda's, sans ghouls, and checked their weapons. It was like watching the unholy Mafia coming in.

Everyone was quiet. No one was talking. And that was because we all had the same question in our minds: where was Dags?

There hadn't been a word. Not one. No asking for money. Not

even a "hahahaha . . . we have him!" from any ugly sources. It was if he'd disappeared off the face of the planet.

Rhonda had called his number over and over until it finally went to voice mail, which meant that it had finally lost power or been turned off. Not a good sign.

Jason used the parlor to display Lex's remains. She'd been embalmed quickly, to prevent any more decay, and dressed in her finest suit. I assumed Jason had known where she lived.

As they gathered, I watched from a corner of the room, paying attention more to the maze out in the garden, now little more than hedges. They were all there, and somehow I knew their names as I looked at them. Emo guy—that was Loki. The Armani-suit guy—that was Brahma. And the list went on, the last of them finally arriving in town and driving straight here. All gathered in one place. Yet I believed it was the safest place on the planet.

Jason tapped a spoon to a glass to get their attention, and everyone turned and nodded to him. A UN rainbow.

"I'm sure you've all heard that Yamato as well as her host were destroyed by the spell."

"This would not have happened if we had had the boy!" Brahma said in a deep voice.

"Yes, it would have," Jason said in a calm voice. "Because I don't believe they have the spell."

Everyone frowned at him. Even me. I didn't see Rhonda. Had no idea where she was.

"But she is gone," Emo Loki said. "Why do you think this?"

"Because in an obliteration—wasn't it foretold there would be nothing? Not even a body?"

There was a small murmur. People looked at one another. I tried to remember more about the book, but there hadn't been anything in it about some all-powerful spell. Just Azrael.

The Archer.

I choked on my drink, and all eyes turned to me. I waved and moved past them into the kitchen. Since it was full of people, I moved past *them* and out to the garden beside the maze. Finding shade was hard, but I was able to. "Azrael!" I hissed and half yelled.

TC was there in a blink. Insta-Symbiont. Just add anger.

"Don't ever call me that." He pointed at me and paused. "What the fuck do you want?"

"Where is Dags?"

"How the bloody hell should I know?"

I pursed my lips at him. "I think you do. Samael was your father."

He took a step back from me and narrowed his eyes behind his shades. Suddenly, he pointed. "You deciphered it!"

"Who is it?" I said.

"It's the name of our creator. You would call him the Phantasm."

I suspected. "But not the one in power now."

"No. My father was defeated by the one pulling the strings now. Betrayed by him. Is that what you wanted?"

I looked at him. "You know Lex is gone."

"No, she's not."

Um . . . I gave him my best WTF look. "I checked. She's gone."

"Lex is not gone. Her soul migrated. Yamato's the one caught now."

Okay, my head was spinning. "You care to enlighten me? Because there's a whole houseful of Revenants in there waiting to declare war on someone. And right now, they're targeting Daniel."

He blinked. "Frasier? He's involved, but I'm not sure how yet.

And to enlighten you—that spell isn't in that large Grimoire. It's locked in the smaller book. Only I couldn't decipher it. But you evidently have."

"You knew where it was?"

"Yeah, well, I helped my sister write the book. How much of it did you read?"

I shrugged. "Only to where she took her first human as a host and Azrael—you—vanished."

"Ah . . . halfway. Why did you stop? Did you see the map in the back? She was supposed to put the rest of the spell in there."

"No, no map. I could only—" And then it dawned on me. "TC—you knew all along. You already know that spell."

"Not the most important part. I do know that the Phantasm will stop at nothing to get the end of it. He didn't obliterate Yamato, but he did put her in a place not even you can get her out of. I'm not sure there's any rescue for her."

I wasn't sad. Not at all. Bitch. "So your sister—Inanna—wrote this book and put this spell in it—" I frowned. "Wait—how could she have put the spell in there unless she—" And then it hit me like a two-by-four. "Either she was the one who stole it, or the one who *created* the spell!"

"Sshhh . . ." He looked as if he would strangle me. "You want them to hear? It's a good thing for them to think the Phantasm did. Gives them strength. The wusses. But what she didn't do was put it in the same book. And that book has a map in it that'll show us where the final piece is."

"But"—I was having a major brain fart on this—"why do you want to bring this spell back?"

"I didn't originally—till I realized what I could do with it. Look, Inanna came up with it when I was young, to use against the Phantasm should he ever hurt me. The spell was given to her by our

father as a means to obliterate himself so that the Phantasm would
have nothing to keep and torture. When the Phantasm found out
about the spell, he wanted it. Has always wanted it. And with you
and me popping up like this—and he realized after that last little
go-round that you *are* that and a bag of chips—he wants that
spell so he can obliterate me, you, and all of them. With that in the
works, he can rule indefinitely."

"I'm just not feeling it," I told him. "I keep thinking there's
something else. Something . . ." I shook my head. "First off, do you
know who's been doing this?"

"No. I don't. And if I did, I'd have already gone after them."

For some strange reason, I believed him. "Okay, how can you
be sure this isn't it? That what's happened to Yamato isn't the obliteration spell?"

"The body remained behind."

Uh-uh. "And are you sure they haven't already killed Dags trying to get that book out of him?"

He started to answer me, opened his mouth, then shut it. TC
removed his shades then and looked away, almost squinting in the
light. His milky white eyes looked in the direction of the gardens.
"Zoë—I don't know." His gaze returned to me. "That Guardian—
he's not something I can read. He's so much like you—vibrates
between both the Ethereal and Astral—" He shrugged. "I don't
know about him. What I do know is that they don't have the book.
If they did and had dipped into the magic inside—especially if it's
the Phantasm riding a human—we'd have known about it because
they would be experimenting."

Okay—something he said snagged my attention. "Wait a
minute—Phantasm riding a human. I thought he couldn't do that.
I thought that was why he made creatures like Fetches, Daemons,
other Symbionts—to do things for him."

"Well, yeah . . ." TC replaced his shades. "There are a lot of rumors out there. Don't believe all of them. And don't trust anyone. You've already fucked that one up more times than I can count." With a deep sigh, he said, "I need to see that book, luv. And I need to see it with the magic you have."

Abruptly, he grabbed my left arm with his hand at the wrist. I hissed as his fingers touched flesh and tried to pull away from him. The mark he gave me flared a bright gold as something stirred inside. I tried to shift, to become incorporeal, but couldn't. "Let go of me," I said through clenched teeth.

His own jaw was set, and he sneered. "Give me that spell."

Oh-ho. No fucking way!

With a final effort, I pushed the change, shifting from human to Wraith. I went corporeal and shoved him backward. The force sent him into the tree. But TC changed as well and sieved through it, landing on his ass on the other side in the sunshine. Cursing, he vanished and reappeared next to me. My left arm was throbbing where he'd tried to take the spell—but I felt it digging in its heels. It was not going to be taken from me so easily. And evidently not by TC.

"You will give me that spell."

"No, you fucking asshole. It's staying with me. It doesn't want you."

"Give me the spell, or so help me, even if I find your precious book boy alive, I'll kill him myself."

"You do that, and I'll put an end to your miserable existence."

I think it was at that moment an alarm clock went off in my head. A realization that this was truth. That I could—as I had become—destroy him. Before, when he'd attacked Daniel and nearly killed him, I'd found I could wail with grief. That power had, in a way, destroyed TC. Physically. But he'd still been there in some form. And we'd made a deal to rejoin and defeat the Phantasm—for different reasons. I wanted to save Susan Hirokumi.

I stared at him. "That's it, isn't it? I *so* have the power to destroy you. To destroy this." I pointed to him.

"Don't be ridiculous," he said. And maybe he believed that. I didn't. "You've already torn me to pieces once—and you brought me back. You can't live without me."

I grinned. "Nor you without me. Because you touched me. We're joined." Taking a step closer, I unfurled my wings. Whereas the sun seemed to diminish him, I didn't notice it. Might be that Ethereal gene running amuck. "You touch one hair on Dags's head, and I will destroy you. You got that?"

"I'm the only one that can destroy the Phantasm, Zoë. *You* got *that*? And if he has your book boy—what you get back won't know you." He grinned. "Sort of like what he did with your cop. Crazy Daniel? Poor Zoë. All the men in her life—she drives them crazy." TC's expression hardened. "Give me the spell."

"Find Dags. We trade."

I had no freak'n idea where that came from. But I liked it. Motivation. On both sides.

He grinned. In fact, he grinned way too fast. "We have a deal. I bring you your squeeze—you give me that spell. And the book."

"Nope. Just the spell. The book stays with me."

"Is there a problem?"

TC and I both turned suddenly to see Jason and Nick standing to our left, between us and the gardens. I hadn't even sensed them. And it was obvious that neither had TC.

"No . . ." I glared at TC. "No problem."

"Good," the Revenant said, and clasped his hands together in front of him. "We have an idea—though a bit risky—that might draw out whatever is doing this."

"Like what?" TC said.

"We're going to have a wake for Lex. Here. At midnight. And we're going to exorcise her soul."

29

MY *life is too complicated.*

I want a new one. And if I'd bought it at Sears, I'd be trading it in right now.

Something simple and quiet . . . like . . . a librarian. Wait no . . . they made that into a bunch of movies.

Geez . . . I don't know. Spin the roulette wheel and just pick something. Anything that doesn't go so fast, so I can get off it once in a while and detox.

Apparently—unbeknownst to me or to TC . . . or Rhonda, Nona, Jemmy (Mom went and got her), or Joe—if you exorcise a magic spell, you also exorcise its creator.

Huh?

Lemme get this straight. So, if you perform a sort of exorcism on the essence of a spell, the incantation vibrates along the silver cord connecting the two entities and, in essence, zaps the creation point.

Kinda like sending feedback down a wire.

Nick liked my description.

Jason—not so much.

It was Rhonda and Loki, whose host name I hadn't learned yet, who presented the idea to everyone.

"Lex's body—the host—was used as a base for the spell. The essence of that spell lingers. Both Tel and I can sense it."

Tel? His name is Tel? You know, in a way he kinda looked and sounded like Criss Angel. "I noticed the markings still sparkle now and then, which means the magic still exists. Rhonda and I talked about it, and it was Erishkegal that suggested an exorcism."

You know, I'd read that name in that journal, but I hadn't heard it pronounced till then. And honestly, I was not ever going to try saying it aloud myself.

A woman stepped forward—the complete opposite of Loki. She was well shaped, statuesque, with long Veronica Lake hair the color of wheat and a husky voice.

Wait . . . too husky.

Oh hell . . . it was a drag queen!

"I've performed a few magical exorcisms in my earlier bodies," she—she?—said. "But all practitioners of magic know spells are traceable with the right countermagic. And Rhonda has that spell. We perform this ritual, and it will lead us to the one who did it."

I leaned in close to Jason. "Why didn't we do this before?"

"Because the bodies all turned to goo."

Oh yeah. Right. And Lex's didn't.

I leaned in again. "Why didn't Lex's do that?"

Jason shook his head. "I don't know."

Rhonda and Tel were still talking. ". . . arrange it for midnight.

But I don't want it a secret. I want the news of this to pass through as many gossips as possible, especially through Abysmal lines." Rhonda grinned at Tel. "With all of us here and on guard, this might be the perfect opportunity to catch whoever is using this spell."

I raised my hand. "Shouldn't we be out looking for Dags? I mean . . . he still has a powerful Grimoire inside of him."

Erishkegal turned to me. "We believe he is already dead, Wraith. Whoever is using this spell has finished it. Yamato's death is the proof. I'm afraid looking for your friend is pointless."

Why you bitch. Bastard. And evidently I started to shift and go forward because she backed up, and Jason grabbed my hand. "Easy . . ." he said.

I looked at him. "But she's wrong!" I hissed. "Dags is still alive. I would know it if he weren't."

"Yes. I believe that. And if it was the spellcaster that took him in order to complete the spell, then doing this will bring him to justice. Everyone hopes he or she will be revealed, and we can find Dags."

But . . . I wanted to tell them that the spell wasn't finished. That Lex's body wasn't corrupted because Yamato still existed in some form. Somewhere. And if they did that spell, the exorcism—would it somehow affect her?

I should have said something. I should have.

But damn her—she stabbed Jason, trying to kill him. She hurt Joe. I honestly didn't give a crap about her.

Well . . . that's not true. I did. But in truth, the only proof I had that she was still in existence was TC's word. And this bunch didn't exactly trust him.

And neither did I.

*   *   *

THE preparations had the whole of the Society busy. Rhonda, Jason, Gunter, and Loki coordinated moving Lex's body as well as the supplies needed to perform the ritual. Mom and Jemmy went home in order to get their "battle gear," as they put it. I really couldn't stop myself from laughing at that one. Oh Lord.

The rest of the Revenants scattered about Atlanta and set the rumor mills flying amid the creatures within the borders of the planes.

Sort of a *Talk Soup* for the Abysmal plane.

The stage set for the event was a warehouse owned by the Society, located about twenty miles north of the estate. I peeked at the warehouse manifest—all of which had to be relocated—and whistled. "Military much?" I asked Rhonda when she shouldered me out of the way.

She started walking down the hall to the main ops, where Gunter was. "We're always prepared, Zoë."

"For what? A war? Do you realize how many guns you have in that warehouse?"

She stopped abruptly and looked at me. After crashing into her, I stepped back. "Yes, I do. And I keep a very close eye on them. Our inventory is more vast than this, and we've actually supplied the US Army on occasion. Now, please, get out from under my feet!" And with that she turned and moved.

I stayed where I was. This was her show. Her element. Me? I was that pesky fly that was going to get swatted. I sighed and turned away, and ran headlong into Gunter.

He stood his ground, his hands behind his back, looking down at me.

I looked up. Wow, I actually looked up at a guy. And I got the feeling . . . real fast . . . he did not like me. "How's the weather up there?"

I got a sneer in response and decided it was time to leave. But before I could, he reached out and grabbed my upper left arm. Painfully. I looked up at him, "Hey . . ."

"I don't like you, or your kind," he said in a very menacing voice. "And if I had my way, I'd lock you in one of the L-6 stasis tubes forever. But Miss Orly seems to think fondly of you—she trusts you. But I warn you, do not get in my way, and do not betray her. If you do, you will have me to deal with."

Oh no he di'int.

I shifted right there, coming to my full height, and looked down at him. And to my surprise, he held his ground. Yeah, I could see fear behind those dark eyes, but he wasn't going to let me scare him. I went incorporeal and slipped from his grasp. "You best watch who you threaten, Mr. Gunter."

He kept his gaze level. "Not a who. But a *thing*." And with that, he turned and left me standing there.

Luckily we had no audience. Just me. Him. The hall.

Pissed did not describe how I was feeling . . . so I shot straight up through the roof of the house and up to the darkening sky.

I think . . . for the first time in my life . . . I'd encountered a racial threat.

AFTER that, I stayed out of their way. Didn't see the point. Just stayed as Wraith and watched from above in the warehouse. It was a nice one, with a well-kept wooded area. Very private, with an electric fence. The perfect place for an ambush. And even if the person responsible didn't get it at first, when they saw this place, they would surely think, well—

TRAP!

I would.

Sitting on the roof, I watched as trucks came and went. Furniture—mostly chairs. Even food. She was having it catered. Oh man. This was so not my idea of an exorcism. All I had to go on was watching *Constantine* or *The Exorcist*, and that was always the victim tied to a bed and priests in robes. Seeing this one performed should be interesting.

Even as I watched them come and go, I reached out through the city for some sign of Dags. Or Maureen or even Alice. Something. Some spark or sound that would let me know he was okay. Anxiety gnawed at my stomach, making it impossible to eat, or even sleep. I'd tried the nap thing as Joe suggested. Even lain down in the bed with him. He'd been asleep in seconds. Me?

Sigh.

Nothing. I couldn't sit still, and I couldn't keep moving. And all I could think about was Dags.

Daniel was out there, possibly being used again. The police were looking for him. Mastiff was heading up the investigation even though he knew there was more at work than a serial killer. He'd do his best to keep the cops away from the Society. But still . . .

TC appeared beside me, no longer dressed in his trench coat but in a black wife beater, to show off his muscles. Leather pants. Lots of studs. "You look like you could step into Woof's and be right at home." Woof's was a local gay leather bar. Pretty nice place.

"The Eagle is more my style," he said. "Your boy's alive."

I nearly fell off the roof as I stood up. "Where is he?"

"That I can't say. He's being protected somehow. A few Daemons saw him. Said he's alive. Or that he's breathing. But they can't get to him."

"But where? If they saw him, then they know the physical where."

TC shook his head. "No. Sit down."

I did.

"These Daemons were being used by something and placed in bodies to do the physical work. The bodies they possessed were completely empty, but they weren't allowed to keep them. So they were used, then tossed away, which leads me to believe what we're dealing with is pretty bad-ass that it can use and control like that. Multitasking Abysmal creatures ain't a picnic, luv."

"Phantasm?"

To my surprise he shook his head. "No. I don't think so. I mean yeah I'll bet anything he's pulling the strings, but what's working here on the physical plane . . ." He snapped his fingers. "That night you and I were training. The hairy thing."

"Yeah."

"It's got something to do with that."

"How do you know?"

He grinned. "Because I'm a fucking genius. One of the Daemons tried to explain it to me, what caught it and used it. He said it was the color of blood and that it wrapped itself around him. And that description was bothering me till just now."

That was the same description I'd have given of that hairy thing that night. "And it turned that Fetch into goo."

He nodded. "Pieces are starting to fall into place. Huh . . . I'm kinda liking this detective shit. But, for right now, I can only report he's alive. Do I get something for that?"

"My thanks?"

"That bastard bit off a finger, Zoë. I don't know why you think I give a shit about him."

"Deal stands. Dags for the spell." Though in truth I wasn't really sure I had the power to give him that spell. I hated to think what'd happen if he delivered and I couldn't.

"Kiss?"

"Fuck no." I pushed at him and he grabbed my arm, pulling me closer to him. I started to struggle, not wanting him to go all tentacles and wrap himself around me.

But to my surprise . . . he didn't. Instead, he pressed his lips to mine and gave me a very short, chaste smooch.

And then vanished.

WTF?

Nightfall came fast, and all the Revenants returned, many of them dressed to kill. What was it with being a First Born and a clotheshorse?

That is Jason's influence, not mine, Mephistopheles insisted, as I entered the warehouse. *Though I can't say I'm not pleased by the feel of the fabric.*

"Sensation is never lost on you, is it?"

Never.

But even as I smiled at the First Born's comment, I stopped inside the doorway, my mouth dropping open. The warehouse had been utterly transformed in a single afternoon and evening!

A fourteen-foot drop ceiling had been installed, sealing off the high vaulted steel beams. Though I could sense there were Society agents all along those beams, dressed in black and out of sight. The floors were covered in padding and a soft beige carpet. To the right was an area for cocktails, coffee, and tea. A bartender wiped everything down. To my left was Loki, dressed in an all-white suit and blue shirt. His hair was extra spiky, and he wore several lip rings, sparkling in the newly installed fluorescent lights tucked inside the drop ceiling.

Okay, *The Exorcist* this was not.

"Feels more like a prom, doesn't it?" Joe said as he came up behind me. He was dressed in his usual, only it was a blue plaid, and made of lightweight cotton, not flannel. "Rhonda's boys usually do it up right."

"Right?" I whispered. "They're going to do an exorcism in here?"

"Oh. No." He pointed to a set of closed, peacock-design stained-glass doors. "Through there."

We moved together through the doors. And prom turned into *Carrie*, real fast.

There was no carpet in there. The floor had been cleaned but not covered, exposing concrete. In the center of the room was a table, where Lex's body lay quietly beneath a red sheet. I could smell the chemicals keeping her body from decomposing—which was a key. A natural progression since the human soul was gone. But for the First Born?

Around the table sat a smaller group of tables, and on those were candles of white, red, and black. A thurible for charcoal and incense. Matches, and a whole array of odd-looking things in jars.

"Is all this Aleister Crowley stuff necessary?" I said.

"Dunno." Joe shrugged. I noticed he had his gun and holster on. "I'm more of a shoot first and *then* mumble the incantation kinda guy."

He put a hand on my shoulder and pointed to the only other exit. Double doors to the left. We went through those and got a grand shot of more woods. Floodlights illuminated the trees around us. "There are snipers all through these woods, on the roof, and in the roof. So, if something comes in, they'll see it."

Wow. I was a little impressed. Only a little 'cause, well, if this thing wasn't solid, what were bullets going to do? I chewed on my thumb as he put a hand on my shoulder again. "We'll find him. He's fine."

I nodded. "I think I know that. TC told me Dags was alive—but he doesn't know where."

"TC was here?"

I told Joe what the Symbiont had told me—leaving out the whole deal thing. I didn't think that was anybody's business but mine. "So we know he's alive; we just don't know where."

"I'm surprised you haven't heard anything from Alice or Maureen. And that bothers me. A lot."

I nodded. "This whole thing does. Exorcising the magic? That sounds like a stretch."

"It is a stretch." He grinned. "It's not real. It's something they made up and put out there so whoever it is doing this will show up."

I laughed. *Not real? Oh my God. Well, no wonder that room was like so overdone in the occult crap. I wouldn't be surprised if a neon pentagram dropped from the ceiling as an advertisement.*

"You okay?" he asked me suddenly.

I looked up at him. "I should ask you that. I mean, given everything you've been through in the past few days. But you seem a little . . . off?"

He shrugged. "Rhonda and I broke up. Kinda knew it wasn't working. She's in love with someone else."

I wasn't surprised to hear this. And I'd always wondered how their relationship had withstood events. "And you?"

"I'm in love too." He gave me a half smile. "But I know when to back off, Zoë. I just can't help wondering if I had stayed—not been so frightened by what I felt when I kissed you—"

I wondered if his toes curled as well.

Joe reached up and touched my cheek. His fingers were warm.

"Maybe if I'd have made love to you first . . . maybe I could have been the one to pop your cherry."

Uhm. Okay. I was going to tell him that popping my cherry wasn't the point of it. But before I could speak, his hand moved quickly from my cheek to my neck, squeezing hard. I couldn't breathe and grabbed at his wrist, trying to break free. I looked up into his face and saw darkness there. And a slow, even red glow in his eyes.

PHANTASM!

30

OMG!

OMFG!

It's here! In Joe's body! I knew it just as I knew I was going to be so superfucked if I didn't do something!

I couldn't cry out—the pressure on my neck was too hard. I started to shift, but he shook Joe's head. "Uh, uh, uh. You become the Wraith now, and I send word to kill the Guardian." He made a sad face. "And we wouldn't want that to happen, now would we?"

Goddamnit!

I stopped the shift and continued to claw at his wrist. I couldn't speak or scream. Why weren't the snipers shooting at him. Didn't they see I was being choked?

"Now, what we're going to do, is walk together inside that warehouse, and we're going to destroy that body. Understand?"

Destroy the body.

Why?

I could only nod. I felt my face turning red as I fought to get air into my lungs somehow. I called out on all channels HELP as loud as I could.

"You shouldn't have done that—"

I heard the hiss and the thump first, before Joe tensed and released his grip on me. I fell backward, stumbling, then down on my ass as I looked up. An arrow was lodged in Joe's neck, sticking out from the right side. He was scowling and reached up and yanked it out, tearing flesh. Joe was bleeding *again*. Damnit!

I wanted to shift, to take him out, but I wanted Dags to be safe. Oh God, he *had* to be safe.

Joe whirled and looked out at the woods. "I know you're there . . . you fucking *bitch*!" he hissed, loud enough for me but not the snipers in the woods to hear.

Who? Who was there? I had my hand at my neck, coughing loudly, just on the verge of changing.

Changing is the only way to defeat it, came TC's voice in my head. He was nearby, in those woods. I could sense him.

But he'll kill Dags!

It's a bluff, stupid. He wants that book. Now attack!

That gave me the go-ahead I needed. I shifted from where I was and launched upward, grabbing Joe's body beneath his arms, taking him higher and up and away from the others, my wings beating as fast as they could.

"I warned you!" Joe said, and reached around and grabbed at my wings. He was messing with my flying, trying to crash us. I screamed at him and managed to bring my knee up and nail him in the balls.

He reacted at first, as if Joe were in control, but then straightened and grinned, and said, "My turn." He reared his head back and cracked mine with his. I saw stars, literally, as I lost control of him, and we both went crashing down into trees and woods. My wings caught on branches and were ripped before I remembered to pull them in close. I hit the ground hard and lay on my side, trying to straighten out my vision.

Now I knew how wrestlers felt when they got that forehead-to-forehead crack.

My God that hurts!

And then, of course, I fell fifty feet from the sky. I picked myself up and looked around, too late to realize that the bastard was coming at me. He tackled me where I stood, and together we rolled over stumps and rocks and smack into another pine tree. Can't throw a rock in Georgia without hitting a pine, ya know.

I shoved him away, using whatever Wraith strength I could muster. Like this, we were both out of our element. Him more so since he was all Abysmal. I at least could interact on this side of the universe within my Wraith body. Though I'd suspected I have more power in the Abysmal plane, I'd been a bit chicken to go test it. I mean, what if I screwed up and got stuck there? No body to bring my ass back!

I wasn't sure what a Phantasm's limitations were when over-shadowing a human. I was thinking not as strict as when they fuse with them. But I was also worried about hurting Joe. He was still human, and he'd already lost a lot of blood. And by the look of the wound on his neck, losing a shitload more.

By this time all the ruckus we were making had sounded an alarm. I could sense people in all directions coming at us, surrounding us there on the ground. I stood just as he did, and to my surprise, he fired some weird-ass purple light out of his left hand at me. Instinct took over, and I held up both my hands, blocking the attack with a blue shield of my own.

Crazy.

This is crazy.

Mental note: *this is freak'n crazy!*

Though his purple thing didn't hit me, it felt as if it'd zapped something 'cause I got dizzy. Maybe it was supposed to do that? You know, make me defend myself so he could zap energy cells.

Villains were cunning like that.

I called up the sword I'd used against the Horror. It'd been different then—all flaming and such. Now it looked like a combination of both ice and fire. Opposites in the planes. I waved it like a big stick and pointed it at him like they did in animes—and damned if it didn't shoot out a white light at him.

I squinted at the bright show and realized I'd signaled "Hey, we're over here!" to just about anybody within a five-mile radius.

Sweet.

I opened my eyes and staggered, seeing him do the same thing. Though I wasn't sure if that was because I got him or because Joe's body was giving out. How much of it was Symbiont and how much human power? I needed to get him out of Joe's body. And that led me to a whole new string of thoughts.

I liked it when I got those.

Phanty had shown himself to me incorporeal several times, as simply a visual of someone. As a clown once, and as a hooded man at the construction site the night I made the deal with TC. And again in the hospital when we were fighting over the Eidolon. It was possible he could manifest as something in the physical plane.

So, why was he actually in a body this time? The only answer I had was that he had intended on manipulating the physical. He needed to touch something *physically* in this plane.

And all I could think about was the book.

But which one?

"They're over there!"

"Don't shout, asshole!"

Well, thanks to Lieutenant Asshole, we knew they were coming. I charged forward with my sword again, intent on ramming him with it, thinking maybe I could bounce him out of Joe's body or something. What I hadn't counted on was him counterattacking with something of his own.

Joe's body.

I saw him throw himself in front of the sword and altered the attack just in time, nearly skewering Joe right through the center. The movement cost me momentum and balance, and I would have fallen if I hadn't unfurled my wings and moved up a little. But not before Phanty made this incredible roll and jump, reaching up and grabbing my ankle right above my bunny slipper.

He yanked me down and tossed me like a dog tosses a toy in his mouth, throwing me a good hundred feet into another fucking pine.

Owch.

I lay on the grassy ground as a hooded figure jumped on top of me. I reached up to toss this bastard off, thinking it was one of Rhonda's men, when the hood fell back and I saw his face.

Daniel.

It's freak'n Daniel!

Oh shit! And he had me in a very precarious position.

My eyes nearly bugged out of my head as I hesitated, and he grabbed both of my wrists and held them to the ground at my sides. He came closer, and I could see—he looked good. He was going to kill me—but he'd look good doing it.

I expected he would shoot me or stab me, or maybe even use some spell he'd found or something. What I didn't expect was for him to kiss me.

Long, deep, and hard.

He tasted like wintergreen. Not like a breath mint, but really of wintergreen. I found myself in a wood of ferns and tall, gnarled trees decorated in moss. And he was over me. But the voice in my head was purely feminine.

Zoë . . .

I looked up at him, not sure if this was a dream or if maybe Rhonda had some nice Tolkien-looking spring meadow on her property. No . . . I could still feel his lips on mine. Somewhere.

Take this and use it . . . it will remove her from his body. I will help you as I can.

With that, the meadow faded, and I was under Daniel. He was pulling back now, letting go of my arms. And I was human again, looking up at the man I'd loved, who'd tried to kill me.

He smiled. "Zoë . . . I'm sorry. I am. I love you, and I don't want anything to happen to you." He reached under his robe and produced one of Randall Kemp's stun guns. "I took this from the police station. Use it."

"Over here!"

"It's Detective Halloran! He's been shot!"

Daniel looked up as we both heard branches cracking under boots. He smiled at me and stood, then helped me to my feet. "I wish you'd told me . . . about the Wraith. I would have understood."

I moved closer to him and tentatively reached up to touch his face. It was real. He was real. And he was . . . "Daniel . . . what happened? You're not . . . you don't want to kill me . . ."

"No." He shook his head.

And then I sensed it. A Symbiont. And as I looked at him I realized . . . no, not a Symbiont.

A First Born.

He was hosting a Revenant now.

And a name came to me from the pages of the book. *Inanna.* "You were in the shop. You took the copies."

"I tried to. But they were already gone."

"There he is!'

And, abruptly, Daniel was gone.

I stood by that tree in the dark, and as they came closer, I tucked the gun under my shirt in the back of my pants. Six or so armed Society agents appeared. Rhonda and Gunter came as well.

"It was Detective Frasier," a voice was saying in the dark. Joe's voice. "He attacked me, then went after Zoë."

That bastard was still inside of him. Lying. I waited until he came forward, helped along by Mom.

Mom! Get away!

Rhonda looked at me. "Was it Daniel? Did you see him?"

I narrowed my eyes at Joe. "No, it wasn't Daniel." And then I pulled the gun, aimed, and fired at Joe.

The blast was brighter than I remembered, but it had the same effect. I'm afraid I kinda caught my mother in the blast as well, but I wasn't going to let that thing linger inside of Joe any longer.

People yelled out, and before I knew it, I was on my front with someone's knee in my back and a gun to the back of my head. Growling, I shifted to Wraith just as one of the bastards fired, then I went incorporeal. The shot went though my left shoulder, and it smarted pretty bad. I stood and faced the one who did that, shoving my hand inside of his chest. *Asshole . . . you do not shoot me. And just for that, I'll take a little of your miserable life to heal me!*

"Zoë!"

I wasn't insane. I was *pissed off*. And when I'd taken my fill of his soul, I turned and pointed at the creature now rolling on the floor a foot behind Joe's still body. "There it is, Rhonda. Shoot it!"

All eyes turned to see the form shift and move as it turned into something more understandable. Once again, it became Mr. Muscles in the hoodie with the hidden face. He pointed at me.

"That bitch gave you that gun. But it won't help you. Tell my sister that—tell all of them I will come for them and destroy each of them just as I destroyed Yamato."

I waited a few beats before clapping.

Yes, I got the look of the utterly insane from those around me, but I just had to reward genius. "That is so much bullshit." I stepped over the body of the idiot that shot me (no he wasn't dead, but he wasn't going to be digesting food well for a while) and approached the Phantasm. Nona and a Society medic were over Joe, treating the wound in his neck. The whole area was lit up from Society flashlights as well as mine and Phanty's luminescence.

Did I spell that right?

"You are so full of bullshit. You have so many people afraid of you . . . but not me. No . . . because I just realized who you are."

THAT got some serious looks, not just from everyone around me but from the Phantasm as well. He reached up and pulled his hood back, revealing the same chiseled redheaded man I'd seen before. He looked like a singer, a rock star, and he was neither. "How dare you . . ."

"Oh, I dare all right," I said. Now . . . let's get something straight. I am *not* this brave. And I was shaking all over. But I wanted to push the situation. I wanted to know what it knew. I wanted . . .

I wanted . . .

I didn't know what I wanted anymore. I had Daniel's kiss lingering on my lips but Dags on my mind.

Puffing up, I stalked forward even closer. In this form, I knew he had no power. What I didn't know was why.

But I would. Soon.

"You." I pointed at him. "You betrayed your father . . . took his throne . . . tricked your siblings into becoming Revenants, then stripped your youngest brother of his memories and his power so that he could do your bidding as you waged war with the Ethereal plane. Am I right? It was you that caused the barriers to be raised. It was you that shut down communication with the Seraphim. You brought the heart of darkness."

To be honest, I had no idea where this shit was coming from until I noticed my left wrist glowing gold again. And then I knew.

These were Inanna's words, coming through the book.

And they pissed him off.

Oh, they so pissed off the Phantasm.

Rhonda took a hesitant step away from Joe. Everyone stood still, the agents with their guns drawn, keeping their eyes glued on something they could or couldn't see. I didn't know. "Zoë . . . the Phantasm has a name?"

"Yes. It's—"

SILENCE!!

That one word blew past me and around me. I winced as the wind kicked up. Trees fell backward, debris spun up and out. A few of the agents went flying backward. I saw Mom and Rhonda bend down over Joe. When it was over with, it looked as if we were standing at ground zero, and everything else was flattened.

But from what I could see, no one was hurt. Not seriously.

No . . . even now the Phantasm hadn't actually hurt anyone.

And . . . he was gone.

I sighed and picked myself out of the debris, shifting back to human so as not to freak out the agents as I tried to help those who got blowed back (yes I meant to say it that way). Two of the agents worked to pick up Joe and carry him back to the warehouse. Rhonda gave orders to get him back to the estate and under lock and key.

"He'll be fine," I said. I realized I was still holding the gun. "This thing blows out the possessing spirit pretty good."

But she was staring at me, as was Mom. Two of the Revenants were there as well, Loki and Erishkegal. Their clothing had seen better days. "How . . . how did you get that gun. They're all locked up. And how did you know that the Phantasm was inside Joe?"

Okay. Here's where I wasn't sure whether to tell them the truth about Daniel—that he was hosting a Revenant now—or about who the Phantasm was.

But then that decision was taken away as one of the agents, along with the Revenant named Dagda, came running up. "Ma'am! It's Jason! He's gone!"

Okay, the disappearing-man chapter ending is getting OLD!

31

I ran faster than anyone else and got to the warehouse. Apparently, it hadn't gone unharmed by the Phantasm's words as he fled. The roof had caved in, taking with it most of the drop ceiling in the front. The area where Lex's body rested was almost unscathed, having had wards put up by Mom and Rhonda. Nick was there, looking completely unhinged.

I grabbed at him and took him to the side. His skin was hot. "Nick—what happened?"

"I don't know. I was here . . . and Jason was on the phone. He's always on the phone. And I noticed that you and Joe had gone through the door. I followed for a while, and I saw him start to choke you. I came back into the room to tell Jason—but he wasn't there. His car is still outside. And his phone was on the ground."

Something . . . took him. For something to take a Revenant—especially one as powerful as Mephistopheles—oh fuck. "Nick, did you recognize all the Revenants here tonight?"

"Yes. There wasn't anyone strange. I just can't figure out where he vanished to."

"Can you sense him?"

Nick shook his head. "That's just it—I can't. It's like he's just disappeared off the planet. Normally, I can close my eyes and feel him. But he's been cut off—"

"Maybe behind a barrier?"

Rhonda put her hands to her mouth. "Oh fuck."

We turned to her. "What now?" I asked, a little more irritated than I wanted to sound.

But Rhonda wasn't looking at me. We were standing in the ritual room, near the body. The double doors leading outside to where Joe and I had been were open. Rhonda pointed at them, and we looked.

There, standing a good distance from the warehouse, at the tree line, was a figure, glowing softly. And I knew instantly who it was.

Adiran Martinique.

My father.

"I'll go." I started forward.

Mom reached out to me and took my hand. She moved in front of me and smiled. "He's not the same man, Zoë. Even in your dreams where he can be himself. Like this"—she glanced behind her—"he's different."

I knew that. Somehow. "And we're on opposite sides?"

"No." She put her hands to my face. "Not really. And I think a part of him knows that. But, well . . . until you deal with the Ethereal, you can't really explain it. But you'll learn why he couldn't stay with me anymore, or with you."

I wasn't sure I wanted to know that. But I squeezed her wrists and moved away from her to the doors and into the night. The closer I came to him, the more distinguished he looked. Not like in a gentlemanly way . . . but in his features. He looked like I remembered him from my childhood.

Blurry.

With each step, I realized I was shifting, changing again. And I paused halfway there because—my hands weren't a dark, mottled black anymore but a soft, glowing gray. I looked at my slippers, and they weren't angry. They were white, and their pink noses were back. I took more steps and felt my wings unfurl and knew somehow they were no longer black but white. Every step changed me until I stood in front of him.

Father to daughter.

Daughter to parent.

Wraith to Angel.

"Hi, Daddy." My voice was small, and I choked back a tear.

His features never really came into focus. Only his shape, and his height. And his smell. I had always remembered his smell.

"Is this how you remember me?" he said in a soft voice.

I sniffed. Nodded. "It was so long ago. When you left. I—I don't have any—"

He raised a hand, and that came into focus. "There are no memories for me to draw from, Zoë. I'm sad inside to know this is all I left you."

Tears pooled in my eyes.

This is my daddy.

And I can't even see his face.

"Sshhh . . ." he said. "Don't cry. I still watch over you when I can. And as you are now is how you look stripped of the Abysmal taint that poisoned you."

I had never considered myself poisoned. Not really. I mean, I knew, in a way, I was. I sniffed again. "Why are you here?"

"Because we cannot let this go on, Zoë. This ridiculous war between the family of Samael. For too long, Sophia has run amuck, and we have done nothing. She has created havoc and must be removed."

I kind of understood him. If I hadn't read that book, I wouldn't have gotten any of it. "The Revenants—"

"Need our help. And yet they will not ask for it. Only one brave soul has ventured forth to beg for guidance. Even now, he bears great torment at the hands of the Phantasm's minion."

I couldn't think of—"You mean Jason? Mephistopheles?" *Ohm . . . huh?* "I don't . . ."

"What Sophia wants more than anything is power, Zoë. And she believes that the ultimate spell, the ultimate annihilation, can be achieved by removing that pesky book from the Guardian. But we like it there. And we want it to stay. So we've taken the precaution of protecting that book with our own defense. Sophia is unaware of our agent, but that is to be expected. She isn't the brightest to wear the title."

So . . . Dags was safe. For now.

"Now, what she wants is the book you hid in the maze. And what her opposite wants is the spell. These two will clash, and it will take Revenant and Seraphim soldiers alike to dispel her power when she gets it."

"But she's not getting it," I said, switching the Phantasm's gender, which was getting confusing. "I won't give it to her."

"True love, Zoë. There is nothing better. I had that love with your mother. And I still do." He smiled. And I realized he did. Because it was him that saved her from the Abysmal, and kept her soul safe until Rhonda could take it and put it back.

This wasn't making any sense. "I don't get it."

"Destiny, Zoë. Love is what keeps you Ethereal in your soul."

And he was gone.

Just like that.

My body ached as it twisted and changed, and I fell forward on my knees. I could hear Rhonda, and Nick and Mom coming up behind me. And when I felt my mother's arms, I buried my face in her shoulder and cried. Oh God, I cried so hard I couldn't breathe.

"What is it?" Nick asked softly outside of my wall of pain.

"That was the first time she's actually seen her father since she was four," Mom said. "And she couldn't see his face."

AFTER a long, hot shower at Rhonda's, I stood in front of the mirror. So many people say this is the worst way to explain how you look. Well, I'm sorry. But a mirror is exactly how I know how I look. And at that moment, I looked like baked shit.

My hair had gotten long . . . too long. I wanted to cut it. Cut it all off. I could see it peeking from behind my hip. Wet. Dripping on the brain-stabbingly white tile of the palatial bathroom. I'd wiped an area of the mirror off with my hand . . . and I was still foggy. But I could see me.

Me.

Me as human. I was still the Latina tomboy I'd always been. Never painted her nails, or bothered with jewelry as a child. And when I was old enough to notice boys, apparently it'd been too late. They all saw me as Zoë. Their best friend. The one with the crazy mom. To see me now . . . the long, thick white streak from my temple the only color I could make out.

My light brown eyes. Dad had called them his topaz jewels. Down to my upturned nose. Other kids called it a ski slope. To my permanently smirking mouth. Mom called it attitude. It was me. And then I looked down at my left wrist, at the golden pattern of Azrael's touch.

Azrael. It felt odd to call him that. I would always know him as TC. The Archer.

I released the hold I kept on this shape and turned. I watched as my skin mottled, my eyes grew black, and my hair spread out from my head in an electric fan, like thin, dark eels searching through the sea of air. My nails sharpened, and my body remained the same shape. But the skin . . .

The skin wasn't my own.

I could remember this shape.

I could remember my first house.

I could remember my last birthday party.

I could remember Daniel's kiss on my lips.

And I could remember Dags's body against my own.

But I could not . . . couldn't . . . remember my father's face.

Tears streamed down my face again. The Wraith is crying. Thunder sounded from somewhere, heralding the night. And I watched as huge, broken, and ripped bat wings with bony joints spread out from behind me.

I thought of my dad's pure white light and compared it to my darkness.

I was a monster.

Someone knocked at my door. "Zoë?"

It was Mom.

I sniffed. "It's open."

And I let her see me like this. Nude and exposed. She stood in the doorway as it opened and smiled at me, her expression so lovingly hers. "You can't scare me, you know. I'm your mother."

"I scare myself."

She came to stand beside me. We both peered in the mirror as she wiped more of the condensation away. "I scare myself too, sometimes. The things I think. Or what I do. But, that's a part of living. Perfectly natural."

I pointed at my reflection. "That isn't natural. It's . . . hideous."

"No, it's beautiful." And she hugged me, careful to avoid the points of my wings. "Because it's uniquely you. I always knew you'd grow up to be a badass. I just didn't know how big a one. Or what kind."

I smiled and released this part of me. I was so surprised at the ease with which I was able to do so, almost as easy as it had become to shed my skin. "I'm not a badass."

"Oh yes, you are. Think about it. You've got the biggest bully on the playground afraid of you."

"And that's right?" I turned to her, not caring that I was naked. This woman had changed my diapers, for goodness' sake. "That I should force her to hurt my friends and family just because she's afraid?"

"No," Mom said, and put her hands on my shoulders. They were warm, those hands. And full of love. "But because another acts out of fear doesn't mean you blame yourself. You choose to help those in need. Think of the one that fears you the most and try to imagine what would ease their fear."

"Oblivion?"

"No, I think you can come up with something better than that." She squeezed my shoulders and moved to the rack beside the door. Retrieving a white robe, she handed it to me and grabbed the brush from the table. I sat in the chair to my right as she brushed the tangles away.

"Mom . . ."

"Mmm?"

"When you go . . . will I be able to remember your face?"

I watched her reflection above my head. Her expression faltered. "Not as clearly as you remember it now. Zoë, don't dwell so much on not being able to remember your father's face. Or the fact that you saw him that way. Angels—tend to shape themselves out of the memories of those they wish to speak to. He wasn't there for solid memories to mature in your mind. It's not a failure on your part, and your dad realizes that."

I kinda knew this. Really. And I'm not usually melodramatic. Never have been. But geez . . . maybe I was due for it.

"Man trouble?"

I looked at Mom's reflection. "Daniel gave me the gun."

She stopped brushing and looked at me in the mirror. "Daniel?"

I nodded. "He was in the woods and gave me the gun. Told me to use it on Joe to knock out the demon. I think it was him that shot Joe to begin with." I launched into an explanation of what had happened when Joe and I had gone outside to talk.

Afterward, she sighed. "Well, I should have known something was wrong with him when he refused one of my crab cakes."

A sin!

"But there's something else, Mom," I said, and looked at her reflection. "Daniel's hosting a Revenant."

Now that stopped her cold. She moved to stand in front of me. "Are you sure?"

"Yes. That was him that day when someone was in the house. Jason sensed it was Inanna—one of the First Borns. She's joined with Daniel now. I could hear her—she was the one that told me she would help us. That's her journal—the smaller one." And then it was time to fess up on the book and what I'd read.

Not long after that, when I was dressed, Mom called all the players together for a meeting in the library, and again I told what I knew. Me, Rhonda, Mom, Jemmy, Nick, Gunter, and three of the Revenants. The others had been told to go to their lairs and prepare.

Yes, Rhonda had said *lairs.*

The Revenants were Loki, Erishkegal, and Dagda.

Rhonda rubbed at her cheek. "Now I'm all confused."

I raised my hand. "Me first."

Erishkegal spoke softly. "I—I didn't realize that Sophia had—"

"I don't believe any of us knew," Dagda said as he sighed. "We were all living our lives in this world, fighting to adjust to this shared existence. Sophia told me there was a great enemy looking for us, and that enemy had created a spell that would obliterate us from the Akashic records."

All of them nodded. They had all been told the same thing.

Sophia had worked her magic well.

"So the Phantasm in power is actually our oldest sister." He snorted. "Just great. What a bitch."

I nodded. "That she is. The spell we're all looking for wasn't created by her to get rid of the Revenants—or by this mystery Phantasm that you all believed destroyed your father—it was created by the first Phantasm, your father, Samael, to obliterate his soul so that his daughter wouldn't have him for sport."

"So who performed the spell on Samael?" Dagda asked.

I shook my head. "I guess Inanna did. My God, this is all so confusing."

Jemmy—who I'd completely forgotten about—sat forward from her perch in the chair at Rhonda's desk. "Not so confusing. Not really."

We all looked at her to find out what the hell it was she meant. We all sought enlightenment on this.

"It's like any other story of familial behavior. A grieving father can't give his first born love—and so she gets all nasty and pouty. He has a lot of other children in order to ease his loneliness, but that doesn't work either. Then one day pouty nasty child decides she wants to be the Phantasm, the ultimate power. She tricks all the others to lock themselves in boxes because a big baddie is a comin'. They do this, so they don't see what she did. But the father knew and created a male child to hide away with his only remaining faithful daughter. He writes this big mojo spell and gives it to the daughter—" Jemmy held up a finger. "She's supposed to obliterate her father—destroy him utterly so that the pouty child don't take him. But honestly, can any of you actually believe she would do such a thing?"

I thought of my own father. "No, I couldn't. I mean I might—"

Oh lawd.

Rhonda hit jackpot the same time I did. "Oh my God—she *changed* it!"

And now it all makes sense.

Kinda.

Wha—?

Jemmy nodded at Rhonda. "Don't you all see? There was no way this child was going to destroy her father. So she made it look like she had. Now, if you performed this ritual on a living body, I'm sure you might get the same results as she got on Lex."

Jason had said Yamato wasn't really gone. They'd all agreed. But no one knew where she was.

Dagda snapped his fingers. "Oh, I think I have it. Sophia had part of the spell, but not all of it, so she's been experimenting until she could find it."

"And my guess is she did," Jemmy said. "She found it in the Grimoire inside of Dags. But it's still not the spell she wants. Otherwise, why possess Joe? Why come here in a physical form?"

"Well, the rituals on us have to be done physically," Loki said as he tapped a black fingernail to his chin. He looked like Rhonda's brother today. Black tee shirt, jeans, high-tops, and lots of gaskets on his wrists. Silver on his fingers. "So he has an agent here doing this for him."

"The detective?" Gunter said.

"No," I barked at him. "Daniel's not involved."

"How can you be so sure?" Gunter said, his eyebrows flying up onto his forehead. "You know something?"

I turned and looked at him. "Do I have to come over there and bitch-slap you?"

There were chuckles all around, especially from Loki.

"Daniel has nothing to do with this." I hadn't told them about him. Or about Inanna. That wasn't for me to say. "Inanna changed the spell, she saved her father's soul, and tricked her sister. But I'm willing to guess the original spell—"

Great Scott!

Is it possible?

"What is it, Zoë?" Rhonda said.

I looked at Rhonda. "The original spell." I held up my left hand, exposing my wrist. "I know where it is!"

32

IT all made sense now as I ran through the maze to the center, where I'd hidden the book. The sun was just cresting the trees as dawn came, but the fifteen-foot-high hedges kept the sun away as I navigated, having memorized the path from when I'd stood out on the balcony. In the center of that maze was a fountain with benches. I'd stashed the book in a paper sack beneath one of those benches.

And when I arrived there, I had to look under each one.

It wasn't there.

Shit.

Did I miss something?

"Looking for this?"

I whirled to see Gunter standing behind me, holding up the package in his left hand. I was a little confused. Was he a good guy with a perverted sense of revenge? Or was he a bad guy who had infiltrated the Society, and I was about to get my ass kicked?

Shadows coalesced on all sides, moving through the sludge of dawn. I was thinking the latter was based more on what was happening. But how could Rhonda not know she had a possessed guy in her midst?"

"That's easy," he said as if reading my mind. "Because I'm not a Fetch, or a Daemon, not even a Symbiont. I'm something she's never come across before. Something not even you can see when it's in front of you."

I pursed my lips and shrugged. "You gonna tell me or keep me in suspense?"

And then I knew. I don't know how I knew. I knew the second I shifted and saw him with Abysmal eyes.

Chimera.

Nope. Never came across that before. So . . .

Mental note: *new thing!*

I held up a taloned hand. "Now . . . I might be wrong, but isn't the Wikipedia definition of a Chimera like . . . an impossible or foolish fantasy?"

He growled. Well, that didn't ingratiate me, did it?

I held out my hand. "Okay, so you're a Chimera. And the moment Rhonda finds out, you are so fired. Give me back that book."

"I'm afraid Rhonda won't be finding out. And as for this book"—he tucked it in his shirt—"my master will be getting it hand-delivered, along with you." I thought he was going to hit me with some big light show, since these kinds of things were mostly all flashy. Instead, he pulled out Randall's gun and fired.

If I'd been in a body—it might have worked. What it did do was hurt. A lot. But I wasn't the former Wraith, who had to move out of her body. I was a corporeal thing now. And that trinket . . .

Eh.

There was a brief look of terror on Gunter's face as he realized the gun wasn't doing what he thought it would. "But—this gun hurt my master. It should hurt you!"

"Uh, dude." I gestured to myself. "Physical creature not riding a human?"

I held out my hand and tried something. I thought about the gun, and, to my surprise, it came to me. I pointed it at him. "Now you, a noncorporeal entity definitely riding a human." I grinned. "Night, night."

Boom.

And out it went, flying.

Boys and girls, whatever you've read about Chimeras, that whole body of a lion, snake for a tail, head of a goat? Well, it's true. All of it. 'Cause that is what I saw stumble to its feet. I think I got too complacent as I watched it, because lo and behold it recovered, reached its ugly goat's head in the pocket of Gunter's jacket, and swallowed the book in two gulps.

Well . . . they say a goat'll eat anything.

Damnit!

And then it was gone. Just . . . poof.

Christ on a crutch.

Picking up the heavy Gunter, I flew up and landed on the deck outside the library. People came running when I landed. Rhonda called in more staff to take Gunter away and treat him. And that was when I saw Joe in the doorway. He looked . . . wonderful. I told them about the Chimera and what it'd done with the book.

"A Chimera?" Dagda said. "It takes a lot to raise a Chimera. And a very powerful spell. It's not something I believe Sophia knew."

Rhonda paled. "Oh my God."

"What?" I said, and held up my hand to ward off the dawn sun. "You know this spell?"

"It was in the Grimoire. That spell. Riding the Chimera. Oh shit, Zoë, they've got access to the Grimoire. They can read the pages!"

But I didn't think that was possible. At least it shouldn't be. And Dad had assured me Dags was protected.

"We have to find them now," Rhonda said. "Now."

Joe reached out and took her shoulder. "And where do we start? Hum? My guess is—and I'm coming at this cold—is that Phanty, this Sophia person, has taken Dags and that book to where she feels safest. A place she controls. A home."

I didn't know what that was. I'd hoped it was in this plane, because having Dags and Jason in the Abysmal . . . "It's not in the Abysmal."

Dagda tilted his head. "Why do you think not?"

"Because neither Jason nor Dags could survive there. Their bodies would die within a matter of minutes." I wasn't about to tell them that Rhonda had survived in the Abysmal a much longer time—no time for that. "Where in this world would she feel safe?"

No one spoke.

Then, "Between."

We all turned to see TC in the shadows. He wore his coat again, and his shades. His gloves were on. He looked ready for a scrap.

"Where?" I said.

"I found him. Came all this way to tell you, and I hear you let a Chimera take the book?" He shook his head. "God, luv, you are not so bright sometimes."

"You!" Dagda shouted. "How dare you show your face to us. You who hunted us."

"Dagda," Erishkegal held out her hand. "Enough. We know now that Azrael wasn't in control of himself."

TC turned a very angry face at me. "You told them."

"I had to," I said. "We know that your sister Inanna didn't use the spell Samael gave her. She changed it. And she put the original spell in that book—the one the Chimera stole. Sophia wants it so she can kill all of you."

And then TC began to laugh.

I did not like it. That laugh was not something you ever want to hear in a dark alley. Vin Diesel unhappy.

We all looked at one another. "You know nothing. All of you. You might have ruined it all."

Ruined it all. Oh-kay. Ruined all of what? I was missing something important.

I held out my hands and shrugged at him. "Okay, which part do we have wrong here? You haven't exactly been forthcoming all this time with the secrets."

"Because they *are* secrets, and they needed to remain so. But if Sophia opens that book—if she gets the spell—"

"No, no." I held up my arm. "I still have that."

Rhonda looked at me. "You do?"

"I told you that, keep up," I snapped before redirecting my ire at TC. "Is there something else about that book?"

TC frowned. "Do you want to rescue your friend? Then we have to leave quickly."

"Not by yourself you're not." Dagda stepped forward. "We want to help."

"You can't." TC looked at them and shook his head. "Not like you are. But there will be a time soon when you will be called. Can you be ready?"

I thought I caught a bit of solidarity there between brothers and sisters. Something I didn't think he was capable of. But then, my relationship with him had changed so much in these past months. We weren't the same people. Literally.

"When you say in between, you mean the borders?"

TC looked at me and frowned. "No. Between, Georgia. Small town out 78. She's got a base out there where she can manifest. Built a connection to the physical plane so her minions could move easily through the borders and not get caught." He gave me a withering look. "You think they named the town 'Between' just for kicks?"

You have got to be kidding me.

He pulled a card from his jacket and gave it to Rhonda. "That's the address. Zoë and I have to go in first, do reconnaissance. I hear you've got some help from the Seraphim's foot soldiers?"

Rhonda nodded. "Yes. They'll come when I call them."

"Then we'll rock and roll." TC turned and grabbed my arm. "Let's motor."

We both sailed up into the sky straight as arrows, and his grip on my wrist fell to my hand. Hand in hand.

Flying over Atlanta as the sun came up was a bit disconcerting. We usually flew at night. Under darkness. Like this, I felt exposed and expected helicopters to come in and shoot us down. TC seemed to know where he was going, so I let him lead me there. We passed over so many trees, and I realized then exactly how green my town is. Atlanta.

We passed over Snellville, then followed Highway 78. TC turned right at a certain point, and we dipped low over the trees, so low in fact it felt as if the tips were tickling my middle. Ahead, I could see a hazy area, where the trees seemed a little . . . unnatural.

He pointed, and the two of us touched down near a seven-foot wall. There was a little space between the tree line and where we were. The wall seemed to vibrate and made the soft hairs on my face stand at attention. "Is the wall electrified?"

"No, not in the way you're thinking. It's warded against humans. They can't see the building from this angle or above."

Well, that explained the hazy look. I figured my human half saw the haze, but my Abysmal self was what let me see the building. "Can we get in?"

"I have before, but that was before all this shit happened. Technically, we're Abysmal, so any lockdown protocols wouldn't be triggered. Then again, your Ethereal parts might make the alarms dance. But then, we'll just have to find out." And before I could say "Wait," he had his hand through the wall.

I ducked. Waited. Nothing happened. He nodded at me as he pulled his hand out. "Your turn."

I made myself incorporeal and shoved my hand through as well. Concrete . . . ick. Not as good. Made my skin crawl, as did the little electrical or magical impulses firing through. When nothing seemed to happen, TC walked on through, and I joined him.

On the other side, there wasn't much. Just a round brick building with a door. The grass was little more than weeds around us. No landscaping at all. "I guess this is supposed to look like this?"

"I guess," he said. "Makes it look like you don't want to go in. Nothing special. And the door doesn't have a handle or any other means for a physical body to open it." He moved closer to it, studied it, then raised his shades as he stared again. "Ah, I see. Come on."

And he moved through the door as well.

I sighed, shrugged, and moved in too.

Now for something completely different. Inside was much bigger than the outside. I looked up at the stars above me, my mouth opening. "Whoa . . ." I said, and my voice echoed. I looked down and saw the same thing. It was as if we were standing in the middle of space with no ending and no beginning. "Where the fuck are we?"

"Between." He moved a few feet in and looked around. "You'll need to see through the façade. You should be able to do it with your eyes. Pretend it's a"—he snapped his gloved fingers—"magic eye thing."

I looked at him. "Dude, you spend way too much time at the mall."

"Just do it."

I dismissed my wings, not needing them in there, and moved forward. I stared at the floor first, readjusting my vision as I would when looking at those old nineties picture-in-a-picture thing. And then—

The universe vanished, and we were inside a round room, just like the round building we'd entered. In the center was a spiral staircase, and both of us looked at it. "I wonder where that goes."

TC suddenly brandished two pistols. Desert Eagles by the size of them. "It goes down." And he started his descent.

"It goes down," I mouthed, feeling anything but cooperative. *Sheesh. Dude is gonna start shooting and wake the whole damn building. Idiot.*

With a sigh, I followed him down—and we went down a long way. There wasn't anything to see around us or below us. Just black. And if I looked at it and not him in front of and below me, then I got dizzy and wanted to fall.

"Don't get sick back there and puke on me."

Now I wish I would. Jerk. Finally, I could see a floor . . . or something. It was concrete, like the one above. We came to the end, and I stood beside him. It was another round room, with hallways branching off in five directions. I looked at each, narrowing my eyes. TC stood near the stairs and nodded. "Pick one."

I moved out, going to each entrance. At one of them—the mark on my arm glowed.

"That's it," he said, and moved in front of me. "Keep close."

I nodded. The corridors themselves were softly illuminated, but I couldn't tell where exactly the light was coming from. The only door seemed to be the one at the end of the hall. The walls were gray like cement, but when I touched them, they felt more like—felt. Yeah, felt.

Like I used to cut out and play with in kindergarten. Mom always made Christmas decorations with it, sometimes ornaments with pouches to put on the tree, stuffed with candy and—

Gah . . . where are these memories flooding from?

Weird.

As we neared the door—

Zoë! Run! It's a trap!

I stopped. I knew that voice. "Mephistopheles?" I said out loud.

TC frowned at me. "You can hear him?"

"I can—"

She has the book! She knows the secret!

"She knows the secret?" I shook my head. "What secret?"

TC cursed under his breath. "I was afraid of that. Well, she can't do anything without that spell."

"But he says it's a trap."

"It's *always* a trap. Don't you watch movies or read?"

Touché.

He motioned me to the door. I didn't hear his voice again, but there was an echo of something. A voice murmuring something. "Do you hear chanting?"

He nodded to the door. Counting down with the fingers of his right hand. One. Two. Three!

We busted in, him first since he had a gun. I moved in after him, baring my old bad Wraith self.

The smell of blood was overwhelming, the coppery, sickening sweetness of it. The room was painted black with silver symbols scrawled over it, looking a lot like Lex's room at the morgue. In the center was a stone slab, and strapped to that slab was Jason.

He was nude, and every inch of his flesh was carved. I yelled out when I saw him, then noticed a movement near him. A figure in a robe. The same robe I'd seen Daniel in.

No . . . not Daniel. This couldn't be him. He was helping me, right? He was a Revenant now. The hood obscured the face, and I took a step forward, seeing Jason's neck with two tubes shoved inside, connected directly into his jugular. "Jason!"

The robed figure turned to us and produced a gun from beneath its robe. It was a normal gun, which can inflict some damage on me—not sure about TC there. And then the robed figure pointed it at Jason's head. "He's not dead yet," came the voice. "But he will be faster if I pull the trigger."

That wasn't Daniel's voice.

That was a woman's voice. A familiar voice.

As in . . .

A Familiar.

I took a step closer, swallowing. "Oh God ... no ..." I said. "Not you ..."

And then she pulled the hood back and smiled at me. "Hello, Zoë. Didn't expect this, did ya?"

It was Maureen.

33

OF all the faces I expected to see under that hood, Maureen's wasn't one of them. I mean, I could even have swallowed Daniel being there, having a Symbiont invading his body. But this?

"Holy shit," TC said. "What the *fuck* are you doing? Ain't you a Guardian Familiar?"

I looked from Jason to her. "How . . . why? Did you kill the others? All of them?"

She nodded, and seemed really proud of herself, like a puppy wagging its tail. "Yes. But I didn't have the whole picture at first, ya know? And then there was Dags, always interfering with being conscious and all. I needed that final piece—that last bit that really makes the spell work. I remember writing it—but you know spells don't stay with you."

Narrowing my eyes at her, I leaned forward. "I'm sorry—did you say *you wrote* it?"

She nodded to me like I was dumb, the gun pointed at Jason's head swaying as well. "Well, yeah. I did it so I could take out these bastards. All of them. Ungrateful assholes, all of them. I'll teach them to turn on me."

"Uhm . . . can you tell me your name? Just so we're on a friends basis."

She bowed reverently, and a bit spookily. "I am your death."

I leaned in close to TC, who still had his gun pointed at Maureen. "I've never dealt with a crazy-ass Familiar before, so I'm kinda out of my league."

"And you think *I* know what to do?" He shrugged and nodded to Maureen. "Hey."

"What?"

"You solid? I mean—you have to be to wave that gun around."

"Well, of course I am. I used to watch Alice do this. Did you know she used Dags for five days straight like this? Kept him alive so she could drain his spirit and interact on the physical plane. So I learned how—and locked Alice out."

I licked my lips. She was draining Dags's spirit. This did not sound good. Nor was I happy to find that Alice had done the same. "Where is Alice now?"

"Oh, she's with Dags. They're both under this room. But it's too late, Zoë." She pursed her lips at me. "I got to the book." She nodded quickly. "I tore out the blank pages—and I kept the ones I needed. And then you came along and yanked out my memories. You stole me from him. And I had to figure out a way to get the book back—but then I couldn't read it anymore."

I think it was at that moment that I realized we weren't really dealing with Maureen. We were dealing with bits and pieces of someone's scattered memories. As if those memories had coalesced into an essence of their own and taken over Maureen's—

Holy—

I reached out and grabbed TC. "Where did she put Samael?"

He stiffened, and I knew I'd hit the secret. How could I have been so stupid. "Inanna changed the spell—I *know* that, TC. Just like I know that Yamato isn't gone either. It's like Jemmy said—how can you kill your own father? She didn't. She simply locked him in that damned book, didn't she? That's why it tried to latch onto Dags—it knew parts of Samael were in that Grimoire inside Dags. That's why it gave me the translation." I looked back at Maureen. "And now some of Samael is in Maureen—tainted. Angry. Oh shit." I hated it when I started thinking deep. But don't be shocked. I am capable of it. It just gives me a headache.

But now it all made sense. The book had lodged inside of Dags, the remaining essence of Samael joining with Maureen, the Abysmic part of Dags. That was why Dags had stopped dreaming. Maureen/Samael had taken control, but only when he slept. And they'd killed.

Two humans, a ghoul, and now three Revenants. All because Inanna had tried to save her father.

I stared at TC. "Through all this time—all these centuries—it corrupted, didn't it? And you *knew* it."

TC's face remained impassive behind his shades. Until, "Yes. When I touched the book, I knew it. I couldn't get to him, but I could sense him. Pieces of him. And I gave it back to you for safekeeping. I didn't know it had already given you the spellcaster's key. The plan was to hold him until the time came to destroy Sophia. And then Samael would take the seat again." He shook his head. "I knew they never should have trusted the magic of the Seraphim."

I blinked. *Holy shit.*

Literally.

"The Seraphim? But what about the Phantasm—"

"Don't you get it?" He looked at me with those milky eyes. "He's already attacked the Phantasm. That's why Inanna is here. To set things right."

"Attacked . . . ?" I shook my head. "Did he kill—"

"Okay, that's enough," Maureen said, and pressed the gun to Jason's head. I'd been keeping track of the amount of blood he was losing. "Now that I have the last piece, I can begin my obliteration." She frowned. "No, I don't like that word. I do like the word *redact*. Yes . . . all of you naughty children are being redacted."

I realized too that Maureen was acting really . . . kinda . . . drunk.

"So you're saying . . ." TC lowered his gun. I freaked.

You lowered your gun. Why are you lowering your gun? Are you nuts. She's obviously nuts. Put that back up there!

Shush!

Ah . . . He shushed me!

"That you're solid now. Like . . . human. And you've done this by siphoning off the Guardian's soul?"

"His spirit, yes." She looked very pleased with herself. "He's just below me," she whispered. *Not. You already said that.*

"Oh, I see. So not so far down you can't find him."

"Oh no. Because I have this direct link to him. I can—"

TC brought up his gun and fired six times, point-blank into Maureen's heart and head.

Her head exploded as did her chest, showering everything with blood.

Blood.

She has blood?

WHOSE FUCKING BLOOD IS THAT?

I went incorporeal as fast as I could and sank straight down. Now don't misunderstand—I did it first to get away from all the blood and gross. Kinda like a reflex. And then I realized it was like she said.

Dags was there.

The rooms were identical. He lay on the table, shirtless, strapped down at his ankles and wrists. His chest—

Oh my God, his chest. The book lay open on his chest, pages scattered about the room. I ran to him and pressed my fingers to his neck. There was a pulse. Weak.

And then Alice appeared as a ghost hovering over him. She turned to me. "Bring . . . the witch . . ."

The witch.

What witch? "The book is—"

"Bring her!"

The only witch I knew was Rhonda . . . who was so far away. I couldn't possibly bring her—

Or could I? We were technically *between*. Maureen had to have been able to bring bodies in and out, right? To perform the spell here, then drop them where they could be found. So—why not bring Rhonda here.

Uhm, how do I do that?

I looked around at everything. The room was a blank, simply a holding place. Except there was a door to my left. Was the door there before? I went to it, thought of Rhonda, and opened it.

Air-conditioned cool blasted in at me as I looked out at the library at Rhonda's estate. She, Mom, Joe—the Revenants. They were all there.

"Zoë! Where did you—" Rhonda stood and ran to me. I'm sure it was kinda odd, seeing a door appear in the middle of your library.

"Get in here! All of you! I found Jason and Dags!"

Everyone piled through the door, Rhonda and Nona first.

Rhonda stifled a scream, but Mom took her hand and put her in front of Dags, facing the book. "Girl, you've got to keep it simple. You put him together once, you can do it again."

I moved to the side, wringing my hands. When I saw Erishkegal, Loki, Dagda, and Brahma, I pointed up. "Jason's upstairs. I think if you go back out that door without thinking of where you're going, you'll see the stairs. Go up. He's there. I'm not sure if he's going to make it."

All of them left then, except for the one called Frejya. She moved in close to Rhonda and put a hand on her arm. "I will help you."

And I watched them raise their hands together, close their eyes. Pages rattled off the floor and rejoined the spine as the book flipped this way and that, turning left and right, as if it were re-sorting everything. And once the book was whole again, both of them put their hands on the spine and pressed it into his chest.

Dags's torso heaved upward, and his eyes came open as he yelled out—a bloodcurdling sound. The only thing that kept him still were the bindings. Once the book vanished, he lay still, and Mom put a finger to his neck. I waited an eternity to hear her say, "He's alive."

My heart wrenched in my throat as I helped them untie him. And then I saw his left palm and gasped. Mom and Rhonda came to look at it. The circle was completely black—the skin burned and charred.

Oh my God . . . what had TC done?

"He'll survive," Frejya said. "Maureen's not dead, this servant. She is merely . . . damaged. Time. Time is God's bandage."

I looked at her, and though her face was that of an Egyptian beauty, she had a Norse name, and her voice was that of age and wisdom. With a nod she moved with ease to Dags and picked him up, tilting so that his head rested on her shoulder. She looked at me. "We will take care of things here. You have business in the other world."

Business. The book. The Phantasm. Where was TC? I straightened and nodded, understanding what she meant. "I don't know what'll happen to her."

"It's okay," Frejya said. "Sophia has had a hard and long life. She deserves a rest. Can you give it to her, Wraith? Can you feel it in your heart to forgive her?"

I looked at Dags resting there and thought of the pain he'd endured. And I thought of Joe and of Jason. I hoped Jason would live.

At that moment, the door opened, and Nick came through, carrying Jason with him. He'd draped a sheet over him, and it was sticking to the bloody cuts. "He'll live . . . I hope," Nick said. "But how do we get back?"

I moved past him to the door and opened it. The library was back, and all of them filed through. All but Mom and Rhonda.

"Where are you going?" Rhonda asked.

I put a hand to her cheek and felt an overwhelming sense of . . . loss. "To grant forgiveness."

34

WHEN the last of them had left, I stood in front of that closed door for a long time. I knew where I had to go . . . I just wasn't sure I wanted to. I needed answers. A lot of them. And I knew that TC was already ahead of me. But would he allow me to do what was right?

With a sigh, I touched the door handle and thought of the Phantasm, of Sophia, the first of the children of Samael.

When the door opened, it wasn't to the city I remembered from before or that alley. There were no talking bricks, not even a talking mailbox. There was only—desolation.

It was a city street, complete with blinking traffic lights. Cars were parked in a scattered fashion, as if their drivers had simply vanished. Dust and debris moved with the wind as it blew the lights on their wires.

I moved along the street, letting a familiar presence pull me forward, guiding me. I came to what looked like a theater, the old kind, with a marquee. Above it read SOPHIA IN PHANTASM!

Moving past the ticket box, I pushed the double doors aside.

Inside, the stage was lit, and all around in the plush red velvet seats were brilliant incandescent balls of light. They pulsed and moved as I passed them. And I felt as if—I *knew* them. They were every-where, illuminating the dilapidated theater. As I moved down the far left row, I saw TC moving down the middle, and behind him was—

Daniel!

Oh my God. How is he here? He can't survive here. Not like that. Not as a—

And then I realized he wasn't in pain, but walking evenly, his face forward. He wore a green peacoat, the hood back. His glasses perched on his nose. Jeans. Sneakers. So normal.

I continued walking to the front and looked up onstage.

There, in the center, bathed in light, was a woman. Or what was left of one. Her skin was withered, her hair gray and lifeless as it covered her body. She rested, curled inside a floating gray ball. An egg of sorts. And when I looked at her, I felt fatigue, and anger, and regret.

Adiran Martinique came to me at that moment, and I could see him clearly. I gasped when I saw him, so beautiful, and I wanted to hide in shame because I was ugly.

"No, no," he said as he took my hand. White and dark. "You are to me the loveliest of creatures. You are my daughter. And like the Guardian, you are a creature of both worlds."

I looked around then and realized that the glowing orbs of light were the Seraphim foot soldiers I had been told about. "You're here to destroy her?"

"No." He smiled. "Never destroy. We cannot truly destroy God's work. But her time has come."

"What will happen to her?"

"That is up to you," he said. "We simply guide, but we don't

lead. You and the Last First Born must figure this out on your own."
And with that he stepped back. TC and I looked at each other and
moved up the stairs on either side of the stage. Daniel—Inanna—
moved as well, coming up behind TC, and we all three stood facing
the egg.

TC pulled out his gun and aimed it.

I put up my hand, and Daniel raised his as well. "No," we said
in unison.

TC snarled at Daniel. "You don't get to decide. Now do what
we promised to do."

I watched as Daniel pulled the small book from his coat pocket
and held it out. "I'm sorry, brother. But I can't do that. I can't mur-
der my sister."

"Yes, you can!" TC roared. "It's what we promised to do. You
said when the time came, we'd bring Father back . . ."

Oh no . . .

I put my hands to my face. This . . . *this* he kept inside of him
all this time. Even I hadn't seen it?

"Azrael," Daniel began, and suddenly I didn't see Daniel anymore, but a tall, dark-skinned woman with plaited hair and black
eyes. She shook her head and held out the book. "There is so little
left of him, and what there is, is corrupted. Sophia tried to use the
Guardian's Familiar to kill him, but he was too cunning and evaded
her. But now those pieces of him, those things we still remember,
are gone. Father is no more, Azrael."

I looked at TC and gasped.

I no longer saw Vin Diesel but a small child of maybe eight. He
wore the clothing of a Sumerian prince. His head was shaved, and
he was crying. "No . . . you said one day . . . we would bring Father
back."

"I know, little brother. And all these years I've kept him. And still . . . until the Guardian came, and then I saw how corrupted and bitter father's soul had become." She held the book out and up. It disintegrated in front of us, simply melting into the air like ashes.

TC went down on his knees, no longer the child. And Daniel lowered his hands, no longer the daughter of Samael.

"I'm sorry, brother," Inanna said through Daniel. "I failed you." And with that, he turned and moved down the stairs.

All eyes in the audience turned to me. Though they didn't have eyes, I just knew it.

I moved to TC and stood over him. I bent down and touched his back, but he flinched and pulled away. "Leave me the fuck alone."

"No," I said. "Whether you like it or not, we're joined. For how long, I don't know. Your pain, in a way, is mine. I'm sorry, Azrael. I really am." With that, I moved to the egg and looked inside.

I heard him move behind me, heard the cock of the hammer. "You move away from her. She doesn't deserve salvation. No rest. Only an eternity of pain."

I shook my head. "No. She doesn't. No one does, don't you see?" I turned to him. "All this time, I've been so worried about my own soul that I forgot I have a larger purpose. I'm here to release those souls who have lost their way. And Sophia lost hers a long time ago. Now it's time for her to rest."

"No!"

I turned to him and pointed. "YES!"

And the power was there. I held out my hand and forced him to drop the weapon, to drop on his knees and bow to me. I was his keeper, he was not mine!

Daughter . . .

My dad's voice made me blink. The power I had. It would be so easy to give in to that anger.

To the hate and resentment that Samael and Sophia had.

I lowered my hand and released him. TC stood, and fixed me with the coldest gaze he'd ever used on me. "Fine—I warned you. Don't. Trust. Anyone." He grabbed his gun and left the auditorium.

I looked back to the egg and pressed both hands to the outer shell. It gave like any shell would and crumbled away, though not like pieces falling to the floor, but changing to dust and vanishing around us. I wondered if the shell had at one time been her protection against the world. She remained suspended before me, bathed in an incandescent green light. I touched Sophia's face, and she opened her tired eyes to look up at me.

"Why?" she said in a quiet voice. "After everything I've done to you."

I shrugged. I was surprised I wasn't angry. Or hurt. Just . . . sad. "I don't care about you, Sophia. Not one bit. I'm doing this because it's the right thing to do. If it weren't"—I smiled at her—"I'd gut you myself." And with that I shoved my hand into her chest. She screamed as I rooted round for her soul, surprised even now that First Borns had souls.

I grabbed it and pulled it out. It was a twisted thing, like a walking stick from a gnarled oak. And with a final breath, I cut her cord and released her.

The power that surged through me was incredible. I lifted my arms high and yelled out with joy! Oh . . . the power that coursed through my joints, healing the muscle aches and pains. I felt myself lifted, high over the stage, above the remnants of the egg. I glowed as my father below me glowed, and I felt everything. And . . .

Nothing.

With a sudden snap, I was in darkness. Total and utter darkness. I couldn't move, and my screams resounded in my own ears, deafening me. My knees were in my chin and I was surrounded by—

The egg.

I was *in* the fucking egg!

Quiet, Zoë, came my father's voice. *The universe cannot have a vacuum. And it cannot exist without a Phantasm. For now, you will be that creature.*

Wha . . .

NO.

DADDY!

Quiet, child. Soon you will grow accustomed to the position just as Sophia had before. I'm afraid you won't be able to move much, or leave, until Azrael is destroyed.

Destroyed? Daddy . . . what are you doing?

Taking control. Soon our soldiers will find him, and you will become the Phantasm. One under our control. For now, just sleep. And rest. You deserve a rest.

And then there was silence.

Utter silence.

Daddy?

Nothing.

DADDY?

SOMEBODY!!!!!!

EPILOGUE

MORNING sunlight brushed against his face, luring him from sleep with the promise of coffee. The smell of it was intoxicating. Rolling over in the bed, he blinked several times and focused on a lamp with a headless Mary Had a Little Lamb.

I'm in Zoë's room. WTF?

Sitting up, he looked at the clock. Eleven in the morning. It was Monday. With a groan, he shuffled into Zoë's bathroom, showered, shaved, and dressed in a pair of jeans and a tee shirt laid out for him. Running a brush through his unruly hair, he made his way down the stairs.

Dark . . .

Nona was in the kitchen, sliding a panful of eggs into a bowl. He could smell the butter, and his stomach growled. She turned and looked at him, a smile on her face. "Well, about time you got out of bed. Sleep well?"

"Yeah," he said, and took the bowl she gave him. He moved from the kitchen to the tea shop. The table was set. Rhonda sat in her place, dressed as usual in black, reading a book. Jason sat to the left of her. He looked better—the scars were nearly healed, and soon his skin would look as if he'd never had an obliteration spell carved into his flesh.

To Rhonda's right was Dags. He looked as he had since coming back from Between. Glassy-eyed. Sitting still. Responding only when spoken to. He got along well enough, and Rhonda believed his condition would improve with time. She and Nona figured it was because Maureen was still out of commission, thus his left arm was useless and bound to his chest in a sling, and because the book got reshuffled when it went back in. He thought maybe it was a good opportunity to fix that book, but Rhonda seemed to like Dags like this.

Alone . . .

Docile. And with no memory of Zoë or much of anything else. Alice appeared every now and then to help him eat or bathe. It was sad. And it was wrong.

On the other side were Tim and Steve, quiet as usual. Tim more so as he faded in and out. Not really trying to be corporeal.

Jemmy was missing, but she'd moved away, saying things weren't right anymore. It was time for the horsemen.

Nona came to sit down, and they all helped themselves. He grabbed up a coffee and treated it as he always had.

Help . . .

He sipped it for a while and watched them. All of them carried on their lives as they had since that day.

When Zoë disappeared. And no one seemed to care.

But him.

His phone rang, and he nodded to Nona as he got up and stepped outside. There wasn't really any need to answer it. It was just a signal for him and an excuse to leave the house.

Down the road to the right stood two men. One was bald and

beefy, with dark clothing and shades. The other was taller, thinner, with a more graceful build, and wore glasses, jeans, and a cotton shirt. They waited until he was within earshot before the bald one spoke. "You hear her?"

He nodded. "Yep. Started yesterday."

The lighter one licked his lips. "You tell them?"

He shook his head. "No, Daniel. I haven't said a word." He looked at Azrael, also known as TC. "But at least we know she's alive. A month, and finally some word."

Azrael nodded. "And I got a pretty good idea where. You in, Joe?"

Joe Halloran nodded and checked the gun in his holster. "Oh, I'm ready." He set it back. "We're gonna need your friend Frejya if we're gonna get Dags away from Rhonda. We need to fix him first." He looked at both of them. "And then, gentlemen, we go find the Wraith."